MARK ROBINSON

EVER SEARCHING

Chalk Stream Books

Published by Chalk Stream Books
www.chalkstreambooks.com

ISBN: 978-1-917056-34-2

Printed and bound in the UK.

PART ONE

Sommovia: Early 1990s

The midday sun shone down onto the side of the mountain and filled the clearing with unfiltered light. Amongst the forest greens the air was clean and still-moving. A borrowed space that could never be owned. The man had stayed on when everything made him want to run. His family depended on his twisted loyalty. Every day he feared for his life. Coercion and cruelty denied him the peace and security he craved and found briefly in this isolated spot.

Climbing out of the cab, he checked the machine's oil and water levels. He took the chance to eat a sandwich and stretch his legs. Now that the engine was quiet, if only for a moment, he could appreciate the loneliness and nature's respite from the increasing madness that threatened to crowd him out. The sound of distant gun fire emanating from the valley below devastated the silence and the rest of his idyllic summer's day.

No excuse could be offered, none would be accepted. Surveying the morning's work, he prayed that the trench was long enough. In the stillness of the air, the drone of a lorry coming up the hill was clearly audible, and he knew the group were on their way. An ugly intrusion, he kept a nervous eye on the track where it entered the clearing.

The lorry, when it arrived some twenty minutes later, reversed onto site just as agreed and parked close by the side of the trench. The first man down from the cab was bare headed and wore no obvious uniform but he gave the distinct impression that all should know who he was.

An obvious leader, made plain by the deference the rest of the group gave him when they finally emerged. Interestingly and unlike him, they wore masks and peaked caps to hide their identity. All, of course, were heavily armed.

No orders were necessary and every angle of view was checked and covered. Two of the group climbed onto the bed of the lorry and without ceremony began the task of unloading. As with their part in the mopping up operation down in the village, they wasted no time in getting rid of the human remains.

By the time it was over, the bodies, all women and children, lay strewn side by side in an uneven line. There was room for more and the man duly watched and waited for orders, conscious that the bare headed leader was walking towards him with something on his mind. Beady grey eyes in a face devoid of humanity stared with unfailing direction but in the end no words were wasted. Sign-language only and the inference was that the day was done and all evidence should be hidden and buried.

With a dismissive wave of his hand, the leader turned and made his way back to the lorry. His reputation would forever infect the clearing. Destined for greater rank and position, it would take a brave man to stop him.

The lorry headed back down the mountain side and the man listened out for the squeal of its brakes as it slowed for the first corner. Tears of relief and distress ran quietly down his face as he made his way over to the side of the pit. Putting names to faces was a one-way ticket to hell.

Before he could stop himself, he was down in amongst them, straightening their limbs and adjusting the angle of their heads, trying to make them more comfortable. He clung onto what was left of his sanity, knowing one day, someday, people would return to look for their dead.

The backfilling went slowly. He waited until the heads and torsos were fully covered, using the softest earth. Heavy stones when they struck could make the bodies dance in an absurd and disturbing way. The last layer of top soil would hopefully lessen the visible scar and encourage new growth to cover his work.

It would be as if they never existed. Towns and villages, their houses all burnt to the ground. Files and papers destroyed along with their histories and evidence of their deaths buried in unmarked graves. Lost forever? Sadly, some will remain so. The rest with specialist help must one day be uncovered and found.

Ever searching, the hunt goes on.

Main Characters

Charles Hanlan: Impresario and wealthy property owner

Amelia Highland: Actor and adopted daughter to Charles Hanlan

Lloyd Hanlan: Charles' son

Claire Hanlan: Wife of Charles, mother of Lloyd. Maiden name, Williams

Nick Sayers: Photographer/Journalist

Libi Sayers: Editor and part owner of Stress Magazine.

Samantha Grant: Public relations executive for NRG Pictures

Sherman Powers: Head of NRG Pictures

Rosalind Powers: Sherman's wife and inspiration for his latest venture

Louise: Powers Personal Assistant

Ellen Preston: Amelia's Personal Assistant

Katie Ley: Understudy to Amelia Highland

Peter Pearce: Newspaper reporter/writer

Jim and Mary Paxton: Full-time employees of Charles Hanlan

Maurice Highland and Jelena Horvat: Amelia's natural parents

Joe Peterson: Ex special forces working in land management

Colonel Bradbury: Joe Peterson's boss in the Army

Sally Stewart: Charles Hanlan's Personal Assistant

Duncan Marwood: Newspaper Editor

Tony Sterling: Head of Sterling Associates Inc.

Marsha Ivanovic: Voice Coach

Alan: Ex-Army officer and friend of Joe Peterson

1. Forethought

England: Year 2000

In places the road narrowed to a single track, a small ribbon of tarmac that wound through a wilderness of uncharted life. To the right windblown trees and thick carpets of reeds hid the sea from view. To the left and beyond fields of rough pasture, the estuary meandered gently inland and was lost from sight behind a rise in the land. At its edges, small flocks of wading birds were dots in the distance, occasionally making swirling patterns of white and black as they flew to settle once again on the soft sand. Ahead the road wound down towards a woodland that partially hid an old church tower. Joe Peterson looked on with a practised eye born out of habit.

Encouraged, he accelerated the van forward and was struck by a surge of nervous energy. For him this was new territory. A track on the left led to the church which was small despite the grandeur of its tower. To the right, the canopy of the trees lost their intensity and allowed light to filter through to ground level. Joe wound down the window and experienced the smell of cedar and pine mixing with the sea-air.

As the van climbed a small rise in the road so the house came into view. This was surprising, given the proximity of the beach and sea beyond. Acres of rough grazing and marshland stretched into the distance where sand dunes kept back the waves.

Joe slowed at a farm entrance. Outhouses and barns formed a courtyard that had shelter from the prevailing winds. Two empty cottages within an acre of grassland were separate from the main house itself. A traditional Suffolk-style property built for purpose, Joe thought it attractive and could see his father's hand in its renovation and new build design.

Tarmac dissolved into gravel as he approached the house and parked next to the other vehicle on the driveway. Leaving plenty of space between his van and a large Mercedes, he opened the door and took a moment to look about him. A gentle breeze played in the tops of the reeds, making a backdrop of sound that was mysterious yet calming. There would be no need to announce his arrival. The front door was already open and somebody was there waiting. Joe breathed in deeply and told himself to smile.

"Mr Hanlan? Pleased to meet you." Joe shook hands with a well-dressed man of indeterminate age. The same height as Joe, Charles Hanlan's eyes were politely intrusive as the two men played out the first seconds of contact. Joe showed no weakness and soon sensed a growing confidence between them. Charles was the first to break away, as if somehow satisfied.

"Come on in. Thanks for coming." They went through to a makeshift office. A large wooden table stood in the middle of a room adorned with drawings and plans laid out in order. Printed photographs were stuck to hand written notes. A great deal of trouble had obviously been taken.

"Your father has been busy as you can see." Hanlan had been about to sit down. "Come on let's go for a stroll and have a look outside. We can go through all this later should it become relevant."

Within minutes he was explaining his plans for the surrounding gardens. It was obvious that Hanlan knew what he wanted regarding many items but when he turned his attention to the farm and marshland areas, he finally seemed less sure of himself.

"My family has been in property for a very long time, as has yours Joe. Your father worked for my father and now for me. There's not a lot Mr Peterson senior doesn't know about the building game, agreed. One thing your old man can't cope with is the land. He won't want the hassle, I know that." Charles gestured with his hands. "This, believe it or not, is really important to me."

Joe looked out over the marshland towards the sea once more.

"It's a specialist field which we will both need help with." Hanlan emphasized the 'we'. "I want to create a wild life sanctuary as part of a huge private garden for the house. Something to attract and fascinate all in one go. A kind of haven." He left the words hanging as if he was hearing himself for the first time.

Joe tried to keep hold of a little professional detachment. Yes, this was the work he wanted now, and yet he sensed that the man had more up his sleeve. By the time they spoke again they'd reached the edge of a small overgrown ditch. Clear water sparkled in places where the tall grasses and scrub bushes allowed a view. Joe could see the remains of an old sluice gate that urgently needed repair.

"The devil is in the detail, Joe. I don't need to tell you that. This is a new kind of business, something for your long-term future. I know a little of what you've been through and I'm keen to give you every opportunity I can." Hanlan sounded sincere. "We all have different skills, Joe, and your previous work in the armed forces has provided you with a rare set indeed." He held his hand up. "Blame me, not your father. I wouldn't take no for an answer. At the end of the day the choice will be yours, it goes without saying."

"I'm moving on. My time in the army is nearly up." Joe spoke simply and couldn't imagine why his recent history had so much relevance.

"And I can help you with that." Charles gestured towards their surroundings as a reminder. "This is where you'll be needed for the majority of the time, I guarantee it. I suppose I'd like to know that I could turn to you for assistance and security if it was required in the future."

Joe Peterson listened carefully trying to plug in the gaps of information not yet revealed.

"An occasional but invisible minder, that's all it would be. But not for me personally." Charles could see that would never do. "No, not for me."

"Who then?" The words were out before Joe could control his tongue.

"It's for somebody far more important than me," Hanlan explained. "In comparison to your work for the army it should be easy, providing she never suspects that you are actually there."

Joe had never watched a hockey match live. The thought had occurred to him as he walked away from the school's main buildings towards the playing fields. Hockey at a posh girls' school was the most unlikely venue and he felt exposed because of it. Perhaps seen as an unsavoury element in isolation he sped up his progress across the finely-kept grounds to pitch number one. It came as a relief to mix with the rest of the spectators that were already congregated on the touch-line.

Joe sidled in amongst the shouts of encouragement and squeals of excitement that were the backdrop to an apparently enthralling game. He knew already that the seniors were playing against the Old Girls. One-one, so the score-board said. Keen parents and pupils followed the ebb and flow of the action. A space finally presented itself and Joe stepped forward, able to see the whole pitch for the first time. His eyes travelled the length and breadth of it. Twenty-two players to choose from and he already knew that Amelia Highland didn't play in goal. No point in coming all this way if your subject had her face hidden behind a protective visor.

That he was standing there at all was down to Charles Hanlan and his persuasive powers. His insistence that Joe "go and check her out" had sounded like a crude invitation. Joe felt voyeuristic and as Wednesday afternoon-activities went, he could never have imagined a more surreal way to assess his need of a job.

One of the players cracked a shot on goal and the thud as the ball crashed into the keepers' pads was heard by all. Desperate defence was required before the danger was cleared, leaving two players to become the focus of attention. Roared on by factions of the crowd, Joe could see that the girl with dark hair was going to be first to the ball. The break was on; a chance to score and take the lead was suddenly dashed as the opposing player cynically hooked her back. The dark-haired girl's lithe limbs and determination kept her upright until inertia and gravity finally took their toll. She landed heavily and slithered to a halt not five metres away from where Joe stood. As the umpire blew her whistle for the foul, Joe watched as the girl immediately sprang to her feet. Fiercely blue eyes blazed in indignation and words of some vehemence and imagination were directed towards her opponent.

Fortunately for all, the umpire was on hand to keep the girls apart and Joe allowed himself to be swallowed up by the crowd as they politely jostled for a better view. He had time to reflect on the violence that was surprisingly woman's hockey and the nature of the words that had been uttered by the girl with a fire in her eyes. He could only hope that no one present spoke Sommovian, as they would have been shocked at the given description of the other girl's mother and the accusation made about her sexual preferences too.

Front line stuff; Joe had seen and heard enough. So that was Amelia Highland.

"She's a school girl, dad, or near as dammit." Joe bent over the architects' drawings that his father had laid out on the office desk at their home. "Not what I was expecting from someone tipped to be a West End star. Not much lovey-dovey in evidence there."

Joe's dad was making coffee in the kitchen. He brought two full mugs back with him and waited for his son to continue.

"If I do work for Charles Hanlan, it's the land management that really interest me. As for Miss Highland's security, I'm struggling to see the need."

His father was swift with his reply. "The man has his finger in many pies, son. His company owns The Theatre outright. We're talking West End, right? From what I've heard his girl has great potential and he's producing a musical in which she will star." Joe's dad confessed he knew nothing further and needed to be careful with what he said next. "Sounds to me as if on certain, special occasions security might be an issue he'll need some help with. You know how it is with these celebrities. Blimey, compared to what you've been through, it should be a piece of cake."

Predictably Joe was not convinced. "That's what Hanlan said. It's not the point. In the army I worked for professionals." He needed more to go on. "Is there a present threat to her safety?"

Joe's dad settled back into his chair to consider the question. He had worked for Charles and if he cared to remember, for Hanlan's father too. But did he really know the man? Not intimately. Property development and maintenance underpinned the man's wealth but beyond that any personal knowledge was pretty much down to here-say.

"The Theatre and more lately his daughter have become the most important things in his life." He took a sip of coffee. "I know he split with his wife and I think she lives in America." Joe's dad shrugged his shoulders. "Perhaps he's just scared of losing his daughter too."

Joe ignored the veiled reference to the issues his own dad had dealt with when he'd been away on tour. "And Amelia never went with her mum, isn't that unusual?"

"Well, that's the thing. I'm surprised I never told you before. Amelia is Charles Hanlan's adopted daughter. Her real parents died when she was only eight years old."

Joe's dad had all but finished work on the house in Suffolk. Grade listing on certain parts of the property had caused no real concerns beyond what was commonplace. That was why Charles employed him. Now he wanted 'Peterson junior' on board as well. Loyalty was not an unfamiliar concept to Joe. It had been a major part of working with army bosses who couldn't afford to let him down.

The old man's opinions had been valuable but he understood that his own mind was the making of his future. He tried a little digging and it soon became apparent that Amelia's birth mother had originated from Eastern Europe. This piece of information was significant, if not a game changer. The links to Joe's previous employment begged the question as to Hanlan's underlying motives in wanting to hire him.

The White Hart was as good a place as any to continue their conversation. The pints of beer purely incidental.

"I think you need to speak to your extended family. Wouldn't do any harm to get the security bods to check the story out. Hanlan knows you were out in Sommovia with UN. but I wouldn't read too much into that. You're out of it now." Joe's dad tried to put his son's misgivings into some kind of context.

The extended family that Joe's dad was referring to was made up of a select few. Colleagues, some having completed their respective tours of duty had remained in the army to further their careers. Training the next generation was a vital role. Joe was aware of others who had left for the lucrative private sector where position, power and money demanded the highest levels of protection. Decent remuneration could not be ignored but the need to feel decent about what you were being paid to do was another subject altogether.

In the meantime, Charles' offer remained firmly on the table. Fortunately for Joe he could rely on advice which was only a phone call away.

In less than a week Joe had some feedback and true to form the outcome was not as simple as he'd been hoping. He knew better than to ask for details over the phone, but was fortunate that a Colonel from his former unit had suggested a meeting where privacy could be guaranteed. Joe made the trip to London assuming that the available information would only be given to him 'on a need-to-know basis.' For the rest he would have to make do and rely on trust.

At what point his invitation from the Colonel had become a summons was surely debateable.

"Here goes nothing." Joe pushed open the office door.

"Good to see you Peterson." Colonel Bradbury shook him warmly by the hand. "Have a seat." Retreating to the other side of his desk he sat for a second in silence while he made an appraisal. "You're always welcome of course, but maybe you hadn't envisaged us meeting again so soon?"

"You might be right there, sir." Joe took a chance. "Not that I'm unhappy to see you of course." He sensed they still had a mutual understanding. They'd got on very well in the past. "Seriously I appreciate your time on this..." He left his words hanging. "So how big is this hornets' nest I've kicked up? I have to assume your enquiries into Amelia Highland's background have some connections to my dealings in Sommovia."

The Colonel nodded. "Raking up history, particularly in Eastern Europe, will likely cause a dust storm, we both know that." He flicked through an open file on his desk. "You were right to contact me by the way. Tell me more of what you do know, and I'll try to give you everything I think is relevant. Fair enough?"

Joe conceded it was the best he could hope for. Charles Hanlan had not been specific over his concerns towards his daughter but it was possible that her mother's country of birth had piqued an interest that was more than just coincidental. He told Bradbury everything he knew and finished by emphasising that he thought that any security concerns were probably based in this country.

"This is a tricky one, Joe." Bradbury made noises at the back of his throat, which suggested he was searching for the right words. "Sommovia is still the problem. I don't need to tell you how volatile the situation can be out there. You saw it first-hand, so know the dangers that communities suffered. Knowledge is power and you supplied us that in spades." The Colonel was sounding very formal. "Many more lives could potentially have been lost. It's only right we should respect your interests in your retirement."

Joe sat very still while he listened to the compliments. He and the Colonel were genuinely aware that the peace-keeping operations that they'd been a part of had failed in so many ways.

"I'm afraid the problems arise around Amelia Highland's parents who were killed when she was eight years old. This would be two years before the unrest in Sommovia bubbled over into open conflict. Most of this is common knowledge and in the public domain, agreed?

"That much I do know, sir." Joe smiled in recognition of a familiar trend. "But I get the feeling that there's more to this than meets the public eye?"

"Perceptive of you, Captain Peterson. What I can say is I'd be happy for you to continue with your new found association. There are complications that I've considered, some of which you are not aware of, and frustratingly some that I don't have the authority to inform you about." Bradbury could see Joe's mind working overtime. "Not as yet. New information could be brought to light at any moment. Not that it will impact on you personally or for that matter be detrimental to Miss Highland's safety and security. However, I would be hesitant to allow her to travel and meet with family in that region at present. No actions are without consequences."

Joe interest was piqued at that. The civil war was formally at an end but it sounded very much as though the UN's former responsibilities were being replaced by something just as important. The territory was familiar; all about protecting humanitarian aid. Joe had invested much of his own time beyond the safe areas and designated exclusion zones, minus his blue beret.

"Do I take it that certain power struggles amongst the greater good are finally being side-lined to give justice a chance?" Joe asked a question that the Colonel could not presently answer. "About bloody time, if you ask me."

"No comment." The Colonel smiled riley. "What I will say, is if you ever fancy coming out of retirement, let me know."

By the time Joe was halfway back to Suffolk, his mind in regards to his own future was made up. Swayed by his trust in Colonel Bradbury and the latter's request that looked to continue their association post-retirement and into civilian life, he realised he was looking for excitement within his new job description.

Charles Hanlan, who was totally unaware of any ongoing research, had been confident that the position of Estate Manager had already been filled. Work to Joe's cottage was entering its final stages by the time he revisited the property for only the second time. The painter/decorator knew his name and bombarded him with questions over colour schemes and finishes, some of which he'd never heard of before. Joe gave his preferences and came to realise his absolute commitment in securing a brand-new job.

Happy to leave the smell of new paint behind, he stood in the road and took in his surroundings one more time. The church and the large Suffolk long house at the end of the driveway were landmarks in their own right. The whole area was suddenly bathed in bright sunshine. An omen of sorts? It would be difficult to turn away from it now. Yes, Sedge House and its adjoining estate would do him just fine.

*

2. Big Cheeses

London and New York

Sherman Powers was egotistical and forthright, but knew he was lacking in heart-healthy fitness. He excused his lack of exercise by way of blaming the paucity of available hours in his busy day. There was nothing wrong with his entrepreneurial skills and the single-minded resolve he'd shown in his role as head of NRG Pictures. A principled man, who rarely compromised when it came to the quality of the films he produced, he was often in direct competition with Hollywood, sometimes aggressively so. He lived with the knowledge that in comparison to his west coast rivals, he'd rarely received the commercial reward to match his critical success. A rich man still, "but not made of money", he had made his own path and trodden it well.

Nearing retirement age, he was mindful of all he still wanted to achieve in business. Many people inside the industry respected him, but this masked a sadness knowing he had very few friends. Walking together in the here and now, he glanced at his wife, elegant and tall, and felt a precarious pride. Clasping her hand, he wondered if she could read his mind.

The streets in London were unfamiliar, unlike the sense of shared excitement as they approached The Theatre in the heart of the West End. Back home in New York and used to the comforts that money and fine planning afforded him, Sherman was surprised to find he was actually enjoying slumming it with the rest of the punters as he entered the foyer. He hoped Rosalind would appreciate the irony of securing a couple of cheap seats, so called, something he'd not had to do for a very long time; not since he'd seen her first perform on Broadway.

As the auditorium lights died the sound of a single oboe sure and clear hushed the audience to an expectant silence. Sherman found he was actually holding his breath as he sat forward in his seat, eyes intent and focused on the stage, waiting for his first glimpse of the actor he'd come to see. The total blackness became darkness, and pin-pricks of light were the stars. The figure of a girl, hooded and caped was visible now as the moon provoked shadows across the stage.

The oboe pitched its final note and was joined by a voice that seemed to come out from nowhere. Nerve-endings prickled up and down his spine and Sherman heard the man next to him gasp. Her spell had been cast and the singer named Amelia could do no wrong. The sun replaced the moon and the scene became clear; morning and life in a better part of town. As the sun rose in the sky, the girl, without her cape now, moved into the light.

The song was a sad one, the haunting melody rippled in her voice pleading with the audience to understand her plight. Amelia sang alone. Amongst the top-hats and bustle, the handsome and the elegant, she stood with the cobbles of the street below her feet. Each cobble a day too many spent separated from her child, taken at birth, so the family name should not suffer the shame of illegitimacy.

The song drew to its end and Amelia walked to side of the stage, she turned and looked up as if to the heavens. The first hands came together in rapturous applause, and it seemed to Sherman that she knew he was there.

In the same way his heart had been stolen nearly thirty years ago, "Ever Searching", playing at The Theatre had allowed Sherman Powers to appreciate how a young talent could capture the hearts of critics and paying public alike. The similarities with that night on Broadway when Rosalind had become an overnight success were all consuming. He drew breath as they stepped out into the night and hailed a taxi.

*

On his return to the Big Apple, the head of NRG Pictures had soon felt the hard yards of a steep learning curve. It might have helped if there had been a normal set of rules to follow. Lines of communication between Sherman Powers and the elusive Miss Highland were almost non-existent. With no agent in sight, negotiation with her step-father had become the only avenue open to him. The frustrations were tangible and the fallout at NRG Pictures was an increasing volume of barked orders from the boss, a bull-mastiff incarnate, who'd suddenly lost his bone.

Amelia wasn't to know, couldn't be expected to appreciate the depth of Sherman's commitment to finding the perfect match, someone to portray the talented beauty he'd fallen in love with. He was nothing if not persistent. It was evident from the little dialogue that had been afforded to him that the young actress, without confirming an interest, wasn't actually saying no. Perhaps parental control was still pulling the strings and tugging at emotional family ties.

The mysteries of untwisting this confusing history would require a dexterous mind, and Sherman knew his limitations. It was something he gave himself credit for. Thus, securing the capture of Amelia Highland was laid at another's door. Public relations executive, Samantha Grant was duly deemed the right choice for the job.

Undoubtedly it helped that she was young and enthusiastic, but only a shallow mind would have failed to notice their shared sense of admiration, disguised as banter, and in her, the business-like qualities that had attracted Sherman's offer of work some eighteen months before.

On moving to New York, Samantha had used her qualifications to gain access to interesting and well-paid work. Even though her secretarial skills were excellent, the environs of office life had proved too dull and claustrophobic to fulfil her ambitions. Table Manners, a Brooklyn based catering company had seen her potential straight from the get-go. Her ability to inspire and galvanise a staid workforce had made her invaluable and promotions duly followed. Sam found herself organising functions, one to the next. It suited her temperament and the money got better with time.

Contracted on specific occasions when a director was shooting on location in and around New York City, NRG Pictures came to rely on Table Manners and inevitably Samantha herself. Sherman had witnessed first-hand the way in which she handled people and more importantly how they in turn responded to her. His reward to the catering company had been a sizeable bonus on a job well done. Personal thanks had been extended to Miss Grant along with a written job offer. In the time it took to ring her father for his valued opinion, Sam already knew she would accept.

"Come in Miss Grant and sit down." Sherman moved from behind his desk and pointed to a chair. "What have you got for me?" He waited until she had settled, before reclaiming his seat. "Lots of research by the looks of it." Watching as she placed type-written text on the desk in front of him, he noted the title; "The Hanlan Dossier". He raised his eyebrows and wondered if Samantha was pulling his leg. "I'll read this later." He placed the notes to one side.

"Perhaps you could summarize?" She was a confident young woman who could look him in the eye, even when his humour left a little to be desired. His mould had been cast too long ago for dramatic change, but Sherman had every confidence that Samantha could take that in her stride.

"Well, I managed to get a little info on his early life." Sam referred to her own copy of the notes. "The rest is pretty much common knowledge; newspaper and magazine articles mostly. His private secretary was reluctant to speak on his behalf. No surprises there."

Charles Hanlan was born in post-war London to parents who had believed their opportunity for a family had long since passed. Charles's father's prolonged absence due to work and a history of ill health that had beset his mother had all but dashed their hopes. In the years after the end of the war, Hanlan senior had invested wisely in property and became a major influence in the rebuilding process of a bomb-struck London. Consequently, Charles had never wanted when it came to finding work. Inherited ambition flowed in his veins but he'd been encouraged to follow his heart. This had become more poignant following the sudden death of his father. The theatre had become a passion that would ultimately bring him acclaim.

Samantha Grant had done her best to pick out the poignant facts. Sherman could see she had done her home-work and was surprised to admit to his own ignorance when it came to Hanlan's past.

"Rarely talks about his family or his private life. Well that much we know." She looked up to check if Sherman was still paying attention. He was. "After his father's death he took over running the family's property interests. By chance The Theatre was part of their portfolio and became his passion. A production company was set up in partnership with a friend." She emphasized the last word. "The friend's name was Maurice Highland." Sherman was nodding his head. "It took them a few years to get it established but now the business goes from strength to strength."

Sam continued with some background information. "Both men coincidently married in their late twenties. Hanlan to a bit-part actress called Claire Williams. Highland to Jelena Horvat, a classical singer, originally from Sommovia in Eastern Europe. If I remember correctly, they first met when she travelled to London."

"Maurice Highland was a writer/director and then went into television." Sherman took Samantha by surprise. "In fact, he made documentaries if I'm not mistaken." She gave him a questioning look. "Wanted to interview my wife at one time," he gave by way of explanation, "it's a small world in some ways, Miss Grant; but do go on."

"Television." Samantha checked her notes. "You're right, but he remained involved in the original business." She gathered her thoughts once again. "Both couples had children, within six months of each other. The Highland's had their daughter, Amelia, while the Hanlan's had a son they named Lloyd. Tragically Amelia was only eight years old when her parents were killed in a traffic accident whilst holidaying in Italy." Sam was obviously moved by this.

"Apparently, Hanlan had encouraged his friends to go away, while he stayed behind to act as guardian to Amelia."

Sam paused and wondered if she should express an opinion. Charles and Maurice had been like brothers according to those in the know. It was no secret that they'd often holidayed together, and this had not changed even after they were married.

"At the time of Maurice and Jelena's trip there'd been speculation that the quartet had suffered some kind of falling out and that was why the Highland's had gone on their own. As far as I'm aware, Charles has never commented on any of this."

Sam put down her notes.

"Even now there are elements within the British press that continue to hound him. The inference is clear, and not helped by the lack of a denial." She sounded frustrated at this. "Not long after the accident, Hanlan's own marriage hit the rocks. By all accounts his wife, Claire Williams, made that very public with a string of affairs." Sam had a final thought. "Interestingly, they've never bothered to divorce, even though they separated some four years ago."

Sherman was nodding his head again.

"If you're right Miss Grant, then we need to be certain about these people. My wife would not thank me for tainting her good name by bad association." He looked disappointed. "Let's hope Miss Highland's parents and their pasts won't put an end to our future plans."

*

NRG Pictures was not alone in finding difficulty coming to terms with the idiosyncrasies associated with

Amelia Highland. The popular press in Britain had hungered for closer relations in order to feed their readers with the latest juicy morsels. Unfortunately for them and even before negotiations with NRG Pictures had begun, it was clear that the promise of fame and fortune carried no favours with her. On the contrary, Amelia was fast developing a reputation for shyness and exclusivity.

There were inevitable consequences. Some editors, still keen to assuage their need for a pound of flesh, were not prepared to ration themselves to the tit-bits of interest being fed to them by the Hanlan dynasty. Instead of the papers making Amelia their target, it became easier to prey upon the over protective step-father and blame him for the untenable situation. Charles was duly forced to suffer the ignominy of a bad and, at times, brutal press. Some assumed his continued silence to be a confession of guilt. Was it more than just family ties that bound the star to the master of her universe? In the wake of a very public dismissal of one of Ever Searching's leading men, there appeared the following in a Sunday paper of some notoriety. The author of the article was a man named Peter Pearce.

"…It would appear that getting too close to the princess of the stage, Miss Highland to you sir, has proved a bad choice for a career. Stringent terms and conditions of employment are inhibitive and purposely so. Is there a danger that her keeper will not tolerate an unwanted red-blooded intrusion into his world of blue? Surely there lies the danger. How can purity prosper and survive in this contaminated world of ours when the nature of pedigree excludes all but the privileged few? Perhaps Mr Hanlan should be aware of the consequences of his design. It is a proven fact that too much inbreeding has a habit of driving you mad…"

Charles mouthed the name of the author again. Peter Pearce, the bane of his life. Even for the mild-mannered impresario, this was possibly a step too far. The constraints of promises previously made and the duty he owed to Amelia weighed him down. Now that publicity was becoming invasive, it was clear that what had remained private could no longer be controlled. It was time for a serious talk with his daughter. One question remained above all others; how much of the truth should he reveal?

Moving through the office he found the key to a rarely used storage cupboard. A metal box, with M. Highland written on its top, lay just inside the door. Once open, a raft of papers with little sketches and some hand written notes in red ink were unmistakeably Maurice's. A loose-leaved book with a headline of School Day contained the best of his creative mind.

Charles returned to his computer and was moved to capture something of Amelia's father in his own words. If nothing else it might help explain how they'd been drawn together. He used Maurices's notes as his inspiration.

...A walk into town was fraught with interest, and sometimes a little danger, and almost always, when the boys strayed off the beaten track. Hidden mysteries of the back-streets where terraced houses and small gardens gave neighbours little privacy, were like gems of insight into an unknown land. Not all outsiders who ventured there were aware of the suspicion and scrutiny that followed their progress. Only one in the small group, the tallest, the most confident, appreciated that their presence and uniform was rarely welcomed there.

Innocent laughter, too loud for the lowly bin-man, must have sounded dismissively contrived. "You think I'm an animal, don't you?" The heavy-handed treatment of a bin-lid sounded a warning to all the boys that they had crossed an invisible line. Only the tall one, with hands in his pockets, felt capable of turning to face the much older man. "Why would you think that?" He asked in polite puzzlement, giving room for some form of debate.

"Stuck up bastards!" A one-line winner from the bin-man ended the conservation.

The other boys moved quickly and ushered their intrigued leader away.

"Is it just because of our school uniforms, or are we really that different from everybody else?"

Younger pupils from the boys-only boarding school had been targeted and suffered too in other parts of town. The word had it that the local fishmonger had taken it upon himself to make a personal point. Cleaning the shop floor using a bucket and mop was standard practice, but the timing of the chore seemed poignant. A final sluice of the shop-floor entrance to coincide with the passing of shiny shoes and trousered turn-ups seemed on the face of it to be a cheap trick and totally unnecessary. The choice appeared clear. Take your medicine and a dose of fish oil whilst walking on the pavement, or risk being hit by a passing car.

An interesting conundrum that the tall boy found both amusing and unsettling. It seemed that camouflage was required or he'd remain an obvious target without it. Suitable for the season but more to hide his uniform, a coat from the local Oxfam store proved worthwhile. If nothing else it gave him legitimacy and more access to a host of new found characters.

A coat and a scarf were essential on that particular, bleak winter day. Pearly-grey sky that was thick with cloud had diffused the daylight and diluted life's colours. Black skeletal trees stood out in contrast to the snow that had been falling since just before dawn. No traffic, few people, just the sound of his footfall in the cold cushion of white on the ground.

The faintest wisp of smoke from the chimney was a welcome signal and offered the promise of further diversion and a more comfortable place to write. The approach to the derelict house on the top of a small rise was a tricky one. Half hidden and forgotten behind a screen of small trees, its part-time residents who dossed down for the night were common enough, but tended to shy away from any regular contact during the day. The boy slipped cautiously and quietly into the house. The front door was missing as was much of the glass from the downstairs windows which made it an infrequent shelter for those in need, but a perfect refuge for those that had an hour or two to kill.

"Come up Mo, we've got a fire going." Another boy's face was looking down on him through a hole in the ceiling.

The faint crackle of wood in the grate got louder as Mo negotiated the stairs. "Hi Charlie. Glad you got here before me." The bright yellow flames and their heat were welcome indeed. Glass in the room's only window gave insulation of sorts and in part made up for the vandalism below. Efforts had been made to enhance their own comfort by using bits of detritus to create benches and seats in the form of a semi-circle around the fire.

Charlie grinned, as did the girl sitting cosily beside him.

"Who's this then mate?" Mo offered his cigarettes to both of them and paid particular attention to the girl as she accepted a light. The girl called Molly swept the hood of her jacket from her head to reveal a round face framed by chestnut coloured hair. Static messed with her style. Long woollen socks and Wellington boots covered her lower legs and were not unattractive, or so Mo thought.

Charlie got up and put another bit of wood on the fire. Charlie was useful, no, he really was. A different uniform, a different kind of school. He spoke the same way though, and besides, did it honestly matter? Not forgetting the girl. Just mates, Charlie and her. Mo had assumed this but never bothered to ask. No, things were definitely on the up, and chance meetings could often lead to something of consequence.

Charlie had skills that nobody else had; Mo could see that. Like mending things, building things at the house; that's how it began. Seriously, the school's theatre company could definitely benefit from someone with his skills. Genius! The school play, held in the summer. They'd need girls to play some of the parts in it too!

Mo wasted no time in setting about persuading Miss Barns, the drama teacher, who was conspicuous, not only for her popularity but that she was very much "a her" and not "a him". The headmaster, from his lofty position could see the benefits in advertising the school's well rounded and inclusive policies. It all hinged on the controlling competence of "Barnsie" and whether she could keep everything, including the girls, intact.

Mo passed on the good news to Charlie the next time they met and warned him that a formal invitation would be put to his school. "I've told Miss Barns we need your talents backstage. And get Molly to come and have an audition." Any hesitation on Charlie's part was easily overcome and the deal was sealed over a few bottles of beer and a shared packet of fags…

The play had turned out to be an unrivalled success, and much credit was duly given to the production team and co/directors of Barns and Highland. Charles smiled to himself. Maurice had always used his precocious talent to seize the moment; it seemed to run in his family. Special dispensation in education to children of the clergy had proved to be a god-send and for that the vicar and his son Mo, had always been truly grateful.

Charles found himself tapping the keys once more. "Maurice Highland, a vicar's son, who would have believed it?"

Charles reflected on his own education and those early years in work. Private school had never been seen as a serious option, not when there was a successful family business to support and one day run. Property was king. His father had been recompensed for his services in managing secret facilities during and after the war in bricks and mortar. Government contracts to help rebuild London had been lucrative.

His father grafted but had paid for his property portfolio with bad health and an untimely death. There was more to life than making money; how many times had Charles heard that from his mother? With her approval he had immediately set out to reform and downsize parts of the business. It didn't stop agents and contractors waiting in line to earn their piece of the action.

Charles had taken considerable risks. He needn't have worried; greater freedom gave him time to invest in other avenues of work and creativity. Consequently, when it had become clear that the business owned valuable property in London's West End, he went into overdrive. Future renovations to The Theatre had piqued his interest and who better to involve in the project than Maurice Highland. If anybody could realise their ambitions and make it a vehicle for their own artistic success it would be him.

It had become a hot topic of discussion during a party being given at the vicarage. The Vicar, Maurice's father, was to offer assistance to a choir from the cathedral in Mezlar, the regional capital of Southern Sommovia. They planned to visit London as part of a tour sanctioned by a more relaxed approach from the country's communist government. The choir manager and his soloist had arrived in Britain earlier that day.

Rehearsal space with access to musicians; what better venue than The Theatre to have at your disposal? Accommodation? No problem. Yes, Maurice had seemingly already done a deal. All that was needed was Mr Hanlan's blessing.

"Mr Hanlan is it now, why so formal?" Suspicion had invaded his every word. "Come on Maurice, what's your angle. I thought it was strange being invited to tea at the vicarage."

"Just doing the old man a favour." They'd both looked towards his father who had been uncovering plates of sandwiches ready to receive his guests. "I've already met them. Nice people and they even speak English." Maurice had tried to sound non-committal

"And?"

At that precise moment the doorbell had rung followed a moment later by the entry of the Sommovian delegation. The vicar dutifully made the introductions.

"You both know Maurice, of course, but let me introduce Charles Hanlan, my son's partner in business."

Charles remembered shaking hands with a grey looking, middle-aged man, and immediately forgetting his name.

"And this is – I'm so sorry, but remind me how you pronounce your name." The vicar had had no hesitation in admitting his ignorance.

"Hello," Her blue eyes had twinkled in mild amusement as she offered her hand. "My name is Jelena Horvat, and I'm very pleased to meet you."

Charles got out of the chair, impatient to be active in doing something that would allow his mind to be flooded by the mundane rather than the vital. A change of scenery and some exercise perhaps? He shut his thoughts down along with his computer, and decided upon a walk. When he returned to his desk some thirty minutes later, he worked on late into the afternoon, considering his options and following them to their logical conclusions. Eventually, and only when he was satisfied, he picked up the phone and dialled a familiar number.

Before leaving the office, Charles picked up NRG's formal invitation and studied the itinerary once again. It was certainly true he had nothing but respect for the quality that was NRG Pictures. Sherman Powers was a dreamer with a reputation for making art out of his films.

"A penny for your thoughts." He waved Amelia's invitation carelessly in his pa's direction.

Sally Stewart, who was ready to leave, continued to stare at her computer screen while she plucked up the courage to answer. "I think it would be good for her. I know cultural differences can be tricky but if you trust in Powers, then she should go." She held her breath.

Charles did the maths and considered the collateral damage of his decision either way. Okay, so two days only; just a visit and with provisos that his daughter must strictly adhere to.

"I know it's late but we need to reply to this. Ready to take some dictation?" He took a deep breath. "Shorthand Sally, before I change my mind"

She already had a pen and paper to hand.

Grateful he'd stayed in London for the weekend, it was something that he'd been doing more and more often. He and Amelia had already planned a late breakfast meeting for the following morning and it wasn't as if he needed an excuse. The last weeks of his daughter's involvement in the show were upon them. It was difficult to believe that a year had passed since the adventure had begun. His ability to find and cherish the gifts of others was matched only by the attentions he heaped upon her burgeoning career. He was aware what the cynics said, some in private, the more courageous in print. Charles sometimes wondered if he really did have a problem in defining between the two.

The sudden thrumming of heavy rain on the car window broke the spell of his introversion. Now was the time to gently separate the fiction from the fact. If the call he'd made to Joe Peterson showed anything it was his commitment to that. One question remained; who would be hurt most by the decisions he was making?

*

The early morning mist was evaporating in the brightness of the sunshine. The air was fresh, more akin to the healthy living of a country life. Amelia cracked open her bedroom window and offered her nose to the world. Pavement puddles sparkled, making the most of their short reflective lives.

The surprising change in the weather was in stark contrast to the conditions Charles had encountered on his journey home last night. Driving the silver Mercedes was always a pleasure and he'd made good time on his way across town to Kensington Green. Not too early, he hoped. Amelia liked to sleep in on a Sunday, her one day off. Confidently reversing the car into space outside her flat he switched off the engine and turned down the volume on his CD player. The music he listened to was important to his work. New songs, new voices; he needed to keep in touch. Rare indeed the actor working in London who had not unwittingly auditioned for him in the luxury of his car. Right now, the song was a familiar one, the voice tried and tested. The best he'd ever heard. Amelia evoked many emotions in Charles, but never more so than when he listened to her sing. Normally he would have waited to the end of the song, but today there seemed a sadness where there was usually pride and joy. A copy of the Peter Pearce article lay open on the passenger seat as a reminder of why he felt that way. Anxiously, he glanced up to the windows of his daughter's flat.

Situated on the first floor, it was one of six new conversions in what had been a large Victorian family house. The property and adjoining gardens were well maintained and the reasonable rents and fees ensured that all the flats were occupied. It was said that the agents carried out a vigorous screening policy on any new incoming tenants. As landlord, Charles Hanlan had insisted upon it. From the day of purchase, he had decided that Amelia should live in pleasant surroundings. Had Amelia herself realized to whom she paid the rent, it was debatable whether she would have felt quite so at home as she evidently did. After all, her purpose in moving there was to have a place she could call her own.

Charles picked up his pace. The curtains were drawn back and she was probably waiting.

"Here goes nothing." Hanlan couldn't remember the last time he'd felt less like seeing his daughter.

The smell of freshly warmed croissants filled the living room. Charles sat upright in a single chair with an empty plate balanced carefully on the arm-rest. Amelia watched as he wetted a finger and gently stabbed at flakes of pastry too good to be left. It was something she'd seen him do a hundred times, and yet today it annoyed her. Still in her dressing-gown, legs tucked beneath her, Amelia snuggled defensively into the corner of her sofa.

The silences between them were prolonged and strangely awkward. Amelia decided that background noise might help. She shifted sideways and stretched out to the radio.

"We need to talk." Charles spoke suddenly, concerned his thoughts would be drowned out by the sound of music. "It's not good when we're like this." He softened his tone.

"What about?" Her bright blue eyes flashed him a warning look.

Despite himself, Charles struggled to suppress a grin and for a split second was reminded of Amelia's mother. Although she'd had precious little time to pass on her experience of the world, Jelena would have been proud to see her Sommovian influence alive in the expressions and demeanour of her daughter.

He was still the subject of Amelia's stare.

"It's at times like this when I feel the luckiest of men." He began to explain. "Most people think that butter wouldn't melt, where as I get to see it sizzling in the pan." He raised both hands to deflect the cushion's path that Amelia had thrown at him. Had she meant to hit him he believed she would have succeeded. He took comfort in the hope of a connection of another kind.

"In under two months' time you'll be unemployed. But before you end up on the scrap heap, we're going to make sure you go out with a bang." They were back to business, back on common ground. Whatever the future held they had agreed she needed to take a break from the show.

Amelia retrieved the cushion and returned to the sofa whilst Charles outlined some thoughts on promotion and marketing. The plan had always been to organise charity performances to mark the end of Amelia's involvement and introduce Katie Ley when she took on the lead-role. Recognition at the BAFTAs had encouraged Charles to create new material as the perfect vehicle to help the transition.

"Jonathan wants to see you tomorrow afternoon to go through the new number again." Charles felt the need to warn her. "Don't be late. It'll be full orchestra, and if they can promise to get there on time, then so can you." He tried to look stern.

They briefly discussed other dates and commitments, including a concert and a charity ball to be held at a venue outside of London. This would involve select members of the cast and backstage crew. Charles ticked off the items listed in his diary.

When it lay closed by his side, Amelia sensed that their discussions were not quite over.

"I've changed my mind about the other thing and I think you should go." Charles frowned and clasped his hands together. "To New York, I mean, if only to get Sherman Powers off my back." He made his decision-making sound suddenly trivial. "A few days away will give Katie a chance with the public."

Amelia could hardly believe her ears. Was this her father speaking? He'd previously dismissed the invitation out of hand. She couldn't hide her delight. She wanted to hug him but instead picked up another cushion and threw it towards him, gently this time.

"There are provisos.", Charles tried to suppress his smile. He liked it when she was happy. "Amelia, seriously now. This is not as simple as it sounds. My wife is not going to like this, not one little bit."

Amelia was confused. What difference could it make to Claire; somebody she hadn't seen for nearly four years? As far as she knew the woman lived somewhere abroad. It came to her. "Resides in America, doesn't she?" The cynicism was real.

"In Manhattan, actually." He saved her the trouble of asking. "And Lloyd too."

"And?"

"I should have told you this, but it was all so confusing at the time. I made a deal with them on the day they left. Stupid of me I know." He held his hands up. "But I was desperate."

"What kind of deal?" Amelia pressed him. It was the first time he'd spoken about his wife and son for as long as she could recall.

"She left on bad terms. It was when you were ill in hospital, remember?" He quickly moved the conversation on. "I told her I never wanted to see her or Lloyd ever again." Charles let the words sink in before speaking again. "I had my reasons, very personal ones." His emphasis and tone denied her further questions. "The long and the short of it? She agreed to leave us, as long as you never set foot in America."

"Me? Why me?" She had every right to ask.

"One reason only. She wanted to hurt me. That's all she cared about at the end." Charles got up from his chair and joined Amelia on the sofa. "She knew the best way to do it too."

3. Big Apple

In down town Manhattan as daytime's light faded, so nature's understudy of neon and bulb warmed to their task. The traffic on the street was moving steadily as people headed for home. The purple-grey sky above the city landscape seemed heavy as evening drew in and the threat of rain was real.

Bene's for a beer. He considered his options and checked his watch to see if he still had time. The young man frequently gave in to the charm of the popular bar with its soft lighting and fragrant aromas of freshly cooked food. But not tonight. Without checking his stride, he shifted his collection of newspapers, recently acquired, from one arm to the other and continued around the corner. A few minutes later and a little further down the street, he shut the door to his apartment with a flick of his foot. Turning on lights with his elbow, he contemplated the stack of newsprint and finally placed it on a desk in the corner of the room.

How informative the articles might prove to be was a two-edged sword. A desire to understand was matched by his fear, and as ever his guilt was intense. He recalled the images he retained at will. Involuntarily he clasped his hands together, fighting emotions and nearly always loosing. A spasm of irritation gradually passed. His continued composure was important as he flicked through the newsprint, page by page. The paper felt brittle from the cold of the journey home the previous night. One careless tear. All should be unblemished, just like Amelia Highland herself.

Only two editions contained anything of note. The discarded and unread were deposited on the floor. On the desk, held down by a pair of red-handled scissors lay the shapes of word and picture he wanted to keep. Through the oval handles, like red-rimmed spectacles, the face of Amelia looked up at him. He consoled himself with the thought that he knew more about her than the journalists who were making money from selling their stories. His anger started to simmer and grow as he started to lose concentration. The name of Alan Burrows stopped him short, and his eyes focused back to the beginning of the paragraph he'd been reading. There in black and white, the words and their implications filtered slowly through to him.

"... at the Parkside Grand for Saturday's Moving Picture Salute to film director, Alan Burrows. Among the personalities who will be honouring the Oscar nominee, it's hoped Britain's Amelia Highland will make a rare appearance as she takes time off from her huge West End hit, "Ever Searching". Speculation has it that Miss Highland is being courted to make her film debut later this year in an NRG funded project. However, the word from London, England is that Charles Hanlan, who owns the production company responsible for "ES", may yet oppose his daughter's defection. The smart money is on Sherman Powers and NRG persuading Miss Highland to take an extended break from the stage and let film have its chance."

*

The pace of life had just picked a notch or two. Within two days of her father agreeing on her trip to New York, she was suddenly and unbelievably on her way. Now that she had some time to herself, Amelia spent it going over her not-too-distant past. Claire and Lloyd leaving the family home near Bath was something she had easily accepted. Neither her step-mother or step-brother had ever been a constant in her life and she'd never felt compelled to ask more about that.

Amelia had been seriously ill and sent home from school. Yes, she remembered that much. Then, waking in the hospital with her father asleep in the chair beside her bed; but nothing in between. What had happened to make Claire go away, and why take it out on her so personally? Only her father could answer that with any certainty.

Amelia closed the pages of her magazine and placed it on the pull-out tray beside her. Her dark shoulder length hair was casually styled and tied back with a ribbon for convenience. Removing her reading glasses, she brushed from her cheek the occasional wisps that had escaped the black velvet's clasp. She was elegance personified. Ralph Lauren would have been proud of his black woven stretch leggings and multi-coloured hand knitted sweater. Amelia made the perfect model. Inside her stomach the butterflies danced and not for the first time she checked the whereabouts of her coat laying folded in readiness for the cold she anticipated at journey's end.

As the 747 banked left on its final approach to Newark Airport, Amelia stared through the small window and captured her first impressions of Manhattan's sky-line. The middle-aged man, sitting across the aisle from Amelia, took the opportunity to concentrate his gaze on the form of the young single woman. Even now with her back half turned, the smooth line of her jaw and the soft sensual nape of her neck prompted his greatest attentions. In turning back, she caught the direction of his stare. If she'd not taken notice of his interest before, it was clear that she was aware of it now. The man felt that his attentions were unwelcome and had even disturbed her. He promised himself to be more subtle in the future.

*

Samantha Grant was late however many times she checked her watch. A mix of heavy traffic at the entrance to the Hudson Tunnel and the inclement weather New York had been suffering from were the causes but could not be offered as genuine excuses. The last few miles to the New Jersey airport were understandably not her most relaxed. In her capacity as public relations executive she was becoming accustomed to the stresses the film business was subjecting her to. Leaving the limo and driver parked illegally outside the terminal, Samantha walked quickly through the arrivals lounge. Her boss held in high regard the efforts she had made in her eighteen months with the company – he had even told her so. She firmly clung to this thought, determined to keep her reputation intact despite the last half hour of highway hell and automotive delay.

Pleased to be moving and making up for lost time, she slowed for a second or two outside a windowed shop-front to check on the state and style of her flax-coloured hair. The reflection she glimpsed was by no means perfect but she was quietly pleased, knowing the care she took at that moment was unusual. Meeting image conscious people was second nature to her now. Wining and dining them on behalf of her boss; flirting with the best and being subtly polite with the rest. Why should it be any different with Amelia Highland, unless of course she feared uncomfortable comparison with her new client's fresh and natural looks?

The question remained unanswered and any drop of unease evaporated as Samantha caught sight of Amelia pushing her luggage across the concourse. She laughed aloud as a man following in her wake crashed into a barrier through a lack of proper concentration. She couldn't blame him really. One thing was certain, Amelia Highland, in her own quiet way had definitely arrived. The next couple of days should prove to be full of interest and Sam was glad of that at least.

The two young women sat together in the back of the limo as it sped along the highway leaving the airport behind them. Amelia filled her eyes with the sight of Manhattan in the near distance and tried to pick out the iconic shapes.

"So, are you looking forward to your visit with us?" Sam asked, making conversation. "I'm so glad you were able to come over." This was something of an understatement and she wondered at just how much independence Amelia had in making the decision. "It's a shame that we have to condense so much into a couple of days."

Amelia considered Samantha's question and came to reflect on what her father had recently revealed. If she was honest, she couldn't quite believe it all herself. The deal that Charles had made with his wife had seemed implausible and extreme to say the least. If nothing else it made her realise how cocooned her life had really become.

Why hadn't she been more inquisitive about Claire's migration? And Lloyd, there one moment gone the next, with no goodbyes. Her illness and trip to the hospital now appeared to be a flimsy excuse for her indifference, if that indeed was what she'd shown.

"I never really thought much about work after Ever Searching. If I'm honest The Theatre has taken over my world. I've learnt to take each day as it comes." Amelia sounded nervous, conscious that her words sounded lame. "You mentioned something about a screen test." Her reluctance was audible and she felt instantly ashamed for not showing Samantha more appreciation. "I've never had to do one before."

"Neither have I, but I hear there's nothing to it." Sam made it sound like she was poorer for having missed out. "Nothing too onerous, it's more about lighting and camera angles, that kind of thing. It's not an audition as such." Sherman Powers was looking nowhere else to fill the role of playing his wife, that was a given. "It'll give you the chance to meet up with the casting director and some of the film crew. We have a small studio built for the job."

With some reservation Sam then went on to outline their schedule and the role NRG had asked Amelia to play in public that night. Publicity was a necessary evil, but she sensed that the young Brit had her reasons for fearing its intrusion. Adapting to her needs and employing a lighter touch might yet prove important.

"I'm sure I'm going to like New York. I've read so much about it." Amelia searched out the skyline again as shafts of sunlight lit up an area of high rising peaks of block, brick and glass. "And seeing you of course. I've been looking forward to that." Amelia sounded rather shy. "We spoke on the phone about tonight's tribute." She hesitated. "It's not something I would have chosen to do on my first visit though. I suppose I'm just feeling out of my depth, being amongst all those famous people. Apart from you I won't know anybody there." A sudden thought struck Amelia. "You are going to be there aren't you?"

She was referring to one of New York's finest hotels, no more than a few blocks walk away from the south side of Central Park. The Parkside Grand, chosen venue for the annual American Arts Museum's celebratory dinner held in honour of those who have contributed most to the world of stage and screen. This year's special guest of honour was a man who had worked on a number of occasions for Sherman Powers, as well as a host of Hollywood producers. Alan Burrows stature as a film director was at an all-time high and America's finest were about to gather to celebrate that.

"Of course, I'll be there." Sam found her response to be protective and naturally warm. "You have nothing to worry about. Sherman will look after you like a perfect gentleman and I'll be there to look after Sherman."

Sam was the only person in the company to call the boss by his first name. Powers himself had not laid down any hard and fast rules. It had become somewhat of a company tradition, one of many that Samantha had not adhered to in her short and sometimes eventful period of employment. If truth would out, Powers didn't object to Sam's wicked breech of office protocol. In fact, he rather liked it, particularly as it came from "the best thing I've had working for me since buying flowers for my wife back in the seventies."

"It'll be fine," Samantha continued, "and don't worry about being a stranger. If Sherman has his way, you'll soon be the toast of the town."

Amelia managed to laugh. "As long as I don't get burned in the process." Standing on stage in the spot light was one thing. Seeking limelight away from work was altogether another. Instinctively she understood that Sherman Powers, in contrast to her father, would not try to shelter her from paparazzi interest.

Sam reached across and touched the actress's arm in a reassuring gesture. "Sherman admits to finding you a fascinating contradiction." Amelia looked up in surprise. "Take it as a compliment." Sam continued, aware that it was not in her remit to talk about this yet. "A well-known actor with a recognisable talent and yet you don't appear to exploit your position. Perhaps that's why you unwittingly create such interest. I happen to admire you for that. It makes a pleasant change in the film business." Sam took a breath. "Listen, let's you and me enjoy tonight and don't worry about Sherman." Her voice took on a hint of sarcasm, "Really he's a pussy cat, he just thinks he can bark."

As they emerged from the tunnel under the Hudson River, Samantha had time to reflect on the impressions the Brit had made on her. Repressed excitement instead of wide-eyed wonderment at seeing Manhattan for the first time; maybe that was because of Amelia's nerves. No mention of the film as yet, which was slightly strange. Wouldn't every young actress jump at the chance to star in a movie? Well, maybe not given her success back home. One thing was for sure, Sherman and his swelling ambition would have to be kept in check, lest he frighten Amelia Highland away.

*

"Lights, camera, action." The small studio consisted of a simple set made up of two chairs turned in to face each other. A low table gave space between them. Three static cameras situated in an arc were pointed towards them, while intricate lighting gave depth to a background that was not really there. Amelia sat much like a deer caught in a car's headlights, wondering what she'd let herself in for. Her surprise was real when a voice from the dark asked the first question.

"Tell me about yourself." If it was meant as a prompt, then it had the opposite effect.

The approach was too contrived and had no chance of working, just as Samantha had predicted. Whispering a few words with the casting director, she slipped out of the room intent on finding some help for Amelia. Fortunately, Rosalind Powers was sitting in 'make-up'. Tall and upright, wide-set features striking and familiar, her grey hair full of body and vitality much like the woman herself.

Hazel-brown eyes, full of focus, turned away from the mirror in front of her.

"That bad, eh?" A questioning look and a sympathetic smile were full of understanding. "Okay, I'm on my way."

Back in the studio, Sam found that the change of mood was palpable. Rosalind, while remaining inclusive, had made her primary task of rescuing Amelia quite obvious. Taking over from her attentive husband who stood in the background, she introduced herself with a handshake and sat down beside her, speaking quietly to the young actress without being overbearing.

Sam watched and wondered as Rosalind held onto Amelia's hand, as if it were the most casual and natural thing to do. It was a small gesture that some might have found too personal, but it seemed to be having the desired effect.

"What do you say to having a chat, just the two of us. Give ourselves the chance to become acquainted. I think I'd like that, if that's okay with you?" Rosalind spoke in even tones and her eyes showed genuine sincerity. Sam could see that Amelia was grateful for that, and it was no surprise when Rosalind decided to take things further.

With an imperceptible nod to Samantha and the casting director, she spoke aloud to the rest of the room. "Ten minutes would be nice, if that's okay with you guys." An order shaped in the words of a request, not even Sherman was going to question the sense in what she'd asked, as they shuffled in line and out the door. "Samantha, could I ask you to bring me some water?"

Now the scene was comfortably set.

"I enjoyed my time on Broadway but I'd fulfilled my acting ambitions when I was still very young." Rosalind sat in the chair across from Amelia and offered to refill her glass. "By the time Sherman and I had got to know each other, I was ready for a change and happy enough to walk away." She smiled with affection. "He will tell you something different; that I sacrificed my career, in a bid to help him with NRG. But the reality is I've never looked back. Well, not that often." She briefly put her finger to her lips. "Don't say I said so, but we're a good team, Sherman and I, and I've loved every minute of working with him."

"You could have gone into film yourself. I heard that Hollywood came knocking on your door more than once" Amelia took a sip from her glass. She tried to imagine how Rosalind had reached a decision to turn those offers down.

"True, but in those days, you had to sign your life away. For sure the big studios were prepared to offer a lot of money but they tied you in to a three or even a five-year contract. I'm not sure that Sherman and I could have survived that long apart."

"You were in love." It was simply said and for the first time Amelia looked as if she was relaxed and enjoying the conversation.

"I was and still am, even if our relationship is much changed from those heady, vital days of independence and the excitement of making something for ourselves. It's what motivates Sherman to want to make a film now. His way of showing his thanks to me, through you." For the first time Rosalind sounded embarrassed. "Anyhow, it's a way of celebrating that we made a life together. These things are important."

Amelia studied the older woman's face and could see genuine emotion in her eyes. "It's interesting that you say that. In the last few days, I've had the chance to re-evaluate my relationship with my step-father and how much I've taken for granted because of him." Amelia wanted to reciprocate with her own honesty. "For instance, how weird is it that I should be closer to him than he is with his own son. I wonder if I should be feeling guilty about that."

"I haven't got an answer for you, every family is different. Looking out for yourself is important but I guess we don't neglect our nearest and dearest. Not easy in our business, especially when you're young." Rosalind looked thoughtful. "Conversely, those around you can get greedy. You do them a favour and before you know it, they're asking for more. It can be lonely at the top and

I'd imagine that's something you can ask your step-father about." Rosalind stopped short of mentioning the loss of Amelia's parents but it was evidently in her thoughts.

"I've very few friends of my own age, it's true. Competition for parts makes it difficult. Jealousy comes with competition and an over protective parent can f… up your private life too." Amelia clamped her hand over her mouth as part of an apology.

Rosalind waved it away and enjoyed that Amelia was happy to expose a little of her true nature. "Whatever happens down the line with NRG, don't become part of this project unless you can feel fully invested in it. You owe that to yourself as well as to us. Compared to some, you have already lived a life; losing your parents at such a young age must have been hard for you." She took a deep breath. "The only advice I can offer, that is if I'm allowed to give it, is to make your decisions from a position of strength and not out of weakness. I truly believe that the comfort that offers you will be your greatest luxury."

From the darker recesses of the studio, hidden behind the glare of the lights, Samantha Grant listened in fascination while making an occasional note to herself. She had always intended to stay but had the impression that Rosalind had invited her to do so when asking for a jug of water. It had occurred to her with some amusement that Sherman Powers would be needing something stronger when he got to see the daily rushes. Rosalind's idea to leave the cameras rolling while she talked to Amelia was proving as useful as it was under-handed.

That the camera loved Amelia Highland was an indisputable fact. The bigger question and of more concern, was how much Amelia might love the camera back?

Amelia was alone and sitting comfortably in a green leather chair. Her top floor surroundings were in keeping with the highest office in the company, because without doubt nobody out-ranked Sherman Powers. That had become apparent as she'd entered the glass fronted doors of 'Sherman Towers'. Sam had felt bound to explain away the title for Powers administrative HQ as 'just his little joke', but left it to others to imagine his strength of ego swimming at the time of the name's conception.

Amelia finished her coffee and rose to stretch her limbs, realising that by rights she ought to be tired. Walking to the window and remembering how Mr Powers had proudly given her a static and detailed tour of Manhattan's landmarks, she tried to get her bearings once again. Situated on sixth avenue, Sherman Towers was in a high-class part of town. The exorbitant price of real estate meant that rent for the area was charged by the square foot and not by the yard. Those that could afford the island's rich urban plane included the likes of CBS, NBC, Time and Life Magazines, all huge corporations. The buildings could do no more than impress. Towards the horizon, the panoramic view of the East River and beyond was truly unique to Amelia's eyes, and she was drawn again to stare at the lights of Queens and Brooklyn on the far side of the water.

She searched for the Queensboro and Williamsburg bridges. One spanned Roosevelt Island; she couldn't remember which. The United Nations building was, she knew, not that far away. What about the Brooklyn Bridge? She ought to see that before she went home. But the winter light had faded quickly. Sight-seeing would have to wait until tomorrow. Amelia raised her eyes to the inky blackness above the buildings as she noticed flickering lights moving across the sky. The traffic from La Guardia and JFK International airports remained as busy as that on the streets and avenues below her.

"Would you care for some more coffee Miss Highland?" Amelia had not heard the office door open. "Mr Powers has finished his meeting and should be with you again at any moment." It sounded as if Louise, Sherman Powers' faithful and long-serving secretary, had delivered that particular line on numerous occasions.

Amelia smiled her acceptance of this news and a top up of her coffee and then remembered a promise as yet unfulfilled. She'd forgotten to ring her father to tell him how she'd got on. "My mobile seems to have died, Louise. I wonder if I could borrow a phone?"

"Yes of course you can." Louise hesitated, wanting to remind Amelia of time zones. "It'll be quite late if you're thinking of ringing home, and perhaps I should have told you, your father has already called. I spoke to him myself and told him that you were here." She felt the need to further explain. "He said not to disturb you, he just wanted to check on your schedule for tonight." She tried to gauge Amelia's reaction to the news. "I hope I did the right thing."

Amelia said it was fine and was left to ponder and puzzle over her father's actions. She'd made him promise not to call but had given her own assurances in return. She found it strange that having taken the trouble, he had not wanted to speak to her in person. Perhaps her protective parent had felt guilty for not sticking to his word?

When Samantha and Sherman finally returned to the office, the latter's face was wreathed in smiles. Amelia looked to Samantha for confirmation that all had gone well. A thumbs up and a small nod of assent was a welcome relief.

"It seems you had a good chat with my wife." Sherman had obviously seen the rushes and broached a delicate subject which took a little wind out of the two women's sails.

"Mrs Powers was so kind and it was really lovely to meet her." Amelia decided to stand up for herself and was rewarded with Sam's look of encouragement. "We had a frank discussion which was very valuable. Underneath her calm exterior she's quite feisty. I'd like to think that there is a little of that in me." Amelia spoke with a confidence that had, until now, been lacking.

Sherman instantly regretted his previous and rather clumsy attempts to gain the young woman's trust. He was more than convinced of Amelia's suitability for his film but recognised his influence would be minimal. Her father would see to that. Also, he had to wonder to what extent his ambitions had been compromised by the honesty of his own wife.

Samantha took the opportunity to reminded him that time was running short. Amelia was gently taken by the elbow and led to the nearest elevator. Still feeling protective but somewhat relieved, she noticed her boss' immaculate manners and reverential behaviour. He appeared to be anticipating the evening's celebrations with a new air of confidence.

"Until eight o'clock then. See you both there." Powers caught the remnants of Samantha's cheeky grin. "Look after my new star, Miss Grant, or else there will be trouble!"

*

It had been suggested that they taxi their way to the Parkside Grand. Less conspicuous than the company limo, Amelia was glad of that and said so. Sam was reassured by the dazzle and sincerity in her show of happiness. Things were looking up.

Amelia was thinking much the same as she absorbed the street-level scenery, whilst making slow but steady progress in heavy traffic across town. It gave her time to revisit her meeting with Sherman Powers and how passionately he had sold his vision in dedicating a film to his talented wife. Rosalind too had been so supportive whilst maintaining a level-headed take on life and showing how in tune she was with the nagging doubts Amelia had. She more than her husband seemed to see the Hanlan family's complex situation might yet prove influential. Her father couldn't give his blessing to her working in America as things stood.

Time enough to meet those questions head-on, and be sure in her own mind of the things she really wanted. Rosalind was certainly right in saying that success, however carefully managed, could be a bind. Oh, too many questions and not enough answers! Better perhaps, to live in the present and enjoy whatever New York had on this evening's menu. Judging by the spectacle outside the taxi's window, the Parkside Grand was going to be a brilliant starter.

*

Nick Sayers was prompt and professional and a couple of hours early. The temperature was dropping and snow was in the air. The welcoming lights and the promise of warmth inside encouraged his steps to the Parkside Grand. Classy and old fashioned, the popular hotel prompted memories of old haunts from his life and work in London. A rare reminder indeed, that could still produce a varied mix of emotions.

British born and in his early thirties, he had few ties and no family left to speak of. Manhattan was home, even if his links were tenuous now that he and his American wife, Libi, were thinking of getting a divorce. Immediate depression threatened to close in upon him and he chastised himself for letting his mind linger on something still too raw to carelessly cope with. One constant remained and was viewed by both in a positive light, and that was his work. A role of contributing editor for Stress Magazine and helping to grow its success, was something that Libi, as its CEO, was keen to continue with and actively encourage. Nick took some comfort from that.

'Stress' had originally been set up in the late nineties as a monthly glossy to see out the old millennium and usher in the new. The magazine had struck a chord with the public and Nick's work had blossomed under the increasing demands put upon it. Writing articles on the exploits of persons past or the futuristic suppositions of the world to come and illustrating them with his photography, he got to travel widely around the world. Nick now had a free hand in choosing his own material and creating a particular brand of journalism. His wife had come to trust his position in the company as much as he did in hers.

What had become blatantly obvious to him was that mutual admiration was needed in the home as much as it was in the boardroom. Healthy pay cheques and bank account balances appeared to be the best that they had in common at present.

Back to work, work of sorts. He adjusted the heavy camera case on his shoulder and headed for the stairs. Tonight was different. The job, a blast from the past. The magazine's paparazzi appointment had conveniently got himself stranded out of state in a snow storm and Nick had agreed to stand in and cover the celebrations made for the director Alan Burrows. In truth he was glad of the distraction. Libi too had sounded relieved when she knew he was keeping busy. It meant once again that they'd found sufficient reason not to get together and talk about subjects of a more personal nature.

Old habits die hard, Nick was the first photographer to arrive. Over the last ten years he'd built a reputation as a dedicated operator, one who never squandered an opportunity to be in the right place at the right time, given the chance. Some of his rivals, particularly in the paparazzi ranks preferred to call him lucky but Libi was sure he had a very good eye. It was why she hired him when he first came to the Big Apple to claim his slice of the pie. That he was tall and handsome, polite and British had, she claimed, always been of secondary importance. He in turn had learnt much from her in those early days and not all of it had been about work.

He paused and looked in on the largest ballroom in the hotel. White linen draped tables circled by chairs filled the dance floor. In the balconies above smaller tables for two were dressed in readiness for diner. Up on stage selected clips from Alan Burrows's greatest films were being projected onto a large screen. Nick identified most of the film titles and realised the potential guest list that would surely come to honour the director of so many successes.

A familiar voice stopped him in his tracks. Tony Sterling, resplendent in dinner jacket, bow tie and patent leather shoes strode confidently towards him.

"What brings you here, Nick?" They shook hands. "Not working? I thought you'd gone on to finer things now." The sarcastic note to Sterling's comment was typical of the man. Not quite a sneer, more of a challenge. He decided to let it go.

"Tony, good to see you. Forgot you'd be in handling this little bash tonight." Nick put down his camera case and took the weight off his shoulder.

Tony Sterling, head of Sterling Associates Inc., a public relations company that had grown in stature over many years. Tony had a reputation as a "power house" in business, the "driving force" behind everything successful. Tony's own words if Nick remembered correctly. He thought that he should explain how the magazine had been let down last moment but felt less inclined to give an update on his own private motivation for being there tonight.

"Usual reception area for the photo-call? Any dos and don'ts?"

"Always on the ball, eh, buddie boy. Oh, and by the way, you'd better have one of these." Sterling brandished a press pass. "Since you were last here, we've had to tighten our security. Only those on the official press list will be allowed in to work the shoot." He puffed himself up. "No exceptions. You can tell the rest."

Nick held his hands up in token surrender. “Okay by me, Tony.” He remembered the farcical shambles of three years ago when he and his colleagues had broken ranks in a manic attempt to corner Robert De Niro. Nobody had really gained but by being patient and polite, Nick had succeeded where others had not. “Any late additions to the guest list, Tony? Any surprises in store?”

Sterling considered his answer, weighing up the pros and cons of giving secrets away. Nick smiled at his host’s dilemma.

“Not that you’re supposed to know but Powers may have a young English actress in tow. Amelia Highland. You must have heard of her.” Nick shook his head. “Meant to be hush hush, don’t ask me why.” He began to move away. “Carol Benton will be looking after the photocall so you’ll get a fair crack of the whip. Just behave yourselves.”

*

Room 805 was beautiful with furnishings and décor that gave a cosy, old-fashioned feel. Amelia lifted her heavy suitcase onto the vast expanse of her bed. With its ornately carved headboard, she thought it an impressive if not slightly extravagant place to lie upon. She switched on the near bedside lamp and stretched out across the pillows to light its partner. The silken cord of the shade that brushed her wrist shimmied and swayed. Amelia allowed hypnotic shadows to fall upon her face and knew that sleep was not far away.

It seemed a shame to wake the sleeping beauty. Sam peered through the partly opened partition doors before stepping quietly through from her own adjoining room. She tilted her head to look more intently at Amelia, believing that at any second the peaceful mask and steady breathing must surely be disturbed by her presence.

"Time to wake up." She whispered but not loudly enough. "Amelia."

One eye opened and immediately closed again. It was the only sign that she'd heard Sam's reveille. Sleep's cocoon gradually dropped away. Stretching magnificently, she smiled and then tried to stifle a yawn.

"You're alive then."

"Yes, I think so. How long have I slept?"

"An hour, maybe a little more." Sam checked her watch. "There's plenty of time before we need to go down but I thought it best to wake you. Some girls take longer to get themselves ready, know what I mean?"

Amelia, now fully aware of her surroundings, noticed that Samantha had already showered and changed. "I only closed my eyes for a second." Keen to reassure, she pushed herself up from the bed. She glanced again at the American. Her dark blue, fit and flared knee length dress contrasted the colour of her hair. "You look great. The style really suits you." Amelia found it hard to look away.

"You're more than kind." Sam felt a little self-conscious. "What have you brought with you? We should have hung it up as soon as we got here."

Amelia peered into the depths of her suitcase. "I hope you'll give me an honest opinion." A black halter neck dress appeared. She held it against her body for Sam to inspect. "What do you think?" Amelia went back to emptying the contents of the suitcase out on the bed. Underwear fell decorously where it lay; brand new and lacy.

Sam could sense Amelia was beginning to panic. “I really like that.” She watched as the young woman wrinkled her nose in uncertainty. “No, I really do,” she said again. “Shower and try it on.”

The moment passed. Amelia gathered her wash things and disappeared into the bathroom. Sam could hear the sound of running water as the shower burst into life. Crossing the bedroom, she tuned into CNN news and was just in time to catch a live report taking place from the street outside the hotel. The cream of Hollywood was expected and New York’s paparazzi obviously agreed. She could see a swarm of photographers waiting patiently for the action to begin. The lights of the Parkside Grand main entrance looked particularly bright, intensified by the clear cold darkness of the night.

The bathroom door opened and she turned to see tiny swirls of steam escape and evaporate into the cooler air of the bedroom. Amelia, tall and slim, wrapped in a large white towel, emerged from the mists. The skin on her face and shoulders glowed, the warmth of the water had both cleaned and revived. Samantha got up from the end of the bed and prepared to leave. Amelia would want some privacy while she dressed.

“Hotting up down stairs.” Sam pointed at the television. “Bet your life Sherman will be in the thick of it before too long.” Sam stopped and turned as she reached the door. “Knock when you’re ready, or give me a call. Okay?”

Amelia did not readily reply and when Sam looked again, she could tell that her new friend was looking troubled. Returning into the room she regained her position at the end of the bed while her mind raced to fathom the cause of this sudden distress.

"Here, come and sit down." She patted the bedspread next to her and waited as Amelia appeared to suppress a sudden surge of emotion. "Tell me what's wrong." She smiled endeavouring to calm Amelia who was still dripping wet, clutching at the towel wrapped around her.

Amelia sat quietly down, trying to find the words that would adequately explain. "I'm really sorry," She held herself still and looked down as she fiddled with the hem of her towel, "I know we haven't known each other that long, so maybe this is too soon but perhaps you should look for somebody else." She spoke with some determination. Tears were not that far away but she would find it hard to forgive herself if they were shed.

Samantha took a deep breath allowing her own tension to subside. She found that she was blushing and chastised herself for not being more detached. What was it about this girl? Regaining her composure, she shifted so she could face and speak directly to Amelia. "Give yourself time." She gently touched the girl's arm. "Tell me about it, if you think you can trust me." Sam rose from the bed and returned from the bathroom with another towel which she placed around the young actress' shoulders.

Amelia spoke for nearly fifteen minutes while Samantha listened intently and with increasing sympathy. In the end they agreed that no final decisions would be made in haste and that the confidences they'd shared would be kept strictly private.

Amelia dried her hair and dressed with speed and having applied a touch of makeup was transformed from bedraggled in bath-towel to beautiful in designer gown. Sam remained in her preferred position on the end of the bed. Although deep in thought, she found time to reflect on the intimate position she'd quickly and unexpectedly found herself in. Could it be that she was feeling proud and happy that Amelia had confided in her, when she must have found it difficult to do so with others who'd known her longer?

*

With a concerted effort, Nick Sayers climbed out of his bed and padded bare foot from the bedroom. His newly-acquired apartment was undeniably clean and tidy, bordering on being bare. There was no danger of him tripping over much which was fortunate considering his half-unconscious state. Simple domesticity had been forced upon him and it continued to act as a constant reminder that he really ought to make more of an effort to create a home.

Coffee in the kitchen. He thought back to the previous night. The job had gone well. Although he hadn't had the time to edit all his work, it was always a relief to get his pictures successfully downloaded onto his computer. It was something he always did before going to bed whatever time of night it was.

He allowed himself a rueful smile. It hadn't taken him long before he'd reverted to type as he knew he would. The constant battle for space and angle of shot plus the persistent calling of famous names had soon shattered any illusions he may have held of latter-day grandeur. Fortunately, Carol Benton, resplendent in sequins, had kept firm control on celebrity and photographer alike.

Nick had actually enjoyed the evening. Even the crude banter, most of which had been at his expense, had been worth putting up with. It was nice in a way to get some feedback from his old adversaries, at least from those who were prepared to admit they'd seen his latest work. There'd been no encouragement for him to return fulltime to their specialist field. Lens-life in New York was hard enough without the competition, seemed to be the overriding message.

Even after a relatively short period away, his memory had tended to play tricks. Nick had on occasion relied on the old adage of shoot first and ask questions later. It was in this way that Samantha Grant had inadvertently become a celebrity for the night. He had taken a couple of shots at an attractive face he felt he ought to recognize. Yes, a mistake, one that anybody could have made but preferably not in such unforgiving company.

Samantha did little to help his predicament.

"I'm flattered. Did you want my autograph as well?" Her teasing grin was only to be expected and endured; her recognition of him, immediate. "Well, my goodness. How the mighty have fallen." There was no more time to talk as Sam moved quietly out of his line of shot.

Behind her Sherman Powers entered the room, a smile on his face as wide as his girth. Who could have blamed him? On his right arm, his wife was tall and graceful. On his left, a shy young woman that few had seen before. Flash units lit up the room. It was a strange thing to witness. The usual calls to secure some-kind of eye-contact were strangely muted and suddenly respectful. Nick could see through the view finder a certain reticence on either side of the big man in the middle.

When Sherman suddenly withdrew, Rosalind's reassuring smile and outstretched hand were the only things that prevented Amelia from running. They walked forward together. Amelia took comfort from her older and more accomplished companion, while her genuine shyness and quiet manner appeared as refreshing as it was believable. Nick was aware of the effect on his fellow photographers. Paparazzi politeness was a rare commodity indeed, as was Amelia Highland.

"Nick Sayers?"

"Yes, speaking." He replaced his mug of coffee on the desk.

"Samantha Grant here. Sorry to call you this early but I wanted to make sure I caught you." Still at the Parkside Grand, she had been assessing the room service menu when thoughts of work had taken priority. Thankfully Louise, Sherman Powers' secretary, had been early at her desk and able to help out.

"Samantha. No problem." He was fully awake. "It's been a while and now twice in twenty-four hours. Funny though, I was just thinking about you."

"Is that good or bad? No don't answer that." She wondered what he'd think if he could see her propped up with pillows in a comfortable hotel bed. "I'm glad we got to bump into each other last night. Hope you got some good stuff by the way." Sam had been doing her maths. "And you're right, it's been a while."

In fact, it had been more than a year. Nick had been on assignment at the Oscars and Sam, had accompanied Sherman Powers on the trip west.

"If I remember correctly, I caught you smuggling photographic equipment in behind the scenes and breaking all the rules." Crisp denominations of bribery had helped him to carry out his latest ruse.

"I never was that comfortable with the way I behaved but it made me good money. At least working for the magazine has made me an honest man."

"I phoned your home number and spoke with Libi." Sam said cautiously. "I hope you don't mind but she explained that you're living apart. I'm sorry to hear that."

Nick wanted to keep the conversation light and knew that the two women had met before when Sam was managing a catering company.

"No worries." He felt uncomfortable and needed to change the subject. "Listen, sounds like you've got something on your mind."

"Just wondered what your work load is like? I appreciate that the magazine takes up a lot of your time but I might have a project that could be of interest." Sam was bending the truth and reacting to a last-minute idea.

"What's it all about?" He was curious.

She considered how much she had a right to say. "I'll be honest with you. It needs agreeing with my boss but I'd see you in a consultant's role."

"That would include promotional stuff for NRG?" Nick prompted.

"Initially not that much. Biographical documentation, mostly. Sorry, I'm trying not to be too indiscreet." Even now she could picture Amelia Highland, wrapped in bath towels, revealing secrets that people would pay good money to hear. "It needs to be handled carefully by someone my client and NRG can trust."

Nick wondered at what he was not being told. "It goes without saying I'm flattered but I'd need to know a little more."

"Truth is if we hadn't met last night then we wouldn't be talking now. That said, I do think it could be to our mutual benefit." Sam immediately felt that her last statement left a little too much open to interpretation. She continued quickly. "Look, you know how it is. There's no such thing as bad publicity but in this case, I feel it could compromise everything." Sam was thinking quickly. "And besides you're British, you understand the language." She listened to the silence at the other end of the phone as the penny dropped. "Why don't we meet later today. Come and meet the girl herself before she flies home." Sam checked her diary. "We won't be leaving the city much before five. I'm dropping Miss Highland off at the airport."

Nick considered his day. Editing and a meeting with Libi were essential. A planned trip to Hong Kong needed to be discussed and finalized. He made a suggestion.

"Maybe we could meet for lunch. How would that be?"

Sam checked her watch and considered her commitments with Amelia, who was still asleep. "Sounds good to me. I know she wants to go sight-seeing but a spot of lunch, as you English would say," she tried and failed with her mimicry, "would do us just fine."

It was agreed. Bene's for one o' clock.

*

The salute to Alan Burrows was deemed an unconditional success and Sherman Powers had enjoyed it immensely. The interest shown towards Miss Highland suggested that top billing would not go amiss. It had been delightful to see she'd not thought once to turn her head and witness the effect she was having. Rosalind had skilfully guided her through the night with a cool reserve and had born with great patience her husband's excessive bouts of bonhomie. Her tight reined and controlled emotion balanced out his unbridled joy.

Truly she had enjoyed her time with Amelia, and yes, she would undoubtedly be a great asset to any film they made. However, Rosalind had yet to be convinced that the deal her husband craved deserved the confidence he set by it. Call it a woman's intuition, but not only her own. Samantha Grant's body language had advised caution; it had all night. What a shame it was that her husband did not always read the signs.

On entering the lobby of the Parkside Grand the next morning, Samantha was there to greet him. When her face did not openly reflect the joy he could barely contain, it was then that his wife's words began to echo and take substance again. Sherman allowed himself to be led to an alcove where their conversation would remain private.

"I need an answer by the end of next month Miss Grant. I've made an approach to Alan Burrows to direct." Sherman sounded in control, even though his thoughts were racing. "You don't think somebody got there before us?"

Samantha shook her head, but couldn't believe that he was naive enough to think that negotiations would be trouble free. On the plus side Amelia had loved her time with Rosalind.

"She's ready for something new, but she's not ours to have until her step-father says so."

"And when will that be?" Sherman was fidgeting. "Look, it's got nothing to do with money Miss Grant, though god knows we could do with a commercial success." He patted his pockets in search of a cigar. "It's to be my last film, my chance to bow out and concentrate on other things I've neglected for too long. My wife for instance, there is no one else." Sherman smiled, the last vestiges of formality falling away.

"I want the chance to say thank you for all the sacrifices she made." He bowed his head.

Sam was strangely moved and took courage. She explained about her idea of hiring Nick Sayers and this was keenly debated before being accepted.

True to form Sherman impressed upon her the need to get their dollars' worth. "You're sure he can help, Miss Grant?" He'd seen them talking at the photo-shoot the previous night. He would have said more but a familiar voice echoed again in his ear. He relented. "I'll leave it to you. I'm sure you know what you're doing." Rosalind would have been proud.

Sam recalled the words the Director, Alan Burrows had spoken when questioned by the press. "You're only as good as your latest work,"

One thing was clear, if Amelia was ever to make a film for NRG, then Sam was going to need all the help she could get.

*

Tony Sterling was also having a meeting that morning. A debriefing with all his team leaders. The importance of clarifying problems incurred during the previous evening was paramount in his eyes. Everybody had their say but it seemed the general consensus was of another job well done. Sterling Associates were nothing if not thorough. When he was satisfied, Tony dismissed his men.

Only one remained. He had been part of the team but was unlikely to work for them again. He was due to go back to England later that day. Reporting in full to his own client would probably justify the reason as to why he'd been sent to New York at such short notice.

"Well, I think that concludes our business here, Mr Peterson. My boys said you handled yourself very well last night. Just the one incident I believe?" Tony Sterling tried to gauge any reaction to his compliment and inquiry. "I sense that I'd be wasting my breath but if you're ever looking for a change of scenery..."

"Thanks Mr Sterling." Joe got to his feet and offered his hand. "I'll be in touch if there's anything more you can help my client with."

Tony Sterling would have to make do with a generous payment for his cooperation and silence over what had occurred.

Joe shut the office door behind him and reflected on the implications of Charles' predictions and the forethought in sending him to New York. One thing was clear. However coincidental and unfortunate the incident had been, there had been little chance of it being avoided.

Lloyd Hanlan had been stubborn to a fault.

His first two attempts at bypassing security at the Parkside had met with firm denial and increasing impatience; the lack of correct press-passes undoubtedly his undoing. The third time he'd almost made it. The need to convince perfect strangers with hearty handshakes that they had definitely met before was essential. Once in line he'd done his utmost to hide amongst their dinner jackets and sparkling gowns. But to no avail.

"Excuse me sir, you're wanted on the phone." Lloyd had feigned deafness before eventually allowing himself to be taken to one side. "If you'd like to follow me sir, there's one in here you can use." The well-spoken guard with an English sounding accent pointed to a door on the other side of the hall.

Once across the threshold Lloyd's sense of foreboding shouted loudly. As he turned with an explanation forming on his lips, the door was shut firmly behind him, joined swiftly by the sound of a key turning in the lock. He was momentarily alone, or so he thought. A fist landed with accurate aim just under his rib-cage. The punch was meant to stun more than hurt, which was just as well. Somebody moved with unexpected speed to grab Lloyd before he fell and with quiet and controlled viciousness led him across the room to what proved to be another exit. Arm in arm like bosom buddies, Lloyd was retained in a vice like grip until he felt the pavement outside beneath his feet.

"You take care now." Another guard with an American accent this time offered some advice.

Lloyd had not suffered from further pain but the threat of further violence followed him down the alleyway as he was allowed to depart from the rear of the hotel. With every retreating step his relief increasingly turned to anger. Somebody would have to pay for the frustrations he'd had to endure.

There'd been no other way. Joe had no qualms in justifying his actions. Of more concern was what had subsequently taken place. Sherman Powers and his entourage had been the next group in to be photographed. A young woman with flax-coloured hair led the way but stayed to one side. She looked familiar; the same woman who had met Amelia at the airport, where Joe had held back so as not to be noticed. Unfortunately, she had responded naturally to his uniform and promptly asked for assistance in keeping a couple of errant photographers behind the ropes. Like them, she evidently wanted clear views of Miss Highland.

As he passed by to do her bidding, he managed to snag the strap of her bag in the buttons on his jacket sleeve. To say that they had come face to face was an understatement. Joe smiled as he recalled his apologies and the hint of amusement in her eyes as they eventually untangled themselves.

"Don't let her out of your sight." He spoke in a whisper but she definitely heard him. It was a risk he'd deemed worth taking in the time that it took to say the words.

And then he was gone.

"Keep a low profile. Don't let my daughter suspect you're there." Simple enough instructions for Joe to follow. Fortunately for him, Amelia had not witnessed the incident but the American would certainly recognise him again. Too late to worry at present. Future problems lay in how he should undertake the logistical nightmare of shadowing Miss Highland back to the airport and whilst boarding the same flight remain unobserved. Imperative to this was the proximity of their respective seat numbers. It seemed impossible to believe that Charles Hanlan, of all people, had not already thought to take care of the details.

*

"With all the flying that I've done in the last few years you'd think I'd be used to it by now." Nick made patterns in the condensation on his beer glass. "I still watch my suitcase disappear along the conveyor-belt and wonder if I'll ever see it again."

He and Amelia sat across the table from each other. The bar and restaurant areas were packed with people. Beer and conversation were in full flow and the popular jazz coming from the sound system was adding to the ambiance. Bene's bar was always a good place to go.

Amelia leaned forward with her arms resting on the table. Her bright blue eyes held his gaze and he found it hard not to stare in return. His only respite came as she blinked, her long lashes gently closing beneath the subtle fringes of her dark brown hair.

"My father lost his luggage once. The baggage handlers went on lightning strike or something," she explained. "Anyhow, he went to Oslo on business and his suitcase ended up on a flight to Rome. To this day he swears that the thing that upset him most, was knowing that his clothes probably had a better time than he did."

In the far corner of the room Samantha Grant was busy on her mobile, trying to get a signal. The weather outside wasn't looking very favourable. Thick flakes of snow were falling again and the chilling wind had increased its bite. She keyed in the number for departure information in the hope of checking on Amelia's return flight later that evening.

Two sets of eyes were better than one. The whispered words of the hotel guard echoed in her head. Sam looked over to where she'd left her two companions and was pleased to see them chatting amiably. Amelia seemed outwardly more relaxed and Nick was helping with that. Last night had been quite eventful for all of them but thankfully everyone had survived. Sam's biggest worry was if Amelia would now regret that she had been so open and honest with her. With that in mind it had been a good call to keep Sherman out of the picture.

The line was busy, so she tried again. Sam allowed herself a small pat on the back. Perhaps she'd got it right about Nick too. Before coming to America, he'd worked in London and would be familiar with the West End scene. He spoke a language that put Amelia at her ease.

"No delays to flights as yet." Sam returned to the table. Almost as one they looked to the window to judge for themselves the state of the weather. The snow continued to fall in wind-blown flurries adding to the discomfort of those that passed by on the sidewalk. Even now they watched as a dark-haired man ducked his head, adjusting his coat collar and pulling the peak of his cap down to protect his face.

"Miss Highland? This is for you" A voice close-by brought them back inside. A waitress stood there, looking slightly amused. She handed Amelia some folded news print.

"For me? What's this then?" She looked to the others, somewhat perplexed.

Neither could reply but both were intrigued.

"How did you know who Miss Highland was?" Sam was suddenly suspicious.

"A guy at the bar pointed you out." The waitress explained. "Comes in here often."

"Still here?" Nick asked.

"Not now," The waitress was beginning to enjoy herself and pointed to the window. "You just missed him."

Amelia waited for her to leave before turning her attention to the misshapen piece of newspaper.

Today's addition, the particular page showed coverage of last night's events at the Parkside Grand. As she unwrapped it, a used sachet of ketchup fell to the table and left a smear of red on a close-up of her face.

There were hand written words that said, "Mind how you go." Amelia pushed it away; her distress was clearly visible.

Sam voiced her opinion. "Somebody with personal knowledge. Your worst fears realised."

Nick raised an eyebrow as he read the note.

"My father was right. I didn't want to believe him." Resignation was etched on Amelia's face. "I told you I might never get to come and work for NRG."

"A very crude attempt to scare you off." Nick cleaned a spot of ketchup from the table with a bar mat. "You didn't recognize the guy in the cap outside?"

"No, but I think I can guess who it might have been."

"So, you know who wrote this?"

"My step-brother, Lloyd most likely. I only found out in the last few days that he lives here with his mother." Amelia was gauging how much to put her trust in Nick. He returned her gaze with no sign of embarrassment.

"My father, my step-father," she corrected herself. "He believes that if I work in America, I risk becoming involved in some kind of vendetta against him. I told him he was just trying to scare me. He's always been over-protective and I think we all know what people say about that." She couldn't keep the irony out of her voice.

"You believe him now, though?" Nick frowned. "Is he capable of arranging a stunt like this to scare you?"

Amelia wrinkled her nose at the thought in disgust. "No, I can't believe it."

"If it was Lloyd outside, why not come and confront you in person?" Sam deposited the soggy newspaper into an empty glass.

Amelia remained silent thinking it through. Obviously, she and Lloyd had history but surely this threat, if that's what it was, must be born out of a hatred; something she did not deserve.

"Looks as if I'm in trouble." She looked to Sam fearing the worst.

Samantha in turn looked at Nick as he rose from the table.

"Another beer for anybody?" He collected the empty glasses on his way to the bar.

*

How quickly the agonies of last night had been forgotten when Amelia had miraculously walked into Bene's Bar. Unfortunately for Lloyd his stomach was still painful. Bruised muscles from the bouncer's punch and numerous beers he'd consumed to drown his sorrows had tipped the balance as a shot of adrenalin too powerful to contain had rippled through him. A hasty exit to the restrooms had been timely. With sickness there was relief and perhaps the faint beginnings of hope. Lloyd stared at his paleness in the mirror above the basin on which he was leaning.

Once recovered he returned to the bar and ordered a club soda. Choosing to ignore a knowing look from the barman, Lloyd took cover in the lee of the man sitting next to him while he considered his next move. Despite his caution, inevitably his eyes were drawn in her direction. Like the sparkling water that fizzed in his glass, her beauty and loveliness still appeared refreshing and pure.

It was warm in the bar, despite the cold outside. Amelia stood and slipped her jacket from her shoulders, draping it easily on the back of her chair. Her multi-coloured sweater stretched tightly over the firmness and curves of her body. He witnessed again a habit born out of earlier years as she combed back her hair with delicate fingers.

Lloyd's confident stare crumbled as Amelia turned her head to look around her. He drained his glass and tasted the bitterness of lemon as a slice contacted his lips. And just like that, insecurity and hurtful memories threatened to overwhelm him once more. Nothing had changed it seemed since those last dark days at school.

She was smiling at the man across the table from her now, how often had that happened when he'd needed her. How could she have been so selfish and blind to his needs. "Get in touch with your feelings," they'd said. "Be honest with yourself and with others." The way to be a better pupil. Well, that is exactly what he'd done – told her how he felt, how he longed to be with her and have her approval, one day her love. Why had she laughed?

A surge of anger, rapid and strong built with each breath and sudden cold resolve made him shiver inside. She wouldn't laugh at him next time. Not if she stayed. Lloyd emptied the sachet of its contents and folded the paper on which he'd written his note. Hurt her slowly, like she'd hurt him. Perhaps then she'd be sorry for what she had done.

Lloyd paid off his tab and buttoned up his coat. A hefty tip secured cooperation from behind the bar. One last look and he was outside the door. "This time, Amelia you won't get your way." Lloyd mouthed the words in a silent promise.

4. Home Truths

The black and white collie-dog ran fast and free across the meadow down to the river's edge. Pausing briefly to view the views and smell the smells, he continued to look back to the path at the top of the rise to check on the progress of his companion.

Timing it to perfection, the collie ran back up the slope and was at Mary Paxton's side as she stepped onto the footbridge. Below their feet the rush of the river flowed quickly away from the town in Wiltshire. On reaching the far bank, Mary turned and headed upstream, while the collie stayed close by. The pathway narrowed and became shadowed by bushes and trees. Above and to the left of them the steep escarpment continued to be bathed in the early morning sunshine. Rows of beautifully built, honey-coloured houses stood out brightly and in contrast to the varying greens of nature.

Eight o'clock, the sound of the bell in the clock tower echoed across the valley and hung in the still air. Mary quickened her pace and decided to take a short cut. The foot bridge by the old mill would take her directly into Church Street, and from there the house was just around the corner. Avondale was its name.

A short cut it may have been, but the direct route called for extra effort. Having passed the tiny Saxon church, the steepness of the climb to the road above made Mary breathe a little harder. Many who were younger than her sixty years would have found it a good test of their fitness. As an avid watcher of television, Mary had often heard and understood the expression, "there's no gain without pain".

When she finally reached the road, she called the collie to heel and together they walked along the pavement to the entrance of the driveway. The house and gardens were among the largest in town. Constructed in the early eighteen hundreds, the 'Governor's House', as the locals called it, was originally occupied by one of the wealthy clothiers of the time. Many similar sized houses had been divided up or converted into hotels and guest houses. Not so Avondale. It had been privately owned from the very start.

Mary and the collie walked up the drive, the gravel surface crunching in tune with their footfall. All being normal she would have taken more time to appreciate her husband's care and attention to detail. The well-manicured lawns to either side and the flower beds and borders with their abundant colours made the ideal setting for a house built of Bath stone. Encompassed by a wall of natural yellows and greys, the overall feeling was one of security and permanence. Unfortunately, Mary's thoughts were far from these things, not because of over-familiarity, for she and her husband loved their adopted home, rather it was the sight of the silver Mercedes parked outside the front door that had held her attention. Mr Charles Hanlan had, it seemed, escaped the city and without warning returned to his home in the country.

Glancing briefly at the Mercedes, Mary went round to the rear of the house, aware that her husband's car was missing from its usual spot in front of the garage. She assumed that Jimmy had been sent out on some errand, either that or he'd been called in to work at the golf club. Outside the back door she bent to stroke and fondle the ear of the collie. With wagging tail, he listened intently as she encouraged him to be a good boy, before padding off into the garden to find a shady spot to lie in.

The house was quiet and devoid of life. Once in the kitchen Mary filled the kettle and allowed her suspicions to simmer. Life would continue but only after a nice cup of tea. Sharing a pot of PG would give her the ideal excuse to find out why her employer had returned without warning. Whatever his reasons she fully intended to give him a piece of her mind. What was the point of him buying her a mobile phone and then never bothering to ring or leave a message?

Mary bustled her way down the hall. She'd decided on a firm but fair rebuke. The choice of words would be spur of the moment but then her tongue rarely let her down. He wouldn't escape, even in his own home. The sight that confronted her as she entered the room however, momentarily banished all harsh thoughts from her head. Although the room was empty of human life, his recent presence was evidenced by a large bouquet of flowers placed on the coffee table in the centre of the room. Propped against the vase was a hand written card, addressed to The Keeper of the House.

"Have borrowed your husband for the rest of the day. He and I have gone to Suffolk and will be back late tonight." signed, "Charles."

The fragrant smell of manipulation was thick in the room, compounded by the fact that her husband was complicit. Two to scold was as easy as one and she'd be happy to do it individually. Mary smiled to herself, knowing that time would not impede her memory or become a healer.

She bent to smell the flowers once more. It was a familiar scent, often used and strangely tinged with sadness, reminding Mary of days when all had not been well in the Hanlan household. The help that she spontaneously gave, even today, was in the form of tough love. But then Charles could take it and always had done; they'd been through a lot together.

With one last look, Mary wandered back to the kitchen. Was it really four years ago that things had come to a head and changed the lives of those who remained in the house? Charles' wife, Claire had never been a permanent fixture. Her emmigration along with Lloyd to the US had put distance between her and a string of affairs that had become uncomfortably public. Putting herself at the mercies of those that reported on such things had been quite devastating. In Mary's opinion the question remained as to why the masses had a right to know, not only your knicker size but more importantly where you habitually left them. No wonder Charles had increasingly used his work to minimize his despair.

Mary spilled her tea stirring it a little too vigorously. However severe the embarrassment, it was the depreciating self-loathing that had taken its toll as Claire had escaped further introspection. Charles, to this day, had never resolved the uncomfortable guilt of failing to connect with his son.

"What a mess." Mary emptied her saucer back into the cup and tried to brighten her thoughts.

And then there was Amelia. Without question the last four years had given Charles a chance at redemption. Her emerging talent, a tonic, and his pride in her achievements, unquestionable. Mary was sure of that.

As sure as she could be that Claire had never understood the meaning of unconditional love.

*

Meanwhile, Mary's husband was settling down in new and unfamiliar surroundings. Not that he was uncomfortable, far from it. The leather armchair suited him very well as did the views from the bay window inside the clubhouse. It was an environment he was accustomed to. The eighteenth green with its yellow flag fluttering in the breeze looked in good nick and recently mown.

Jimmy Paxton's position of course manager at his local club had been an ambition fulfilled and something he'd only recently retired from. At a time when Charles Hanlan had employed his wife at Avondale, they had decided to move into a self-contained apartment within the main house. From their humble beginnings, their new-found status was uniquely felt and admired by their friends in the town. The one thing they'd lacked in their life had been the blessing of children.

How ironical then that Charles' wife had found no fortune or joy when her pregnancy tests had proved positive. New beginnings? More like the beginning of the end. From budding actress in a marriage that should have afforded her every advantage, to motherhood and early retirement in a blink of an eye. Charles was to blame. His part in the making of their son had effectively ended her career.

Jimmy had always tried not to be too judgemental, but then his work had allowed him to distance himself from the ensuing and unhappy conflict. The daily damage done within the household had been reflected in the eyes of his wife. Not that it had always been so. Early days at Avondale were exciting, especially if Charles and Claire had friends staying over. Extended weekend visits by the Highlands were often the social highlights of a busy calendar.

The sudden and tragic deaths of Maurice and Jelena were shocking and left a desolate hole in everyone's heart. Charles had found no way to disguise the sorrow he felt. Young Amelia who was now their houseguest instinctively picked up on the tragic and life changing consequences that impacted on them all. Mary had witnessed it most, but Jimmy had been drawn to see for himself, an eight-year-old girl coming to terms with strange feelings of abandonment.

He saw too how Claire had initially taken on the role of mother that Amelia was in desperate need of. However, Jimmy couldn't shake off the impression that she had used the child as some kind of leverage in her battle against Charles, who in his grief had buried himself deep in dealing with Maurice's affairs. To counteract the pain, Amelia's happiness had quickly become his crusade. Not through love, not at first but out of a sense of loyalty to his friends, now gone.

For Claire, the circumstances had become something of a diversion that allowed her to forget the frustrations in her marriage. The subtle change to this came as Charles began to adapt too well to his role of guardian. His lack of affection shown towards their own son, Lloyd, hurt her deeply. The final straw had been his petition to adopt the little girl. Amelia had very quickly outgrown her usefulness.

Predictably Claire had retreated and she took Lloyd with her, thus depriving Amelia of a playmate and a brother. It never occurred to her that the reverse was also true for her son. The little boy she'd not really wanted had become an asset and security against the total rejection she feared from her husband. With their relations at an all-time low, Claire requested more freedom to pursue the importance of her own life. She immediately returned to London to rekindle the numerous associations and friends she'd known before Charles. She had missed the buzz of living in the city, readily acknowledging how life in the country had failed to satisfying that, "something indefinable" that she needed.

The fallout was often ugly. Jimmy Paxton and his wife saw it all. They more than most had good reason to feel aggrieved. On the day Claire and Lloyd packed their bags, in the midst of a vivid storm that had flashed and crackled in the hills around Bath, Mary was officially informed of her change in status. From "daily help" to "house-keeper and mother" in the space of a day.

Jimmy was alone on the golf course that day, seemingly oblivious to the dangers, as if provoking nature to strike him down. To believe that a child could be callously discarded was more than he was prepared to understand. Only later that evening would his mood begin to lighten. His return to the house had been slow and ponderous as the rain remained unrelenting. Jimmy hadn't rushed inside. Instead, through an open window he'd watched a little girl playing with a wooden spoon and a mixing bowl. The smell of fresh baking and Mary's kind words permeated the air and had somehow coaxed the little girl-lost to the warmth of the kitchen. The dreadful tears of earlier were no more, replaced by a beaming smile encased in cake mixture and matched only in beauty by the happiness that shone in the eyes of his wife.

From that day onwards, life for the Paxton's would take on a new chapter, something that neither of them would have changed for all the world.

Jimmy shook off the memories and returned himself to the present. Thoughts of what might yet become an unexpected twist to his future were exciting.

With economical effort, Joe Peterson set another chair down alongside Jimmy's. He made sure not to block the views that the older man had been immersed in.

"Doesn't get much better than that." Jimmy nodded towards the window. The yellow flowering gorse that lined the fairways framed a picture.

"Different to what you've been used too, though? Boxdale, wasn't it? Up in the hills above Bath?" Joe had been doing his homework.

"Yeh, but it still makes you want to get out there and play." Jimmy smiled. "Not that I had much time when I was working. More of a gardener these days and the house at Avondale needs a lot of looking after." Jimmy found it difficult to take his eyes away from the big skies so close to the Suffolk coast. He wondered if Charles, who was elsewhere in the clubhouse, was thinking of taking up golf and applying for membership. "Thank you for the invite, Joe. I'll admit the setting certainly makes me feel right at home."

"Just as it was meant to," Joe was totally unfazed and seemed to be dispensing with the small talk. "Mr Hanlan suggested it when he told me you were coming today. A long way to travel, but hopefully you'll find this second property to your liking and see it as a worthwhile challenge." Joe pointed to the window. "It's less than two miles away from where we're sitting now." He lent forward in his chair so that they should not be overheard. "Mr Hanlan's in here somewhere having a meeting with their board of governors. He'd like to involve them in securing the surrounding land as a conservation area."

Jimmy had been told as much by Charles in the car. He studied the younger man and decided to be frank. "Seen a few things in your life I'm guessing Joe, but not brave enough to invite my wife today?"

"Looks as if we've both been briefed and responded to good advice." Joe was grinning as he stood. "Come on, let's go and have a stroll outside before we meet up with the boss again. See if we can make a little sense out of what this is all about."

*

Mary was awake and lay listening to the sounds of the night. The luminous dial on her old-fashioned alarm clock told her it was a little after three in the morning. She could hear the strength of the wind in the trees outside, the curtains at her window were swaying to and fro. She was aware of movement of a different kind on the drive directly beneath where she lay. Her employer and his cohort were making good their return to Avondale, betrayed initially by the sound of tyre on gravel. The security lighting that spanned the front of the house was now constantly and a little annoyingly activated by their comings and goings.

She hoped the trip had been worth their while. Certainly, she knew better than to get out of bed to ask them. In the time that it took them to fully and finally enter the house, Mary had turned over and once again returned to the peace of her sleep.

The following morning Charles locked himself away in his office with much on his mind. Amelia's trip and the three weeks following her return from America had been problematical. Sherman Powers had been purposely kept at arm's length in a bid to keep his daughter focused during her final weeks with the show. Quoting 'It's not over until the fat lady sings', had gone down like a lead balloon. The chocolate brownie that usually accompanied her morning coffee had stubbornly remained untouched.

The contact he'd received from his wife, the first in years, had not been pleasant. A hand written letter showed how hard her pen had been pressed onto the paper. He recognised the hurt of old wounds that had no chance of healing. Her accusations that he'd broken his word were impossible to deny.

Sending Joe Peterson to New York had been essential, judging by his report. Lloyd's attempt to secretly approach Amelia, further proved that his son still carried the baggage that had blighted his teenage years. One thing was abundantly clear; by trying to do right by his daughter, he'd exposed her innocence to the madness of his family in exile.

In the short-term, matters closer to home required his attention. His own inconsistent use of Avondale was causing rifts and unease. Negotiation and Mary Paxton were not entities that usually played out harmoniously. His inconsiderate behaviour had created a problem that needed a swift fix. Seen in isolation his lack of sensitivity was a wobble rather than a major fall from grace. In repetition it had become a tired excuse.

The smell of cooking from the kitchen and a bottle of red wine left to breathe on the dining room table gave him hope that the frost might be thawing. The stark and lonely place setting spoke of punishment dished out with his dinner. Mary was still speaking without talking to him. A loss of appetite prompted a growing sense of conviction as Charles dared undertake the walk of shame to the kitchen, armed only with two extra glasses and the untouched bottle of red.

*

A week later, the healing process and getting back into Mary's good books was still a work in progress.

"Jimmy Paxton, I can't believe you knew all about this. More to the point that you didn't tell me. Moving house? Whatever next? Dragged from one end of the country to the other!" Mary accentuated her exasperation in a bid to mask a growing excitement.

Jimmy had heard it all before.

"Don't exaggerate woman. This is Suffolk not Scotland." He ignored her scowl. "Think of it as a holiday. It might be the only one you get this year." Jimmy looked out through the leaded-light windows that framed a picture of buff coloured stone and rich green grass. "You like it really, I can tell."

"Well, it's not like Avondale." Mary sniffed in a superior way. Then she smiled. "But you could be right." She had to concede. "Are you sure this is our room?"

"That's what he said." Jim turned just as Mary lowered her ample bottom onto one of the twin beds, testing the mattress for comfort and forgiveness. "Want to push them together?" He stifled a laugh as she treated him to another of her looks and so offered the logic behind his suggestion. "Just in case you get cold during the night."

"Jimmy Paxton, please behave. Why don't you make yourself useful and go see that nice young man, Mr Peterson?"

Jimmy needed no second invitation and in a shot was descending the stairs. Bless her, he could still hear her talking. "And get out from under my feet for a change."

Unfortunately for both of them this was very much a working trip and not the holiday that might have proved advantageous to Jimmy and his provocative suggestion. Vehicles at that very moment were on route with the rest of the furniture that Charles had ordered for the house some months before.

At the first of these deliveries Mary had quickly taken charge, laying down her own specifics of the law that all should abide by. The promise of tea and biscuits was real but the threat still remained. Woe-betide a careless scratch to paint work or dirty foot-mark left on the carpet.

Jimmy walked out into the kitchen garden at the side of the house. The attention to detail was obvious. Its renovation matched all the workmanship carried out in the house. There was much to explore. Passing through a gated archway, he turned and followed a well-worn path that wound its way through tall grasses and within seconds he was in the midst of a wilderness. It was what he loved most about the place. He could only hope that Charles Hanlan could appreciate the treasure that was Sedge House.

Jimmy made towards the landing stage that allowed private access to the river. Rising above the reeds he could see a single mast with a pendant fluttering in the breeze. With any luck Mr Peterson would be found there.

Sure enough, the man himself was working hard in the midst of what seemed like a small flotilla. The creek was not only home to the sailing dinghy but a small rowing boat and a canoe that seemed ready for use.

"There's a paddle in there if you want to give it a try." Joe spoke without looking up from his work.

Jimmy smiled as he saw where Joe was pointing. "Not today mate, but thanks all the same." He took a moment to admire the wooden boat house that the young man was building. "Looks as if you've been busy. Not much more to do by the looks of it."

Joe conceded that it had actually taken longer than he'd expected, due in part from having to use a boat as a working platform. It gave him food for thought. "The roofing timber is being delivered tomorrow, if you fancy giving me a hand."

Jimmy needed no second invitation. "I'm up for that providing you don't want me to walk on water."

A little later that day Jimmy was struggling to put his thoughts into meaningful words. The confidences that Charles had made known, invariably led to many questions and stong opinions.

Joe temporarily quit from varnishing the hull of the small rowing boat. It was a last-minute job that he really could have done without. Now he waited with his brush hanging in mid-air for Jimmy to collect his thoughts.

"I guess you can never be too careful, but that's not the point." Jimmy was talking about Charles Hanlan. "I know he thinks a lot of you Joe, but he surely can't expect you to take on the family's responsibilities." He looked enquiringly at the younger man. "It's crisis management of the worst type, particularly if his son is as mixed up as Charles claims. Okay, so you succeeded in Manhattan but what if she wants to live and work there? You can't become a permanent bodyguard. She wouldn't have it and neither would you."

Joe already knew that to be true, although the thought of spending time with Amelia Highland… He cleared the fantasy quickly from his mind. It was obvious from their conversation, that Jimmy was not fully aware of the impositions that Joe had worked under when Charles sent him to New York.

"Something you should know. Amelia doesn't realise I work for her father," he admitted. "Officially we've never met and that's how he wants it until this is over."

"Until what is over? More deception, more…" He searched for the right word. "…more manipulation. We can't be having any more games, not now."

Joe was inclined to agree. He weighed up how much more to reveal. The last thing he wanted was to put the older man in harm's way. On the other hand, another set of eyes would be useful. He came to a decision. "Let's finish up here." He checked his watch. "I've got to be in the village for a meeting with the concert hall manager at eleven thirty. Security checks and that kind of thing." Joe offered by way of abbreviated explanation. "Want to tag along?"

"Is that an invitation freely given or do we both need to seek permission?"

Joe laughed out loud.

"Fair question, Jim; you deserve an honest answer. I've put a good team together and later I'll introduce you to the rest of the boys. That is if they haven't already been given the sack." He nodded in the direction of the house.

Jimmy was quick on the uptake and with realisation there came a sense of sympathy. So, removal men of an unusual calibre, used to working in the harshest of conditions, were once again being put to the test. He wondered if "the boys", as Joe liked to call them, had ever come across a drill sergeant like his wife before?

5. Past Ports

It had been a close-run thing but they'd made it. A month and more had passed since Amelia had visited New York. Samantha Grant had been busy in planning their itinerary while Nick had been abroad working for Stress Magazine. Although lines of communication remained open, the exchange of positive information was frustratingly slow. Sam hung on to an optimistic view that Charles Hanlan could be brought on-side with NRG's ambitions and Sherman Powers' desires.

Nick Sayers just had time to re-pack his suitcase before making his way back to the airport. The anxious look on Samantha's face was transformed as she spied his tall frame making speedy progress across the terminal building to check-in. She hoped he was glad to be there. He looked well at least. His face was deeply tanned and his hair shone. The light blue denim shirt he wore showed off both to good effect. The trip to Hong Kong to report on the changes since the transfer of sovereignty from Britain to China had perhaps been a success.

Sixty minutes later the Airbus took off out of JFK International and came onto its first heading for London Heathrow. Nick and Sam had been lucky and found a row of seats to themselves and accordingly made best of the extra room. As the jet climbed towards its cruising altitude they sat contentedly, deep in their individual thoughts. Despite the air-miles chalked up in recent weeks, Nick could admit to a sense of excitement knowing he was on his way back to Britain. His last trip home had been a lonely affair. This time it felt like being part of a team with the added compensation of working with a friend. He glanced across at Samantha and found that he was already the object of her gaze.

Sometime later Nick was aware of movement beside him. He couldn't remember falling asleep and for a second or two he imagined he was at home with Libi. His eyes were heavy and remained closed ready to sleep again. His new reality was flying high while Libi remained on the ground. He shut down a stab of pain and listened instead to the hum of the engines, reassuringly constant and steady.

Sam was still snoozing peacefully, her head resting on his upper arm. A hint of perfume and the smell of her hair, he breathed in deeply and gradually opened his eyes. Moving as little as possible, fearful of waking her, Nick looked around him. Other passengers seemed to be stirring and the cabin crew were once again busy with their duties. He noticed that at some point during the night, Sam had thoughtfully spread a blanket over both of them.

Dawn at thirty-five thousand feet. He gazed through the cabin window at the merging layers of light. Deep blue above fading towards the horizon. Vivid pinks and reds that heralded the sun. And below in the shade, an inky blackness like a blanket on the world.

He took it all in. He made himself stare. Perhaps it was tiredness, a build-up of emotion or the sense of failure. Thinking of Libi when he was most vulnerable was becoming bad for his health.

"Would you like something to drink?" Samantha's voice fortunately broke the spell.

Nick re-joined his surroundings and was glad to be back. He smiled and took the orange juice she held for him.

"Onwards and upwards." He raised his plastic cup in salute.

"Okay, I'll drink to that." Plastic met plastic. Sam didn't pretend to understand his meaning, and now was not the moment to ask. Later perhaps. There was plenty of time.

With the breakfast service finally cleared away, the crew were preparing the Airbus and its passengers for the end of their journey. An air of expectation filtered through the cabin as landing cards were handed out and people searched for pens and passports. Sam took the opportunity, whilst filling out her card, to give Nick some reading material.

He raised a questioning eyebrow that begged an immediate answer.

"I did some research while you were away in Hong Kong," She seemed somewhat amused. "It won't bite you. Just some background info on the Hanlan family. I think you'll find it interesting."

Nick took the loose-leaved file with caution and Sam was reminded of a student who should be revising for their exams.

'Somebody's been busy. All your own work?" He flicked quickly through the pages.

"A mixture of easy access on the internet and copies of newspaper articles, as it happens. Your old friends on Fleet Street have been busy." Sam was referring to members of the British press. She pointed to a name on the top of page five.

"This guy for instance seems to have made a career out of keeping tabs on Charles Hanlan." Sam didn't particularly sound as if she approved.

Nick checked it out.

"Doesn't ring any bells." He said and then hesitated for a second. "Anyhow he seems to have given us plenty to read."

Sam returned to the business of filling in her landing card, while Nick settled back in his seat and considered the reasons why he'd felt it necessary to lie. Peter Pearce, sometime mentor but never a friend. He should have guessed that of all the likely candidates Pearce would come out top of Samantha's list. Reading some of the inflammatory quotes, he could hear the vitriolic words as if spoken by their author. It was a reminder, should he need one, of the damage that Pearce's pen could inflict. There was unfinished business between them and he'd already put himself in an awkward situation with Samantha.

Final landing checks were being made as he handed back the file to Samantha with a promise to read it later. Buckling his seat-belt he waited while she finished applying a hint of make-up.

"How much influence does Hanlan have over Amelia's career?" He pointed at the file that Sam had put away. "I mean, considering what she went through as a child, he's been a huge part of her life right from the time her parents passed away."

"A great deal, I suppose. Like any normal parent." Sam tried to put herself in Amelia's place. "Only natural don't you think?" She immediately thought of her own father and how supportive he had been to her over the years.

Nick was more sceptical. "Can't really call their situation normal, can you? Having influence is all very well but they're in business together; tied at the hip." He didn't want to be crude. "What's the old adage? Never expect to own your kids."

"Ownership sounds a little strong to me. Adoption, yes. He could have sent her back to Sommovia, I grant you. Perhaps his loyalty to the Highlands was stronger than we give him credit for." Sam thought about the present situation. "Circumstances are about to change. She tells me it's a joint decision for her to leave the show."

It was a good point which they discussed. The idea that as an eight-year-old Amelia would have been better off living with Hanlan than return to a country that was on the verge of war seemed logical. They agreed her present career path seemed reckless when there was so much to resolve within her family.

Nick returned the conversation to the subject of his previous lie. "This journalist, Peter Pearce has had some rather scathing things to say, insinuating that Amelia is locked up after dark in her ivory tower." He had instantly seen a familiar pattern.

"That started when Hanlan got rid of her first leading man. The press implied he was jealous of the chemistry between them." Sam remembered her conversation with Amelia at the Parkside Grand. "She definitely thought he'd overreacted. I guess parents can't be right all the time. There were moments in New York, when she seemed so confused." Samantha confessed to a feeling of responsibility.

Nick wondered if she was in danger of becoming too personally involved. "It's why you're so good at your job."

"Meaning what?" She was unable to make the connection.

"Because you care. It matters what happens to others." He was thinking of the mistakes he'd made. "Not everybody plays by the same set of rules especially when there's a need to sell newspapers."

Sam nodded and they lapsed into silence as the cabin crew made their final checks. Bright sunlight flooded the cabin space as the plane turned onto its final heading. With London directly below him and Heathrow just a few miles away, Nick tried to decide if he was glad to be home.

By the time they'd cleared customs and arranged transport from the airport, half the morning had simply disappeared. The relief at having reached their hotel was palpable. Situated off the Bayswater Road, The Randolf was in spitting distance, with a following wind, of London's Hyde Park. Not that Nick could have proved that one way or the other. Despite his continual intake of mineral water, juices and anything else the airlines had had to offer, his recent and prolonged high-flying travels had left him dehydrated. When they'd finished signing in at reception and their luggage was safely on its way up to their rooms, he made a suggestion.

"Fancy a pint?"

Sam shook her head in disbelief. By all that was normal Nick should have been dead on his feet. "Remember we're going out again in a few hours' time." She reminded him while allowing herself to be led to the bar. "If you don't get some sleep soon, I'll be going on my own."

"Out" was a trip to The Theatre and a meeting with Amelia. Sam was anxious to see how the young actress was dealing with the pressures she must be feeling from all sides. Ever Searching continued to draw deserved acclaim. Sales of the new song and the constant demand for tickets had encouraged the Hanlan dynasty to put on extra shows. Individually, Charles had taken the unprecedented step of donating the proceeds from two performances directly to charity. Amelia had phoned Samantha with the news. It was plain she couldn't disguise her annoyance at this unexpected extension to her involvement with the show. Yes, she wanted the charities to benefit, but the suspicion remained that her father was constantly putting obstacles in her way. Sam did her best to keep an upbeat view. As a priority she wanted to shield her new friend from the rumblings of discontentment and impatience that were reverberating down from the top of NRG.

To a casual observer, Charles Hanlan might have seemed impervious to those details that did not directly impact upon the show, such was his dedication and focus. Ticket revenue and sales of the new song had apparently outweighed all expectation. Sam was sure that Amelia's final appearance in London was guaranteed to draw a huge response from invited guests and celebrities alike. When you considered the various charities of choice and the decent cheque they could expect, Amelia's frustrations paled to insignificance. It had surely become a matter of pride.

*

London Pride, two pints of it had definitely hit the spot. Sam had even tried a sip or two but couldn't agree with Nick's assessment on the value of its fortifying effects. In the end she'd allowed herself a glass of dry white wine and was surprised at the difficulty she'd had in refusing a second. Drinking at lunchtime, not something she was used to, could do that to you sometimes when the company was good.

A short ride in the lift to the second floor was where Sam and Nick parted company with a promise to meet in the lobby for five. Samantha closed the door behind her and was pleasantly surprised by the size of her room. Posh but not pretentious, she would find this a pleasant place to stay for a few days.

Her luggage had been left at the foot of the bed. One suitcase and a travel bag. She couldn't be bothered to unpack it all now. Kicking off her shoes and loosening her skirt, Sam crossed to the window to close the curtains. She looked down into the street below as another taxi pulled up outside the hotel entrance. There would be time enough, she decided, to cross the Bayswater Road and walk in London's famous Hyde Park.

In the subdued light, the traffic noise outside seemed a fainter, more distant sound. The last of the buttons unfastened easily and Sam tossed her blouse onto the armchair in the corner of the room. Her skirt came next. With a few feminine wiggles the short Armani slid over her hips and down to the floor. As she stepped nimbly out and to the side, a lazy flick with her right foot sent the designer garment looping through the air. To her mild surprise it landed perfectly, if a little untidily on top of her blouse. The effort to hang and fold them was suddenly too much. She gave little thought to anything else as she collapsed onto the bed pulling the duvet up and over her.

6. In the Smoke

While some slept, London and the majority of its people enjoyed the early summer sunshine. In offices and on the streets alike, short sleeves and light cotton dresses were the order of the day. The latter in numerous pastels like flowers in an urban garden were catching the breeze. Voyeuristic enjoyment and outright assessment were a new game to play that day. Smiling faces suggested evidence of increasingly optimistic moods.

One who was not so enamoured with her day, anxiously waited for her bus to come to a grinding halt. A few minutes late, she did not let this detail distract her from her anxious mood. All journey long the slow-moving patterns of traffic and the lights that controlled them had been against her.

When her feet touched the pavement, the bus was still moving and her lack of athleticism was put to the test. She did well to cling onto Amelia's freshly dry-cleaned costume-dress as she stumbled. It was a poignant reminder, if she needed one, that exercise might help with her increasing lapses of dietary control.

"Bollocks, it's too hot." Ellen Preston, twenty-six, was Amelia Highland's personal dresser and assistant, sometimes friend. The last hundred yards were taken more sedately. It was an easy decision to make.

With The Theatre in sight, Ellen took a moment to consider her increasing fits of pique. Sex or the lack of it was a legitimate reason but in truth and more to the point, these final shows were certainly taking their toll. A yearlong routine, suddenly changed, and they were expected to cope. Amelia was not the only one to be feeling the pressure. The extra workload was affecting them all.

"Another week of this and then you can put your feet up." Ellen had been quite vociferous. "And what about me?" was what she wanted to say. Soon, it would all be over. Another lead would take Amelia's place but it wouldn't be quite the same.

"Nothing I can do about that." The show apart, Ellen considered whether the same was true for her relationship with her boyfriend. He seemed more intent to tinker on his ailing classic car. "Both need a service perhaps?" Ellen often talked to herself when she needed to test an idea. A new set of injectors for the car and the boyfriend too? Well, anything was worth a try in a quest for a decent ride.

By now Ellen was approaching the main entrance. Already a queue for the sale of returns was forming outside the box-office window. Some lived in hope she supposed. One young man at the front of the line seemed particularly on edge. While showing signs of impatience, he was studying the iconic bill-boards and Ellen saw an opportunity to have some well-deserved fun. Coincidently the costume that Amelia wore in the photograph was the very gown that Ellen carried in her arms.

Without further thought for her lateness and for no other reason than to lighten her own disenchantment with the day, she joined the young man in his appreciation of Amelia's pose.

Lloyd suddenly realized he had company. His first thought was that the young woman was trying to push in and take his place at the head of the queue. He took a couple of paces towards her while checking to make sure that nobody else had sneaked up and taken him by surprise. To add to his problems, he could tell that the woman was actually going to speak.

"Just checking I've got the right dress." Ellen made a show of studying the poster again.

Lloyd looked at her as if she was mad.

"You're talking to me?" He spoke in a way that showed he had no intention of encouraging a prolonged conversation.

Ellen forced a nervous smile before beating a hasty retreat. How wrong she'd been to stop in the first place. "Sorry, I thought you were somebody else." She explained whilst trying to put as much distance between herself and the aggressive young man.

As Ellen headed for the stage door at the rear of the building, she was aware of a voice calling out to her. In her haste she nearly collided with Ben Evans who was acting as security on the door. With no time for pleasantries, she simply stabbed a thumb in the direction of the street.

"Don't let him in."

Ben was left scratching his head in wonder. What was it this time? A quick perusal of the busy street outside gave him no clue as to the potential trouble poor Ellen had got herself into this time. She really was quite an eccentric girl.

It was too late now. Lloyd had finally recognized the significance of the dress, sheathed in its flimsy polythene cover. "Shit!" If he'd not been so anxious to get rid of her, he might have made something of his opportunity. How could he be so dumb? Any attempt to retrieve the situation was lost as he watched her disappear into the building.

Lloyd stabbed a match on the side of the box. The phosphorous burnt, engulfed by flame as he cupped his hands in a protective way. The end of the cigarette glowed as the tobacco took and pungent tendrils drifted into the air. His second of the day, but then he didn't really smoke. No chance of becoming dependent unlike some of his friends back in New York. His knowledge of suppling his peers was preferable and had become very profitable. That was his addiction; that and gaining revenge.

Lloyd's last few days before leaving for England had indeed been very lucrative. His earnings when combined with a generous allowance meant that money would not be a problem. The cost of his return ticket that was now safely tucked away in his wallet had been a small price to pay. The excitement of daring to intrude into his father's domain once again could only be matched by the dread of being found out. He still found it difficult to shut out the humiliation he and his mother had felt at effectively being kicked out of the country into exile.

His anger returned swift and sure, fuelled by the memories from when and where long-reaching choices had been made in a matter of hours. Whatever the circumstances, just how easy had it been for his father to decide between him and Amelia. Darling Amelia! Christ, he'd only been seventeen. It seemed like yesterday.

...The house to himself and with nothing to do. Mary and Jimmy Paxton away for the weekend and his parents spending rare time together up in London.

The prospect of 'doing a little' to help his father in the office had been enough to put him off joining them. His choice to stay at home meant Lloyd had become easily bored.

That was the trouble with living in a small-town, miles from London. To make matters worse his friends at school had talked of great plans for the holidays, something he now viewed with envy and frustration. In contrast, ducking the family trials and tribulations seemed all he had to look forward to.

Rarely alone, Lloyd had strolled around the house looking for some kind of diversion. His father's study and Amelia's bedroom were both off limits without their specific permission to the contrary. Amelia always guarded her privacy, while his father's study had never been a comfortable environment. On entering the latter, the smell of leather and polish were a powerful reminder of the owner's place in the world. Lloyd had briefly toyed with unfamiliar buttons on the desk-top computer. In the end the confusion of wires and cables to printer and fax machine had proved a huge deterrent. Caution somewhat killed his pioneering spirit.

Just as well. Views of the garden rarely induced much response in him. Manicured lawns and borders full of flowers would mostly pass him by. Not so an object as big as the taxi when it came onto the driveway.

The relief when it proved to be Amelia returning from school had allowed his guilty conscience to subside. On the other hand, he fervently hoped that her visit would be fleeting. Her growing indifference toward him after their recent involvement at drama class had done nothing for his confidence. Despite this, he'd watched her enter the house with a weird fascination.

Up close she'd looked ghastly pale and unusually weary. The flu-bug that he'd recovered from had obviously now claimed his step-sister. The outbreak at school was an epidemic and any signs of illness would have left them no choice but to send Amelia home. She'd have hated that.

Lloyd offering his sister support must have come as some surprise to her. If being useful had seemed out of character, Amelia never had the strength to question his motives. Not that she knew it then but there would be a price to pay. What followed that evening had not been planned and certainly had nothing to do with a young man overcoming his boredom in a natural way.

"Amelia Highland, darling."

Somebody was speaking her name. Lloyd was rudely interrupted from his unpleasant review.

"Oh, Highland's the best I've ever seen, by far." A man with a loud voice, occupying an even louder blazer was holding court with his friends. Lloyd could not escape the jarring, well-educated tones. "Of course, this is the fifth time we've been to see the show. Isn't it darling?" Blazer turned to his wife for confirmation. She smiled her assent not wishing to interrupt her husband who was now in full flow.

Quickly irritated, Lloyd diverted his attention to the two teenage girls who were with the party. Both were pretty and smartly dressed for the occasion. They had cleverly removed themselves from the rest of the group and were definitely laughing at Blazer who continued to demand the attention of the others whether they liked it or not.

Lloyd casually sidled over to be nearer them. He could smell their expensive perfume. One of them made eye-contact but only briefly, then half turned so that he could no longer hear what she was saying. Lloyd knew their type well enough. Unapproachable, untouchable, stuck-up China dolls. Until you found their weakness and their secret desires. Just like Amelia?

Blazer invaded his space once again with screeching incredulity.

"Mean to say you don't know who Amelia Highland is?" One of the couples were forced to exchange nervous glances at each other, their ignorance cruelly exposed.

Lloyd watched with badly disguised amusement as one of the girls, apparently his daughter, finally came to their rescue. "Come on daddy, not everyone's an expert on the theatre like you." She came over and took him by the arm. "Besides it makes mummy jealous. She's scared you'll leave her and run away with every actress you see."

Blazer coloured with embarrassment but never got the chance to reply. The doors to the theatre were finally opened, an announcement encouraging them to have their tickets at hand. It seemed that all concerned could move on and breathe a sigh of relief.

Lloyd stubbed out his cigarette and was surprised to find he felt like lighting another. Suddenly he was nervous. Images of Amelia sitting in Bene's Bar filled his mind. Once again, he would watch without her being aware.

*

Samantha Grant paid off the taxi-driver with a handsome tip and asked for a receipt. She had at her disposal a generous expense account which was likely to take a beating over the next few days. Unusually, she was carrying cash. Rather too much of it in her opinion.

Sherman Powers had asked her to go shopping on his behalf. At Harrods no less.

"I need a present for Rosalind." Samantha had been getting ready to leave for the airport. He'd thrust a brown envelope into her reluctant hands. "And get something for yourself, while you're there."

Sam would have protested but he'd waved her away.

"You're doing me a favour. And besides I always think it means more when you buy a gift with paper money."

Sam peaked inside the envelope.

"A thousand times more, I should say."

Sherman pointed a finger at her.

"All I ask is that you spend more on my wife than you do on yourself. Blood will be spilt, yours first and then mine." Sherman frowned and tried to be serious. "She has a nose for such things, Miss Grant."

Sam had done her best not to laugh and miserably failed. Fortunately, her giggling had been infectious and for once her boss had been quite unreserved.

Items from Harrods were easy to choose and came gift-wrapped on request. The stock of Amelia Highland was a one-off and might not be easily bought. Sam felt that Rosalind, unlike her husband, would somehow survive if the package went missing.

Nick was waiting on the pavement, checking settings and viewing histograms on the back of his camera. The light was fading and he needed shots of The Theatre building from the street outside. Sam thought he looked the part. Every movement and gesture suggested competence and a love for what he was doing. A professional at work, who she hoped, might think the same about her.

Ben Evans was back on duty at the stage door when Sam and Nick finally announced themselves. They were late but not overly so. He asked them to wait while he made the appropriate calls and told them that signing the visitors book was essential rather than quaint. As the ballpoint was left to dangle at the end of its string, Ellen Preston pushed through the swing doors and introduced herself, welcoming them both with a nod of her head.

"Good timing actually. Amelia has just finished in make-up." Ellen brushed aside their gratitude and made a quick appraisal of the two strangers she'd heard so much about. She did her best to be cordial even though they were here to change the status quo. "Amelia's certainly been looking forward to seeing you again." She turned to lead the way.

Sam and Nick exchanged expectant glances and quickly followed in Ellen's wake. She explained that the majority of the dressing rooms were on the first and second floors. Not so Amelia's, which was situated right by the stage.

"With the number of quick-changes we have to complete we can't afford to be too far away." She pushed through another set of doors and they immediately found themselves standing in the wings at the side of the stage. Nick was surprised that the area was so much smaller than he had expected and realised that the first row of the stalls could only have been thirty or so paces from the street outside.

It was a unique experience. Backstage at a major London theatre with less than an hour and a half to go before curtain up, Nick had assumed he would find a hive of activity but instead the place was deserted with not the slightest hint of chaos. He guessed practice made perfect.

Pausing with genuine interest, he was struck by how dark and dingy the place appeared to be. Back-clothes and screens invaded the space and brick walls at the back were all painted in black. A dusty odour, totally unique but not unpleasant and a smell of oils on canvass and cloth filled the air. A vaguely familiar whiff of spent pyrotechnics and smoke too.

Nick's eyes were drawn upwards following the lines of ropes and cables, three or four stories high. He guessed they controlled the different backdrops and changes in scenery. The suggestive powers of illusion with lighting and clever set design had always fascinated him and to a degree he had used this in some of his photography. It was said a good designer was worth his weight in gold to a show. He checked out some of the art work on the screens stacked at the side of the stage. Seen up close like this and in poor light, they looked a little ridiculous and fake. From afar and with the permission of imagination, he could only guess at how effective they would be.

The backstage crew were beginning to arrive and Nick decided to move out of their way. Time to find the others and begin to earn his fee.

"You look like a little boy lost." A newly familiar voice caught him mid-stride.

Amelia smiled and lightly kissed his cheek in a greeting she was happy to make. In full make-up she had to wipe away a small smudge of lipstick from his skin with her finger and thumb. She stood back in concentration, with a teasing look in her eyes, making sure her attentions had been successful and that no lasting damage had been done.

Nick was pleased and embarrassed all in one go. He too stepped back and made a show of studying Amelia.

Her costume was certainly something. The period gown showed off her slender figure to fantastic effect. Drawn tight to the waist, there was red velvet below that fanned out until it brushed the ground. Above, the white cotton chemise accentuated her every breath.

"It's not all mine, you know." Amelia followed the direction of Nick's eyes. Her own seemed to sparkle as she added. "But it's nice to have props in the theatre, don't you think?"

"Better to have secrets and keep us all wondering, that's what I would say." Nick tore his eyes away and tried to be serious for a moment. "You look great, but how are you really?"

"I'm fine," she said. "Concerned about all the fuss I seem to be causing but glad to see you none the less. I hope you haven't put off other work just to be here?" There was genuine concern in her voice.

"No worries. I only hope I can do some good for all concerned." He could see her brighten as soon as he spoke.

"So do I Nick, I really do."

He was aware of the presence of more backstage crew. Their privacy was becoming more public by the second. Amelia took him lightly by the arm.

"We can talk about that later though." She quickened her pace, heading for her dressing room. "Samantha will be wondering where we've got to."

Sam was hungry and even though Nick had wanted to stay for the performance, he too could no longer ignore the need to refuel. Daylight had all but gone and there was a definite chill in the air, yet Soho still teamed with life as they walked the back streets eyeing the choice of restaurants. They slowed outside the welcoming lights of an Italian and in checking the menu the decision was made. A table for two in an ideal spot by the window where they could relax and watch the rest of the world go by.

Both chose pasta and agreed to share a bottle of dry white wine with their meals. Nick helped himself to bread and olives, while Sam, feeling decidedly guilty chose to decline. Her calorific intake and the damaging increase of alcohol she'd recently consumed would have to be watched. In sharing time with a certain Mr Sayers, she was growing to enjoy unaccustomed habits under his influence. Nothing to worry about, not yet, and who actually cared? Well as it happened, she did. Nick was not the only one to have noticed the enviable effect of period costume on the female form. It was an image that Sam had decided could dishearten if she let it.

"She seemed happy to see us, I thought." Sam moved the candle on the table so it wasn't shining directly in her eyes. "Especially seeing you, Nick." She fluttered her eyelids gently mocking him.

"Yes, well." He took a moment to think. "There's no denying Amelia has good taste and the camera really loves her. More to the point, where do we go from here? Despite my obvious charm, I think you'd be unwise to rely upon it working on her father." Nick was laughing even though he'd made a serious point.

"Funnily enough that's exactly what I'm hoping might make the difference." Sam nodded her head when it looked as if he'd not heard her correctly. "Hanlan inquired about you by name, and wants to meet up. I've gone ahead and set it up for tomorrow."

Nick made a face. "Isn't that a bit strange?" He sounded slightly suspicious. "I can't imagine your boss being too happy about that."

"He doesn't know anything about it," Sam explained, shrugging her shoulders. "And I've already said yes to Hanlan's request." She'd thought it through. "Sherman will have to accept my judgement on this."

"Interesting." Nick was feeling slightly uneasy, trying to imagine what motivation might be behind this. "You'll be there as well, I hope?"

"No, not initially. He wants a private talk with you."

Nick topped up Sam's glass with wine as he absorbed this latest piece of news. "I'm sorry?"

"That's how he wants it, and besides I'm already meeting with Amelia at lunchtime tomorrow." Sam had briefly considered if she was using this as an excuse for not being invited. "It'll be fine, Hanlan knows you're working with me." In truth she was feeling a little put out. "You'll need to go to his offices here in London. I have the address, it's not far from here." She handed over a piece of paper.

Sam sounded as if she was taking this a little too casually and certainly Nick didn't understand why. "Surely you need to meet with him first," he reasoned. "You should be the one selling him the deal, don't you think?" It made absolute sense as far as he was concerned.

"I'll get my chance later in the week. I've an official invite to the last of the charity performances. He's also organizing a party for cast and crew and a small concert for friends of the show. We'll be needed for that too." Sam went on to explain about the venue in a place called Suffolk, a couple of hours north of London. They were to travel up the day before as his invited guests. "That's when he'll be happy to talk about Amelia's future. I have his assurance on that."

"Well, that is something at least. I'm not sure I'd have your patience. But I still can't help wondering what he wants with me?" Nick was still worried.

Before Sam could answer the waitress returned to their table loaded with food. Conversation died as a mark of respect to the pasta and the hunger that consumed them. The chilled white wine was crisply dry and complimented the penne to perfection. Sam said as much, but could see that Nick was impatient to hear her thoughts on his previous question.

"Hanlan says he has a story he wants you to hear. He knows you're a journalist and I believe he thinks you're the right person to tell it to." Sam had made sense of his reasoning once she'd got over her initial disappointment. Looking on the bright side it was the means to an end and might help to justify her idea of recruiting Nick in the first place. That was how she now intended to sell it to Sherman Powers, when she next got the chance.

Nick was still unhappy that Samantha was not getting the respect she deserved.

"Well as long as I don't blow the whole deal before you've even got started." He knew from experience how damaging an innocuous clash of personalities could sometimes be. "Anything else I should know about?" He tried to sound as put upon as he dared.

"One more thing." Sam responded, taking the opportunity. "Hanlan has asked that you do some homework on that journalist we were talking about before." She studied the frown on his face. "The one who wrote that article I showed you. You read it on the flight over here."

Nick took a breath and allowed himself a wry smile while Samantha searched her memory for a name.

"Peter Pearce is the one you're looking for," He confessed and was resigned to his embarrassment. "A name I know quite well as it happens. Eat first and then I'll feed you a story.

*

That night Lloyd Hanlan had stood with the rest of them, if only to see her reaction to the applause that was freely given. He sensed they knew her run was nearly done and felt compelled to express their emotion in a most traditional way. Amelia's performance deserved the standing ovation and their acclaim and it seemed that five minutes in, that those around him were communicating not just adoration, but even feelings of love.

"She can do that to you with her eyes closed." He muttered under his breath. The couple standing next to him were too much in the moment and paid little attention as he forced his way past them with little finesse.

He left them to it and headed for the exit. The noise in the theatre was giving him a headache and he was aware of a need to escape. Lloyd descended the last flight of stairs two at a time, eager to be outside and away from the madness.

A few minutes later his feet struck the pavement, his stride lengthening and taking him away. Street after street, emptying his head, just concentrating on the act of walking. Gradually and much to his relief, a rational idea began to take hold and calm him.

What he needed was an ally to keep his spirits high. Someone to get him closer to the goal he had set himself. Lloyd allowed himself a smile. Chocolates, if his guess was correct, and an apology full of sincerity, if he was to have any chance at all. It wasn't much to go on and luck would need to play its part. Was it really too much to hope that one day he might escape from living his life in her shadow?

7. Fronting Up

The underground garage at the back of the offices wouldn't be open until seven o'clock, so Charles Hanlan had left his Merc parked in the road outside. A chilly wind was gusting strongly with the arrival of the dawn, made apparent by the scurrying progress of a single sheet of newspaper. Halting the offending piece of litter with his foot, he deemed it clean enough to pick up and return to a crowded waste bin nearby. Peter Pearce and trash-talking, came to mind.

His offices were the original buildings gifted to him by his father when he'd first joined the business. To this day Charles still enjoyed a sense of pride every time he unlocked the doors and went inside. Where would he be now without the start his father had given him? The contrast in their relations with those he had with his son stabbed at him sharply.

Refusing the lift, he made for the stairs. As his only concession to the taking of exercise outside the membership of an infrequently used gym, Charles could almost hear the ringing endorsements and encouragement of both Mary Paxton and his daughter. Thick as thieves those two. Charles would not miss their nagging for all the world and could not wait until they were altogether again. For that he'd have to wait for the concert in Suffolk and the private party at Sedge House.

Charles deposited his briefcase on the desk in front of him and with it another air-mailed letter of warning from his wife. He had made the decision to show it to the journalist, Nick Sayers, whom he was meeting later that morning. If nothing else it would affirm the seriousness of the situation and justify his reserve in allowing Amelia go to America.

For the next two hours he tackled the in-tray, neatly stacked in order of importance by his P.A. This part of running the company had initially proved a burden to him, a necessary evil forced upon him by the death of his friend, Maurice Highland. How he'd missed the energy and confidence the man had in making things happen.

Memories of Amelia's mother, Jelena, invaded his thoughts. Would she be proud of the way he had raised her daughter? Over the years, Charles had used her as his guiding benchmark in everything where Amelia was concerned.

Charles changed programs on his Mac and scrutinised the graphics and design work for the up-coming refurbishments of The Theatre. At the end of the year, he wanted to improve the backstage capabilities for special effects and increase computer communications. The whole project had become a bit of a nightmare. The Theatre was a grade listed building where preservation was seen as paramount. Adhering to the rules was a battle that often inhibited and hampered the art for which the building had been created.

The problem lay beneath the stage. During the Victorian era a series of hand-operated winches along with trapdoors and moveable platforms had been installed for the very same reasons that Charles wanted to modernise now. The problem this time round was that his builders would have to install the new equipment without removing the old. Although none of it had been used for years, time had elevated the contraptions to museum grade status with a value all of their own. Charles highlighted the star of the show on his screen. A hydraulic pump was the largest and most interesting obstacle of all that used to control the rise and fall of the heavy velvet curtains. Controlled by a set of valves, it had been the most efficient way to handle the weighty problem of opening and closing the show. Redundant maybe, a national treasure for sure, it didn't change the fact it was also a bloody nuisance.

Charles heard the hum of the ascending lift. Eight-thirty already. The peace of the early morning was about to be shattered.

"Morning Mr Hanlan." Sally Stewart brightened up the dullest of days. Despite her distracting hustle and bustle, Charles coped better behind the confines of his own desk when she was around. In her early days a dancer, now in her mid-forties, Sally was still very trim. He was in awe of her sense of fashion which she carried off with confidence and aplomb.

"Morning Sally."

The return of greeting had barely been aired before Sally was in full stride. Not a fast talker by nature, Charles had soon figured out it was his presence that made Sally hyper. Her phone manner and communication skills with the others were in contrast to the way she was around him. It appeared there was nothing he could do to change that.

"Best left well alone," he'd decided. It suited her and besides she was bloody good at her job. With Maurice gone, Sally had become the closest thing to a partner that Charles would ever want. Her knowledge of the theatre was invaluable and more importantly she had adapted well to the office environment. She could type as fast as she could talk and the computer held no fears for her.

Sally was busy arranging things on her desk.

"...and you'll see that I've left you a pile of papers to..." Charles stopped her short, proudly showing off the fruits of his early morning work.

"All done. You're impressed I can see." He pointed to the chair opposite him and asked her to sit. Sally was temporarily silenced as she complied to her boss' invitation, elegantly crossing one knee over the other. Charles cleared his throat whilst collecting his thoughts.

"The concert and party on Sunday, Sally." As if she needed reminding of it. It had fallen to her to do most of the organization. Constant contact with the house in Suffolk had kept Mary and Jimmy Paxton in touch with catering plans and associated arrangements. "Now, travel. We agreed you'd go up the day before?"

"I'm driving up on Saturday morning, and I've booked all the B & Bs." Sally sounded excited and in truth she'd thought of little else. A chance to see the property he'd been keeping under wraps. She couldn't remember the last time she'd had a weekend outside of London.

"Right. That's what I wanted to talk to you about." Charles felt he was being insufferably coy. "I wondered if you'd come as my personal guest?"

Sally had gone quiet again, her face was a picture.

He warmed to his theme. "There'll be things to get ready for the party of course, and we need to finalise arrangements in the village, but stay on after its all over. You'll have plenty of time to look around the house."

Sally could see he was sincere.

"I'd love to," she replied before giving herself the chance to say no.

Determined to carry on the good work of earlier, Charles was back on the phone. Roger Dukes, manager at The Theatre had been in contact twice already. The charity shows were causing headaches and all the available staff were stretched to the limit. Delegating duties was at a premium. There was local and national radio to accommodate, along with television news teams who would be covering the events. Security was a major priority and needed to be increased.

Half way through the morning Charles took a moment to drink a cup of tea and reflect. His P.A. was noticeably quieter than usual. In fact, she was hardly speaking at all, just smiling.

"Oh dear." He spoke quietly to himself and wondered if Suffolk and the planning of it was fast becoming recipe for disaster. Charles returned her smile with one of his own.

No doubt others would make of it what they wished, not to mention Claire, if she ever found out. There'd be a time to confront those issues later.

"Courting trouble, Charles," he spoke to himself and was instantly reminded of a promise to ring Joe Peterson. The scheduled meeting with Nick Sayers was imminent too. What he craved was certainty and something to give him hope.

Charles picked up the latest letter of warning from his wife and lifted the phone to his ear. The ring tone rang twice before the quiet and yet proficient voice of Joe Peterson answered.

"I'm outside the restaurant now…Yes, I've already checked inside." Joe was economical and yet concise with his answers. "No sign of your son as yet… If he is spotted, one of the boys will stay with your daughter and Miss Grant; agreed?" It took a moment for Charles to reaffirm their pre-made plan. "And tomorrow Miss Highland will be with the photographer all day." A statement rather than a question. Joe was keen to keep a tight grip on the situation. It led him directly onto his next point.

"The traffic out here is doing us no favours. I have a suggestion to make. How easy would it be to persuade your daughter to lose her car for the next few days? Much easier for surveillance purposes and no need to second guess her every move."

Hanlan quickly appreciated the sense in this but was quick to point out that "he knew not what he asked." He would do his best and that was all he could promise.

"I'll call you back, Joe. You've given me an idea." Charles cut the connection. More was undoubtedly required to assist the young man in all he was being asked to achieve.

"Sally, get me Marsha Ivanovic's number, while I quickly phone Amelia."

Charles scribbled a note to himself on the pad by the phone just as Sally announced the arrival of Nick Sayers.

"One moment, Miss Stewart, this must come first."

*

...He wanted her badly, that was something she knew for sure. Something chemical, almost tangible simmered and scented the air; this despite his show of detachment and resistance to all her teasing. The thrilling question remained. How long before she would pay for all her cruelty towards him? Not long now, all being well. She wasn't fooled by his calm indifference as he bowed with irony, holding the door open and allowing her to pass.

The actions of a gentleman? No, only a ploy. Now with the stairs ahead of them he had created the perfect opportunity, not only to ogle but to make advances on her from behind. Turning her head would have only spoiled the fun. Climbing the stairs, she moved sedately at first, putting distance and safety between them, but couldn't resist accentuating her wiggle in a provoking and naughty way. She'd done it now, there'd be no escape.

A glance back to make sure he was following and seeing that his eyes were intrusively intent, she dared not wait a second longer. Bolting for the top of the stairs, the race was on and she would do her best to win it. The sound of their feet on steps echoed loudly, as she fumbled in her purse for a front door key.

Reaching the landing and suppressing squeals of frightened delight, she anticipated inevitable surrender, while at the door the thrill of it made her clumsy with the key. As sounds of his exertions grew louder in her ears, she prepared herself for the worst, still shockingly exposed as he came at her from behind and finally touched her. Words of negotiation were lost amongst the squeals of delight.

Begging him between giggles, unsubtle hand allowed her some respite to concentrate her efforts and gain access to the flat. One snaking arm never left her, a hand on her torso, he managed to close the door behind them with a flick of his foot. Walking wasn't made easy as they shuffled in tandem, his other hand creeping beneath the hem of her skirt. Now the flimsy restraints and last line of her defence were being put under attack…

Amelia was suddenly and disarmingly awake. The chaotic landscape of her bed matched her confusion and shock as the dream faded away to nothing. It would have been easy to reproach herself because of the promise she'd made to control these troubling emotions. The frustration that she contained within the privacy of her bedroom had everything to do with how she'd been taught to behave.

The break-up of the family had taken on new and disturbing connotations. She was aware how little thought she had given to it until she'd gone to America. Memories of her illness and subsequent stay in the hospital were vague at best and something she'd totally underrated. Four years later she was having to resurrect an uncomfortable past she'd thought dead and buried.

She remembered being sent home from school and Mary Paxton not being there to receive her.

...Undeniably, like it or not, Lloyd had been her lot. She could remember a sense of disquiet, but knew that her choices were limited. His search for strong aspirin and a promise of something hot to drink were the best that she could hope for. Her bed was where she truly needed to be before another bout of dizziness hit her. Discarded clothes remained in a heap on the floor, as Amelia stepped into the shower in an attempt to stop her shivering.

Perhaps she might have picked a more appropriate garment from the top drawer of her dresser. The silken nothingness with a neck and hem-line that did their best to meet in the middle. It was a nightie, what had she cared? Saved for occasions of fantasy when feeling unashamedly sexy about herself, it would be hidden beneath the bed clothes.

Hot liquid plus the rattle of capsule and pill, Lloyd had been as good as his word. Encouraging her to sit up and take her medicine, unbeknown to a delirious Amelia, he'd watched in fascination her efforts to comply. Little moans and groans had punctuated her labouring, while the cut of her night-dress had also come under stress. For Lloyd at that moment the site of Amelia had suddenly become more vital than his own next breath.

If she'd had any doubts as to Lloyd's motivations in kindness, she might have been surprised to find out that the boy himself was pondering certain contradictions. For instance, what was it that made him feel unexpectedly tender towards somebody that his mother had openly encouraged him to despise? Could it be that her look of frailty and paleness was easier to contend with than the usual confidence and radiance she exuded? Was it that she actually needed him for a change when self-sufficiency had appeared to be her only goal?

She had found it hard to swallow. The sugary-sweet liquid with its kick in the tail neither revived or gave any hint of relief. Later, in a haze of delirious sleep and fitful awakenings, uncontrollable shivering made mockery of the patch-work patterned quilt she'd pulled up under her chin. If Amelia had been even faintly aware of someone tending to her, she would have known it couldn't have been Mary.

Alcohol and pills had proved a volatile mixture, and with the sickness, a suspicion grew that her trust had been misgiven. Hands were where they shouldn't be and an enveloping shadow weighed her down. A voice in pain, but not her own. Dizziness taking her away, oblivious to anything more…

Amelia suddenly needed to be active. Nothing was clear and nothing was comfortable. Enough time had been devoted to scouring the past for now. Better to stay in the present. Lunch with Samantha for instance. Yes, something to look forward to. Her feet found her slippers as she sat on the edge of the bed and reached for the phone. A message from her father, no less… well who else would it be from?

*

You had to know it, to have any hope of finding it. A small brass plaque on the wall by the entrance was the only clue as to what was hidden inside. Too public a place to meet with Amelia? Samantha Grant could relax in the knowledge that the choice of restaurant had not been hers. Apparently, Amelia and Ellen, who was also invited, often came there when spending time together away from the theatre. "Aperture" was an unusual name for an eating place, she thought. Walking off the street and now down the stairs to the bar, the murmurings of conversation drifted up to meet her. On the walls of the stairwell framed photographs were hung with enough space between them to show that each print deserved to be there. Now the restaurant's name made sense. Sam was aware that Jeff Sayers would have appreciated the subtle lighting employed to create the gallery-type effect. She wondered, and not for the first time, how his meeting with Charles Hanlan was progressing.

Sam had her name checked on the booking sheet by a very polite, if somewhat serious looking girl, and asked if she wanted to hang up her coat. For a second, she struggled to give a coherent answer, her mind still not focused in the here and now. In the end she declined the offer and asked to be shown to her table. She thought that engaging a little more with her powers of concentration would be important in negotiating the rest of her day.

The restaurant was busy and she kept her eyes focused in front of her, trying not to invade on the space of the other diners as she passed by. The table shown to her was set for three places and she decided to sit where she could observe the rest of the room. Sam relaxed and began to appreciate the understated elegance of her surroundings. Stylish handwriting on blackboards articulated the promise of artistic culinary design.

She'd just ordered a sparkling water from the waiter, when she was conscious of a lull in the conversations from the other tables around her. Sam witnessed their easy high-jacking as all of a sudden there was a rival to the chef's speciality of the day.

Amelia too, like Samantha before her, kept her eyes to the front as she walked across the room towards her. She smiled, quickened her pace and arrived at the table before the waiter could pull out her chair.

"A drink for you, Miss Highland?" He recovered his composure with a smile of recognition.

Amelia made herself comfortable and looked to Samantha for help in her choice. The two women kept each other company with sparkling water, saying little of importance until the glare of public attention had dissolved to a less intrusive level.

"So, what do you think?" Amelia asked, without looking around her.

"Stunning." Sam too kept a narrow point of view.

It was unsettling for Ellen now with Amelia about to leave. It had not become an issue until her trip to

New York, but now only a few days remained before her friend took her final bow. Ellen was acutely aware of feeling left behind.

Perhaps it was presumptive to call Amelia a friend. They had shared much in the last year. If nothing else, Ellen could boast that of all in the company, she remained closer to Amelia than most.

Considering the future, Ellen could take comfort from knowing that her job was secure. The contract she had with Charles Hanlan Productions was on-going and she'd already agreed to work with the next leading lady. Like Ellen, Katie Ley had been with the show from the outset, so they knew each other well. As Amelia's understudy for the last six months, she deserved her chance to lead, but that was of little consolation to Ellen who considered, with no disrespect to Katie, that working with the best had become a bit of an addiction.

Ellen remained deep in her thoughts and allowed home-grown worries to creep up and overtake her. Their private mode of transport, her method of escape from the madness, continued to prove unreliable. Worse still, her boyfriend was plainly suffering from problems very similar to that of his car. The combination was painful, and both were in serious danger of being traded-in.

She took stock one more time. Amelia, the car and her boyfriend. One was giving up, the second was playing up, and the third wasn't getting it up. Ellen's powers of positive thinking had been undeniably disconnected at the mains.

The subsequent invitation to join Amelia and Miss Grant, the American film company executive, for lunch was a surprise and much needed shot in the arm. A trickle of optimism was a bonus and had gone a long way to convince Ellen that the tide of destiny was about to turn. On her way to the restaurant a few minutes behind Amelia, the thought of meeting new challenges and experiencing new horizons was suddenly a potent tonic to mix with the changes. Like working in New York perhaps? Anything was possible, like winning the lottery. There was always that hope to cling on to.

"We need to keep our wits about us." Samantha Grant was speaking whilst pouring Amelia another glass of water. Ellen was acutely aware that of the three, she was the only one to be drinking alcohol. Miss Grant was speaking again and Ellen realized that it was mainly for her benefit.

"If Mr Hanlan's son was the man we saw in New York, we'd be silly to treat it as an idle threat." Sam sounded apologetic, not wanting to accuse Amelia's step-brother without the certainty of proof.

Ellen's attention was already wavering. Really? She found it all a little melodramatic. What she wouldn't give to have such powers of attraction. In her opinion Amelia had always guarded her privacy to excess and that was puzzling for someone who should be milking her success for all that it was worth. So, what if you attracted a few cranks now and then? Surely it was a small price to pay.

She endeavoured to find some genuine sympathy for the situation but knew it to be a sham. For the first time since she'd known Amelia, it felt like a gap had opened up between them. Nobody's fault perhaps, it had most likely always been that way. Looking now across the table at the designer labels and beauty that she would never possess, it was plain that Miss Grant and Amelia belonged to each other, while she had probably done well to hang on this long.

Ellen emptied her glass. Her fourth give or take a glass or two. Tears were about to be shed and it was time to leave. The last of her pride would not allow her to show them how hurt she really felt. Making excuses of not feeling well she rose from the table, asking as she did so, to be allowed to pay her share of the bill. The American, of course, refused the offer and Ellen, with a pang of guilt was witness to Amelia's genuine concern.

"What's wrong Ellen? Wait, let me come with you."

"Please don't." The words sounded harsher than she wished to convey them, but they had their desired effect. Ellen said her goodbyes and left the restaurant alone, holding herself together just long enough to make it to street level. In a moment of pique, she decided that the American accent could be tolerated for just so long. Once on the pavement, the tears fell uncontrollably as it hit her that her happiness lay in the hands of those who would never understand.

Once outside Aperture, a picture of abject despair, Ellen made no immediate attempt to hide her watery scars. A saddened heart worn defiantly on her sleeve; she knew it was a poor way of seeking attention. Her reliable routine would be changed forever in a matter of days and while others moved on to the bigger and better, she was in danger of being left too far behind. Her self-imposed depreciation bordered on being self-indulgent, she knew that.

As her tears dried, she reached for tissues from the depths of her bag to make much needed and timely repairs.

"On your way back to the theatre?"

A trans-Atlantic voice came from nowhere and put a temporary halt to her cosmetic endeavours. With embarrassment she just had time to blow her nose.

"I don't talk to strangers, particularly strange men." She blurted out, and began to walk quickly, not wishing to offer him any encouragement. She did however risk a glance to confirm that she'd met this particular man before.

"I'd like to apologize to you if that's okay?" Lloyd settled to his task, aware of her caution, and who could blame her for not wanting to play in his game. "We're not complete strangers, I should point that out." He slowed his pace hoping she would too. "Outside The Theatre? I think I frightened you. I really would like to tell you how sorry I am." Lloyd held out his hand in a time ordered manner but made no attempt to touch her.

Ellen slowed and came to a standstill, her eyes flickered from his face to his outstretched offering of reconciliation and back again. "You were outside on Monday afternoon." She spoke the truth but her words sounded more like an accusation. She could vividly remember his flash of hostility.

Lloyd could see it written on her face. "Stupid of me, the way I reacted. I know what you must be thinking." He gently took hold of Ellen's hand. "I'd like to explain. Perhaps you'd allow me to buy you a coffee or something. Whatever you want and no strings attached." He tried a smile to show his contrition. "If nothing else I'd feel a whole lot better about myself if you could find a way to say yes."

She didn't respond, not at first. Her mind was racing, while coming to terms with his possible identity.

"Please?" Lloyd made a last throw of the dice and then he was silent.

Ellen made him wait for her decision even though her answer would certainly be yes. "All right, a quick one. Coffee, I mean." She responded to his smirk. "I'm working tonight and I need to go home and change before that." Intrigue had overtaken her previous caution and the warnings given by Samantha Grant were easy to recall. Could it be she'd found a way to be useful to the cause and take back some control?

A gentle squeeze of her hand and a nod of her head sealed the deal and she allowed him to lead her to the corner of the street.

"I've got a car parked not far from here. I could give you a lift if that's what you need. If that's not being too presumptuous?" Lloyd seemed to be making progress at last and was consequently feeling better about life in general.

Coincidentally Ellen Preston was too. In the end they flagged down a taxi and were happy to share that as well.

*

"Take a seat, Mr Sayers." They shook hands across the table. "Thanks for coming at such short notice. What's it like being back in London?"

Nick made himself comfortable and took a moment to evaluate his host.

"Oh, I have mixed emotions to tell you the truth, Mr Hanlan." Nick felt that intelligent eyes were assessing him too. "I've lived in New York for some years now and I can honestly say I've not missed this place too much. I was a freelance photographer based in London as you probably know, but never felt really settled here."

Hanlan made no judgement. "So, coming back to visit had no bearing on you agreeing to work with NRG then?"

"No, not at all. Meeting up with Miss Grant in Manhattan was purely coincidental. We've known each other for some time and she was keen to have somebody on board who speaks with a native tongue." Nick held up his hands. "Her words not mine. No, I'm only here as a consultant to help with the control of publicity surrounding Miss Highland."

"Very formally put, but you're a journalist at heart. Getting an inside story has to be a more gratifying way to make your money?"

Nick could not disagree. "Of course, a story, but something of consequence and certainly not at any cost. The difference for me is Stress Magazine. I have no deadlines to keep. My editor is also my wife and I'm lucky I can be flexible." There was an irony to what he'd just said in view of their virtual estrangement.

Hanlan, if he was aware of Nick's predicament, wasn't letting on.

"Then if I understand you correctly, I'd say you were in a small minority. You're in a fortunate position, because ethics and the press don't usually sit at the same table. Or am I being over sensitive? You've no doubt read certain articles written by a former colleague of yours." Hanlan made sure he had Nick's eye. "I notice you don't need to ask who I'm talking about."

"Peter Pearce, of course."

"The very same. I've never had the pleasure of meeting him but he seems to be under the impression he knows me intimately." Hanlan spoke with heavy irony.

"You've never thought of putting him right on that, or making a complaint to his paper's editor?" Nick had wondered why he didn't do more to defend himself and the relationship he had with his daughter.

Hanlan ignored the question and reached for a piece of paper laying on his desk. "And just to add to my discomfort, a letter from my wife." He waved it in the air. "Claire seems to be closely acquainted with Pearce and his style of journalism. She mentions him by name. It's as if they're tied at the hip when it comes to these very personal attacks." Although wounded, he sounded hardened to the nature of what had been written. "I'd love to know what I've done to deserve this kind of treatment."

Nick remained impassive although he had his own opinions as to Peter Pearce's motivation.

"I'm funding my own problems where Claire is concerned." Charles felt he should explain. "When my wife left the country, we agreed on terms that were meant to protect the family." He paused to emphasise the importance of what he said next. "Amelia is an innocent in the midst of this present mess. Leaving the show for America compounds my mistakes but I'm okay with that as long as she's safe. What is important is that she gets her chance."

It was difficult for Nick to comment on what was becoming a confession.

Hanlan drew breath before speaking again. "I need to keep her away from my son," he said with some conviction. "Allowing her to meet up with NRG was always going to be a gamble, which in all honesty I'm beginning to regret. The information I have suggests that Lloyd is here right now with heaven knows what on his mind. I'm to blame for that in so many ways."

Nick tried to unpick the implications of that. He needed more and wondered if Hanlan knew of a specific connection between Claire and Peter Pearce. "Let's take this separately. Putting the estrangement of your son to one side, no one can blame themselves for the fiction Peter Pearce writes. I'm an expert on that."

"Oh, and why is that? I know you worked on the same paper at one time." Charles had prior knowledge but not all the facts.

Nick hoped that what he said next would not backfire on NRG. "Look I'm happy to be open with you. If you were wondering, I've come clean with Samantha Grant." He made a proviso. "To be fair to her and my present job description, the flow of information has to be a two-way thing."

A knowing smile played on Charles' face but never quite reached his eyes. "So, you do want a story."

Nick said nothing and sincerely wished he'd had a camera to hand. Across the other side of the desk there was an interesting portrait of man weighing up the odds.

"Cards on the table Mr Sayers?"

"Face up." Nick nodded his head.

"Before you continue." Hanlan offered him coffee, no doubt a ploy to break the tension and give them the opportunity to get their thoughts in line. "Look let's keep this off the record for the time being and see where a little integrity gets us, shall we?"

Nick had to laugh. "I can promise it makes no difference to me."

"You're right, and I'm prepared to take you at your word." Hanlan bowed his head in resignation. "I interrupted you, please do go on."

Nick put his empty cup back in its saucer. "A few years ago, the paper gave Peter Pearce full reign to follow a suspect in a murder case. It went on to make headline news." Charles nodded his head. "Anyway, Pearce asked me for help to carry out surveillance on the man's house. Initially, I thought it was all above board. The paper made good on headlines that mocked the deficiencies of the police. As it turned out the wrong man was convicted, thanks in part to what we had become embroiled in."

He wanted to ask for more coffee. It had taken some of the formality out of the meeting, if not the intent with which Hanlan was listening to his confession.

"You spoke earlier about trusting each other. It's not easy admitting my mistakes. I was young and inexperienced enough to believe that we were on the side of justice. Thankfully modern forensic science came to the man's rescue. Huge compensation payments were made to him. Pearce was unrelenting and continued to stick by what he'd written. Once you cross Pearce you're his enemy for life." Nick rubbed his face as though suddenly tired. "You asked me if I was glad to be back in London. Perhaps this explains my mixed emotions."

Hanlan took it all in. "Thank you for being so candid. A difficult thing to have been involved with. But in light of what you've said, we need to figure out the connection between Pearce and my wife. I mean is it possible that they knew each other before she went to America?"

This question was a shot from out of the blue and yet easy enough to answer. "Putting it bluntly, yes, it's more than likely." He was aware that too much truth could hurt as much as being deceitful.

"With respect sir, your wife was a regular on the London party scene. The kind of territory that Pearce was happy to frequent. Saw himself as some kind of undercover agent if you like, digging the dirt on those he felt deserved it, unless it suited him otherwise." Nick emphasised his words. "Remember we hunted in pairs. For a time, I made a crust being out on the street, waiting to photograph the evidence when it staggered out the door."

If Hanlan felt that Nick had been too easy with the facts, he gave no sign that he'd taken offence. He was however capable of tapping the ball back over the net. "Glad to see you decided that life in the gutter was not for you." Both men took the opportunity to study each other.

"The Sunday papers loved it of course. Happy to dish the dirt." Nick held his hands up. "I'm accusing no one, you understand, but Pearce loved a circus and who's to say he wasn't its ring master."

He did not want to speculate but it seemed possible that Claire Williams, while still making the news, may have benefited from Pearce's protection. "What I can say is that Pearce knew your former partner, Maurice Highland."

"How do you make that connection?" Charles looked shocked as he absorbed this latest revelation. Was it something he should have known about before?

"I did a bit of digging and his name is credited on some of Highland's documentary work." It had been simple to find that much out. "By association your wife may well have come to Peter's attention. The world of celebrity is smaller than we sometimes think. I used to photograph the same old faces time after time."

They mulled this over but reached no firm conclusions and Nick felt he was missing the relevance of certain connections that the other had made. "Forgive my ignorance, but I'm struggling to see why your son may be a danger to Miss Highland?"

Hanlan's face clouded over. The question was valid and would need answering as a show of their mutual trust. It was too late in the day to back out now. Charles was being asked to open a whole new can of worms and in the process spill the beans.

Nick leaned forward to show that he was paying attention. It was too late to refrain from asking difficult questions. He hoped Samantha Grant would see things his way.

"I've never considered divorcing my wife for good reason." Charles leaned back in his leather up-holstered chair. "Okay, I still support Claire even now, and that does afford me a degree of control. We might lead separate lives but as you've already gathered, she has specific needs, things she might not find easy to afford if our situation were to change." He wasn't taking any pleasure in what he said.

"I bought her off and Lloyd was part of the deal. It's been four years since I had direct contact with either of them." His promise to keep the children apart had seemed so easy then. "When Amelia stepped off the plane in New Jersey, she unwittingly stepped into a no-go zone. By letting her do that I've potentially put her life at risk." He reached for Claire's letter, "... and I quote; he wants to right the wrongs that have made his life hell."

Nick's simmering frustration came to the boil. "I get that you want to protect her, but both your children have their own lives to live. That's not something you can control forever." He could see that Hanlan had immediately taken offence at this. "Miss Grant and NRG are offering Amelia a huge opportunity." He would not be interrupted. "Since the incident in New York, your daughter blames herself for her ignorance, or even worse, her indifference. Let's be plain. Either you embrace the family's problems or there'll be nothing left to save."

When Charles eventually regained his seat, it took him a moment to appreciate that he'd actually left it in the first place. His options were limited and Nick was waiting for some kind of reply.

"I'll tell you this much Mr Sayers. You're implying Amelia deserves all our sympathy. And you're right, no child deserves to lose both her parents at such a young age. Consequently, Lloyd has become a victim too. If I was a cynic, I might try to blame my wife for that." Charles took a deep breath. "Admitting one's own guilt does not in any way excuse my behaviour. I'm sure you can agree with that."

Charles was looking for some common ground. "To be truthful, my son and I parted company the day he was conceived." He tried to qualify his remark. "I have always provided without giving of myself. Lloyd is still my dependant. Financially he does very well by me. Emotionally? Well, we never did get to open an account."

Hanlan was at last beginning to open up.

"With Amelia, it was different. She felt like family right from the outset." His voice softened. "When Maurice and Jelena didn't come back, she was all that I had to hold onto."

"But why should that impact on your wife and son?"

"Jealousy and disappointment were factors, that's for sure. When Claire got pregnant that was the beginning of the end for us. Lloyd was an innocent party and should have been treated accordingly. Truth is, we have never had the same connection."

Nick didn't push the point. Who was he to judge? "Separating when you did, I can understand, but why banish them from the rest of your life?

Charles looked at him and simply said. "That's a very good question."

He went on to fill in the gaps as best he could. It was true that relations with Claire had seldom been easy. The physical attraction between them followed by predictable periods of relative calm had sustained them. These had been the good times, put to best use by discussing Lloyd's welfare and erratic behaviour.

"Compromise is a little overrated when it comes to negotiating with Claire." Charles began with an observation. "Lloyd had been showing encouraging interest in drama. He even asked to attend a few theatrical workshops that Amelia was heavily involved with." He admitted to not consulting Amelia as to her feelings about this.

"I wanted to be impartial and gain Claire's cooperation." He readily admitted to is ulterior motives. "I'd just entered into negotiations concerning The Theatre that required an uninterested press. As for Lloyd, I thought it might do him some good." Charles was keen to justify his actions.

"It worked for a while, but I made the mistake thinking that we'd all turned a corner. That went straight out the window the day Amelia was taken ill at school."

He painted a lurid picture as he told how Claire had descended upon him earlier that afternoon demanding attention in a way that he found hard to resist.

Fellow diners enjoying lunch at a famous restaurant would have been forgiven for believing that their much-publicized split was rapidly healing. The journey back from London had been fraught with pleasant dangers, she'd seen to that. Charles spared Nick the detail and himself the embarrassment. It was evident he found it uncomfortable reliving it now.

"When we finally got home, I knew instantly that something was wrong. The house was in complete darkness and Lloyd would never have thought to be that frugal unless he had something to hide. Claire thought nothing of it and couldn't understand the fuss I was making."

Once inside the house, Charles had waisted little politeness in listening to her opinions. "I didn't know for sure that Amelia was there, you see, and yet somehow I sensed…" He was suddenly angry. "If only I'd got in touch with the office sooner, I'd have picked up the message about Amelia being sent home from school."

Charles told Nick the rest. There didn't seem much point in keeping it from him now. He told of feet that barely touched the stairs, of his intuition and the unbroken silence within the house. The dread and fear that consumed him while he made his way to her room. The sight of spread-eagled legs and a rag-doll body lying prostrate upon her bed. Dull matted hair and a face partially hidden as though from shame. The smell, the stench of vomit that had made her slightly revolting to him, if only briefly.

"And the bed." Charles spoke slowly, seeking control. "It was obvious… unmistakeable." He paused, not daring to look up from a point of focus somewhere on the desk in front of him. "How could my son…?" He didn't finish it.

"I found him locked away in his room. I practically begged him to tell me what had happened, but to no avail. Claire was laughing and trying to make light of it." Charles looked as if he was reliving the pain.

"Amelia ended up in hospital?" Nick tried to help by filling in the gaps

Hanlan nodded. "There was so little time. All I could think about was getting them out of the house." He explained how Lloyd was allowed to pack a few things into a bag before being bundled, along with his mother, into a taxi taking them away.

"I just had time to put Amelia into a spare bed, so the paramedics wouldn't see the state of her room."

Nick could hardly believe what he was hearing. "You took a calculated risk doing that."

"Yes, I did. And I've lived with the consequences ever since. It was damage limitation, pure and simple, because the truth would have crushed us all."

Nick still was not convinced, and it must have showed.

"Just imagine if the press had got hold of it. You in your former life and the likes of Peter Pearce would have had a field day."

Nick had no answer to that and allowed a silence to fall between them.

*

The aroma of freshly brewed coffee made Nick look up from his work. It was definitely one of his favourite smells. Drinking it black, or with a dash of cream, it didn't much matter to him, just as long as it was hot. Picking up the silver jug from the tray, he tipped a little white onto the black and waited for the mixing clouds to tell him when he'd poured enough. The bar of the hotel in which he and Samantha were staying was fairly deserted which was just as well. Nick had scattered his notes all over a table to the floor beneath it. Under the watchful gaze of the barman who had delivered the coffee, he was doing his best to make sense of the random handwritten text.

For one moment only, the barman felt inclined to offer his help. However, on closer scrutiny he thought better of it and was heard to comment that his two-year-old daughter had a scribble more legible than Nick's.

He was duly thanked for his observation, and politely told to go away.

"How's it going?" Nick asked the question without looking up as the chair next to him was lightly engaged.

Samantha leaned over to witness him put pen to paper. Like a patient with a doctor's prescription, she was left to trust that the scribble would make sense to someone. Before she could say something, another coffee was delivered to the table.

"Don't thank him, he's really rather rude." Nick warned her. "Thinks his daughter is a better writer than me."

Sam looked quizzically from Nick's notes to the barman. She picked up the bill for the coffee and signed it to her room. The barman thanked her and made a show of checking the room number and signature.

"First legible thing I've read this afternoon," he spoke directly to Samantha. "Glad you signed it and not your friend," he added and turned quickly away before Nick could reply.

"Have I had a good day? More to the point, what about you?" Sam reflected that only a couple hours ago she and

Amelia had agreed how easy it was to have him around. Was Nick now doing his best to frustrate the hell out of her?

He could sense her impatience. "I'll come to our friend Hanlan in a minute, How's our star?" It seemed a poignant question to ask.

"Somewhat distracted I should say. Lunch was not a great success." Sam explained about Ellen and how it had affected Amelia. "She's got a great deal on her mind and I'm afraid that Ellen has just added to that. Obviously, she was nervous about you meeting with her step-father but on top of that I sense she became aware today how her leaving is going to impact on the people she's worked closely with." Sam sounded deflated. "Sometimes I get the feeling she's just trying to please everybody else and that includes us." She watched as he nodded his head in agreement. "My fear is that if she can't commit fully, she hasn't a chance of convincing Sherman she's the one."

"A major disappointment to all."

"So come on, tell me you had more success." The look she gave him made it clear she would not be put off a moment longer.

Stacking the sheets of text into a pile, he wondered where he should begin. "I made notes as you already know." He smiled wryly, knowing that humour would figure little in what he was about to recount.

"You couldn't make it up even if you tried." Nick described the scene that Hanlan had found on returning to Avondale, four years ago. Sam had immediately suggested they retire to a more private table in the hotel lounge.

"They found Lloyd locked in his room. Wouldn't come out, at least not while Charles was trying to beat the door down."

"What about Amelia?" Sam looked devastated. "She was all on her own."

"Out cold by all accounts. Had already been terribly sick." Nick felt no obligation to protect Charles. "He did say he wasn't trying to hurt the boy. Just trying to find out what drink and drugs she'd been given."

"Sounds as though her sickness was probably what saved her."

Nick agreed. "Obviously Charles went with the ambulance and stayed with her through the night. She didn't wake until later the next day. The doctors didn't feel it was necessary to pump her stomach. There was nothing left to come out."

Too much information. Samantha pulled a face. There was another matter that she needed to ask about.

"And was she interfered with? I mean, had she been raped?"

Nick could only shrug his shoulders. He'd asked the very same question of Hanlan.

"We don't know the answer to that one." He said it simply and waited for the expected response.

"What do you mean? They didn't check?" Sam was flabbergasted.

"No evidence to make them think it necessary."

"I'm sorry?"

"He cleaned her up."

Sam was temporarily speechless. She looked at Nick for confirmation that she'd understood him correctly, before using the very words that he had uttered under his breath in front of Hanlan.

"F…ing hell."

It was the first time that Nick had heard her swear.

Sam needed a drink, but first a breath of fresh air. She and Nick walked up and down the road outside the hotel for a few minutes whilst they both gathered their thoughts. She tried and failed to imagine how Hanlan had coped with the dilemmas of the night. As a woman it felt that Charles had dealt with the problems in a biased and unemotional way. Most perplexing was how he had managed to broker a deal that removed Claire and Lloyd so quickly from the house. Perhaps it had always been thus for the Hanlan family.

"And when she awoke, I'm guessing Amelia couldn't remember a thing, which is why she's never spoken about it." Sam gave a hollow laugh. "Jeez, I bet Hanlan couldn't believe his luck, could he?"

Nick didn't immediately answer.

"You don't agree?"

"Initially I reacted just as you are now." He held his hand up to fend off her protests. "Even when she was out of danger, there was the question of what if she'd got pregnant?" He shook his head. "Think about it. Who was he really trying to protect here."

"So, what you're saying is he waited for nature to decide and then act accordingly?" Sam didn't sound convinced. "We're assuming that Amelia still hasn't a clue what took place."

Nick thought it likely. "Ignorance is bliss or the truth at all costs?" He realised he was echoing decisions that Charles Hanlan had made.

"It had started to spit with rain forcing them back inside. As it must have been for Amelia when she'd returned home from hospital, there was a sense of unreality to the steps they were taking. Without question, a young woman's vulnerability had to take precedent over what to tell Sherman Powers.

"I've got to tell him something." She argued.

"How can you? Not without Amelia's consent, you can't." Nick was right. He watched as Sam weighed up the situation. "Ever played a game called Consequences?" Sam shook her head. "Well, you are now." He put a comforting arm around her shoulders. "We need a plan and as it happens… Come on, I'll buy us a drink while I explain."

8. Risky Decisions

Lunch time drinking usually made her sleepy. Not this time. Although the young man's apologies had seemed sincere, she remained resolutely suspicious. The decision to share a taxi back to her place was fuelled by adrenalin and was all about making up for her negativity and lack of spirit at the restaurant. What had Miss Grant said? Something about keeping your wits about you. Was this now a case in point?

He was using a bogus name and his accent seemed overdone. An hour ago, she'd been listening to the real thing. Harry kept up his incessant stream of chat and charm unabated. If this was really Lloyd Hanlan, then it wouldn't be long before the subject of his sister came to the fore.

The taxi turned into the top of her road and Ellen reached for her purse.

"I'll get it." Harry, the gentleman was not short of a bob or two judging by the size of his wallet. Seconds later they were closing the front door of Ellen's ground floor flat.

"Come on in and sit down. Make yourself comfortable." She was aware that the state of living room left much to be desired, Ordinarily, it wouldn't have mattered. "Sorry the place is such a mess." Her keys and handbag joined the general confusion and lost themselves on the dining room table. She felt he was being remarkably cool. "Tea? You Americans probably prefer coffee. By the way, thought this might interest you." She gave him the latest program for Ever Searching before going to put the kettle on. A glance at the clock in the kitchenette confirmed her fears. Once again time was against her and still no sign of his true intentions.

Of the two of them, Lloyd had more stamina and practice for the game they played. Despite her valiant efforts Ellen was becoming anxious. It dawned on her that making a call to The Theatre was more than appropriate. She didn't want to make Harry too suspicious but how grateful would Miss Grant be if she could send a warning?

"I need to shower and get ready for work." Ellen silently cursed as she remembered the battery on her mobile was flat. She was just about to plug the charger in and grab a fresh set of clothes when Lloyd spoke up.

"Amelia Highland was in New York a week or so ago. But you knew that of course."

Ellen stopped dead. Surprised, she flung everything onto the bed and hurried back down the corridor.

"Yes, that's right. Did you see her then?" She poked her head tentatively into the living room.

"Yeh, but only on tv." Lloyd looked relaxed. "I knew her from drama school." He nonchalantly sipped his tea.

Ellen was taken aback. She hadn't expected him to be quite so frank. "Are you planning to meet up while you're over here?"

Lloyd feigned indifference. "I hadn't planned to. She's too famous to be bothered with the likes of me." He seemed to be making lame excuses. "I doubt she would even remember."

Ellen didn't quite know what to think. She'd been sure that Harry was only using her to get closer to Amelia. She had a suggestion. "I could mention that I'd bumped into you."

"No, that's kind." Lloyd smiled. He put down his cup and saucer. "Look, I've kept you long enough. You're probably going to be late as it is. Thanks for the tea though."

"That's quite okay, but you don't have to go." Ellen didn't want to sound too keen. "Look at least let me call you a taxi. Give me half an hour and we'll share one back into town."

Lloyd checked his watch. "Okay, you've convinced me."

"I won't be long, I promise." Relieved and yet mindful, she knew the game was still on. "Put some music on if you like." She spoke loudly from her bedroom as she began to undress.

"Ellen, I've been thinking about Amelia. Maybe I should try to make contact. If you've got an address, I could drop her a line."

So that was it. He didn't know where she lived. Hardly surprising when she considered how jealously Amelia guarded that information. Question now was how should she proceed?

"Write her a note and I'll save you the postage." Ellen thought it a sensible repost. "There's pen and paper somewhere on the table."

Lloyd did not immediately reply. It was obvious he wasn't impressed with her suggestion. Now she remembered from their first meeting how angry he could be. Locking the bathroom door, she perched her bum on the toilet seat. One thing was certain, she was never going to give him Amelia's address in London.

Rivulets of water cascaded down her body as she turned to the source of the shower. Shampoo, thick and creamy, splattered heavily on the bottom of the bath and meandered between her feet. Ellen rinsed her hair until it squeaked clean between her fingers. Grabbing a couple of towels, she unlocked the bathroom door and cocked an ear in Harry's direction before tip-toeing along the corridor back to her bedroom.

He was sitting on her bed, searching the drawers of her bed-side cabinet. In her surprise she dropped one towel but managed to hang onto the other.

"What are you doing?"

He didn't answer, never made a sound but held his head in his hands looking totally forlorn.

"Are you unwell?" Despite her state of undress, Ellen moved towards him. It looked as if he was shaking, perhaps even crying. Recalling her own distress her heart went out to him.

It happened so quickly. Lloyd sprang from the bed in a bid to push past. He swung his right arm out blindly. Whether he meant to or not, the back of his hand struck the side of her face.

Only when she reeled away and fell to the floor did the stinging pain bring tears to her eyes. She couldn't believe it, not at first, but with comprehension there came further alarm. Surely, he wasn't going to do it again?

As she picked herself up and turned to face him, indignation added to her distress. The bath towel she'd been clinging to was lost to the floor. Standing naked and exposed with the taste of blood on her tongue, she used her hands and arms to cover herself. In despair she watched him move in on her again.

Retreat appeared her only option. She had to hope that space might give her time and appeal to the better part of his nature. As she attempted to step backwards her feet became entangled with one of the lost towels and with that her balance was gone. There was no time to scream and despite his threat she actually reached out forlornly towards him.

She toppled like a tree. Whether Lloyd was hesitant or he was just too late, there was nothing he could do. When she finally hit the floor, the sickening crack as her head hit the edge of the door was as heart-stopping as it was loud. Lloyd watched with fascination as her chin snapped forward and seemed to smash into the top of her chest.

Silence invaded the room. Ellen appeared to be dying. Despite the horror of the moment, he still had time to notice her breasts, white and fleshy, quiver and subside as her breath escaped in a steady wheeze through her open mouth. Scared eyes looked up at him and for one brief second, he could have sworn she was trying to speak.

All his instincts told him to run. Fear and anger squeezed and twisted his gut. Once again, he'd managed to snatch tragic failure from the jaws of certain success. With one last look Lloyd took flight and bolted. The one thing he clung onto was Ellen's party invitation he'd found in her bedside drawer. If only she'd told him about that before, things could have been different.

Sedge House in Suffolk was now fated to be his last chance to get back at his father.

*

Joe Peterson had but a few seconds to make up his mind. If using his instincts was what set him apart then ignoring them now might prove disastrous. True, the young man would soon be out of sight, and yet something held Joe back. The front door to Ellen's house remained open and this seemed significant.

By the time Lloyd had turned the corner at the end of the road, Joe was already on the move. His trespass into Ellen's home was justified by the lack of reply when he called out her name. His automatic and experienced reactions were life-saving when he eventually found her lying on the bedroom floor.

Her pulse was slow and even but her breathing very shallow. The angle of her head looked unnatural and was the greatest cause for concern. Kneeling down beside her, he was aware of blood from the back of her head seeping into the carpet. Joe quickly took stock and decided Ellen must be carefully moved. Her nakedness allowed him access to skin which he pinched in places to check on her natural reactions. In the same moment he released her feet from the towels that they'd become snagged in.

Her eyes suddenly opened and Joe tried to reassure and explain that he was there to help. Cradling her body by tucking one arm around the top of her shoulders, he slid the other beneath the tops of her thighs. Her skin felt cold and clammy. Very carefully he lifted and moved her forwards, inch by inch, all the time watching her face. Gradually her chin that had been tight to her chest began to shift and her breathing became easier. Sliding his hands out from beneath her, he laid the towels to either side of her face to restrict further movement.

He finally covered Ellen in blankets from the bed to help counter the effects of the shock she'd be feeling. When he was content that she was out of immediate danger, he used the house phone to call for an ambulance. By design his mobile remained unused in his pocket.

Back in the bedroom Joe remained at Ellen's side until he heard the sound of an approaching siren. By this time, she was listening and comprehending his gentle instructions. He finally told her that professional help was on its way.

Minutes later Ellen Preston was in much better hands. Joe had watched discreetly from behind the wheel of his car, as two paramedics hurried inside the property. More than anything he hoped that she'd be fine and that he'd made the right decisions. He drove away leaving the ambulance and its flashing lights, necessarily blue and conspicuous, drawing the attentions of attentive neighbours.

Of Lloyd, unfortunately, there was no sign.

Fifteen minutes later he gave up his search. Hearing the siren must have sent Lloyd underground. A shop, a pub to hide in. A passing taxi or even a bus, there was certainly no way of knowing which one he'd chosen to make good his escape. Stopping the car Joe punched in Charles' number on his mobile phone.

"Have you called anybody else?" Hanlan had quickly absorbed the news.

"Not directly. Do you want me to?"

Hanlan thought for a second.

"If Ellen's okay, she'll be able to explain what happened. It'll be out of our hands. My preference would be that we spoke to him before deciding the best way to proceed." Hanlan was trying to make sense of it all. "Why did he leave her like that? Panic?"

Joe found it impossible to answer the question, but was angry that innocent people like Ellen were being put at risk. "Perhaps it would be better to put the authorities in the picture. I include myself in that. You don't want this coming back to haunt you." There was a deep sigh on the other end of the line.

"I hear what you're saying but if anyone makes that call it should be me. And don't feel responsible for loosing contact with my son. You did right by Ellen. She might have died if it weren't for you." The consequences of that were not lost on either of them. "Next time just pick him up anyway you have to. Looks more and more likely we'll have to involve the police, but understand this; I take the responsibility." Charles sounded resigned and somewhat dejected.

It was a reluctant admission of defeat but the truth was his son had left them with few options. Hanlan went on to briefly discuss his meeting with Nick Sayers and highlighted the possible link between Pearce and his family. By the end of their conversation, he had relented to Joe's insistence on taking advice from his lawyers. The rest was all about damage limitation.

"As you suggested, Sayers will go with my daughter to Suffolk and she's agreed to leave her car there. I'll find out which train they plan to return to London on."

Everything they spoke about was plausible but Joe's ability to protect Amelia felt compromised, now that Ellen Preston had been so badly hurt. Once again, he worried that his boss was taking chances with other people's lives.

"Security will be increased at The Theatre for the last show, but that'll be on me." Charles was firm on this. "There's no point your boys getting mixed up with the police and my own security. I'd prefer if you were at Sedge House checking on preparations there. Let's keep to the plan. Get everybody out of town and up to the party in Suffolk. After today, I'd say it's imperative."

Joe was glad that Hanlan was making necessary compromises but was keen to push home his point of view. "We must be seen to be accountable. An independent witness, somebody like Miss Grant for instance. Let's face it without her backing, your daughter's chances of going to America are zero."

"You're probably right. No more delay. Okay, Miss Grant it is." Charles thought for a second before finishing up. "I've only met her briefly but you have my permission to tell her everything you know."

*

"I thought I ought to warn you." Libi Sayers voice sounded small and distant over the phone.

"Where are you? Not still at the office?" Nick propped himself up and turned on a bedside light, squinting in the direction of his watch. Just after one.

"I'm just finishing up and about to head home."

He did the maths. Another long day for his wife at work in Manhattan.

"What's up?" Nick was fully awake now.

"Apparently rumour has it that you're having an affair. Not just one but probably two."

Nick took his time. "Right, okay. Surprised I have the energy." He tried to inject a little humour while he gauged how much credence Libi was giving these revelations. "No doubt these rumours come from reliable sources."

"The usual news trails. One word and it spreads like wildfire. Nothing in print but hold the front page." She sounded tired.

"And your reaction?"

"Need I say. No smoke without fire means all the guys at the magazine have been acting strangely around me. How am I supposed to feel? Look, I know we're not exactly getting on these days, God knows why but I trust you'd have the courage to tell if something was going on." She was trying to sound confident. "Wouldn't you?"

Despite the seriousness of the situation, Nick had to laugh. "How I wish you were here now." He spoke with feeling. "I do miss you."

"Sounds like you just need to get your end away." She tried to keep her tone light.

"Who would you suggest?"

"Spoilt for choice? Ask Miss Grant or Miss Highland." Libi hesitated. "Roll over and ask one of them now."

"Libi, don't." He could tell she was hurt. "We can both guess who's to blame for this. It didn't take him long to find out I was back in town."

"You mean Peter Pearce. Will you never escape from his clutches? Look, I'm tired and I need to sleep. We'll speak when you get back. Promise me, please." This was progress of sorts. "One thing's for certain, we can't carry on like we are."

"Okay, you're right." Nick wished her a good night. "And Libi, I'm sorry."

She put the phone down. No time to explain what he was sorry about.

Only a matter of minutes later there was a tap at his hotel bedroom door. He padded bare foot and turned lights on as he went to answer. Samantha was standing there, wrapped in a coat.

"Come in, what do I owe for the pleasure?" He stood aside and ushered her in. "Sorry, not the best thing to have said."

"I tried to ring you but your phone's been busy. Thought I should come in person," she started to explain.

"Just been talking to Libi."

Sam looked surprised and sheepish all in one go. "Ah. You might need to ring her back when you've listened to what I have to say." She steadied herself. "Sherman thinks we're having an affair."

Nick climbed back into bed. "Take a seat." He actually smiled. "My wife has already told me. And guess what? Apparently in my spare time I'm knocking off Amelia. Let's hope Sherman isn't aware of that?"

"Your wife? Oh shit, how can she?" Sam blushed. "I mean who's been spreading these lies?"

"Take a guess."

They looked at each other. "Not only me but Amelia too? That's a pretty big appetite you have." Samantha sat on the bed, stealing some blanket to cover her feet.

"What about Sherman. Plenty of understanding there I hope?" He winced as Sam pulled a face.

"Not especially, but that's to be expected. I've been summoned back to New York. Don't worry, it's not your fault." Sam tried to sound calm. "He wants me to attend an important meeting." She shrugged her shoulders. "That's what he said."

"Did he say why?"

Sam shook her head. "Said it could change his decision about taking Amelia on."

"Serious then. I hope he's not playing games with you." Nick reached the obvious conclusion. "I guess that makes me redundant."

"Not so fast. I've rigorously denied everything and told Powers Amelia needs your protection. That's if you want to carry on."

"Really? How ironic. Libi will absolutely love that."

"Yes, well, in view of what we've just talked about, I'm going to call in at Stress Magazine on my way to see Sherman." Nick was about to protest. "I'm being selfish about this. The more I can do to put Libi's mind at rest, the better it'll be for me. That's if you're okay with the idea?"

He reluctantly consented to this. Samantha shouldn't have to feel responsible for his wife's state of mind and he told her so.

She was already thinking ahead. "This plan you cooked up with Hanlan, to put pressure on Pearce through his editor, Duncan Marwood, seems flimsy at best."

Nick was unable to contradict her. "I know we need to do more but it was the only way I could get Charles to even consider fighting his own corner. Take what we can from it. An invitation's been sent for Marwood to attend the final charity show."

Sam reminded him of his duties concerning NRG and their publicity campaign. She stifled a yawn. "God, it's almost two o'clock. I'm meant to be at the airport in a few hours' time." She extricated herself from the blanket that had been keeping her warm.

Nick got out of bed. "Safe journey. Let me know how it goes." He kissed her cheek and then she was gone, tip-toeing down the corridor. At least his new found reputation had not been enhanced by unscrupulous photographers waiting outside to snap at the evidence.

He ambled back to his bed. It was difficult to imagine how things could get any worse. The mention of

Stress Magazine had sparked in him the briefest hint of inspiration. He allowed himself a few minutes more to calculate how long it would take his wife to drive out of the city. He punched in the numbers and she answered his call almost immediately.

"Libi, it's me again. No hear me out. Like you said, we've nothing left to lose. Here's what we should do."

9. Road Trip

It was hard not to be envious. Amelia's flat in Kensington Green oozed style and understated class. In total contrast to his own bleak, mid-town Manhattan excuse for a home, the rooms reflected something of the woman Amelia might want to become. The girl that had opened the door, now stood in reflected and flattering natural light. Interestingly, she still possessed an attractive awkwardness that should be captured before it was lost forever.

Amelia was in good spirits, despite the news from her father that Ellen had been taken ill and wouldn't be around for a few days. She'd shared this latest news with the photographer as he set up his equipment.

"Not too early is it, Nick?" She watched as he struggled with a fiddly tilt and pan mechanism underneath the camera stand.

"Have more respect for your elders please Amelia." He spoke with aloofness, much like a teacher to a cheeky pupil. "Don't forget I'm interviewing you. Let's hope you're as free and easy with your personal details as you are with your wit."

She stuck her tongue out, pointed and delicately pink.

Nick pressed the shutter release and with a practised eye glanced at the screen for proof of exposure. Gorgeous. He zoomed in to check the focus and depth of field and saw that her crystal blue eyes were clear and sharp.

"Are you stuck in that position?" Amelia was still in playful mood.

He took a second to decide on his reply. "Just wondering how much time I'll need in photoshop to brush up your features and make something of this shot." He tried to keep a straight face.

There was no winner or loser in their tongue in cheek dialogue. Nick was impressed that for one still young, Amelia had an innate ability to know how far the banter should go. With this part of the photo-shoot over, He was relieved when she agreed it was time to hit the road.

"Where are we going? Charles said you had something in mind?" She drove her BMW out onto the road. At the first junction she signalled to turn left and was immediately allowed to filter into the heavy flow of commuter traffic. Amelia waved thanks to a young executive-type who had gallantly given way.

Nick had to smile at the power of beauty over the beast that is conventionally man.

"There's a place your father would like you to see. After Sunday's concert in Suffolk, he's hosting a party."

"I'm well aware of this. And?"

"Well, the venue is a little out of the ordinary. He said Mary Paxton would appreciate your input on the final details. We could go straight there but I do have a suggestion."

Amelia glanced at him expectantly. "Well?"

"How about we go and visit an old friend of yours on the way up there. Taking your father's advice, I made a call to your old voice coach, Miss Ivanovic." Nick was slow but sure with his pronunciation not wishing to waste the painstaking coaching he had received from the old lady herself. He was rewarded by a beaming smile that lit up Amelia's face. "She's promised to dish the dirt on one of her 'biggest success stories'. I think they were the actual words she used." Nick added with a grin.

"You really spoke to her?" Amelia was excited and yet fretful. "God I've been meaning to go and see her for ages. I hope she's okay."

"Miss Ivanovic told me to tell you that she's fine, but what would you care! And said something about you being too grand to think of visiting her anymore."

Amelia laughed out loud, seemingly unaffected by the scorn the old lady had poured upon her. "She's not changed, by the sound of it." Her face told a story. "Nick, you should have heard her sing, like an angel one minute, like the devil the next. Her range and control were just out of this world." Amelia used alternative hands to help with her description, one hand on the wheel, the other making patterns in the air.

"She's originally from Sommovia?"

"Just like my mother and me. Its why we connected."

Nick considered Amelia and her complicated identity. It was something they hadn't talked a great deal about before.

"Is that how you see yourself, as Sommovian? Things have changed so much in that region over the last two decades."

"I was actually born out there. My mother was living in England but she made the trip back there especially to have me. My real father, by all accounts, wasn't impressed. In contrast my step father has always encouraged me to keep those ties alive." She thought for a second. "The civil unrest and eventual war have made that difficult. I keep in touch with my aunt, Deana." She looked embarrassed before finally admitting. "It's funny but I have very few memories of my real father." Amelia attended to some loose strands of hair that were tickling her cheek, whilst keeping her eyes firmly on the road. Nick had seen her do this before and knew it to be a habit born out of nerves rather than necessity.

They came to some traffic lights set stubbornly at red.

"Despite the troubles Sommovia is special. Have you ever been?"

"Never had the chance. Perhaps it's time to change that and get some insight into your family's culture."

"A summer holiday out there would be perfect. Perhaps I should spoil myself once the show is over. Mind you, the war ripped families and whole communities apart. I'm not sure how welcome I'd be." She thought for a while, and then brightened. "I do speak a little of the language; mostly the swear words." They were on the move again. "All this stuff about me being in danger. We haven't a clue what that really means, compared to what many have been through."

"You sound a little disappointed at that. As if a little danger wouldn't go a miss?"

Amelia's attitude suggested the question was an awkward one to answer.

"Makes you know you're alive." She shrugged her shoulders and seemed uncertain. "Depends on the danger. Besides, you shouldn't be asking me things like that. If you knew the truth about what I really miss, you might think differently of me." Amelia tapped her hand on the steering wheel while thinking about what she wanted to say next. "The bad part of being good is having to make compromises." She decided to keep things light. "The good part of being bad is how nervous that can make other people feel." Her tapping hand she made into a fist and lightly punched his arm. "Maybe you should be asking yourself the same question."

"How do you mean?"

"A married man living a single life."

Nick felt he was being challenged. If nothing else his conscience had been pricked.

Amelia took charge of the silence and changed the subject.

"So, you actually spoke to Marsha Ivanovic." She seemed genuinely impressed. "A very proud lady as you probably gathered."

"She's certainly very proud of you. Says you have a kindred spirit, a survivor of an uncertain start to life." He spoke kindly. "Was she adopted too?"

"She became a sort of refugee. She did the adopting, one country for another. She left not long after my mother died but always spoke fondly of her time teaching at the University in Mezlar."

Once out of London, Nick felt more inclined to relax. He was supposed to have kept an eye on the traffic to see if they were being followed. Amelia was correct to suggest that any danger she was in would pale into insignificance when compared to the well-documented atrocities that had been carried out where she was born. Never the less, what price should one put on any life? Splits in any family usually meant there would be casualties and no ready winners.

Once on the motorway Amelia drove at a speed that gave him concern for his personal well-being. "When do we take off?" His comment promoted another dart of her tongue which made him smile. While he continued to focus on the darker side of matters, Nick thought about his next question and knew it had to be asked.

"Ever come across a man called Peter Pearce?"

"Who?" Amelia looked confused,

"He's a newspaper man, a journalist."

"Can't say I know him." She glanced briefly at Nick as if to say "should I?"

"Thought your father might have mentioned him in passing. You and Charles are an obsession of his."

"My father tells me not to read the papers." She said it quickly and then wondered if she'd been too dismissive. "Why do you ask?"

Her simple explanation sounded more like an excuse and was exactly what Nick had expected to hear. He wasn't prepared to let it go. Reaching inside his jacket pocket he produced and read from the guest list for the charity concert in Suffolk. "Peter Pearce has an invitation, which under normal circumstances would not be a problem. It's only fair you should know of his reputation."

There wasn't time for him to finish what he wanted to say. Signpost-reading and direction-finding took precedence. Amelia asked him to open the map at the appropriate page while she drew on all her concentration to remember the way.

Marsha Ivanovic lived up to Nick's expectations. The animated greetings between teacher and her former pupil were worth the trip all on their own. Unfortunately for him, his own reception was somewhat muted. This was understandable but he felt confident that in time she'd come round. Ms Ivanovic held onto Amelia's arm with no immediate sign of wanting to let it go. He was left in their wake to fend for himself.

Language became Marsha's shield and she used this to exclude him from their conversation. To her credit Amelia tried to include him whenever she could. Her use of Sommovian was rusty at best and she'd often lapse back into English. At one point she appeared to suffer from a severe tongue-lashing herself. Nick had made the mistake of showing his amusement, which in turn encouraged the formidable Marsha to transfer criticism of her former pupil to the state of British culture and by association, British men. A sudden change of language at this point reclaimed and included Nick in this.

Amelia's support of his position had held no sway. All looked lost until the moment he spoke in an aside to her. "How great would it be to take some shots of the two of you together." The old lady's hearing had proved to be in rude health. Appeasing Marsha Ivanovic's ego had finally broken the ice and proved a better way to melt her heart.

"Why do you keep apologising?" Amelia was teasing him again.

Leaving Marsha Ivanovic in tears as she waved goodbye from her garden gate, Nick was reassured to see that Amelia was in good spirits as they continued to travel east towards the Suffolk coast. That was until he said the word, sorry.

"Look, I don't mean to upset you. All I'm saying is that I understand why you might not want to read your own press. You probably crave the chance to be normal."

"And you think I'm not normal?" Amelia feigned her indignation.

Nick had backed himself into a tight corner with seemingly little chance of escape, not at least for another fifteen miles. He tried to fight back. "I just thought you might be worried about becoming more independent. You know, away from your overprotective father. You have to be sufficiently prepared for the likes of Peter Pearce and the damage he can do."

"If you say so. He'll be my guardian wherever I go, remember that." Amelia was about to say more.

"Go on."

"Better to be in my position than yours."

"Oh, what have I done now?"

"Well, if you don't mind me saying, look at your own situation. Married but separated. No other family; travelling the world but always on your own. Not sure I see the sense in that?" Something else occurred to her. "Why are the British, well, so bloody British?" She picked up from where Marsha Ivanovic had left off.

A silence fell between them, invaded only by the noise of the car upon the road.

Amelia struck the final blow and punched his arm again. "I didn't mean to upset you."

Nick relented. He absorbed her criticism like a sponge and realised that in some respects she was telling the truth. The confidence of youth had cut through his personal bullshit. He looked across at her while she was thankfully quiet. Soft focus and filters would have been a mistake where this young lady was concerned.

"What do you suggest?" he asked eventually.

Amelia spoke without hesitation and with welcome levity. "I think I'll come and live with you when I'm working in New York. You're a little old." It was said without malice. "But still attractive I suppose." Amelia placed her hand on Nick's knee.

His head hit the roof of the car.

Amelia didn't stop laughing until they crossed the boundary and had driven into the middle of the village.

Minutes later and Nick was speaking through the open window of Amelia's car asking for directions. Outside the village pub, an old man with an even older dog at his feet had seemed a good bet for tapping into local knowledge.

"We're looking for Sedge House, I don't know if you know it?"

The old man bent his back, his eyes bypassing Nick's face to take a better look at the owner of the legs on the driver's side.

"I should do. Worked there on the farm long enough before I retired." A thought struck him. "Are you something to do with the marquee that's going up?"

"You could say that." Nick tried and failed to regain the old man's attention. "We're on the right road then?" He was ignored.

"I recognise you, young lady, from somewhere?" He spoke directly to Amelia. "You're his daughter, the one in that London show."

Amelia bombarded the old man with one of her cutest smiles.

"You've met my father then?" She leaned across the car and again settled her hand on her passenger's knee.

"'Course I have. He's done well to buy that old place when he did too. I can't believe all that work he's had done to it." The old man sounded impressed and proud. "I've been giving him and that young Joe advice on the wetlands. You know, marshes and the reed-beds, that kind of thing. Proper gent is your old man."

Amelia was struck dumb. This was something she knew nothing about, unlike the old man who was quick on the uptake.

"Your first trip here then?" She failed to respond. "Just follow the signs for the old church and go on through the wood. You'll find the house and farm buildings at the end of the track."

"Thanks for your help." Nick just had time to raise a hand before Amelia pulled away.

She drove on in silence and ever-increasing speed until she reached the woodland. Only when she glimpsed the house for the first time did she make some kind of comment. It sounded ugly and in Sommovian, allowing Nick to make up his own translation.

"What's he been up to now?" She said in English.

*

Mary Paxton first warmed the pot before making the tea. A minor detail but one that was reassuring. Amelia had watched it happen many times before. From where she sat at the large kitchen table, she could feel the steady warmth of the Aga on her back. Mary Paxton and an Aga, as a security blanket it didn't get much better than that.

"It was as much of a shock to Jim and me as it must be to you." Mary thought twice before deciding which cupboard door concealed the fridge and the jug of milk that she was looking for. The country kitchen was of such proportions she still hadn't got the layout imprinted in her mind. Despite wanting to side with Amelia's frustrations at her father's lack of tact, secretly she had fallen in love with the house the moment she'd entered its door.

Amelia wasn't quite ready to give up just yet. "Why here? And more importantly, why didn't he tell me anything about it?" She was about to pout but knew that it would have little effect on Mary. "And who's this bloke,

Joe? The old man from the village says he's looking after the place and lives in the cottage up the road."

"I don't really know dear, but he seems very nice." Mary poured the tea. "Jim says he's done a really good job on the gardens and all that swampy bit beyond." Mary smiled and put a small pair of binoculars beside Amelia's cup and saucer. "I bought them with me from home. Thought you might need them. Finish your tea first, why don't you, and then go and find my husband. He knows more about this than me."

Somehow, Amelia doubted that.

Jimmy Paxton watched her walking from afar, her hair shining in the occasional sunlight. The clouds that had been thick and grey since early morning were breaking up in the strengthening wind. The shallow pools were full of life and movement as ripples on the surface of the water made the mallard and shellduck bob up and down. To his left, a little ringed plover scampered across the silt, halting here and there to feed where the tiny waves lapped the shore.

Sitting in the hide with his elbows balanced on the window ledge, Jim lowered his binoculars to focus his eyes on the familiar figure he had come to know. A young woman who had a lot on her mind, although he could see no outward signs of this as she looked around her, taking in the sights and sounds. No airs and graces, a natural beauty, in a place that man and nature had uniquely designed. It seemed to Jim that both deserved to be safeguarded with sympathy.

Amelia covered the last quarter mile at a sure and steady pace, following Mary's directions to the letter. Instinctively she kept to the best path, missing the boggy bits and trying not to disturb the birds. She carried a small pair of Leica lenses in her hand. A gift from Jimmy, her enjoyment of them the real prize.

The man himself returned his eyes and thoughts to the pools. In the near distance a male marsh harrier briefly fought and then took to the wind, flying low across open ground before following the ditch on the edge of the marshland. What better timing. Amelia's capacity to be moved by such things was infectious and he was glad that she had come. It would be interesting to see if she was still happy to open up and talk with him.

The open door briefly circulated the air but he did not look round, preferring to wait for her to negotiate the mildly uneven and creaking floor before benching her behind beside him. Jim continued to track the harrier.

"Female in the reeds?" she whispered.

He nodded as he lowered his binoculars. "That perfume's nice on you or are you using the new shampoo my wife thought you might like?" Her shoulder length hair, the colour of night was a tucked behind a delicate ear. She took up the flight of the bird of prey in her glasses as it hawked over some gorse and gave them gorgeous views of creamy wing patches and dark brown belly bits. As if to order the sunlight pierced through an opening in the clouds.

"Flatterer. Mary said you'd be here." She rummaged in her pocket and produced a packet of polos. His favourites. "You forgot these." She raised an eyebrow questioningly and took one before handing them over. "Or were you hoping that I'd think to bring them down for you?"

She knew him well enough.

"Thought you might want to talk." He was thoughtful himself. "A lot seems to have happened in a short space of time." Jim watched and waited to see her reaction. For a while she continued to scan the wetlands as though he'd never spoken. Undoubtedly pent-up emotion simmered within her. He sighed with compassion and was reminded of a time when this girl had been affected in similar ways. Time for change? Maybe. Time for others to start acting with responsibility? Definitely.

10. Pond Life

Why could Sherman Powers command and seemingly acquire whatever it was he desired? Sam was feeling used, the possible result of an uncomfortable flight from London and an immediate summons by the boss to an address on the upper west side of the city. All this before she'd had a chance to go home for a change of clothes. She was only too aware how the click of finger and thumb grated and aggravated a latent desire to rebel.

Apparently, Sherman had chosen their present location to keep a beady eye on a modest but lucrative project. Man-management but not necessarily a welcome presence for the young director, if Sam was to hazard a guess.

"We're going for a walk, Miss Grant." Powers was being very formal and there was little warmth in his greeting. He had yet to inform her as to why she'd been summoned, and more to the point, who they were going to meet.

Powers guided her away from the set. Lights, cameras and the action of a hundred extras were suddenly forgotten as they approached the edge of Central Park. Sam had the impression that this was not a walk for recreation's sake. She kept pace one step behind him. His quiet calm did nothing to improve her mood.

Once inside the park, Sam noticed rare beads of perspiration on Sherman's brow. His breathing rate increased as his speed of step faltered. An audible grunt led to an alteration in direction and Sam could finally see the end of their road and her boss's relief and satisfaction.

The lone figure of a woman was sitting on a semi-circular shaped bench set back in a cul de sac. Although outwardly relaxed, Sam judged the woman's poise to be somewhat contrived, with one leg crossed over the other. The seat was bathed in late sun and dark glasses hid the woman's eyes. Sam was keenly aware of being thoroughly appraised.

No one spoke, not at first. Sam was determined to be polite despite her mood and frustration. "Hello, I'm Samantha Grant." She offered her hand which, after some hesitation, was finally accepted. The grip was limp, as was the smile. Sam shivered involuntarily without knowing why. As the woman made to stand, Sam caught the whiff of a peculiar smell.

"What's all this about?" Sam turned to Sherman, looking for him to lead.

Sherman wouldn't be hurried. "You're like me. You like to know all the facts." He finally addressed her, "But that's only made possible if you've done your research. I like to keep an open mind as you know. I thought you ought to hear this in person."

Pompous ass! After all she'd done to protect him. Sam had a sinking feeling that this was not going to be good news. Good or bad she could do without the dramatics and sincerely wished that they'd just get it over with.

The woman spoke.

"My name is Claire Williams." She paused for effect. "I've simply come here to put the record straight, and to warn you."

"See what I mean, Miss Grant…"

"Williams is your maiden's name?" Sam cut across him.

Claire removed her sunglasses as a cloud helped to filter the strong light. "I use my maiden's name. Call me what you want. My story's still the same."

Sam steeled herself and it took every ounce of self-control to keep a lid on her temper.

And then silence. Suddenly Claire was hesitant and unsure of herself.

"How about going somewhere different? I could do with a drink."

It was a stale smell, slightly sour, and unfortunately it had become part of her. Samantha reappraised it and even wondered if there wasn't a hint of death about it. Claire Williams was a drunk, there was no denying that. Twenty minutes in the same car, was time enough spent. No perfume could mask the fact that booze was a large part of her day. Sam watched the older woman slump without ceremony into the generous leather sofa in Powers' penthouse suite. Flawed skin and dull eyes were the visible signs of the abuse her body was suffering.

"What will you have Mrs Hanlan… I beg your pardon, Ms Williams? Bourbon, Scotch?" Sherman seemed happy to host the party all by himself.

"Perhaps coffee would be more appropriate." Sam tried not to sound too unkind.

"Not for you to say, Miss Grant." Sherman scolded her. "You should be thanking Ms Williams for coming forward, not offending her."

Sam felt herself blush with embarrassment and wondered who's side her boss was really on.

"Something wrong Sherman?" Another voice startled them. A familiar voice that made them turn in unison. Rosalind, a picture of elegance and poise glided across the carpet and did more to mock Claire Williams than any words Sam could hope to find. She always belied her age and radiated a feeling of health and self-knowledge that was like a breath of fresh air.

"Rosalind?" Powers tried to smother his surprise.

"Don't be such a bully dear, the girl is only doing her best for you." Rosalind stooped to kiss her husband lightly on the cheek and in doing so effectively stopped any repost. Turning her back to Sherman she nodded civilly towards Claire Williams before sitting next to Samantha. If anyone needed a sign. "I'd certainly prefer some coffee at this time of day."

Sam's smile was nervous and she would have gladly died. Unsure of what was happening between her bosses, it looked for all the world that she was in danger of becoming crushed between them.

"Let me get you some." Sam offered but Rosalind gently shook her head.

"I can't stay." She was giving hope to her husband. Respite of sorts. "I'll see you later, Samantha. Just thought I'd let you know I was here." It was a message to all in the room.

Rosalind turned to her husband, who by now was the colour of crimson.

"I really came to remind you we're out to dinner tonight." She looked suddenly concerned. "Keep it in context, Sherman. I know your intentions are worthy, but it's not a matter of life and death. Think of your heart."

To his credit, Sherman made no attempt to retaliate. Instead, he gently ushered his wife towards the door. If he did so only to make sure she crossed its threshold, then it was worth it. She kissed him once again with a promise not to return. When he turned to the room it was obvious that the atmosphere had been irreversibly changed.

Sam was now fully engaged and intrigued to watch Claire Williams and hear what she had to say. Ice clinked against the side of her glass and she spoke between sips.

"If only I could have been that strong. "A half laugh died at the back of her throat. A compliment to Rosalind or plain simple jealousy? Nothing could disguise the bitterness Claire had seemingly found at the bottom of her glass. Sam saw a look on the face of a woman in pain and was moved to regard it a sobering experience.

"It's not easy losing your husband to a child." The implication of Claire's words seemed to hang in the air. Sherman sat quietly letting her dominate the room. An unsmoked cigar lay within easy reach should he feel the need.

"Somehow, she always got her way in the end. Charles wouldn't have it any other way."

Sam shook her head in disbelief.

"People think she's had it hard." Claire pointed directly at Sam. "Believe me, she was tough even at the age of eight, so save your sympathy. It's something she induces but rarely needs. Besides..." She actually belched. "Do you really want to take on all the negative publicity that I can provide? And I will if you continue with this nonsense."

Claire wagged a bony finger in Sherman's general direction.

"Anyway..." She stopped to catch her breath. "Not content in ruining my marriage, then she started on my son. Believe me, he and I have been hurt enough. The last night..." She could not finish her sentence.

Claire studied the smear of lipstick on the rim of her glass.

"Well, what did she expect? Wearing a nightdress that couldn't keep her navel warm." Claire was rambling, almost talking to herself and trying anything to embellish her story. The images she portrayed were disturbingly clear.

Even so Samantha couldn't help but wonder if some of Claire Williams story was too near to a truth that Amelia couldn't bear to remember. She banished the thought immediately, ashamed of herself and her disloyalty to a friend.

"Oh, it's possible." Claire must have read her mind. "Amelia is not welcome here. This is our home now." She was on her feet, swaying slightly as she looked down at Sherman, crowding and invading his space.

Sam listened to the desperation in a voice that, if nothing else, showed the apparent sincerity of a woman's distress.

"Charles can't renege on his deal. I won't let him. It's a crying shame when the first real emotion a father gives his son is that of jealous rage."

Claire said no more and judging by Sherman's face, even he found that to be a blessing. It looked like she'd simply run out of steam. Professing the need of a bathroom, she gathered herself and left the room.

Whether she meant to return, in the end she wasn't given the choice. Down at street level a little while later, few if any bore witness to the actions of a kindly NRG employee as he assisted the erratic progress of a middle-aged woman to the back of a company limo. Had Sherman seen for himself the polite and smooth efficiency of the man as he closed the door on any protestations, he would certainly have been surprised by the conspiratorial nod he gave to the tall female figure who was standing just inside the foyer.

Feeling genuine concern, and certainly more than she'd showed earlier, Rosalind watched the limo pull away from the side-walk and was heard to reflect to no one in particular.

"Sometimes we just need someone to help us."

It had come as something of a relief. The truth was perhaps easier to live with if her boss was up to taking his medicine straight from the bottle. Reality rarely matched the romance in which he'd wrapped his fantasies.

"So, you want me to forget it, is that what you're saying?" Sam was angry and would no longer stand for his brand of vitriol.

"No, I'm not saying that." The old man, too, was hurt. "Now that I understand what Amelia has been through..." He couldn't find the right words.

"Well, you know now." Sam made gestures to show her frustration. "Nothing has changed. She still has the talent. I can't believe you'd throw away the chance to have her work for you."

"I'm selfish and I like my own way. Always have." There was contrition in his voice. "You're right in one respect. Miss Highland does deserve our respect whatever Claire Williams might have to say." He finally sounded relaxed. "I have to protect the integrity of NRG and more importantly that of my wife. Go back and do what you can."

Sam was already half way to the door.

"Bitter?" Nick repeated it aloud. "An understatement if ever there was one."

"It's good to hear a friendly voice on the other end of a phone." Sam was recalling her late afternoon meeting with Claire Williams.

Nick was comfortably ensconced in Hanlan's new office at Sedge House. "Do you sense that her threats are real?"

"On the face of it, I'd have to say yes. She definitely holds Amelia responsible for the breakdown of her marriage. Incredible, that she could be jealous of a teenage girl." Claire had been adamant of her condemnation. "I mentioned Peace's name like you suggested and that definitely touched a nerve."

"I don't suppose she was very complimentary."

"Not sure I would totally agree. I tried to lead her on. She said something about loyalty and that journalists could not be trusted. The only bright spot in my whole day."

"Listen you, go carefully or spare me."

"You're not like that though. Integrity over dough, is the Sayers way."

There was a lull while she awaited his measured response.

"Well considering I've yet to see the colour of NRG's money, I think I can call myself exempt from any criticism."

Their banter died away.

"I didn't get a chance to drop in on Libi by the way." Sam was hesitant, feeling her way. "What? What's the matter?" She sensed he had something to say.

"Lucky you didn't really." Nick cleared his throat. "If you're not already sitting down, then find a chair." He decided to keep it short and sweet. "The story goes that Libi is hiring Peter Pearce to do an official piece on Hanlan and Highland." He heard Samantha splutter. "My wife has bought into the lurid gossip and is out to get revenge."

"You're taking the… She surely can't believe that you and Amelia…?"

"Who Libi? I did wonder. But no. Privately, she's prepared to believe in me. In public, she's a woman scorned."

Sam remained confused. "What's the point?"

"Charles seems determined to get all his enemies under one roof. A one-time opportunity for all to vent and voice their troubles. Thanks to Libi, Pearce is now officially being paid to come to the party."

"You mean he's being lured to this house in Suffolk?"

"Exactly. My biggest concern is how your boss is going to react when the shit hits the fan. This certainly isn't going to do you any favours."

"Well, Claire Williams has already put a dent in Sherman's perfect world." Sam was aware of changes in her own motivation and her loyalty to NRG. "Good on Libi, though. Can't have been easy for her."

"No, but then in some ways Pearce has been casting shadows over us for years."

"Talking of enemies. Any news on Lloyd?"

"Not that I'm aware of." Nick explained. "I gather Hanlan has his people out looking for him."

"His people? Who are they?"

"He's hired his own security team, all ex-army. Apparently, he had one of them in New York for Amelia's visit."

Samantha had a flash of instant understanding but kept her thoughts to herself.

Nick was still speaking. "Charles is prepared to accept that there's a link between Pearce and his son. If only we could find him."

What was done was done. Sam brought their conversation to a close.

"I leave you for one day and look what happens."

"No regrets then? Sorry if this further complicates the picture with Sherman."

"Look, I'm on the way to my apartment and then on to the airport. I'll be in London early tomorrow morning, okay? Where are you now?"

"Still with Amelia. This place called Sedge House has been a bit of a shock for her." Nick checked the time. "We're staying here overnight and then taking the train back to London in the morning." He could sense her concern. "It's all been agreed. Amelia's spending valuable time with the housekeeper and her husband. Possibly the two remaining and trusted friends she has in the world right now."

Sam felt saddened by his comments but seriously hoped they weren't true.

11. Commuters

Joe Peterson wasn't an avid consumer of the popular press. A broadsheet buyer at the weekend, mostly for the tele and the sport. Naturally he kept abreast of the serious world but found political bias off-putting in the extreme.

However, that morning an article written by the journalist, Peter Pearce, had tempted his interest.

...The troops are gathering; the fight has already been joined. Mighty forces from America are in town to try and steal the princess away. The dangers of harm appear to be real. Limb from pretty limb, the pull of independence draws her away from the clawing fingers of a desperate man try to cling on. The question remains as to how much pressure may safely be exerted without leaving traces of his disturbing intent...

Enough was enough. He got up and threw the paper into the nearest bin. The clock on the arrivals board ticked over. Travellers from New York were in baggage reclaim and would be coming through customs any time soon. Red-eye flights were traditionally problematical and not only for the passengers that regularly flew them. Joe belatedly put a hand in front of his mouth and tried to stifle a yawn.

Late finish last night and early start this morning. Pretending to be a colleague from work, he'd decided to visit Ellen Preston in hospital and found her parents sitting at her bedside. They'd been eager to share in their distress. Ellen had evidently suffered a fractured skull.

Still heavily sedated, the word from the doctors was encouraging but full of caution. He hadn't stayed long but had received thanks for his concern.

The arrivals lounge was suddenly busy. Another flight load weighed down with their luggage were exiting customs. Joe played at being a proper chauffeur by holding up a card with her name written in felt tip pen. They certainly looked to be a cosmopolitan bunch. As it turned out, he would have been hard pressed to miss Samantha Grant.

A curious smile played out across the whole of her face. "So, we meet again, Mr Peterson." She put down her bag and shook his hand.

"Good morning, Miss Grant. Let me take that for you. If you'll come this way, it's only a few minutes' walk to the car."

*

"The train arriving on platform three is..." much like any other early morning commuter train heading into London. On the outskirts of town this rather unfashionable station had been well chosen for its links to the underground network. Less crowded than many others, the passengers waiting on the platform tried to predict their potential comfort as the train slowed and eventually stopped. Only one of them had a professional camera. Only he remained static, counting the carriages as they passed him by.

The automatic doors slid open on carriage number five and of the few to disembark, Nick Sayers was the first, carrying a bag in both hands. As he stepped down onto the platform, a single flash from the camera bathed the side of the train in a stark, white light. Following closely behind, Amelia seemed to become distracted and lost her footing.

Teetering somewhere between the platform and the train, the gap was wide and inviting her fall. Fortunately, Nick had the presence of mind to drop the bags and catch Amelia around her waist instead.

The camera unit flashed one more time and captured the action. In the aftermath Miss Highland appeared unhurt, if a little unnerved. She straightened her dress and looked somewhat embarrassed. Most importantly the shots were in focus and adequately exposed. While making his exit, the photographer congratulated himself on a job well done and his luck in getting the tip-off.

Why him? Who cared? A single shot safely in the can, earnings guaranteed. An exclusive for Stress Magazine. Amelia Highland in the arms of her boyfriend. Now that had to be a first.

*

The early morning sun lay low in the sky and shone strobe-like through the gaps in the houses striking the car as it passed them by. Yesterday's meeting with her boss and the unfortunate Claire Williams was still fresh in her mind. Full of bad feeling, Rosalind's intervention had been timely and welcome. Now back in London the waiting car and handsome driver she found herself sitting beside was some compensation for the sleepless night she'd had to endure. Sam settled into her seat as they picked up speed and progressed eastwards away from the airport.

"Well, you certainly get around." It hadn't taken Samantha long to figure it out. She'd watched with interest as her driver had performed his chauffeuring duties with quiet efficiency. The stark contrast to his clumsiness at their impromptu coming together at the Parkside Grand Hotel in New York had made her wonder.

He got there before her. "How's your arm Miss Grant? No lasting damage I hope." Joe Peterson sounded cheekily sincere.

"I'm fine, thanks for your concern. An interesting way to introduce yourself, I thought."

"Yes, well. Not very subtle, I admit." He stole a quick glance in her direction, taking in the shape of her legs and the way her knees were bent together in a well-practised and feminine way. "Wrong of me I know, trying to sweep a girl off her feet like that."

"Was that what you were really trying to do?" Samantha feigned surprise but stopped short of saying whether he'd succeeded. She reluctantly steered the conversation back to a more serious train of thought. "I take it we're definitely on the same side then?"

"We are." Joe felt he ought to explain. "That's why I made sure we literally bumped into each other that night. I work for Mr Hanlan's estate in Suffolk but on occasion I get sent to keep an eye on Miss Highland. I have previous experience." He tried to play it down. "I assume you've been made aware of Mr Hanlan's concerns."

"I have indeed." Her work had been made doubly difficult.

"I understand you were there at Bene's bar. I'm sorry to ask but what were your impressions?"

"At the time I thought it was college boy humour, taken too far. In hindsight and with recent knowledge? I met with Lloyd's mother and that puts a whole new perspective on the threats that they've made."

"I have to agree. Everything suggests we have to be vigilant." Joe was thinking of Ellen Preston and wondered how much more he should say. "Despite trying to remain incognito, I should have made my warning more obvious. Lloyd gate-crashing the hotel party was not part of the plan."

"What happened to him, by the way?"

"Escorted from the building by security and put back onto the street outside." Joe described with editorial license the measures that had been used.

Samantha tried to contextualise what she'd learnt in only the last few hours. It begged the question as to how candid she should be where Amelia was concerned.

"Has Hanlan ever told you what caused the final break-up of the family?"

"No, not directly, but talking in confidence with Jimmy Paxton we've put two and two together." He didn't vocalise his conclusions.

"Jimmy and Mary keep house for Charles, I'm guessing." This must be the couple that Nick had mentioned.

"Lovely people." Joe explained their history. He felt inclined to include Samantha in all that he had discussed with Charles. "You'll have to keep this to yourself until it's made official. After your meal at Aperture, Lloyd made a play on Ellen Preston. They ended up going back to her place." He paused to emphasise his next point. "There's no way of knowing exactly what took place but she ended up in hospital with a fractured skull."

"What? You've got to be kidding me. This just gets better and better." Samantha sounded angry but somewhat resigned.

"As I say, I can't be certain what actually took place." Joe paused while negotiating a busy intersection. "He certainly didn't stick around to give her assistance, that's for sure."

"Or plead his innocence. I hope she's going to be okay." Samantha remembered Ellen's sudden departure from the restaurant, but that in no way explained what must have taken place later. "Look, have we got time to grab a coffee? In view of your candour, I've probably got a few things I should be telling you too."

Sam described her meeting with Claire Williams. They'd stopped at a small independent bakery that did coffee on the side. She added a spoonful of brown sugar to her cup, aware that Joe was watching her stir.

He raised an interesting subject. "Has anyone talked to you about Amelia's real parents? They have no obvious bearing on the present situation, but it's easy to forget them in all of this."

"It would probably add to a complicated situation. Claire mentioned them in passing but only to explain how much her own life had been put upon in their absence. Amelia tells me she has no surviving relatives in this country on her father's side. Her family in Sommovia, those that have survived the recent war, rarely make contact." She looked questioningly at Joe.

"No matter, I'm just curious. It's a difficult subject to bring up in conversation. I know she hasn't been out to visit her aunt since well before the conflict started."

"A subject that you know something about, I'm guessing?"

Joe smiled ruefully, aware that he might be backing himself into a tight corner. "Yes, I've been out there as part of a UN initiative."

The smell of freshly baked bread permeated their senses as a new batch was dispatched from the kitchen. Aware she was letting Joe off the hook; Sam thoughts went in new direction. "My new found partner in crime has also been busy in my absence." She related some of Nick's madcap scheme.

Joe prompted her to explain the logic behind permitting the photographer and his wife to become involved in something that was not really pertinent to either of them.

"It's a small world. Peter Pearce's rumour mill is starting to grind everybody down including the Sayers. At last, it seems Hanlan wants to fight back and Nick came up with this dubious plan. I'll be interested to see how far he's prepared to go with it. I think you'll find Libi will ultimately make that decision. Credit goes to her though. Her magazine is paying for Pearce's entrapment."

Joe seemed to accept that, so they went on to discuss future events. If she was honest, Sam had lost all sense of time. Thursday morning already, and with the weekend approaching, the next forty-eight hours were going to be vital. The last two charity shows in London were later that day, culminating in a red-carpet event for celebrities and their cheque books. Friday was to be transition day. Sam thought that Joe was very succinct in all he had to say and treated him to a smile that contained real affection. If it surprised her, it brought Joe to a stuttering halt.

"Sorry, do go on," she said.

"Some of the theatre technicians and stage management staff will travel to Suffolk and work through the night. Then on Saturday morning a small number of the cast will arrive for a lunchtime sound check ready for the concert later that day. They'll be a reception at the hall for local dignitaries." Joe explained it was nothing more than a public relations stunt as part of Charles' integration into becoming a local. "It'll give us some respite before the party gets going."

Sam was gradually getting up to speed. "And that's at Sedge House? Nick tells me that Hanlan owns the place."

"Bought it a year and a half ago. My father oversaw the renovations and I've been running the place on my own ever since." Joe told Sam of the heavy plant work he'd done in restoring the wetlands area under the supervision of conservationists and wildlife trusts. He would have said more but was conscious of not wanting to bore her.

"And you live there permanently?" Sam was trying her best to imagine his lifestyle. From the moment he'd started speaking she could see he was content with his work. The one area that Joe had so far neglected to talk about was what he'd been doing prior to his involvement with Charles Hanlan.

"You've obviously had experience with running security and that kind of thing?" Sam made a statement and yet asked a question too.

"In slightly different circumstances." True to form, Joe felt reluctant to speak about the army and the undercover existence that had once been his life.

"You don't have to tell me if you're not comfortable. Perhaps you're not allowed to." Sam kept her voice light and easy. "Maybe later, if you can."

He took this to be a serious invitation, and knew instinctively it would be easier to talk to a perfect stranger than his family. It was a constant conundrum and something he'd been taught to guard against. For now, he could promise nothing.

"You're right, maybe later." Joe regretted not being more open and covered his discomfort by checking his watch. The atmosphere inside the cafe had been warm and intimate and it would have been nice to have stayed longer. "We'd better make a move."

As they left, they thanked the lady behind the counter and once outside walked side by side to the car.

"Hopefully the party at the house will encourage Peter Pearce and Lloyd into the open. That's when we all need to be on our toes. Mr Hanlan has informed the police of his plans and would like you to be there too, as a witness." Sam looked unsure. "Amelia would appreciate it, and as it happens, I would too." Joe was speaking the truth.

"Let's hope that my boss approves of the outcome, that's all I can say." Samantha patted his arm. "For what it's worth, I am glad to be here."

Joe found it difficult to say more. "I'll drop you off at Amelia's apartment. I think she and Mr Sayers will be waiting there."

"And where are you off to after that Joe?"

"Back up to Sedge House. There's lots still to do before Saturday night and the party." He walked around to open the car door for Sam. "When this is over…" He got no further because his mobile phone began to ring. "Mr Hanlan. Yes sir. Twenty minutes, we're on our way now."

12. West End

"Make your bloody mind up mate." Lloyd was blocking the doorway, oblivious to the fact that others were finding it difficult to get past him.

The landlord of the White Hart had been watching the young man with his empty glass for some time, and if there was one thing he couldn't abide, it was a punter not putting effort into his drinking.

"Buy yourself another and you can stand where you bloody like, within reason." He spoke as he cleared the empties from a table by the window. "At the moment all you're doing is stopping others from getting to their pints."

Lloyd immediately felt under pressure. His chosen vantage point offered him clear site of the stage door on the opposite side of the street. As it happened another drink wouldn't have gone amiss but the problem lay in revisiting the bar and what he might miss outside. The large form of the landlord was another problem he could well do without.

For once in his life Lloyd decided to keep the peace and relinquish his place, making a show of taking his empty glass with him to the bar. A sarcastic nod of approval that followed him across the room did not help his petulant mood that could have threatened to boil over into something more serious. "Bollocks!" He wasn't best pleased to find he was not the first in line to be served.

Pint in hand and once again back in his favoured position Lloyd and the landlord exchanged silent glances. Something in the facial expression of the former convinced the latter to believe he should make no further quip or comment. He retreated with the remaining empty glasses in hand and left the angry young man to continue with his vigil that had come at the reasonable cost of a pint.

*

Peter Pearce had taken extra care with his appearance and it reminded him of times when making an impression had been important. Bluff and bluster were easier to pass off when no one questioned your right to be there. That was then, things were different now. Personal invitations were much harder to come by and Pearce understood that burning his bridges had repercussions.

Another dollar, another day. It wasn't often that a self-proclaimed cynic like Peter was taken by surprise but today excitement fizzed in his veins. His jaunty walk to The Theatre mirrored his mood. Press Identity in hand he passed by security with the beginnings of a satisfied smile. Scrutiny came with the territory but his presence seemed to have caused little consternation. Should he be worried? No fight required. No spice to get his juices flowing. He realised his hunger for information must be tempered by Miss Highland's kindness. Perhaps he should be wary not to over indulge.

Ben Evans felt he should warn all departments about the dubious stranger in their midst. The journalist's reputation preceded him and it had been a struggle to remain polite.

"Don't worry Ben, it'll be okay, I promise you." The words came out of hiding.

A nod of approval and the pat on the back he received from Nick Sayers who emerged from behind a blackout curtain were of small compensation.

"You're sure Mr Hanlan knows about this? I find that very hard to believe." Ben did well not to say anything too uncomplimentary.

"Come in." Katie Ley, Amelia's understudy opened the dressing room door and ushered Peter Pearce inside. The buzz around The Theatre was tangible. The penultimate show, a matinee, was upon them. In Ellen's absence Katie had been busy working behind the scenes. "I'm all finished here for now. Remember you haven't much time." She spoke directly to Amelia who was sitting in front of a multi-bulbed mirror doing the finishing touches to her make-up. She was wearing an oversized dressing gown to cover the state of her undress. She had a pair of flip-flops on her feet.

"I'm outside if you need me." Katie repeated a message to Amelia that Peter Pearce could not fail to comprehend.

Pearce raised a questioning eyebrow.

"She's a good friend and feels responsible. Curtain up in under an hour." Amelia rose from her chair and tried to hide her anxiety.

Pearce looked directly into her bright blue eyes and found it difficult to look away. Finally, he lowered his gaze to her outstretched hand and somewhere beyond.

She decided to change his point of view by removing a pile of her clothes from the sofa and trusted her modesty to luck. "Make yourself comfortable."

When Pearce eventually sat down, he found himself sitting next to a pair of knickers that had eluded Amelia's grasp.

"Miss Highland, a pleasure at last." He tore his eyes away from the garment. "I never expected to be sitting here. How intimate." He nearly laughed at his own joke.

"Thought it was time that we actually met." Amelia tried to keep a friendly tone, knowing what she was about to say was edgy. "You have the advantage of knowing more about me and my family than I do about you." She tried a smile. "That's if I'm to believe what I read in the papers."

"Glad to be here, it goes without saying, although I am intrigued as to why I've been made so fortunate. Perhaps you'd like to explain. I'm assuming you want to be interviewed."

"How interested would you be in an exclusive?"

"Very much so."

"What if I traded an interview for information?"

"Information? About what in particular?"

"I'd like to know why you seem so obsessed with my family."

Pearce thought about that for a second. "Obsession, is that what you think? It's part of my job description to be curious. Take you for instance. I may not be your greatest fan, that's worth pointing out. I certainly don't hold your step-father in high regard, but you're both in the public's eye and good money is spent in supporting you."

"I can see you're not into self-promotion. I understand that you have pre-conceived ideas but perhaps your exposés rely too heavily on hearsay and inuendo. Ever thought about writing fiction? It might suit you better." Amelia suddenly sounded dismissive. "I sense we both need to move on."

"Certainly, you do."

"And you don't? That's pathetic." Amelia knew immediately she'd overstepped the mark.

Peter Pearce's face coloured. "Careful Miss Highland. Remember I'm your guest." He recovered. "Oh, and on the subject of full disclosure, is it you or Nick Sayers I have to thank for my invitation to the party in Suffolk?" He removed a photograph from an inside pocket of his jacket. "Definitely not from your father, that's for sure."

Amelia bowed her head and attempted to hide her distaste at his arrogance. "You haven't answered my question, Mr Pearce." She held her ground but continued to gaze at what he had in his hand. "Do you want to show me that?"

"Happy to oblige, but later, I think. It has value and anything I tell you comes with a warning. You may not like the message." Pearce looked to be in control again. "You're young and resilient with plenty of time to heal. Give me proper access to Hanlan and we can all talk together. It'll lessen the risk of having to repeat myself. Besides you'll want to ask him questions while they're still fresh in your mind."

For the first time Amelia felt a chilly menace to his words. "That suits me. All I want is the truth from you."

For the first time he questioned her motivation, sensing a trap. "Not playing with me, are you?"

More inuendo. Amelia flushed in embarrassment. "It's a trade-off. I'm finished with this show and ready to move on. NRG are my ticket out of here." She used her arms to point out the deficiencies of her surroundings. "I can't afford to be involved in abusive mud-slinging between you and my father." It made perfect sense. "So, here's the deal. I'll give you the access to my father but you don't get to publish until I've secured the contract with NRG." Amelia's reasoning was sound. "A few days is all I need."

Peter Pearce feigned disbelief. "Suddenly, I'm your new best friend? You're making me nervous."

"Then walk away. Forget we've had this conversation. No pressure." Amelia leaned forwards. "You haven't had to live in the spotlight and be kept under lock and key. Soon I'll be truly independent, free to do and say what I want."

Pearce was staring at the widening gap at the top of Amelia's robe but for once his mind was on other things. "Why not get your new man on the job. He seems to know how to support you." The photographic evidence of that landed in her lap.

She took a quick peek and was secretly pleased. "Nick's too close to NRG. I can't afford to jeopardise that. Besides I've no guarantees that you wouldn't stab me in the back. Ethics and trust are words you might want to find the meaning of."

"Cheeky bitch." Pearce was used to the caustic comments.

"Just make sure you get your facts right. Someone whose opinion I value tells me you don't always manage to do that."

Pearce's face clouded over, some scar tissue briefly giving him pain. "Sounds like Sayers has been spilling his guts. Never was one for taking the pressure."

Amelia decided to ignore the intended slur. "Come to the house when the party is in full flow. I'll bring my father and we can talk in private." A theatre bell sounded. "I'd love to chat some more but I have to get ready now."

Just as Pearce was hauling himself up from the sofa there was a knock at the dressing room door. There was no mistaking the voice on the other side.

"Are you decent?"

Amelia was immediately to her feet and opening the door.

"Oh, it's you! I have someone with me." She stood to one side.

On cue, Nick reacted angrily forcing Amelia to make a grab and hold him tight.

"See you've landed on your feet then Sayers. Your wife, remember her? Told me I might find you here." Pearce's comments were typically barbed. "When you're in better humour, we must have a chat about old times." With that Pearce pushed past and was gone.

With a giggle, Amelia let Nick go. "Sorry about that. Shut the door. I need to get changed." She briefly kissed him and then spoke again. "I didn't want you saying anything contradictory."

"A simple shush would have probably done, not that I'm complaining." He touched his lips and then became serious. "Well, how did it go?

"It was good, I think. Hope I didn't overdo it. Pearce tried to scare me with the photograph just as we'd hoped." It was left lying on her make up bag. "We look good together."

Nick shook his head and wondered if she really understood the calibre of man she was taking on. "Let's hope for all our sakes he took the bait and we can pull this off." He made to leave.

"It's alright, don't go." Not for the first time she was happy to get dressed in front of him. In the few weeks that he'd known her she'd displayed a variety of traits and disguises. From delicate petal to sharp pointed thorn. It was sometimes difficult to decipher when she was acting or simply being brave.

She was beautiful. That was indisputable; and nearly naked.

"Dirty old man."

He looked up in surprise.

"No, I don't mean you." She was laughing, totally unabashed. "I'm talking about Pearce." She pointed at the sofa. "The pervert. He's only gone and pinched my knickers!"

*

Lloyd Hanlan's hand was on its way to his mouth when it slowed and stopped. While his eyes never left the street outside, he managed to feel the edge of the nearest table and set down his beer. His full focus of attention was on the man leaving The Theatre.

It was predictable that his jacket would catch the glass and send it spinning to the floor. Only the landlord's surprising agility ensured its survival, thanks to a one-handed catch. Lloyd saw nothing of this, and was oblivious to the single digit salute that bade him farewell.

The infamous Peter Pearce in the flesh. Lloyd blinked in the brightness and despite his better judgement, felt compelled to follow. In the circumstances, he had no other choice.

He was reacting to fear, stemming from the near hysteria his mother had often exhibited when Pearce's name was mentioned. It was ingrained; a mistrust of the press who liked to steal secrets and make them public. His mother even believed that some of them had the gift of reading guilty minds.

It begged the question now that Lloyd was back in Britain, as to how poignant was Pearce's presence, presuming it was at Amelia's invitation?

The smug expression on the journalist's face told a story and all of it seemed bad. Lloyd had to believe that she'd done some kind of deal. Why else have an enemy come to her door? And where in all of this was his father? The nightmare of their last evening at Avondale still haunted him and it seemed further humiliation loomed large.

Lloyd crossed the road and turned down an alley just a few metres behind Pearce. With his eyes, intent on his prey, the choice to use violence seemed the only way out. Gritting his teeth, he made his hands into fists.

Ahead, and without warning Pearce came to a halt, his voice echoing in the dingy, narrow space between the buildings. Lloyd did his best to make sense of it all, while feeling the immediate surge of adrenalin begin to dissipate. He turned to hide his face while reaching inside a pocket for a calming cigarette.

Pearce was on his phone. "All set for the party in Suffolk. She says she'll give me everything then. Look, as sure as I can be. Oh, and by the way, on the other subject. When I left her, she had him wrapped up in her arms. Of course, with justification."

He waited for an answer. "No qualms now and worth every penny. You'll soon get it back when you print the story in your magazine. Don't worry, I'll be in touch." Pearce clicked shut his mobile phone. Without further thought or delay he carried on in the direction he'd been travelling.

Lloyd in contrast was frozen to the spot. Although he'd only eavesdropped on half the conversation, it didn't take a genius to guess that Pearce was negotiating with a buyer. All that was required were the final details that would bring him the bigger prize. Perhaps there was still time for Lloyd to intervene? He looked around him. Other people had appeared in the alley and Pearce was nearing its junction with another busy street ahead. All too public for what he'd originally had in mind.

Suffolk it was then, a kind of do or die.

*

Libi Sayers slipped her mobile phone back into a pocket of her shoulder bag specifically designed for the purpose. She smiled at the others and looked, if all truth be told, a little embarrassed.

"Talking with the enemy." She explained. "It doesn't seem right, especially in this particular environment." She was actually sitting in Charles Hanlan's office chair.

Across the desk Sally Stewart fidgeted, sharing in Libi's discomfort. She'd made up her mind to hold her tongue lest she make things worse by trying to be nice.

"Was Nick there with them, as we planned?" Samantha asked a difficult but relevant question.

"He got there just as Pearce was leaving." Libi seemed to hesitate. "Amelia seems to have taken matters into her own hands a little. Let's hope he reacted in the right way."

"I'm sure he will have been fine." Sam tried to sound confident without being absolutely certain what Libi's last comment was referring to.

"You seem to know him better than I do, which doesn't say much for the state of our affairs." Libi tried not to be angry, knowing she was suffering a weird kind of jealousy.

Sally squirmed in her seat and looked around the office desperately searching for a reason not to be there.

Libi was aware she needed to stay calm. Boarding last minute on a flight to London had certainly upset her natural rhythms. It was still a shock when Samantha came over and gave her a sympathetic hug. Genuinely, she thought a slap would have been more appropriate. She held herself quite rigid in the young American's brief embrace. It would have been too easy to have melted and responded to heartfelt emotion, but so much harder to cling onto her professional pride.

"Sorry." She looked somewhat chastened. "And thank you Samantha. You didn't owe me that. Don't worry I'm truly committed to doing my part in Nick's hairbrained scheme." In the guise of a scorned wife looking for revenge, she had been amazed at how much raw emotion had sustained her performance. "My vendetta against a cheating husband, made negotiations much more believable. Paying Pearce in advance, helped to tip the balance."

Libi had been careful to leave nothing to chance by painting a picture of Manhattan's newsstands crammed full of his work. "Front page cover, Peter? Well, I'll give it some thought. Depends on the headlines and how powerful we can make them."

"What I don't get is why he's not done this before?" Samantha had some concerns. The stakes were high and she feared Pearce might want to trade his story to the highest bidder.

"Believe me Sam, he won't get a better offer anywhere else. Right now, I believe he lacks the proof to write his final chapter. That's why he wants to confront Hanlan." Libi could see that Sam was unsure. "Timing is everything. He's got one decent shot at this."

"Why not buy him off and save all the hassle." Sam was playing devil's advocate.

"Not unless you're prepared to credit his accusations and gamble on the public's perception. It's better getting him to commit and then we can discredit him once and for all." Libi suddenly sounded more convincing.

Sally Stewart could contain herself no longer. "Mr Hanlan is taking a huge risk with this." Her voice faded to a near whisper. "I believe in him. I know that much."

It was an innocent remark and yet it spoke volumes. Her confidence sounded loudly in Libi Sayers' ears.

Samantha left the two other women to pack up the office. It was obvious that Libi felt there was nothing more she could achieve by staying in London. As Sally was driving directly to Suffolk, the offer of a lift was gladly accepted. Perfect company, if Libi could cope with Sally's nervous energy. Interestingly she never once asked what her husband would be doing and it implied an independence that seemed a little unhealthy.

As yet she'd not had the chance to speak with Charles Hanlan, bar a handshake and exchange of pleasantries. This struck her as ironical given the job that Sherman Powers had originally sent her to do. Sam planned to put that right by attending tonight's charity show. She was determined to be in at the sharp end. Never before had she relied so heavily on others to succeed on her behalf. Success or failure, whatever the outcome, she was determined to hear the arguments and have her say.

*

A black-tie affair on a carpet of red. A mix of rock star, politician and minor royalty were arriving in a constant stream. The early evening cloud cover above London had trapped the heat of the day. All the visible stars of earthly design were shimmering in the flash lights of the gathered paparazzi. Trusty steel barriers on either side were adequate but large numbers of eagle-eyed security guards were the front line of defence. In briefing his charges, Charles Hanlan had emphasised the need to be vigilant but gave no specific reasons as to why this was important. Highly polished leather shoes squeaked in anticipation and to order.

Nick Sayers was there informally, watching journalists and small pockets of Tv. crew secure their interviews. He was glad he'd been given no particular brief or instruction to add to the pressure of the night. Determined to be discerning and selective he was able to mingle with the most charitable and more popular celebrities as part of The Theatre's family. A recognition of the stars would add flavour and content to his work, but he felt no burden to fulfil an editor's wish-list and for that he was grateful.

Inside the foyer Amelia and some of the main cast members were lined up to greet their audience and to thank them for their generous support. Nick was fascinated by the interaction between Amelia and her guests, some of whom had been famous for as long as she had been alive. It appeared her demeanour under these circumstances was carefully used as some kind of shield and he'd seen her act similarly in New York. She inspired fatherly protection and attraction in equal measures, while women of varying persuasions greeted her with a mixture of cautious admiration and not a little envy.

He tried not to laugh and was found out. Amelia flashed him a look that told him he would pay a price for his insolence and then another that warned him of approaching trouble of another kind. Her father had appeared and was standing only a few feet away.

"Just like her mother. Disarmingly beautiful and wicked all in one go." Charles Hanlan had Samantha by his side as he cast his experienced eye over the proceedings. "Not sure she really enjoys this much."

"She seems to be coping well enough. I told her to make the most of it. Who knows when something like this might happen again?"

"There speaks someone who will, like my daughter, recognise when it's time to move on. Variety is an important spice to life and something that Amelia might need more than most. Making films in America could be good for her."

Sam feigned surprise. "You're not scared of losing her?

Charles gave her a look that she could have interpreted in different ways. "Not if you're there to look after her. Remember that." He half turned away, giving her no chance to respond. "I see the king of the Sunday papers, Duncan Marwood has just arrived. Let's go and have a word; strictly off the record." He gave her a reassuring smile. "We stick to the plan. Agreed?"

Both turned in unison leaving Nick and Amelia to ponder the likely outcome. Act two, scene one, must rely on improvisation.

"Mr Hanlan, Miss Grant. What's this all about?" Duncan Marwood tore his gaze away from the activity going on outside the tinted glass window to acknowledge both before returning back to his view. He was people watching. The seats in the circle and stalls below were beginning to fill. He tapped the glass with his knuckle. "I assume we can't be easily seen."

"Correct." Hanlan gestured for Sam to take a seat while he remained standing, waiting for Marwood to re-focus his attention back inside the room. "Neither seen nor heard."

The studio's lighting was purposefully subdued. Consoles of switches and various computer screens adorned the space providing technical backup to backstage management should anything go wrong with the primary systems.

"Nothing being recorded then?" Marwood swung away from the window and sat in the nearest chair, a little removed from Samantha and Charles.

"Not unless you want me to?" Hanlan perched his behind on the edge of a table, waiting for a reply that never came. "I'll come straight to the point then and ask you what your policies are regarding supporting staff in times of controversy." Charles was sounding very matter of fact. "We all have to abide by rules and regulation. Self-governance in the newspaper industry, when adhered to correctly, is something I support and admire. Given that loyalty means absolutely nothing these days, tell me how you cope with an employee like Peter Pearce on a daily basis?"

Marwood was not surprised. "I'd like to say it's none of your business but in this instance, I can understand your cause for concern. Peter can be a law unto himself on occasions. Dogged to say the least, once he gets his teeth stuck into someone it's not that easy to drag him off."

"A colleague of mine tells me that Pearce believes himself to be above the law." Sam spoke wryly. Her voice had an edge. "I gather your predecessor paid the price in full. Surely, once bittern twice shy, Mr Marwood?"

"So, Nick Sayers is working with you. I saw him in the foyer." Marwood looked thoughtful. "You're referring to events that took place way before my time, Miss Gant." He gave her a consolatory smile. "Nick was young and over sensitive in my opinion and don't forget it was the police that made the false arrest, not the staff at the paper. Nick's done alright, no need to worry there. Have you considered that perhaps Peter has a more convincing story this time?"

"The Devil's in the detail." Sam tried not to antagonise even though she was vexed that Jeff's predicament had been passed off so lightly.

"You have a vested interest, so I can understand your need for control." Marwood spoke to Charles with genuine reason. "Let's face it, you're a famous man, and it has to be said, not adverse to using the press in publicising your show."

"For which I pay handsomely, as you well know. We're talking about my privacy and that of my family. If Mr Pearce wants to write fiction, then let him write a book." Hanlan was visibly trying to control his emotions. "Tell me one thing if you're able. Why me in particular?"

Marwood calmly considered his reply. "People like Peter, with huge chips on their shoulders, are motivated differently from the rest of us. You can't predict what gets under his skin. It makes him edgy, and yes, a pain in the arse." He gave a casual shrug of his shoulders but was less cynical with what he said next. "Peter believes you owe him big-time."

"Sorry, I don't understand."

"As it happens neither do I, not fully." Marwood stood up and stretched his back. "You talked about writing fiction. It's my understanding that's what Peter had planned to do with his work. I know what you're thinking but he suffered some early setbacks. Talent is a gift but having the right connections is king. Cast your mind back when you and Maurice Highland had the backing of readymade money. You could afford mistakes and still recover from them." Marwood came to a halt without fully making his point.

"Is that it?"

"Yes, at present. Intriguing though, given the strength of his feelings. Maybe you should revisit your memories? Or wait to read about it in the papers."

Silence fell between them. Sam felt she ought to intercede. "Writing in the public's interest is all good and well. As an Editor, you have responsibilities. The paper can't afford to get this wrong."

"Telling me my job again, Miss Grant?" Marwood wasn't impressed. "Where should my loyalty lie? I don't change sides purely because things may get uncomfortable."

"Peter Pearce has." Sam tried not to gloat.

"Has what?"

"Changed sides." Samantha confirmed it. "The money has already been banked."

"Don't talk rot." He couldn't help himself. "How do you know this?"

"Ever heard of Stress Magazine?"

Realisation dawned on Duncan Marwood's face. "Very clever Miss Grant. I suppose I need to thank Libi Sayers for this? And you Hanlan." The implications fizzed in his head. "Okay, so where are we going with this?"

"Hopefully nowhere." Sam looked to Charles for his blessing. "No, we mean it, but it's going to need your co-operation."

*

Another sell-out, another success. One night could seem like any other if you let it. The secret, as told by those of more experience, had encouraged Amelia to cherish these special moments. If she'd needed reminding, there were twelve hundred people to reassure her as they stood in a single salute. The rest of the cast were caught in the moment and burst into spontaneous applause as the house lights went up to reveal the flash of clapping hands and smiling faces. Amelia found herself sandwiched between public and professional adoration.

Flowers rained down onto the stage from the front rows of the stalls and the boxes to the side. Amelia seemed frozen to the spot unable to suppress her own tears of emotion. Then she too started clapping her hands in the hope of deflecting some of the attention onto the other actors. She was aware of feeling exposed as a peculiar form of panic took hold. Out of the corner of her eye she saw salvation standing in the wings and she beckoned towards her father. A few seconds later Charles Hanlan stood beside her centre stage, self -consciously shielding his eyes. Instinctively she clung to him and for a moment she became a child again, glad of her father's supporting arm.

Charles bent and kissed her cheek and whispered something in her ear. Amelia could hardly hear above the noise of the crowd as he ushered her forward again, where she bowed her head one last time.

Life's rich tapestry was becoming a complicated picture. The different threads, although full of colour were pulling in different directions. Even in celebrating her final performance, Amelia was too aware of her tenuous position. It had happened to others in their careers.

Here and now, she was about to abandon the show that had made her a star. Where was Ellen when she was needed for her straight talking and ability to cut Amelia down to size? Certainly, she was coming to realise there was much she would miss if she went to America.

Messages and cards were strewn upon her bed along with a large bouquet of flowers. It was the only one she had brought back from The Theatre. The cast and crew had shared in the rest and been happy, mostly. The one dissenting voice being that of Gavin from the chorus, who was obsessing over a potential clash of colours with his newly painted living room.

Amelia's mobile gave notice of a rare incoming call. Not many people had access to her number. The voice that she heard was reassuringly familiar.

"Thought I'd better ring you. I've been tying up a few loose ends with your father and I'm afraid he's confirmed a little bit of bad news for me to pass on to you." Samantha explained she was phoning from a waiting car outside her apartment. "I'm hoping you'll join me."

"I'll come down immediately. What's going on and where are we going?" She could tell it was something important.

"I'm afraid it's Ellen. She's been in an accident and has been taken to a hospital not far from here."

Sharing the back seat of the car a few minutes later, Amelia listened with growing concern as Sam told her of what she knew. "Your father has just confirmed it and put me in touch with Ellen's boyfriend, David. He's there at the hospital with her now. Don't worry, she's in good hands."

Amelia sat in silence and felt angry with not only herself but with her father. The reputable hospital's address was well known and exposed him once again to his selective treatment of the truth. He'd obviously had prior knowledge about Ellen's condition, or why else would she be in a private room paid for in his name?

David met them outside while getting some air and led the way through the labyrinth of corridors once they were inside. He was plainly in a state of agitation and felt compelled to share in all that had been made clear.

"She says she fell and cracked her head. Says that nobody else was to blame." He shook his own. "Needless to say, I'm not sure I believe her. Obviously, there's something she's not going to talk about with me." David wanted to be angry. "Maybe you might have better luck, Amelia." He sounded disappointed, but finally admitted. "We haven't been getting on very well and if I'm honest, I couldn't blame her even if she has been seeing somebody else." He tried to minimise the hurt in his voice. "Maybe that's why she's asking for you."

Amelia tried to put David's mind at rest but came to realise that in concentrating exclusively on recent problems of her own, she hadn't a clue what Ellen had been getting up to.

13. Scenery Change

Samantha Grant was tired but found it difficult to come down from the busyness of the day. After leaving Amelia at the hospital, late night travel out of London had been trouble free, sat as she was in the back of a chauffeur-driven limousine. A call ahead had alerted Mary Paxton to her estimated time of arrival and it was a relief to finally be in Suffolk, knowing there was little more she could achieve.

Sitting alone with a hot milky drink in front of her, she tried to process the day's tension and strange excitement that had been fully immersive. True to her reputation, Mary had done all she could to make her feel welcome. Sam nibbled on a digestive biscuit and tried to ignore the delicious looking slice of lemon cake, aware of the kitchen clock ticking loudly in the background.

Of all the foreign visitors and strangers invited to visit Charles's Suffolk home, she was the only one to be staying as a guest at Sedge House. Sally Stewart and Libi Sayers had been found comfortable accommodation, a little removed, and on the outskirts of the nearest village. Although she enjoyed their company it was a relief to be separate from them now. With a resurgence of energy Sam kept herself busy with calls to America, and more importantly to Nick in London, keeping up to date with all his latest news. She finished her drink and looked at the clock one more time.

The meeting with Duncan Marwood had gone better than expected. The editor had managed his temper and that had revealed much about the paper's relationship with their star reporter. Patience had been worn thin over time. In light of this, Sam wondered whether it was better to keep one step removed from anything that might discredit NRG.

Who was she trying to kid? Better to be fully committed to the cause and be damned with the negativity that Sherman Powers was most afraid of. There was much that could yet put an end to his interest in Amelia Highland. Nobody was perfect. Sometimes it was a matter of trust. With that in mind, why was she questioning the logic of Nick staying put in London overnight, given Libi's fragile state of mind?

"Hope I'm not disturbing you." The back door opened and Joe Petersen walked in from the night. He was wearing jeans and a lightweight fleece, all in black. "Just doing my rounds, and I saw the light on. Everything okay?"

Sam was very happy for the intrusion. She too was casually dressed in denims and a light blue shirt. Out of her normal work attire she felt a little self-conscious. At least his presence was another excuse to be busy.

"Time for a coffee? Although I've no idea where anything is." Sam got up from the kitchen table thinking a thousand things. She couldn't remember the last time she'd brushed her hair.

"Actually, I've a couple of things I still need to do."

"Okay, sure."

"You could come with me." Joe made a professional appraisal. "You might want to put another layer on though." He felt the American was feeling a little out of her comfort zone. He guessed the chill air outside the warmth of the kitchen was probably the least of her problems.

"I'll be two seconds." She ran for the stairs and her room on the first floor. Amelia had promised to supplement her travelling wardrobe with many things including a woollen pullover. Mary Paxton, the deliverer of comfort, had plundered Avondale of all that was useful and had insisted that Sam help herself. She was grateful for that now and the revival of self-confidence that tingled in her newly brushed hair. Last reflected checks in the mirror on the bedroom wall seemed essential. A stick of gum and a dab of perfume behind both ears were the final extras.

"Nothing will happen here tonight; this is all about just in case." Joe spoke as he and Samantha walked out under the porch light, closing the back door quietly behind them. He laughed. "More than my life would be worth, if Charles thought I actually believed that."

"You're planning for the worst then? Tell me how that goes."

"Happy to but why don't I show you instead. We're all in this together."

The renovated barn next to the covered yard was part of the working farm. Formerly used as a feed store it had now become an office for Joe. The smell of freshly cut hay, mixed with the night air, was a backdrop they shared, as Samantha stood close in a narrow cone of incandescent light while Joe found the appropriate key to the door.

"Welcome to my world." Joe ushered Sam inside as the strip lighting flickered into life.

It took a second or so for her eyes to adjust. "This is different." She immediately noticed an armchair in one corner of a room that was otherwise sparsely furnished. A desk and two other chairs were adornments to an area that mostly comprised of work surfaces. "Not sure I'd go as far as calling it homely."

"Take a seat," Joe pointed to the armchair. "It was surplus to requirements in the cottage so I nicked it and put it in here. Not that I get to use it that often. I wouldn't want you getting the wrong impression."

"You have television too." Sam blinked in fascination. "Ten of them and counting. How many of those did you nick?" They were actually monitors which Joe had carefully positioned on shelving just above head high. There was wiring everywhere and all were attached to outside cameras. "Infra-red?" Sam had seen similar before.

"They swap over automatically as soon as the light drops below a certain level." Joe proceeded to activate them one by one as part of his test procedure.

"Install them yourself?"

"With help from a mate of mine. They're on loan and he comes as part of the deal."

Sam made an educated guess and gestured towards the equipment. "A home from home, your kind of place?"

Joe didn't confirm or deny it. Instead, he asked a question of his own.

"What about you? This can't be what you were expecting when you started working for NRG." He was keen to see her reaction.

"Perhaps not, but then my boss is very much like yours. I've learnt the hard way. Never second guess where his demands will take you next."

"That could be interpreted in so many ways."

"Every day is an adventure. Some good, some bad I guess."

"And this one?"

"Well, today, seen in isolation? Let me think, when did it start? Up then down and now steadily rising again."

Joe turned away at that point as a small alarm went off on one of the monitors. A fox was clearly visible outside the hay barn on the other side of the concrete yard.

Sam was sorry about that. She needed to talk.

"Well, the system seems to be working, but we won't be using it fully until tomorrow night."

Joe turned to find that he was being studied.

"Just you and your mate; is he army too?"

"Not anymore. Works in the private sector. There's one or two more. You'll see them tomorrow. People I can trust."

Sam got to her feet and wandered over in the direction of the monitors. The fox had moved on and there was nothing to be seen.

"It's a strange world you live in Joe."

"Only as strange as the people who make this kind of job necessary."

"But you gave it up once, why come back to it? You must feel isolated living here."

"It's only temporary, and besides, like you said, every day is different. Tomorrow night, and it could be all over. We hope for the best, prepare for the worst and pray no one gets to spoil the party."

*

When the next day dawned, the air was humid and still. Unnaturally so for that time of year? Mary and Jimmy Paxton were mulling it over, coffee and croissant there only companions, bought in anticipation of Charles' return to the house. He was missing out, having never made the journey from London the previous night. Not so his daughter who had surprised them by arriving via taxi all the way from Kensington Green in the early hours. Mary had naturally assumed some kind of falling out between Amelia and her father. Nothing new there and nothing that couldn't be fixed. The details could be dissected in the clearer light of day.

Jimmy too knew when to keep his own council and did so while he cleaned and put away the breakfast things. If Amelia needed a second opinion when she finally surfaced, no doubt she would seek and find him in her own good time.

*

As the last plate was washed and dried, Charles Hanlan was actually not that far away. With Nick Sayers as a passenger, his Mercedes was making good time on the near deserted roads.

Both men were ill at ease. Nick had been editing his work late into the night and Charles was still brooding over his interview with Duncan Marwood. The question remained, could the man be trusted or would he confront Peter Pearce regardless of their agreement? He'd already reserved the right to back out from an outcome he no longer controlled. As Miss Grant had rightly said, they could only hope that his paper's response would be sympathetic, now that they could no longer profit from Pearce's story.

The connection between Maurice Highland and Peter early on in his career was undisputable; checks had been made. If through the business he'd been unfairly treated, then Charles would be found guilty as charged. Money and copyright? Why hadn't Pearce made more fuss at the time?

No, this was personal. Charles understood how ghosts from the past could be difficult to bury.

If dredging through his failings was meant to be cathartic, they remained his greatest point of weakness. Scar tissue threatened his heart. Almost daily he celebrated his love for his daughter and mourned the death of her mother.

Yes, Jelena used to induce feelings that took you to the edge of reason. Love her or hate her, to remain impartial and indifferent was almost impossible. High spirited, immensely opinionated, she could be startlingly beautiful and disturbingly brutal all in one go. Maurice had been the only one capable of selective deafness and measures of arrogance to survive the high-powered vagaries of their fiery relationship.

And yet Charles had always assumed that in time she would have mellowed and become even more desirable. If only she were still living. There, there it was. An admittance of guilt. If falling in love with someone's potential could be seen as betrayal then Pearce and his logic were soundly based.

Was that what it was all about? Loving Amelia as his daughter had nothing to do with his unfulfilled desire for Jelena, right? Besides, how could Pearce have subverted what could have been insightful exposition into thinly vailed and vulgar fiction?

Hanlan's marriage to Claire clouded the picture. Might have Pearce used leverage against her to get insider information? Something of weight to help tip the balance in his favour. Charles had to assume that due to Jelena and Maurice's' untimely deaths, only Claire had the power to shed light on an already complicated situation.

Charles sucked in a breath and let it out slowly. Claire, his wife, a serial chaser of fame and fortune. Her saving grace, she'd made no secret of the fact. Not to Charles.

"It's all about power and position," He spoke without thinking.

"I'm guessing you're not talking about driving your car now." Nick had his right foot pressed into the footwell. "Speeding runs in the family, I see."

Charles ignored the sarcasm. "Marwood, yesterday. When I was with Miss Grant, implied that Pearce lives with a permanent chip on his shoulder. Money, love, maybe it's both. Young and impressionable? Romantic notions crushed? When you worked with him, did he ever mention me by name?"

"Not that I can remember." Nick couldn't help himself. "Maybe that's not so bad. Romantic notions?" There was a second or two before they both began to laugh.

It was a pleasant release.

"Sorry. Just thinking out aloud. There's something I'm missing here." Peter Pearce had issues, but Charles had them too. Blinding himself to Claire's ambitions and appetites had been all about self-preservation, pure and simple. Used as a foil to dull the longing and most definitely the lust, she'd become a short-term fix while he had waited for Jelena. He could picture her in one of her continental moods, when Maurice's armour of total indifference had provided a calculated form of jousting for all their entertainment.

As for involving himself with Claire, Charles could only conclude that he'd acted like a coward, relying on short term solutions while all the time he'd been waiting for the bigger prize.

14. Arrangements

The kitchen at Sedge House was as good a place as any to have their council of war. Charles sat at the head of the table opposite his daughter who seemed convivial if not outwardly friendly towards her father. Mary was pleased and relieved to see that at least. Down one side sat Nick and Samantha, on the other were Jimmy and Joe. Mary stood to pour coffee for those that wanted a refill.

It was the first time that they'd had the chance to all be together. Charles alluded to this when he opened the proceedings.

"I'm going to start with some apologies, in particular to you Miss Grant, for keeping you at arm's length. You have been extremely patient and also very helpful to me and my daughter right from word go. I can only imagine the kind of pressure you've been under from NRG and I intend to speak to Sherman Powers on your behalf very soon." There was brief eye contact before Charles moved on.

"Amelia, I've already spoken with you, but I'll say it for the record. I fear this may be a difficult day for both of us with much that could go wrong. I fear we will see no winners even if our plans prove successful. We've looked at all the options and our choices are limited now that the police are likely to become involved." Amelia looked determined enough.

"I suggest we concentrate our attentions on enjoying this afternoon's concert as much as we can. Plenty of smiles and keep the atmosphere casual. Hopefully all the musicians had an early night and remained teetotal." Charles made a face. "We'll take what we can and deal with the party as a separate item."

"On a separate note, the generator giving power to the marquee is receiving last minute checks and will have attending security from this moment on. With the forecast of an approaching storm, this may prove to be vital. One thing to remember is that Joe Peterson is totally in charge when it comes to matters of our safety. If at any time he asks you to do something, don't argue, just do it." This piece of advice seemed to be aimed mostly at Amelia, which seemed to tickle Jimmy Paxton.

Charles chose to ignore this playfulness and re-iterated his words with a serious stare.

"Is there anything you wish to add at this moment, Joe?"

"Thank you, Mr Hanlan." Joe cleared his throat before confidently continuing. "Just to say, that after the concert and reception are over you will be picked up and driven back here. The idea is that you should go with the same car and driver on both legs of the journey. Remember we are not expecting trouble but I would rather be over cautious than foolishly under-prepared. With that in mind, there are additional staff on hand to guarantee your safety. Their team leader is a colleague of mine called Alan. I'll introduce him to those of you who have not already met him. Any problems or concerns, then he's your man." Joe looked directly to Charles for some kind of permission to carry on.

"Mr Hanlan's son, Lloyd, was involved in an incident in London a couple of days ago. He was seen in the company of Ellen Preston and we know he has access to a rented vehicle. We can only speculate that he was trying to find out Miss Highland's address in London. Of course, we should not lose sight of the fact that he is part of the family." Joe's words were preconceived and practised.

Charles gave a slight nod of his head.

"However, it's worth pointing out that Ellen ended up in hospital in a serious condition. Mr Hanlan and Amelia have both been able to briefly speak to her. The police are now interested in ascertaining Lloyd's whereabouts." Joe was aware of Charles looking up from the table, "Accident or attack? We need to ask the question. Ellen thinks he panicked, believing her to be dead." Joe let the words sink in. "It's not my job to make assumptions, either way. It's likely that Lloyd won't be too far away come the end of the day."

"With tonight's party carrying on after dark, some of you will be aware of the security camera set-up we have in place around the house and farm buildings." Joe glanced at Samantha who actually blushed. "Jimmy has kindly offered to man the office later and keep an eye on things from there. So be careful what you do from now on. Everything will be recorded." Joe had come to the end of his speech. "I think that will do, thank you sir."

*

A small cavalcade of cars left Sedge House just before noon with the concert venue no more than ten minutes' drive away. They were clearly visible once they'd exited the wood and made the steady climb to the junction at the top of the rise. As Lloyd watched he thought they looked like a funeral cortege and visualized the passengers all dressed in black. From his position on the bridge over the river, he knew it wouldn't be long before they passed him.

Time enough to hide. The concert venue as a place to isolate Amelia from the rest of her entourage seemed out of the question. Her continued silence was paramount and his freedom may yet rely upon her coercion. Memories of that night at Avondale and how much information she'd passed onto Peter Pearce might yet prove crucial.

*

On the other side of the estuary, a lone figure wearing borrowed boots, followed the path over the hill and paused to take in the view. Flowering gorse and fresh green reeds framed the creek and the natural stone tower of the church on the far side of the estuary. It was a beautiful place, wild and lonely and unlike anything she'd seen before. Had Libi Sayers known in which direction to look, she too would have seen the cars as they slowed at the crossroads; intermittent and sparkling reflections of the sun on smooth metal giving them away.

One by one they turned right and disappeared behind lines of bushes and low trees. Similarly, the sun, making its final bow, was hidden by darkening clouds that brewed and thickened. Just as forecast, the scene before her changed in atmosphere and matched her own mood. Dull and flat and full of foreboding, it seemed that stormy weather was not that far away.

*

Sally Stewart and Katie Ley had been busy all morning, carrying out sound checks with the orchestra in unfamiliar surroundings. The concert hall itself was much in keeping and the centre piece of a new age retail park created out of old commercial businesses. Right now, the inside space was filled with music. In Amelia's absence, Sally had acquitted herself well in singing the penultimate duet, leaving Katie to close out the show. Ever Searching was definitely in transition with a new name topping the bill.

Sally exited stage left and walked straight into Charles Hanlan who had just arrived and been listening in the wings. "No need for you to audition." He smiled to show his appreciation. "A woman of many talents, you never know when to stop working." Once again Charles found himself beholden to her. "Seriously though, you were supposed to be taking it easy this weekend."

He tried to sound more business-like. "Take a note, Sally."

She nearly panicked.

"In your head then. I'll remind you later."

She nodded.

"Give yourself a rise."

*

A strange day had just got stranger. Samantha's emotions were working overtime. Sharing a car with Amelia had allowed them only whispered conversation. Both had much on their minds and privacy was hard to find. Sitting side by side, holding hands became their compromise but said much more than nothing.

Now, on the steps to the foyer Sam was met by a well-known figure, who by rights, had no business being there at all. Rosalind Powers; Sam nearly curtsied and her mind went blank as she began to panic.

"Pleased to see me, I hope?" Rosalind smiled. "I said I'd be here when you needed me."

"You did? I mean you did. And I am very glad to see you." Samantha was trying to recover her composure. "You said, needed."

"I did, and I am. Needed."

"That bad, eh?"

"Well, let's focus on the good news. Sherman is missing in action. A touch of gout. I bribed his doctor to tell him he couldn't fly." Rosalind raised her eyebrow. "You'll be pleased. No, don't try to deny it, it's perfectly all right." She thought for a moment. "There is no bad news really, but I do want to have a chat with you, preferably with a glass of champagne in my hand." She could see Samantha's confusion. "Do what you have to and don't mind me. Stop worrying. Things will work out just fine." Rosalind smiled her reassurance.

*

"You do it every time."

His mind was full of many things and once again Nick had failed to knock before entering Amelia's dressing room.

"I'm sure you do it on purpose."

"Just good timing." He shut the door quickly behind him. He turned to find her with hand on hip and in playful pose.

"Seriously Nick. The sound of a zipper and you just wander in."

He mumbled an apology. "I was thinking about Libi and got distracted." He turned his back.

"Don't worry, I won't tell her." Amelia was less angry than her words might have implied. "Can't find a thing in here."

Curiosity got the better of him. "What are you looking for?" She was discarding clothes in every direction. Essentially, she was naked, with her head stuck in a suitcase. One for the album. "Did you get your knickers back from Pearce?" The question seemed suddenly relevant.

Amelia laughed. "I thought you were thinking about your wife?" She considered her present state. "Some things are better kept private, agreed?" She suddenly looked serious. "You're too good for me, so I feel safe with you around me." She brightened again. "We have fun, don't we?"

Amelia looked alluring and he would miss her. He tried to smile. "I'll let you get on. Forgotten what I'd come in to say. Maybe you've just said it for me."

Next thing she was in his arms with the touch of her skin in his hands. Her gentle embrace was a mix of comfort and sadness.

*

Tiny splashes of rain made indents in the dusty ground and tapped lightly on the slate tiles of the old brewery buildings. From inside the hall the faint but unmistakeable sound of thunder could be heard somewhere out to sea.

Amongst the murmur of hushed conversation and growing excitement Charles surveyed the scene inside the hall and cast his eye upon the lone, empty seat at the front of the auditorium. It was a nagging reminder that as yet no one had seen nor heard from Peter Pearce. Charles played around with a list of possible reasons, the most likely that Duncan Marwood had reverted to type, warning his colleague of the trap that'd been set for him.

One last minute decision to ask that the Sayers' should stay away seemed sensible in hindsight. Reducing the possible targets in Pearce's line of sight was preferable. With Samantha's approval, Nick and his wife had promised to join them later at Sedge House, by which time Charles hoped to have a clearer picture of the journalist's intent. Compassion in business was rare but he thought that Libi was most deserving. She'd exceeded all expectations in helping, not only NRG, but him and his family. Charles was happy to reciprocate, aware she had incurred great cost and sacrifice of a personal nature.

The concert was about to begin. Rehearsals were over, now was the time for the songs to be sung.

*

Outside in the strengthening wind, the faint sounds of orchestra and voice confirmed that the concert was still in progress. Rather than attend as he'd originally planned, Peter Pearce was passing the time in ways of his own choosing and in places where he felt more at ease. The weather had been threatening and now, flurries of rain forced pedestrian traffic on the thoroughfares to seek shelter in the shops and cafes. The art gallery too, was making the most of increased attendance. Local artists would be in profit, judging by the number of times the young supervisor had been disturbed from her reading and asked about pricing. Pearce had thought of engaging with her and would have done so but for his need of the loo. Beers over lunch in the nearby hostelry were taking their toll. He settled for complementing her on her choice of author and was happy to see this as a small victory of sorts. He didn't like to ask her where the toilets were though.

"Across the courtyard, diagonally to the left," were the directions given to him by an older shop assistant working in the deli on the ground floor directly beneath the gallery.

Pearce exited the shop and looked to the sky. Another distant roll of thunder echoed in the distance and the leaves in the trees seemed to shiver and shake in response.

Pulling his collar up, he set off in determined stride. Half way across the courtyard he was aware of a man on a converging course. A familiar figure? One he ought to know? A gust of wind-blown rain made him bow his head.

The other man was quicker and had disappeared inside a cubicle before Pearce could get close enough to make him out. He took his time and was just zipping up when he heard a toilet flush behind him. Important hand washing gave him the chance to study the mirror on the wall. Their eyes met in reflection and instant recognition. Both tried to remain cool and calm.

The fleshy teenager had become a man, his features more angular and defined than when he'd last seen them. They conjured up vivid memories and Pearce knew then that Lloyd was lucky to resemble his mother, making it harder to judge him in the same way he did his old man.

"How's America treating you? Lloyd? If I'm not much mistaken."

The younger of the two was not ready to answer and by activating the hand drier gave himself more time.

"Not interested in going to the concert. Obviously, not your kind of thing." Pearce persisted, raising his voice.

"Questions, questions, Mr Pearce." Lloyd's voice was suddenly loud in the quietness of the room. His anger was controlled and his hands were dry. "Always hiding inside the columns of your newspaper and now I see you twice in two days. Want to tell me what is going on?"

Pearce showed that he hadn't quite understood.

"I saw you outside The Theatre yesterday. How was Amelia by the way?"

"You mean you don't know." Pearce took an educated guess. "Not welcome? Not invited? Shame on them. Tell you what, tag along. Come as my plus-one to the party." He saw some hesitation. "Don't worry, you're not my type, but I am serious. You have rights. It's a family affair."

The sound of approaching footsteps helped Lloyd make a quick decision. Somebody else was in need of the gents. Yes, he'd tag along but only while he found out what Peter Pearce was really up to. Self-protection was everything. How strange? Only yesterday he might have struck out without thinking.

"Okay, you're on." To refuse now would have been churlish. "You never bothered keeping in touch with Claire?"

"With your mother? Water under the bridge." He didn't elaborate further. How many times had he wished that had been possible?

The two men walked back across the courtyard, taking advantage of a brief respite from the rain. Meanwhile, the latest arrival to the gents got quickly onto his phone.

"Joe? It's Alan, I'm still at the old brewery buildings. Guess what, the proverbial storm is on its way. I've literally just bumped into Pearce." Lightening filled the sky. "He's not alone… No, a male, early twenties…" Alan laughed. "Yeh, it did make me wonder, public toilets and all. Look, from the bits I could hear, it could be Hanlan's son. They mentioned a woman's name. Yes, Claire, does that mean anything to you?"

15. Party Time

Twisting the bottle and not the cork, Mary was pleased to see the caterers were doing just fine. She might even allow herself a glass of champagne before the evening was out. The beautifully decorated marquee was gradually filling with people. Guests, as they arrived, were escorted from minibuses and small coaches by rain-coated men with large umbrellas. Despite the weather the mood remained upbeat. The backdrop of Sedge House outlined against the stormy sky drew appreciative glances as white flashes of lightning forked down onto the sea.

The anticipated excitement was half the enjoyment and the thrill of occasion was shared by those who wanted a special part of something they had never experienced before. Old friends and new acquaintances circulated in a convivial atmosphere that was of their own making and in no way predictable or staged. The food, the wine, the incidental dancing and the music were in tune with everything that had been hoped for.

With the last of the guests safely sat at their tables, Charles Hanlan gave a formal welcome to all, and thanked a list of people for making the day happen. He disguised any anxiety he was feeling by bringing the speech-making to a premature end. "It's a party. Read the instructions on the side of the tin," was his wish for the rest of the evening. His final task which was met with rapturous applause was the introduction of his new leading lady, Katie Ley.

Amelia seemed intent to keep alert to all that was happening around her, while circulating and talking with those who begged her attention. Mary Paxton was glad that Rosalind Powers had made it her duty to be an ever-present companion, never leaving her side. A wonderful older woman was Rosalind, who understood what real life was all about. That was what she had told her husband as their paths crossed much later that night.

Jimmy had listened, thought for a moment and then replied.

"A bit like you then dear."

Mary had done her best, but failed to hide her smile.

*

Once he'd started you couldn't shut him up. Lloyd flicked ash from his cigarette through the partially opened car window and realized with some horror the lengths to which the journalist had gone. A one-man mission, an obsession, he probably knew more about his father than he did. If Lloyd had had any fears that Pearce might pump him for information, they were soon dispelled. Half the evening gone and still they'd gone no where near the party.

"I'll drive. I know the area. Made it my business ever since Hanlan bought the property." Pearce chuckled to himself. "Got to know one of the brick layers working on the extension. Settled a few of his gambling debts; well, the paper did. I've even had a guided tour."

The boast was worth making. Pearce took the main road out of the village before turning left and following the road along the southern side of the estuary.

"But why? Why are you going to such lengths? I don't understand."

"You don't understand?" Pearce sounded incredulous. "It's all about power and his need to control. He loves running and ruining lives." He took a sideways glance. "Exiled you to get you conveniently out of his way."

Lloyd was still confused and to a certain extent grateful. Pearce appeared to be unaware of the real reasons why he and his mother had left. The journalist had not let that bother him and had seemingly concocted his own theories.

It was dusk by the time they reached the woodland on the approach to Sedge House. The shape of a church tower outlined against the darkening sky encouraged Pearce to pull the car over. As they came to a halt, the gate to a graveyard with a path threading its way between the headstones was plainly visible in the headlights.

"Still too early to go to a party." Pearce cut the engine and the lights.

Lloyd felt reprieved knowing he was reaching a point of no return. They sat in silence deep in their thoughts.

"What did you mean when you said – get me out of the way?" Lloyd's courage was beginning to fail him.

Pearce took his time. "Mate, no offence but aren't you being a bit slow?" He stared into the gloom. "You became surplus to requirements and look where his preferences inevitably lay."

Amelia's name hung in the air between them.

"It's tragic when families get torn apart. She shouldn't have died of course." Pearce was off on a tangent. "Jelena Highland." He wondered why the young man had gone quiet. "You were only a baby but I'm telling you, they were close those two. If I had to guess, I reckon they got caught in the act."

Lloyd was shocked at how casually it was said. "How do you know all this, or is it purely figments of your imagination?" The mention of death had freaked him out.

"I was there and in at the start. Your mother and I were something of an item. Thought we might have got married. I was planning to ask her when that bastard, Highland fleeced me and stole my ideas."

Lloyd was having trouble believing his ears. "So, you knew her even before she met my father?"

"Claire? Met her when I was writing and producing exclusively for Maurice. You won't remember dear old Maurice." Pearce spat the words out. "Didn't like competition but loved taking the credit for himself. Stole my work and dropped me like a stone."

"That means you were indirectly working for my father."

Pearce wasn't listening. "Both of them were to blame. That's how your mother got off with Hanlan, as soon as she realized there was no way back for me." Emotion filled his words. "I stuck around and played second fiddle, just in case she changed her mind." He laughed aloud but it sounded hollow. "She was always up for that, was your mother."

Despite the harshness, remnants of affection filtered his words. Pearce turned on the overhead light and watched Lloyd pull another cigarette from his packet.

"Hanlan was selfish and took her for fear of missing out. He never loved her, your mother, not like Jelena. Never loved you either, did he mate?" The question was a statement. "And look what eventually happened. He was the one who fixed it for them to make that Italian trip."

Pearce took one of Lloyd's cigarettes but didn't light it. "Always thought there was something fishy about the way they died. I'm not saying he killed them, certainly not Jelena, but I've been out there to the scene of the accident. It was a straight piece of road…" He left the words hanging.

"What are you implying? Even I know that's twisted thinking. And what has any of that got to do with getting rid of me?" Lloyd was incredulous.

"I'll give you one guess." Pearce made it sound so obvious. "You were never going to make him money, let's be fair, not with your skill set. No fault of yours but a proud man can only take so much disappointment. Besides, he never got to see Jelena Highland again and have her for himself. He made damn sure that no one was around to see him have her daughter."

There was a shocking silence until Lloyd snorted with laughter that was laden with contempt.

"You stupid shit. What are you saying? I hate him for sure but try to be real. He wouldn't have dared and certainly wasn't capable. Too much the gentleman, unlike me. When I finally got my chance, I took it." The boastful words were out before Lloyd could stop himself. They seemed to echo disastrously around the interior of the car before he could even be sure he'd said them.

"You what?" This was not what Pearce had wanted to hear. "You and Amelia." He shook his head, trying to make sense of it. "But I have the proof..." This couldn't be right and, in every way contradicted what his reliable sources had said. Searching and sifting the tenuous evidence of jealous actors, he clutched at salvation. One way or another he'd been taken for a ride. "What... did he double your allowance so you'd take the blame and then disappear?"

Before Lloyd had the chance to deny it, Pearce re-started the engine and turned on the headlights, the full beam effect dramatically contrasting their surroundings. The front wheels span and kicked up the dirt as Pearce reversed and then made the car shoot forward.

"Let's go and ask him for ourselves, shall we?" Pearce shouted indignantly as he accelerated away.

Lloyd was pinned to the back of his seat and heard alarm in his own voice as he begged for Pearce to slow down and try and see sense.

*

"Sorry if we're gate crashing, but we couldn't stay away." Nick and Libi who had climbed out of the back of a taxi stood, hand in hand and were talking to Joe and Samantha. "We won't be going inside to the party." They were dressed in casual attire. "But we're happy to help out in any way we can."

"That's kind of you. Eyes on the ground, the more the merrier." Joe was aware of their nervousness and tried to put them at their ease. "Sam will show you how to access the main house if you want to make yourself comfortable. No sign of our players but we know they can't be that far away."

"Might be able to help you with that. We passed a car parked on the side of the road." Libi wanted to be helpful. She wanted this thing that Nick had with Pearce to be over. "I saw a cigarette being flicked out of a window."

Just at that moment static and storm-induced interference crackled on Joe's radio.

"I've got movement on the road; a car being driven fast, moving away from the church coming your way. It'll be with you in a couple of minutes." The sound of a high revving engine could be heard echoing against the walls of Joe's cottage as Alan made his report from the cover of the porch.

"Understood, we have visual." Within seconds bouncing beams of bluey-white light picked out the canopy of trees either side of the track. Instinctively Joe checked that security on the entrances to the marquee were all in place and picked out Samantha who was looking on anxiously while moving to one side. That was before the noise of the crash.

To those that actually saw it, the car appeared to run wide as if out of control, with the direction of its headlights hinting at impending and unavoidable disaster. The splintering of fencing was clearly audible above the high revving engine, seconds before the car flipped over and rolled. Everything else was down to pure luck. Instead of careering on its roof in a straight line, the car tumbled and slid to the left. The fast-moving wreckage passed cleanly between gateposts at the farmyard entrance, before tipping over one more time, coming to rest the right way up.

Joe was already running and fearing the worst. Security lighting positioned on the farm buildings clearly showed the damage. As he reached what was left of the vehicle a slight smell of petrol filled the air. Peering in through the driver's side window it was easy enough to see Peter Pearce sitting behind the wheel. Joe carefully reached inside to switch off the ignition and make things a little safer.

"Are you hurt?" Joe could see a pair of eyes blinking at him. "I'm going to reach past you now and undo your seat belt." In leaning across, he could clearly detect alcohol on the man's breath. "Peter, can you hear me? If you're not too badly injured, we need to get you out of here as quickly as we can."

Peter Pearce was now fully conscious and able to move. A large bump to the top of his head and a thumb jarred on the car's steering wheel, his only physical damage. Joe concentrated on getting the man out of the car but was keenly aware that the passenger seat was mysteriously vacant.

"Where did he go? The stupid bastard pulled on the handbrake." Pearce exclaimed.

"Don't worry we'll find him." The voice belonged to Jimmy Paxton who spoke over Joe's shoulder. "Picked him up on the cameras. I know which way."

Somebody else did too and was in pursuit. Ahead, the figure of a woman could be seen sprinting up the road.

Samantha, who had bemoaned the fact that she had nothing to wear to the party, was suddenly thankful for her little black dress and comfortable loafers. No high heels to contend with and lucky too, that she'd been slower off the mark than Joe. From her starting position slightly to the left she'd seen a figure exit the car and begin to run away. His low crouching action seemed to indicate he might be injured. However, within metres he'd straightened, increasing his pace and veered to the right before disappearing behind the nearest farm building.

The exhilaration of running took Samantha by surprise as her feet kicked up a spray of water from the surface of the track. She could see where Lloyd was heading. She'd walked the same route with Joe the previous night. Ironically and unwittingly, he had given himself little option of escape and was heading for the creek where all the small boats were kept. She slowed to a jog; her own progress made more difficult by the darkness at the back of the buildings. Long wet grass licked at her legs as she turned the corner and continued on behind the hay barn. Lightning from the receding storm briefly highlighted the ground in front of her and evidence of a well-worn path gave her encouragement. The upstairs windows of Sedge House in the middle distance soon came back into view and gave the blackness more perspective.

What of Lloyd? He could have doubled back and be coming towards her; she couldn't be sure. Now that the storm had abated, the situation felt less desperate and it was tempting to wait for others to arrive. Even though she continued to move forward, she found herself hoping that Joe would suddenly appear.

Two things happened simultaneously.

"F… it!" A man's cursing was clearly audible.

At the same moment Sam could see low-intensity lights flickering into life beyond a slight bend in the path. The reeds made it difficult to get a clear view but she was sure that they must be the staging lanterns out by the boat house and at either end of the jetty. She was not far away now and very close to Lloyd.

The clonk of wood on wood preceded a splash as something fell into the creek. Samantha put her courage in both feet and ran towards the bend in the path. By now her saturated loafers were squelching rudely with every step. What confronted her was a scene of some confusion. Lloyd who had been attempting to turn the rowing boat around had inadvertently dropped an oar over the side. Stretched out on the jetty, with both arms and half of his torso angled down towards the water he was making a desperate attempt to lay hands on the vital piece of flotsam.

Samantha saw most of it and guessed the rest. In locating what he sought at the end of his range, Lloyd had lost balance and begun to topple. His last gasp attempt to fling the oar back into the boat had him pawing at thin air and losing any hope of salvation. He did manage to grab the boat's painter and use it to pull himself up and away from the water, but physics finally won out over his struggle. Involuntarily he was pulling the boat back towards him. Sam heard the sickening blow as the sharply angled bows connected with his head and then there was nothing more. She arrived at the jetty just in time to see Lloyd slip, fish-like beneath the surface into the narrow gap left between the boat and the jetty. And then it was as if he'd never been there at all.

*

The sitting room at Sedge House was dominated by the inglenook fireplace. It made you feel welcome and included. Oak beams and panels of exposed brickwork had been treated in ways to show them off to their greatest advantage. The effect was made complete by the solid timber floor covered in a richly coloured, patterned rug. A period picture, but not cottage-cosy, thanks to the higher ceilings and an uncluttered approach. Pearce was no expert but the bureau and side-table must have cost a pretty penny and matched perfectly the stylish leather upholstered chairs.

He was sitting in one of them now, quite close to a small fire that was burning in the grate. Despite the accident or maybe because of it, the feeling of comfort and relaxation was truly overwhelming. An empty cup of coffee and large tumbler of brandy were the hospitable advantages of being cared for by Charles Hanlan's staff. Pearce struggled a little knowing that he liked the woman called Mary who had showed him nothing but kindness and yet hated with a passion the identity of the man who had asked her to take care of him.

His thoughts inevitably returned to the car crash. Lloyd, the little bastard, had pulled on the hand brake, seemingly losing his bottle and making good his escape. Pearce adjusted a small bag of frozen peas over the growing bump that had appeared on top of his head. It was a reminder that things could have been worse.

Just at that moment the noise of footfall and muffled voices emanated from the kitchen at the end of a connecting hall. Pearce heard the back door open and shut a few times as people came in from the night and the party outside.

Mary Paxton was the first to re-enter the room.

"Are you warm enough Mr Pearce? Would you like another coffee?" She didn't wait for him to answer. "I'll bring some in for the others when they get here and you can decide then."

Pearce drained the last of his brandy and proffered the tumbler towards her in an unspoken plea.

"A small one then." It sounded as if she didn't exactly approve. "Mr Hanlan will be coming to talk to you in a little while. He has guests to say goodbye to."

Pearce looked confused and raised his left wrist. Only now did he realize that his watch was no longer working. The glass front was missing and a small hole had mysteriously appeared in the centre of its face.

"It's nearly midnight." Mary was prepared to be firm but kept her tone friendly. "Stay where you are and I'll bring you a refill. You're having quite an evening, I think."

If they'd been a breed of dog then the fur on their backs would have stood up on end. Charles Hanlan circled the room before seating himself in a similar chair on the opposite side of the fireplace from Peter Pearce. Both remained silent which was gratifying and preferable; words were inappropriate when all they wanted to do was growl.

Not to be trusted and left to their own devises, some semblance of civility was achieved by the entry of two women who immediately followed Charles into the room. One was expected, the other a surprise, particularly to Peter. Amelia took up a familiar position at one end of the sofa directly in front of the fire. She made herself comfortable and even had the good grace to smile at Pearce. Libi Sayers in contrast appeared decidedly edgy but eventually took her place beside Amelia, deciding for the moment to keep her own council.

"Not sure the company is appropriate with what I've got to say to you." Pearce put down his bag of peas. "Surely not in front of your daughter." He shook his head and regretted it instantly. "And don't think I won't ask the difficult questions and somehow be embarrassed, Hanlan." Pearce's eyes settled on the women and he tried a smile that looked more like a grimace. He warmed to his theme. "I have to wonder where the boyfriend is, or should I say spouse, depending on your point of view of course?"

Of the two of them Amelia was the one to react. "Talking with your mouth full, Peter. Full of your usual crap."

He ignored the rudeness. Although they'd never met in person, he felt confident he'd guessed correctly. Outward signs of Libi's inner belief showed a determination that his words would not hurt her.

She was glad that her husband's presence had not escalated the situation further. To have him fight with Pearce would have been a distraction and she was determined that nothing should undermine the last few hours they'd spent together. Despite the tension, the fire in the hearth was giving her welcome warmth.

Peter Pearce was about to make some further comment when a young waitress from the catering team arrived carrying a tray full of cups, followed closely by another who had been entrusted with the coffee pot, milk and sugar. Mary had carefully loaded the trays in the kitchen herself.

"And I thought the party was over." Pearce looked expectantly about him. "Or am I the lamb about to be slaughtered, eh Charles?" He got no reaction. "Your son certainly had a good try." He felt the top of his head. "And now you're going to finish me off?"

At that moment Mary returned with Pearce's tumbler of brandy. He smiled and thanked her, taking hold of the glass.

"Not poisoned?" She shook her head disapprovingly. "Your health then madam." He sipped the liquid and savoured the taste. Returning the glass to a little side table, it was apparent that his movements were hampered and that he was starting to feel pain.

"Perhaps we should take you to a doctor. Seriously, how do you feel?" Charles spoke to Pearce for the first time.

"I'm touched, I truly am, but surprised that you're not more worried about your son. You ought to be out there looking for him, instead of feigning concern over me."

Charles did not respond, allowing Pearce his aggression.

"Couple of snakes in the grass, you two." Peter diverted his attention back to the women sitting on the sofa, not content to let things be. "One offering me… I'm not quite sure? Cleverly done Miss Highland. The other prostituting her magazine." He spoke directly to Libi. "We had a deal Mrs Sayers, remember? The money is already banked and non-refundable. So where do we go from here?"

Libi shrugged her shoulders. "It's up to you Peter, the offer of the article still stands, providing you can give me my moneys-worth and the magazine doesn't get sued in the process." She gestured towards Charles Hanlan. "It seems your protagonist is ready to fight back."

Pearce thought about that in view of what Lloyd had previously let slip.

"What's he paying you, honestly?" He proffered his uninjured thumb in Charles' general direction. "Getting me here under false pretences." He shrugged his shoulders. "It's your money to lose."

Just at that moment they heard the back door to the kitchen open and slam back in its frame. Seconds later Jimmy Paxton entered the room, his expression was a picture of concern.

"Just got word from Alan, Joe's mate. He says they've located Lloyd, but there's trouble. Reckons Miss Grant and Joe are out on the water trying to fish for him."

"This I've got to see." Pearce scrambled awkwardly out of his chair. "Come on Hanlan. If you're lucky he might drown and do us both a big favour."

Hanlan was also slowly to his feet. He didn't much care for Pearce's growing exuberance and thought it the right to pull him up in his tracks.

"Be careful what you wish for Peter. Blood is thicker; you know how it is."

"Do I? You'll have to do better than that."

"It's your biggest problem Pearce. You're too narrow minded. Squeezing the facts until they fit your fiction."

They came face to face in the middle of the room. "Lloyd might be my responsibility now, and into the future, I accept that. Broaden your mind, Peter. Maybe it's the past that we need to truly understand." Charles saw growing bewilderment in the other man's eyes.

"Perhaps we should both speak to Claire about that."

16. Up the Creek

Samantha was thinking coolly and logically which was why she gave a high-pitched scream. Needs must. A call for help, just before she dipped her head below the surface. The uninviting dark water was cold and shocking as she tried using her outstretched arms and even her feet to make contact with the drowning man.

The small rowing boat that Lloyd had struck his head against was now drifting on the outgoing tide into a narrow stretch of water. Sam was becoming frantic; she'd last seen him lying face down on the surface alongside the jetty. He wasn't there now.

She took a few deep breaths and was about to go under for a fourth or fifth time when she saw something floating in the wake of the boat. Pale light from the jetty lanterns cast faint but helpful shadows. It appeared that a mooring rope from the bow of the boat was wrapped around one of Lloyd's arms. Casting any doubts aside, Sam struck out in her best front crawl. Her only hope now was to get to him before the boat was taken by the strengthening current out into the main channel and from there down towards the sea.

Where was she? By the time Joe Peterson reached the jetty there was no sign of either of them. The rowing boat had gone too, or at best been taken; an obvious choice if Lloyd intended to make good his escape this way. Of more importance to Joe at that moment was finding Samantha, and quickly. The sound of her scream for help was still ringing in his ears.

He nearly tripped over a pair of loafers and a small black garment left by the edge of the staging. A clue at least and some hope at last. Sam was in the water and by design rather than by accident. He shouted her name and was immediately rewarded by an answering call that ended in a gurgle.

Joe moved quickly to the boat house where he hoped his canoe and paddle would still be found. A memento from his army days, he had used it to keep himself in trim. It was unstable and not easy to get into. Once on the water, Joe soon found his balance and a powerful stroke to match.

Leaving the lanterns on the jetty behind him it took a minute or so for his eyes to adjust to the darkness. He was aware that the wind speed had dropped now that the storm had passed. It was easier to hear against a background noise of rustling reeds and running water. Sounds of splashing close by gave him hope. Lifting the paddle out of the water, allowing the canoe to drift on the tide, he kept his eyes scanning the near distance.

The main channel was metres away, made obvious by the increasing speed of the flow. Joe was ready to call out again when suddenly he saw shapes in the water. Maybe a head, as if someone was swimming on their back. Then something else. Coughing and spluttering as Samantha came up to the surface in a frantic bid for air.

"He's unconscious… Hurry, I'm getting weaker by the second."

Joe's decision making was instant and made easier as the drifting boat was caught in an eddy by some reeds. From the canoe Joe knew he could do nothing and yet with the aid of a better platform he knew there was a chance of saving them both. Ignoring the noises of her exertions, Joe paddled past heading directly for the boat. Once aboard he left the canoe to its own devises and immediately began hauling in on the trailing rope that hung over the side. Sam screamed in fright as Joe pulled harder, dragging Lloyd from her grasp and over towards him.

"Don't worry, I've got him. Swim and save yourself."

With an unknown strength Joe grabbed Lloyd by his shirt collar and pulled for all he was worth. It was a balancing act as the boat threatened to tip over. The harder he pulled the closer he came to falling in himself. Worryingly he'd lost sight of Samantha.

Lloyd's body landed heavily in the bottom of the boat and Joe was unsure if he was still alive. It didn't seem to matter as he was instantly back to the side, scanning the water once more.

"Where the hell are you?" He called with dread in his voice. There was no movement or sign of her. He called again and was relieved when her voice came from somewhere behind him. Stumbling from one side of the boat to the other, a fortunate break in the clouds allowed moonlight to illuminate the immediate vicinity. Samantha was clinging on for her life to the discarded canoe.

"Joe, I can't hold on much longer."

Unceremoniously pitching Lloyd on his side to release an oar, Joe poled the boat away from the reed-bed and back out into the flow of the tide. Finding the other oar easier to come by, he rowed the rest of the way, periodically checking for direction over his shoulder. Seconds later and with seconds only to spare before the boat and canoe slewed ever further out into the main channel, he made a grab and finally had hold of her.

She had nothing left and made no sound as he lifted her bodily from the water. Joe was immeasurably thankful her weight was half that of Lloyd's. In contrast to his previous actions, he was particularly careful in how he laid her down.

"I'm okay." Her voice was weak and she could not stop shivering. "Get the boat… I'll check on Lloyd when I've got my breath back." It was all she could say.

By the time Joe had the craft under some semblance of control, there were signs that Lloyd was at least alive. Sam had straightened him out into a position that looked more comfortable than the one that Joe had dumped him in.

"Take my sweatshirt, do your best to keep warm." Joe tried to lighten the mood. "Not the best conditions for a swim."

Sam would have smiled if she could have stopped her teeth from chattering and in truth, she fully understood that they were not fully out of danger. Despite their predicament she was glad that Joe was there.

"Come here and sit beside me. Careful now. Try to keep out of wind."

Nothing could have stopped her from doing just that. Clambering carefully over Lloyd's body in the bottom of the boat, she found shelter from his arms as he encircled her frame.

"No point in trying to row against the tide." He whispered and when she nodded. "There's a shingle beach further down towards the point. I'll try and get us in there."

Again, she nodded not trusting her voice. As she turned to him in the darkness, he kissed her lightly on her forehead and once on her nose.

The sound of voices and occasional pinpricks of light moving inland gave hope to the boat that their true predicament was realised. Jimmy Paxton could surely be relied on to guide the others across the marshland to the dyke that led down to the sea. The boat was no longer in danger but Joe knew that help would be needed if he was to care for his passengers once they got ashore.

There was only one way back to Sedge House from the beach and negotiating the dunes in the pitch black wouldn't be easy. By the time the boat touched gravely sand and was safely landed, Lloyd was still unable to walk. Joe remained cautious as he carried him through the shallows, over the shingle and further up the slope. His priority was Samantha, still huddled in the bottom of the boat. No wading in the water for her. She too was lifted and carried, still shivering violently from the shock and the cold. Finding shelter in the lee of some scrub bushes, he removed his shirt, using it to rub her down and restore some circulation.

"Try to keep moving. I ought to check on Lloyd again."

Their chaotic slow dance came to a close. Sam was reluctant to let him go. "We missed the party," she mumbled.

"There'll be others." Joe kept his thoughts in the present. "Keep calling out so they know where to find us. That'll help to keep you warm."

It was a relief to hear her voice from somewhere ahead of them and confirmation that they were back on dry land. Guided initially by Jimmy Paxton's lantern, the hastily assembled search and rescue team made good progress across the uneven terrain. A line of varied torch lights scanned the ground and seemed impatient to make more speed. Finally, and only as they reached the top of the dyke, did Jimmy give permission for Alan and the rest to make independent tracks. Jimmy was left to bring up the rear.

Piercing beams of light picked out white legs that must be Sam's, and further on Joe's crouching form as he tended to a figure who remained flat on the sand. Jimmy arrived to see three of the boys taking control of Lloyd, getting him back up the slope using blankets as a makeshift stretcher.

In the chilly breeze Jimmy was aware of Samantha's near nakedness and instinctively took off his light weight jacket, draping it around her shoulders.

"Jimmy, thank you, I'm fine."

Joe joined them in the light of the lantern and was able to see her properly for the first time.

"That was heroic and quite some audition, if you were hoping to make a film. Your boss would be proud."

"Don't ask me to do it again." Sam tried to laugh but felt more like crying. She was coming to realise how lucky she had been.

"You two, come with me, there's something you should know." Jimmy had waited for the others to move on before leading them away from the beach. "We'll go to the hide on the edge of the lagoon."

It took them a while and they walked in silence. Sam was acutely aware that she could have done with some shoes. Once there, holding his lantern high, Jimmy ushered them inside.

"Watch out for the wooden floor; I don't want you getting splinters." Jimmy lit the way and got Sam to sit down on one of the benches. She was drying out but still felt cold.

"The police are here asking all kinds of questions." Jimmy's words came out of the dark. He sounded worried. "Joe, looks as if Ellen Preston's parents must have kicked up a fuss. They're here for Lloyd, but they are very keen to talk to you regarding what you witnessed."

It came as no surprise, and was something that Joe had been expecting. Who could blame them? Going to the hospital and showing concern for Ellen had been a natural reaction and perhaps, a forgivable mistake.

"Look, take a couple of minutes to get yourselves together and then I'll get Samantha back to the house. Mary is there waiting for you." The use of her name seemed to soothe the situation. "Joe, you go straight to the marquee, I've told the police that you weren't trying to leave the country and will meet them there. I've said nothing about Lloyd in all this, so be careful." Jimmy declined to express his opinion further. "I'll wait outside, but don't be too long." Leaving the lantern he moved away and left them to say their goodbyes.

"Let me go with you." Sam was insistent.

He shook his head knowing that there was nothing that she could do to help. "Mary would not be very pleased if you did." It was the only answer that might convince her. "Besides, I'm not sure you're really dressed for the occasion. We don't want to give the police the wrong impression."

A sudden flurry of windblown rain came in from sea. The small wooden hut gave protection and seclusion and in the inky blackness any inhibition was instantly lost. Joe held her firmly in his arms. It felt right in the moment and Samantha had no reservations in responding in kind.

But there was no time.

Jimmy and Mary were waiting, and more importantly the police.

Two figures silhouetted against the light were waiting for Alan's group as they found their way to the back of the house. Head bowed but conscious at last, with a blanket draped across his shoulders, the prisoner looked down trodden and defeated. On regaining his bearings, Lloyd soon understood the mood of his guards and knew that everything had been irrevocably changed. Even so, the last few steps from the wilderness onto the manicured lawn should have had more of an impact as he approached certain condemnation and possible arrest. In truth he lacked the wit to feel anything other than tiredness and crushing humiliation.

What then of his feelings on finding that the police were in fact Peter Pearce and his father? Instant relief gave him hope that a mix of derisory comments and ludicrous excuses might yet come to his rescue. Beg for mercy or go with attack? If only he could rid himself of the confusing pounding in his head. He never got to make the decision, for while Charles was dumb and hesitant, Peter Pearce showed no fear.

"Well look at what the cat dragged in. No offence of course." Pearce acknowledged Alan's presence and noted his intention to remain close at hand. "Left me for dead, eh Lloyd? Not very friendly. It's becoming a nasty habit you're picking up there."

There was no response.

"Moral fibre, son, ever heard of it? And I don't mean the stuff in your breakfast cereal."

Another voice joined the debate.

"A slice of humble pie wouldn't go amiss, either."

A blue satin evening dress, rhythmic in motion moved into the wasted light that streamed through the dining room window. Legs and torso joined in cautious rhythm through her hips, but her arms, which were bare remained firmly folded. When she came to a halt, Amelia kept herself separate, a little to one side of her father and Peter Pearce.

"Ellen sends her love, by the way." She looked straight at Lloyd, without blinking. "Yes, still in hospital; knew you were concerned. As is she about pressing charges. We thought attempted murder, might do." She let her words hit home. "What do you think?"

Lloyd looked visibly shaken, as did Charles, while Peter Pearce looked on in pure fascination.

"That was an accident. I thought she was dead, there was nothing I could do." Lloyd's croaky voice blurted the words out into the night.

"And?" Amelia was incredulous. "So, you just left her?" Cold contempt and hostility blazed in her eyes. "Is that what happened to me?"

Peter Pearce was waiting for Lloyd to fight back in what could only be described as a one-sided affair.

"Go back to New York, when you get out of prison, brave little brother. And don't worry," she paused as if making a decision. "I've no intention of going there myself. Not now."

Just at that moment blue coated officials appeared.

"The only one who needs protection now is you." She looked towards Peter and Charles for a second. "No doubt your father and mine will get together to sort it all out."

With that Amelia spun on her heels and left the men to their collective confusion, and within her own mind, the fear that she should have taken the trouble to say more. There was no more time to worry.

A paramedic and two policemen took control of the situation. And Lloyd, not for the first time that night, was taken in hand.

17. Calm After the Storm

Officially Claire Williams was visiting out on Long Island and in truth she was very glad to be there. A boarding school with extras and a fancy name that had become code for this particular kind of institution. In the weeks that followed, term time had strict rules and familiar routines. A popular place, she even made friends. Her absence from home, although necessary, produced mixed feelings in the two men who had different reasons to miss her. Bizarrely, both felt less guilty because she was gone. For Peter Pearce, Bene's for a beer could be openly spoken of, rather than be wrapped up in the deception of going out for a breath of fresh air.

"Not that she ever believed you." Lloyd could speak of his mother with a new sense of acceptance tinged with regret. He too was spending time in a correctional facility to help him see the error of his ways. The likely outcome of a forthcoming appearance in front of a parole board, would depend on continued good behaviour and reliable testimony given on his behalf.

Peter Pearce listened on his mobile while taking another sip and acknowledged that Lloyd was probably right. "I'll be going into rehab myself if I don't cut back on this stuff." He touched the beer glass with his fingers. "Accepting your faults is the only way forward. I think I can speak for us all. Better to frequent the bars and sip cold ales than sit behind them, eh mate?"

"Very funny."

"Seriously though, this is your last chance. Another f… up and they'll throw the key away."

"I know, I know." Lloyd sounded weary and slightly defeated. "You're definitely flying back for the hearing?" The question was tinged with desperation.

"Wouldn't miss it for the world. Your Mother has made me promise." Peter paused for effect. "You do your bit, I'll do mine."

He cut the call and reached again for his beer. Next to it and on the table in front of him was a curled-up copy of the latest Stress magazine. He used his free hand to flatten it out. It was well thumbed and dog-eared despite having just rolled off the presses. A photograph taken by Nick Sayers adorned the front cover, under the headline of – "The only girl to have said no."

"Well, I wouldn't say…" Peter Pearce didn't finish the sentence, glad that Lloyd was not present and that nobody was there to hear him. Setting a good example, something that his son could be proud of would take a great deal of effort; misogyny still ran in his veins.

Amelia Highland's head and shoulder pose was in fact a very good photograph. It gave an insight into her character as well as showing off her physical charms. Headstrong, challenging, comfortable in her own skin, Nick had managed to capture a unique and privileged snapshot of intimate change. He'd alluded to it in his introductory piece, describing Amelia as a butterfly still drying her wings.

"Very prosaic." It went against the grain to admire Nick's work but in this case, it was difficult not to. He could only hope that the feeling was mutual. Under Amelia's picture, a caption of his own name appeared. A feature article, a world exclusive, of which he was the author. Unlimited access to the King of the Theatre and a personal take on why his daughter would not be going to make a film with NRG.

Libi Sayers, the fixer, had been as good as her word. Even now Pearce wasn't sure how she'd managed to persuade him and his old adversary to sit in the same room. A few weeks ago; impossible. His own hatred, sniping at Charles, had been hard to give up.

Peter smiled to himself. The dented pride had not been unique or a one-sided affair. For Charles and Peter, washing their dirty linen in public had proved the most radical form of therapy. Despite their reticence and subsequent bruising picked up along the way, they had agreed to look to the future rather than regret what had gone on before.

Peter flicked through the pages. No longer the original hard-hitting question and answer piece, the article had become a platform for confession and both had taken the stand. The relevant blood tests and Charles' diagnosis of infertility were indisputable facts that had made a powerful introduction. Rather by chance than acting on any suspicion, Charles had explained how a series of minor complaints and a doctor's investigation had made it clear that Claire had not been faithful to him. He'd digested the implications along with his prescription while coming to terms with the knowledge that Lloyd could not be his son.

"I had mumps as a teenager. I never gave it a second thought. So, when the doctor confirmed the need for birth control was all but irrelevant, Claire was already pregnant. To be honest, and this is where it gets difficult, I was more worried about any future relationships than the one I was already in."

"You had designs on Jelena Highland. You always hoped that one day she'd be with you."

Charles had not disputed Peter's assumption.

"I never asked Claire who she was sleeping with. I certainly never realised it could have been you." It was an awkward moment. "Why did you continue to have anything to do with her after the way she treated you?"

"Getting my own back, pure and simple. Trying to hurt you and take revenge on Highland. I never did my sums when it came to apportioning blame." Peter referenced the Italian trip. "When they died like that, I actually felt cheated. I wanted recognition for the material he stole. With him gone you became the next best thing to target."

The stolen material? There was no proof of that. However, Charles didn't require much persuasion to believe that it was probably true. Maurice had been quite ruthless and always got his own way. To be fair, the marital arguments he'd had with his wife, Jelena deserved to be judged in a different light.

And that was where the confession became more difficult for Charles. Admitting to stepping back, allowing them to bicker and bully each other was the least of his crimes. That he'd not been able to confess his love for someone else's wife, not even to himself, highlighted his own failings.

"We were so young." The words were as lame as the way he spoke them. "I became jealous and thought I was missing out. Succumbing to Claire's advances was a total cop-out. I ruined her life and my actions impacted heavily on you." By association Lloyd had also been affected. "Jelena always said she'd eventually go back to Sommovia. I remember her saying this country was no longer a proper place to bring up her child. She claimed the British were morally destitute…" Charles wondered if this might still be true. "… although that never stopped her taking advantage of the good things in our culture while she continued to live here."

"And Maurice, what did he have to say about that?"

"Maurice? He didn't seem bothered. Well initially I didn't think so." Charles remembered his own desperation. "I was the one who tried to convince her, almost begged her to stay. You can see how crazy that was." Charles shook his head, trying to rid himself of the memory. "Doing my best to keep them together while deep down I wanted her to myself. I pretended my interest was purely about the business. That's why I persuaded them to go away together, although deep down I think they were running on fumes. I was buying time." Charles made his excuse. "By agreeing to take care of Amelia, I'd made certain that Jelena would definitely be coming back."

But she never did. In the article Pearce had not held back in detailing the mysteries surrounding Maurice and Jelena's disappearance. Whether either was still alive by the time the car had come to a halt at the bottom of the canyon, nobody could say. "It was a straight piece of road." Pearce was unconvinced, while Charles lived with knowledge that without his intervention and interference Maurice and Jelena might still be alive today.

It was the first time that Pearce had genuinely felt sorry for Hanlan. A watershed moment that had had a powerful effect. Learning about the burden of holding onto regrets and atoning for your mistakes, well, Charles was way ahead of him. Peter could only hope that by writing the article for Stress Magazine, he was part-way to beginning the process for himself.

"Another beer?" Peter was half way out of his seat. He stopped and thought about it, in the time it took to refold the magazine.

"No, I think I've had enough for today."

*

When it was obvious that Amelia Highland had rejected the chance to work in America, Samantha Grant was kept busy on other NRG projects. In some ways she felt her work in England had ended in failure and that her status within the company had been severely dented. Fellow colleagues, so it was whispered, wondered if the tag of golden girl had been misplaced or permanently lost.

In truth, there was a measure of mixed emotions on both sides of the Atlantic. Rosalind Powers in particular had confessed her relief that the film would now not be made. Flattered? Of course, that her husband had wanted to honour her, and by his choice to cast Amelia. In reality, it just wasn't her style

"Besides, I'm not dead yet, Sherman. Better to wait until I am." Rosalind's take on the inevitable had been the final nail, and a stake through her husband's heart. He'd been sullen and unapproachable for the next three days but not enough, she noticed, to put him off his food. Never the less in her determination that she should make amends, Rosalind had used her husband's self-imposed isolation and sulk-time extremely well. If resurrection was seen to be the ultimate miracle, then her hastily conceived and audacious plans might yet prove to be pivotal.

It was the article in Stress, written by Peter Pearce that had caught her imagination. Two feuding school boys on the road to becoming friends. At least that was how it came across to her. Rosalind wondered if she may yet have ideas to turn things round for NRG. Success would depend on Amelia but in ways that might be surprising. Her absence continued to tug at Rosalind's heart. She could only guess at the hidden scars and latent damage that the young girl carried inside her. In all the commotion and drama at Sedge House it would have been easy to overlook and diminish the effects it must have had on her.

She confided in Samantha Grant. "But it has to be much, much more." She sounded passionate, waving her copy of the magazine in the air. "That's why we need Peter Pearce and Sedge House to be a part of it. See the real story we've witnessed. You, more than me were in at the sharp end." Rosalind didn't require a hard-sell approach to be convincing. "There's unfinished business with Amelia too."

Samantha surprised herself by how much that meant to her. The thought that this might just be the beginning proved a powerful boost.

Rosalind got up from the couch and helped herself to another cup of coffee. Louise, Sherman's secretary was keeping a lookout in the outer office for signs of her boss.

"Forget what you're doing here and go back to Britain. Take Mr Sayers if he'll go with you. Leave me here to explain everything." Rosalind could see hope and dismay in Samantha's expression and knew in an instant that she must definitely go. "Don't worry about Sherman." She spoke with determined affection. "If I have one suggestion, take some time to give your private life a chance. No guarantees, but I would say that's probably a good idea."

18. And Later

Once again back in Britain, Nick Sayers had stayed in London whilst Samantha had planned a detour to Suffolk.

"Just following orders," had been her ready excuse in pursuing unfinished business with a certain ex-soldier. "As you'll be aware, we have a weird kind of history that includes swimming and boating. I never got to say a proper goodbye to him."

Rosalind Powers had made sure she spoke to Nick before they left and asked him to keep an eye on Samantha. "She seems a little fragile to me. Her confidence is low despite her heroics."

She referred to his upcoming meeting with Charles Hanlan.

"I was truly inspired by what took place in England. It makes for quite a story. I'm still trying to placate my husband." This seemed to be taking all her sweetness and determination. "There's no point in getting him excited and then it all goes tits up. Sorry Nick, I'm being crass, but presently he's like a child who's lost his favourite toys. More importantly tell Amelia to keep the faith." Whatever she had up her sleeve, Rosalind knew it was important to keep in touch.

The route from Heathrow to Hanlan's offices was becoming all too familiar.

"What brings you back here so soon?" Charles welcomed Nick and tried to keep his interest casual.

"Some follow-up work for NRG and revisiting old friends." Abiding by Rosalind's strict rules of confidentiality, he kept his answer simple. Fortunately, this did not preclude the opportunity to discuss a subject very close to both of their hearts.

"I had to tell her if only to fill in the blanks. Personally, I think that she remembers more than she's prepared to admit." Charles held his hands up in mild resignation. "Amelia is adamant I should have told her what went on much earlier. Maybe she's right. There was no winning whatever I did or didn't say."

"Suspected rape or at best, interference. How did she take it?"

"Better than I expected; quite philosophically really." But Charles didn't sound sure. Underlying revulsion burned hotly as if to scold him.

Nick jumped back in. "A difficult subject to process. Has it jogged her memory at all? I gather Lloyd is still not prepared to talk to you or even admit his guilt."

"Peter Pearce has taken on the responsibility of father-figure. Not before time."

"Pearce?" Nick was confused, if not a little astounded that Charles appeared so ready to concede his position. "And you're happy to trust his judgement?"

"In view of everything else that has happened, I don't have a lot of choice. Apparently, he and Lloyd first spoke about it on the night of the party. Lloyd panicked and thought that Pearce was planning to lift the lid on a pot of trouble. Look, we've spoken at length and we're agreed Lloyd must admit to his failings and understand their consequences. What he let happen to Ellen Preston is truly unforgivable." Charles shook his head. "Amelia seems more distraught about that than anything he put her through."

"Lloyd has got off pretty damn lightly, whichever way you look at it."

Charles did not disagree. "Whatever the nature of the establishment he's ended up in, it's a prison of sorts and he'll live with a criminal record for the rest of his life. I'm to blame as much as he is in a way. Claire and I should have dealt with the problem. Made sure both the children received the attention they deserved."

Halan was contrite. "Too busy fighting."

"Ultimately, if Amelia requires help, I'll see that she gets it. Turning down the film in New York was her own decision." Charles seemed keen to give an assurance. "Even Claire is prepared to accept that circumstances have changed. For that I have to give thanks to Peter. I never thought I'd hear myself say that."

Charles leaned back in his chair while making a decision. A small smile appeared on a serious face and then threatened to get larger.

"Anyhow, putting our troubles to one side, what are you up to for the rest of the day?"

Nick looked around him searching for an ally. No Sally Stewart to help him escape. "Nothing especially. What 's on your mind?"

"You'd be doing me a personal favour." Charles checked that he had permission to continue. "You must have done wedding photography before."

*

The marriage of Ellen Preston to David Ward was a small and casual affair. In a tranquil setting, the Registrar and her faithful assistant wore happy and infectious smiles throughout. Confidence emanated from her and supporters of the nervous bride and groom took great comfort from this. There was collective relief that only passing reference was made of the traumas that Ellen had recently undergone. Pale in complexion, a little less sparkle in her eyes, it would be a while before she was fully recovered. It was noticeable how tightly the bride held onto her husband's hand throughout the ceremony.

Amelia was a witness and signed the register, while Nick, who would be taking her back down to Avondale as soon as the reception was over, was glad to find his photographic talents had not been called for beyond his personal interest.

The reception itself was held in a private room at the back of the pub and was the perfect place to relax and celebrate. Real ale in barrels, iced cold lagers, whites and reds, roses and champagne. The buffet dinner had food to die for, simple fare but beautifully presented and plenty of it for every taste. Amelia had not planned to stay for long but was made so welcome she found it difficult to leave. She chatted and mixed with both sides of the new family who treated her as if she were one of their own. It was only as the party was nearing its end that Ellen's parents took Amelia to one side for a private and more serious conversation.

It was about the man that had saved Ellen's life. They wished to express their regret for any trouble they may have caused him. Involving the police had seemed their only option. Of course, now that they understood what had actually happened... but he hadn't come forward, had he?... and that had made them suspicious. They'd wanted to thank him in person but understood he was a very private man... and yes, they were gradually coming to terms with it all. Ellen had insisted on her innocence and in view of her marriage to David, that was probably just as well… wasn't it?

Amelia felt a tinge of guilt.

A small commotion interrupted the conversation as Nick Sayers indirectly came to her aid. Aunt Edith, on David's side of the family, had apparently been on the Guinness right from the off. Unfamiliar high heels were blamed initially. Her ungainly dismount from a bar-stool on the way to the loo had probably proved her true undoing. Not that she was drunk, well, perhaps a little squiffy, and that could be blamed on the champagne rather than the pints. Praise for Nick's intervention was later given, who in catching her had received an unfortunate blow to the eye. Aunt Edith`s nose was duly powdered where under different circumstances it might well have been squashed flat.

Cue, time to leave. While Nick was consoled by a glut of middle-aged women, Amelia took time to say a heart-felt goodbye to her friend.

"I've missed you not being around, and I'm sorry for what happened, more than you know."

Ellen hugged Amelia with emotion that was about to overflow.

"I'm not sorry, not really, not when you see what I have now." She gazed across the room at David before turning back. "I was going to leave him. I didn't tell you that. What a mistake that would have been. These past few weeks, he's been absolutely brilliant."

Ellen dabbed at the tears that ran down her face, but she wasn't alone in this. Nick was doing something very similar.

New York to London, an unexpected wedding and then straight on to the west country. Nick had slept well and laid-in before going into town. He happily took Mary's collie for a walk and saved a busy woman another chore. He and the dog soon got their bearings in what was unfamiliar territory for one of them. It was as they reached the path by the river that the collie pulled harder and became impatient to show him the way.

Later in the garden at Avondale, bright colours pulsed from the broad planted borders and flowering shrubs surrounding the patio where they sat. Sun-bathing was very much in order and judging by her colour Amelia had been practising it for most of the day. Nick surveyed the scene through his one good eye and wondered if he hadn't gone to heaven. They were reliving his big moment from the previous day.

"Next thing she elbows me straight in the face." He removed his sunglasses

Amelia came closer to check the swelling under his left eye.

"Don't touch it woman, it bloody hurts." Nick swatted away her probing finger while Amelia struggled to keep her facial expressions under control. She sat back in her sun lounger, casually trailing her fingers through the nearest bobbles of blue. The smell of lavender permeated the air.

They fell into silence. She sat up and reached for her sun cream, offering the bottle to Nick before using it herself. Shoulders and arms were liberally dealt with, her hands moving over her skin with poise and grace that seemed to him, almost balletic. Hitching her short skirt even higher she started the process on both her legs.

"Have I ever told you how beautiful you are."

"Yeh right." Amelia continued with what she was doing, totally unconcerned that he was looking on.

"It doesn't worry you that I say that?"

"Well, no not really. I mean, I know you're being sincere and all that, but I trust you. Besides you're a happily married man, again."

"Thanks in part to you of course." Was it only a few weeks ago that he'd held Amelia in his arms? Nick smiled at the memory. "It never really bothered you though, me being around?"

Amelia stopped what she was doing. "You were there to help me and I was grateful. All I wanted was to give you something in exchange. Nothing happened." Finished with the sun-cream, she sat back and seemed to come to a decision.

"I remember what he did to me, if that's what you're wondering." As she spoke, Amelia looked towards the house and up at her bedroom window. "Not all of it but enough to guess at the rest."

"And?"

"And I need to be able to trust in people again." Amelia thought back to the previous day and how Ellen had been with her husband. Self-consciously she laid her hands in her lap. "I can't go on suppressing, well, me forever."

"Is that what you're doing? Keeping yourself in check?"

"By all accounts I'm just like my mother, who for all the good things she gave me was not always conventional. You might say that's a good thing? But knowing me as I do, I can't be certain I didn't lead Lloyd on."

At last Nick began to grasp her true inner feelings. "Some men use that as their excuse for the inexcusable. Lloyd should have seen you were vulnerable. He drugged and fed you alcohol. Don't judge yourself too harshly. You've had dubious role models. Claire for one, who was…" Nick struggled to find a seemly description, "… not adverse to using her charms to get what she wanted. As for your mother's reputation, don't believe the worst in her. If Samantha was here, she'd be telling you the same. She thinks your gorgeous." He saw movement by the kitchen door. "Besides you've always had Mary's influence to guide you. Now who could be more virtuous than her?"

Just at that moment a familiar voice warned them of her own and imminent arrival.

"Too much sun will make you wrinkle and too much talking will make your throat dry."

Nick could see Jimmy grinning in the background.

"And don't think I'm bringing tea out here for you. You've both got legs." Mary did not look in any specific direction. "Some more obvious than others, I see. Try using them. We're in the kitchen, the tea is poured and I've baked a cake."

19. With Joe

Joe Peterson was not alone but remained focused on the job in hand. Walking around the farmer's market he was compelled to consider his various options. Following meetings with wildlife conservationists, protection for the newly created pools and low-lying islands at the back of Sedge House was now top of his agenda. Four legged predators in the shape of foxes and badgers had proved unerringly stubborn when it came to looking for a meal. A suggestion too, that grazing cattle could become natural controllers of this special habitat had prompted Charles and Joe to understand that stock fencing was essential if these problems of trespass were to be overcome.

The clock-tower in the middle of town struck eleven and Colonel Bradbury, out of professional habit checked his watch. His voice on the phone had sounded insistent, which by the very nature of his rank was to be expected. Joe felt fortunate that his former superior had made an effort to see him in person. They strolled together in silence before choosing a quiet corner of the livestock market for their informal chat.

"Just happened to be passing on my way up to Lincolnshire. Thought I'd give you a heads-up on the latest from Eastern Europe." The Colonel looked very much at home in his country tweeds as he surveyed some of the saleable young-stock. "Encouraging developments. Much needed, Joe. The U.N. have pussy-footed around for long enough and were in danger of losing all credibility." Bradbury could not hide his obvious and deep-seated frustration. "Anyway, that's another matter for another day. We finally got the green light to go in and make some arrests. Both men were in charge of prison camps. Small fry, but it's a start." A small smile broke out across his face. "One in custody and the other was shot whilst trying to escape." The Colonel undoubtedly saw this as a sign that justice had been done. "Tracking down war criminals in Sommovia has been given priority status at last." Sarcasm tainted his words.

"How strong is the appetite to go after the bigger prizes?" Joe could imagine how invincible the most powerful perpetrators of crimes must be feeling. "No reprisals, I'm hoping?"

"Not that I've been made aware of. But then no action is devoid of some reaction. Many of them seem to have gone to ground and surrounded themselves with their own supporters. Of course, in part it's thanks to you and agents from other countries that we have the knowledge of who these people are."

Joe just simply nodded his head.

"Moving on." Bradbury cleared his throat and assessed Joe's lack of reaction. "Apart from the obvious benefits of making these arrests, there are some optional add-ons you might be interested in." He wanted to give some positive and personal feedback. "Firstly, it gives me the freedom to expand a little more on Maurice Highland and his tragic death, something we first spoke about a few months back. However, I tell you this with serious reservations. Are we clear on that?"

"What you don't know can't hurt you?" Joe understood that the Colonel was taking a risk and putting his faith in him to act accordingly.

"It'll bring things full circle, Joe. The smart money suggests that Maurice Highland actually died in Central

Sommovia and not, as it was reported at the time, in Italy with his wife. Remember this all happened before war broke out." He made no hesitation in offering this information. "The circumstances behind the death are still a mystery. The coverup was definitely politically motivated and this is where the complications arise." Bradbury paused for obvious effect. "The next targets under consideration for arrest will definitely make headline news and for very different reasons. The Southern Sommovian government is under all kinds of pressure to release its secrets and keep Eu leaders appeased."

"So, why were Maurice and Jelena Highland's deaths hushed up? Surely, they'd be seen as inconsequential figures in all of this."

"A good question and one that our special friends across the water don't want to answer at this time. Let's just say that our government was leaned on and told to toe the line. We agreed to fake the story of the car crash in order to deflect attention away from a so-called 'investment'." Bradbury hoped that Joe could read between the lines. "At a critical time for the causes of regional independence it was deemed too inflammatory to make public. War was inevitable. But why our allies thought it necessary to pander to criminals, is controversial to say the least."

"Politics." Joe offered. "It sounds like the various councils of war gambled heavily to get better returns."

The colonel wasn't about to argue. "One man from Britain, tragically killed. We were told not to quibble about where he was found." It sounded a little too simple. "The fight for independence in the region started with the end of communism, but ethnic cleansing was rife long before then." He shrugged his shoulders. "Whatever happened to the Highland's, the investigation was quashed because no one was prepared to upset the fragile status quo."

Joe absorbed the implications before asking the inevitable question. "If they flew out to Italy, why then go to Sommovia?"

"That's a matter of some conjecture, but we believe it had to do with a family dispute. Jelena appears to have driven herself across the border and Highland followed her later that same evening. He was familiar with her family's village and probably guessed that was where she was headed."

"Not running away then. The rumours were rife."

Bradbury could only surmise. "Family loyalty means everything in Sommovia. You must know that better than most. Jelena could never have imagined the danger she'd be putting herself in, or predicted the final outcome that did for her husband. Her daughter was safely in somebody else's care. Maybe that gave her false bravado."

Joe sensed that the conversation was coming to a close. Was he now to be rewarded for his patience and find out the true purpose of Colonel Bradbury's visit?

The man himself was checking his watch and in the time it took to do that, came to a decision with a statement of trust. "If I'm permitted to offer you one piece of advice, then now is a good time to grab what's left of the summer and go dip your toes in the Adriatic for a week or two. Sightseeing, that kind of thing. Go for a drive away from the coast, there's a beautiful place on the way to… I've got it written down somewhere." Bradbury fished around in his jacket pocket before handing over a neatly folded envelope. "See the country in a different light now that the war is over. I think you'll find it useful, educational even. Just keep in mind that knowledge is power and must be used carefully. I've said much more than I was supposed to. I'll leave you to make the right calls as you see fit."

*

Six weeks had slipped by before Samantha Grant went on the water again. Having made the decision to do so, it seemed best to go back to the place where she had nearly drowned. Had it become an issue for her? She'd had very little spare time to give it much thought. A strong gust of wind made the boat heel over. Holding onto the jib sheet, Sam leaned out over the side as Joe had taught her. The noise of rippling water beneath the bow was infectious and at that moment she felt there was no better place to be.

"Ready about." Joe gave warning before turning into the wind. The boom swung across and the sails lost their shape and their certainty, as Samantha athletically transferred her weight to the opposite side of the boat. Once on their new tack she could see they were passing the shingle beach where they'd managed to get ashore the night of the party. She remembered how Joe had carried Lloyd to safety before coming back to spare her getting wet and cold again. These were memories that had sustained her during a difficult period back at work in America.

The boat was picking up speed again and the wind ruffled the surface of the water. Sam looked at Joe as he adjusted the mainsail while keeping a firm grip on the tiller. There was a reassuring confidence about him, that was agonizing too. She was painfully aware that since arriving at Sedge House, they'd not even so much as touched.

Joe sailed to the mouth of the estuary before turning the boat to run with the wind. Within minutes the shingle beach was upon them once again. The tide, which was high, would soon be on the turn. Joe shed the wind from the sails and seconds later there was a gentle scrunching sound as the bottom of the boat touched coarse sand. With the sails downed and roughly stowed, they paddled ashore pulling the boat up the beach behind them.

"Thought we'd go and look at the hide, if you'd like to?" For the first time Joe wasn't so sure of himself.

They scrambled up and away from the water, just as they'd done on that memorable evening. Sam looked around her and was intrigued to see how even in daylight the dunes were a wonderful wilderness, a desolate delight.

"Not sure I can wait until we get there." She tried not to be shy, hoping her encouragement was not misplaced.

Joe came to an immediate halt and bending down felt the warmth of the sand with his fingers.

"Sand or splinters, Sam? It's not much of a choice." He pretended to be serious.

Sam took little time to consider her options and began immediately unbuttoning her shirt.

Sand or splinters, it didn't much matter. In the end she had to contend with both.

Postscript

Sommovia

One day and totally out of the blue a man appeared. A foreigner who seemed quite at ease with himself and with the place he was visiting. Tall and tanned, a working man, who held himself much like a soldier.

Not that it was a huge surprise to see him. It was what some locals had feared and most expected. It was as if he was giving out a gentle warning for what was to come. Deana's plans for work in the café did not change and she diligently remained close and on hand if required.

He, this man and his lovely girlfriend spent most of the morning in and around the village. It was past midday when they began asking for directions to the old house and tower that was a popular place for sightseers before the war.

Much had changed in the intervening years. Bigotry, racism, rape and murder the backdrop to a recent history that had made the village more insular. Close family were all that some had left to protect. Deana who owned the bakery and ran the café had recently welcomed the return of a sister back down from her mountain hideaway, back to the place where she had been born and raised. The celebrations were muted but the feelings of relief to have her back were obvious to all. Lena is now much changed from the gregarious and beautiful spirit she'd once been. Her greying hair barely hides the scar to the side of her head and the lines on her face can only hint at how much she has suffered.

The sisters' cousin had tried to make his peace with the world by putting crosses on maps to show where the graves are. The authorities had given assurance that there would be no retribution as a reward for his full confession. The slate has been wiped but could never be cleaned. True identities were buried as fellow countrymen and women fought their boundary-wars. Only days before, they'd lived as neighbours.

Lena has no memory of this. She touches the scar the bullet made. This is the one remaining link to her previous life. That the bullet was meant for the centre of her head is something that can't be forgotten or denied. She doesn't smile but the café is home to her now. She loves to bake and make delicious pastries. It must be a natural talent. The local villagers praise the flavours and her simple, childlike artistry. This is what gives her pleasure and the reason she gets up every morning. She works alongside her sister whom she doesn't remember. Deana is content with that and has never tried to change it, maintaining it's better to give love and show that you care. Better that than having no sister to love at all.

The foreigner and his girl have a need for coffee. He doesn't rush the process and allows the air in the café to settle. Joe Peterson speaks a little Sommovian and that helps to break the ice. He seems to know who he's speaking to. He never says so, not outright, but Deana understands this and is naturally defensive.

She decides to take a semblance of control and show Joe that she's not afraid of him. They sit and drink a coffee together, preferring a table outside the café. They talk in hushed tones and look intently across at each other. Studying each other's expressions is to appreciate the spirit of the words as they speak them.

The girl called Samantha prefers to watch from inside and not take on the language barriers that make understanding impossible. Meanwhile, Lena works in the kitchen and knows nothing of what is taking place; isn't aware that her future-life is the subject of a difficult conversation.

And then Samantha becomes more animated. She stares out through the window and sees Joe and Deana are now standing. After some hesitation they embrace but the process looks awkward and unnatural.

Both come back inside and Deana is doing her best to hold back some tears. Again, Samantha senses that this is out of character. There's a tension within all of them that makes her feel emotional and full of despondency. That changes when Deana comes over to hug her as well. The deep breaths and tentative smiles somehow make the difference.

With perfect timing the door from the kitchen swings open and Lena backs her way into the room. She's holding a tray of freshly baked cakes and wants to show off how busy she has been. As part of their ritual, she offers her sister, who is more intent on drying her eyes than eating, the first of the batch for her approval.

Perhaps of more significance was Samantha's reaction to selecting a cake of her own. Speaking in plain English to Lena she said "thank you, they look great". It was fascinating as all froze in the moment to anticipate what her reaction might be.

Initial confusion was all too predictable as she said nothing to show her understanding of Samantha's compliment. It was only as Lena returned to the kitchen and the door began to close, that all heard her say, "You're welcome."

PART TWO

Additional Characters

Deana Horvat: Sister to Lena.

Marin: Mature student at Mezlar University.

Kaira Maes: Dutch anthropologist and translator.

Gabriela Simic: Jelena Horvat's school friend.

General Berislavic: Sommovian war hero. Father of Slavco.

Helen Matic: University lecturer.

Migration

"So, Helen, I'm guessing Sommovia has its own Tourist Board. I'm told it's a beautiful place to visit. But I can't believe you're actually going to live and work there."

"Why sound so surprised? I've always wanted to go to Europe. My surname is surely a giveaway. I have family connections out there. I'm proficient in speaking the language."

"Presumably your immediate relations left for good reasons, back in the day. Why now the attraction to go back? Tell me it's Paris you're going to and I'd get it. I've never even heard of Mezlar."

"I'm not sure why you're playing at being so ignorant."

"Because you've got it all here in Australia. With your musical talents and teaching abilities you'll be so much in demand. I know that other Eastern European countries like Yugoslavia are more accessible now the Iron Curtain has started to crumble, but things are far from stable; probably about to get worse in the short term."

"Ah Ha, the geography teacher returns."

"Just being sensible. I'm losing a valued colleague and friend here."

"But we don't have an organ."

"I'm sorry about that. I'll grow one especially."

"I'm drawn to it. Playing dramatic pieces in church or even a cathedral. I'd take that all day long. It feels like I'll be closer to the centre of the world. I'll make friends and travel to other parts of Europe during the holidays."

"And in the meantime?"

"Look after your kids and that husband you're so proud of. I can fly back and visit. In the meantime, I'll miss you."

"So, tell me again. Adriatic islands and a coastline to soak up the sun on. Lakes and mountains. Culture and art steeped in history. I suppose it has potential, but don't be owned by it. Eventually we want you to come back to us."

1. Sommovian Teens

Early 1970s

Fresh snow falling, although beautiful, came at sensitive times that winter. With power to inspire playground joy and alternate cravings of hibernation, this could change with the light in the sky; sometimes vivid and appealing, sometimes dull and depressing. For two sixteen-year-old girls, realising their dreams would depend on new shoots of potential surviving the snow-melt and into the spring.

Making cushions of their coats and sitting on a wall side by side, they compared the colour of their skin and decided that one had an unfair advantage. Starved of meaningful light, bare limbs were exposed to absorb much needed vitamin D. Arm to arm, leg to leg, variations in pigmentation were inspected with interest and duly commented upon.

"It's got something to do with the amount of melanin you have in your system and the sun's reaction with your cholesterol." Gabriela, the darker of the two, was trying to remember her biology. "And remember my mother's family originally came from Spain. That's why we're so different in colour."

Jelena nodded and wished for the summer when she'd wear her bikini every day the sun shone. "It's the only way I can ever be as beautifully brown as you." She spoke with feigned irritation knowing that her friend could never be that bold.

Gabriela frowned. "You're the lucky one, just you remember that. You get all the freedom." She folded her arms across her body and shivered. "Come on, I'm getting cold sitting here. Let's go and walk along by the river."

They took the wooden steps down the slope towards the fast-flowing water that looked as cold as ice.

"It's such a shame your parents are so strict with you. I bet it's not the same for your brother. He gets away with blue murder. Well, that's what some of the girls say." Jelena knew she was introducing a delicate subject. She waited for a reaction but didn't get one. "And what about the boy that's taking such an interest in you? You must be driving him crazy." She couldn't contain herself any longer. "He must be ready to pop!"

"Don't be disgusting, Jelena." Gabi giggled but was somewhat resigned. "He knows it's not possible while I'm still living at home."

"So, you're going to wait until we both go to university? That's still a year away. I couldn't wait that long." Jelena put her hand to her mouth and pretended to be coy. "In fact, come to think of it…"

"You haven't." It was a statement rather than a question. "I thought as much." Gabriela reached out to touch her friend's arm. "And that's fine by me." She smiled. "I wondered if you'd get around to telling me."

"You're not mad at me?" Jelena shrugged her shoulders. "I made up my mind and well, one thing led to another. It's only happened the one time so far."

To Gabi it didn't sound very romantic but she decided to keep that to herself. "Let's be honest, it was never a competition I was going to win. And not something we could easily synchronise, not unless you're into that kind of thing."

"Gabriela Simic! How could you say such a thing?" Jelena was laughing. "What would your father say if he could hear you?"

Walking down to the path by the river thinking their own thoughts, Jelena took Gabi by the hand and felt that they had never been closer as friends. Swinging their arms to and fro, they instantly became twelve-years-old again and forgot to be world-weary and cautious. Light weight cotton dresses highlighted their care-free movements to make exquisite and innocent shapes framing their bodies.

It was a snap-shot of time that could never be recaptured. Life for these girls, and for their country would eventually change. Lust for power would become the driving force behind a groundswell of reaction. Years of dictatorship was creating a deep-seated identity crisis and small pockets of nationalistic feeling would soon bubble to the surface.

Not that this effected the girls directly, not straightaway. Good exam results meant that they could live out their academic dreams and go to university. Planning immediate futures and celebrating their friendship consumed them in the present. One was naturally artistic and the other more practical and scientific. Jelena was outgoing and Gabriela more reserved. They had decided this was a good combination. Together they were central to the social gatherings amongst their fellow students. Jelena's great singing voice and playing the guitar took the lead, while Gabi remained constant and true with her own sense of humour. There was never serious competition between them and Jelena was happy to admit that Gabi was becoming a beautiful woman who could attract an audience all of her own.

Never living in one another's pocket and invariably claiming a separate set of friends when they were apart, they would always retain a special bond and bring each other up to speed. Sharing a bedroom gave them privacy and the opportunity. It was something they looked forward to whenever they got a chance.

"Not being too obvious but I'm going away this weekend with the cathedral choir. I only mention it if you did want to have someone over to keep you company."

Gabi was not going to help Jelena out. "And?"

"Well, I'm just saying. I don't want you to get lonely and miserable. I know how much you'll miss me, that's all I have to say on the matter."

Both girls burst into a fit of the giggles as they knew the direction this conversation was taking.

Jelena was on a roll. "I realise science is totally different from music but the teaching practices must be similar. You know, experiments and chemical reactions. There must be someone who could give you some oral tuition?"

The giggles continued for some minutes.

The cathedral choir had a growing reputation and the powers-at-be were keen to capitalise on their potential. Travel arrangements for a European tour and an injection of much needed cash allowed Jelena her chance to go to London. While the cat was away one little mouse was brave enough to come out and play. Encouraged by her closest friend, Gabriela Simic did make time for some extracurricular activities. The subject required some privacy and did not appear in any syllabus. Being open-minded, her natural shyness made her vulnerable to cleverly designed approaches.

The young man with grey eyes who was always on the lookout had made his moves appear friendly and welcome.

Not the kind of 'tutor' that even her risk-taking roommate would have approved of, he selected his prey like any natural born predator would have done. He interested her sympathies by explaining that he was soon to go away with the army.

Gabi chose blindness, aware that a leap of faith was required if she were to overcome matters that had become awkward. The need to remove an obstacle and have an experience made her unnaturally careless in her choices.

An outsider to the campus but someone who obviously knew the lay of the land, the young man called Slavco proved a slow burn with seemingly generous expectations. A part of him wanted her to be in love with him. Foreign, yes, but surprisingly beautiful, he took what he came for. Not that she refused him, not at first. His easy victory soon turned into bitter disappointment when things became physical. For Slavco it became a mental aberration he blamed purely on Gabriela's inexperience. The sense of abject failure scarred him deeply. A painful, one-time affair that had far reaching consequences.

Gabi too was hurt, minor bruises and some scratches. The real wounds were more about recrimination and self-loathing. For days she kept all this to herself and believed the world was too cruel for a young woman like her.

From the depths of her depression a phone message made to the University took her completely by surprise. The young man's commanding officer had made that call with evident concern for her wellbeing. Not wishing to embarrass her further, he did offer excuses for the soldier's unbecoming conduct. Falling short of a proper apology, none the less, he conceded that both perhaps should have taken more care.

While others would have taken offence, Gabriela took what solace she could muster from these wise and heartfelt words. All seemed better, all was well, until she found herself in the early stages of pregnancy. As the end of term approached, the prospects of returning to her family loomed large and scared her witless. There was only one friend she could turn to.

"I didn't even get to enjoy it." Gabi's intermittent tears increased to a flow. "And there's me telling you to be careful." She rested both hands on her stomach. "This is going to bugger up all of our plans."

Jelena was failing to keep the anger and her own guilty feelings in check. Gabi's parents had been too strict in their upbringing. She, on the other hand had made sexual interaction sound so easy.

"He could have worn a condom. Or kept it in his trousers. But then again that's not what you were looking for." Jelena held on to Gabi's hand. "You were so unlucky. Maybe we should have synchronised having sex together like you suggested." She tried to inject a little humour.

"He may have been a bastard to me but I'll have to keep the baby." Gabi tried to show a smile amongst the tears and then thought of home. "Maybe I could live in your parents garden shed."

It was a throw-away comment but it got Jelena thinking; a way to make amends. Somehow beautiful Gabriela would survive this and come out on the other side.

Velko Horvat, Jelena's father, was not a wealthy man but he was a planner and uniquely good at his job. Musically minded and good with his hands he had set up his own business in repairing and maintaining church organs. Over the years he had spread his net far and wide and was happy to travel away from home, sometimes for days at a time. When he made money, he tended to save it and when he had made enough, he invested it. Property was king and he understood its value. Jelena's sister, Deana, was a home loving girl who was happy to be in and around her community. The village was crying out for a café and particularly a bakery. When shop space became available, he had the means to secure it. Others who knew Velko well were able to provide short-term loans at small returns knowing that the business would benefit all in the end. New ovens, beautiful furniture complimented the building's new façade and Deana provided the love and the attention that made success a certainty.

Velko did not stop there. Churches and even the cathedral in the capital city, Mezlar, began to employ him on a regular basis. The money he made was good enough to broaden his horizons. Holidays taken on the coast encouraged him to increase his property portfolio and in due course he bought a large apartment on the outskirts of a little fishing village. Little did he know at the time that this would literally become a life-saver for his family.

Gabriela's worst fears of dismay and total rejection never materialised. Her parents were as understanding as they could be, once the initial shock waves and the inevitable tsunami had run its course. Life was not easy for Gabi but she did manage to finish her first year at university before returning home to have the baby the following summer. Her family became insular and rather secretive in the hope that their daughter's misjudgement wouldn't be viewed too harshly by others with spare time and nothing better to do with it.

The summer season was drawing to a close. The large apartment near the coast with its private outside space had proved very useful to Velko's close family and friends who were lucky enough to be invited to use it. It prompted an idea that once considered was thought too good to ignore. The offer to purchase additional land from a neighbour at a knock-down price gave them the chance to build a two bedroomed, self-contained annex. There was one voice in particular which became prominent and was much in favour of this new development.

Velko, although late in life, was ambitious. He submitted the plans and was pleased to see Jelena's interest in the project grow from the moment new ground was broken. Free time that summer was spent with Gabi and her baby boy and included frequent visits to witness the new build's progress in action.

"You'll need somebody to run the place once it's built and then we could rent it out." Velko pretended to look puzzled. "You know, get some revenue out of the investment. I know Gabi would bite your hand off if you were to offer…"

"I hope you haven't made promises you can't keep, Jelena." Velko did his best to sound a word of warning. "But as it happens…" The rest of what he said was drowned out in squeals of delight. Velko was heard to make some derogatory comment about how conniving his youngest daughter had been.

The deal was done with much relief to the Simic family who collectively felt a great weight had been lifted from their shoulders. The day she finally moved in with her son, Luca, was something that Gabi would always be grateful for.

Jelena was going to miss her and the baby. She felt that keenly on her first night back at her digs in the city. Daytime work was a distraction. What she missed was their quiet evenings spent together, planning ahead for tomorrow and into the future. Dreams were important.

Regular trips with the choir to Europe and particularly London had opened her eyes to new horizons. Jelena was one step ahead of the rest when it came to making friends in a strange country; Maurice Highland had seen to that. The tour had been deemed successful and the choir had achieved notoriety with the promise of further excursions the following year. In Jelena's humble opinion that was one year too far into the future.

Settling back into a semblance of routine took some effort as did putting up with her new roommate who was nice enough, but just not Gabi. Jelena found herself staying out of an evening much longer than she wanted to. That was until she had an altercation with a man dressed in Army uniform wanting to know the whereabouts of her missing friend.

"Look, I haven't the time to piss around. I need to know if the baby she's had is mine or some other bastards." His piercing grey eyes held their stare and his demeanour seemed as fierce as the crew-cut he'd given to his hair. Throwing his cigarette down into the space on the pavement between them, the soldier named Slavco, stepped onto Jelena's left foot as if he meant to extinguish her as well. "And don't try to deny it. Your new roommate was happy to tell me all about it once she understood the need for cooperation."

At that moment there was a shout from further up the street as a group of students exited a bar and saw that Jelena appeared to be in trouble. Too many for Slavco to take on alone, although for one moment he fancied his chances. All too public for what he had in mind.

"We'll speak later and I'll want answers." Slavco didn't run but sauntered away with a middle finger raised in reply to the group's jeering and false bravado.

Jelena was relieved to have found a pride of lions to escort her home. Once back on campus, the sight of her new roommate being attended to by her friends brought the seriousness of the situation back into focus. Slavco had been unrelenting in his ability to shock and bully. For all concerned, it seemed that difficult decisions would need to be made and quickly.

To date all in Slavco's Army career had come easily. Fast-tracked by his father to officer status with few capable of matching his drive and determination, it was ironical that having his manliness put to the test had become his greatest weakness. Being near the University had revived awkward memories. Yes, she had been beautiful, easy to dominate and definitely easy to have. Not that it had worked out well. In the space of an unsatisfactory minute, she now had gained the power and possessed a part of him she'd had no right to take.

That irked him greatly. No one should be able to deny him, particularly a girl of mixed-race descent. In these fractious times, girls like her would need friends in high places to protect them. A baby was no use to him, not where his work would undoubtedly take him. Later perhaps, when his country had forced those who didn't belong to pack their bags.

As tensions grew Slavco was aware that scandal might yet destroy his reputation. The relief he felt to be back on duty was palpable and those that he commanded felt the full force of his pent-up frustrations. Trouble was coming. His father would be forced to take on the highest position of responsibility. Civil unrest would last on and off for years. By the time the newly acclaimed General found out his son had a child, it was purely a matter of time before the powder-keg exploded. The slow burning fuses had already been lit and in a country so divided, north and south. Innocents closer to home would bear the General's attention, whatever their creed or colour.

*

2. Marin's Mix

Sommovia: Early 2000s

The chalet-styled cottage had orange-tinged tiles on its roof and dark blue shutters at all of its windows. The front door was of seasoned oak and looked newly treated with restorative oils. The garden was large and mostly cultivated to the growing of fruits and vegetables, in part protected from the prevailing winds by small trees. On the outskirts of the village the property was set back from the road. It had an air of mystery about it. All summer long the washing on the line gave hints to the identities of the couple who had recently moved in. I passed by most days on my way into the centre where I met up with the rest of the men.

Who am I? A man in his late twenties who was about to become an incidental witness to a chain of events that would change his life forever. If I feel privileged now, that was not how my life felt before this all started.

Six years on from the uneasy end of the war, construction was king again. Foreign investors had returned to the parts of Sommovia that had suffered from displacement and the excesses of ethnic cleansing. Plans for development were received with cautious expectation. Burnt-out houses were to be demolished, the ground relevelled and new foundations laid with the desire to start again.

It was something that I lived with; an emotive and personal subject. Few seemed to remember that my ex-girlfriend had been forced to flee our part of the country.

Her family members had never been given that chance. Nationalism is a dirty word in my vocabulary. It's a subject that deserves serious discussion but something I rarely want to mention with any of my friends.

Towards the end of the summer my desire to work full-time was tempered by my other interests. It gave me time to plan my second year at university. The music practice I'd regularly been neglecting sat heavily on my conscious. It was now or never. I'd put money aside for that very purpose and to be honest I craved diversion. My ex had eventually succumbed to her growing depression through the loss of family and her home. A drug-induced and lonely suicide had only added to my heartbreak. Mourning is natural, but should not become self-indulgent.

Days off were my new luxury and cycling into the village to buy coffee and sit by the river became a habit. My presence didn't go unnoticed and locals often stopped to ask me if I was looking for part-time work, cash only. One in particular became insistent but I never accepted. Something about him struck me as odd. When I asked around others spoke of his lonely reputation and hinted at a secretive and chequered past. On a positive note, he helped to solve a mystery. I learnt he was one half of the couple renting the brightly coloured cottage.

Days later, while biking by I met with the other incumbent, a woman. She happened to be out in the garden collecting her laundry from an old-fashioned washing line. Hung from a hook on the corner of the cottage to a post by the vegetable garden, a well-worn track led the way. White with embroidered edges and light as air, a small lace handkerchief escaped on the breeze and floated towards me.

Definitely a tricky challenge, its rescue became immediately vital. I achieved my goal but my bravery lacked any sense of self-preservation. If she was aware that I came to grief she hid it well. Male pride and rigid crossbars don't always go comfortably together. Taking time to compose myself I watched her take down the bed sheets and pillow cases. Her white summer dress with small red flowers in an occasional pattern, looked fresh and appealing. Much like the woman herself. The outline of her body was as obvious as I was in staring at it.

Nothing was said as our eyes eventually met and I reached over the fence to return the handkerchief. To say she was an older woman with grey hair wouldn't do her justice. Her skin was almost flawless apart from the scar to the side of her face, and her movement was still athletic if not graceful. She smiled, I seemed to remember, nodded her thanks and in the same moment she stretched up to kiss me before turning back to her laundry. Instantly I was smitten and infatuated in a very school-boy way.

Towards the end of what proved to be a very dry summer, and with the harvest of barley and wheat all completed, the risk of fire in the valley was utmost in people's mind. I briefly worked for a farmer to help take all the straw from the fields by tractor and trailer. Burning the remaining stubble was an old fashioned and money saving practice that was now deemed bad for the environment. I'd been told many stories of unscrupulous actions that were fashioned as accidents. Fields set ablaze causing burnt straw to fall from the sky like dustings of snow. It was dangerous to the village, and could easily set fire to barns and storage facilities. Most people were much more cautious now.

In the weeks before returning to university I kept an eye out on the house and garden. It became a game of chance and I was happy to wave whenever I saw her. She always stopped and nodded her head to show that she'd recognised me. Then one day I heard her name mentioned in passing and found myself jealous that others should take an interest. The lady with the scar was called Lena. She now worked with her sister in the café on the other side of the river. It was enough to make me change where I bought my coffee and yes, it became my guilty pleasure. Sitting outside with books by my side, I would see her come out from the kitchen, stacking buns and cakes on the shelves. What can I say. There was something special about her.

It wasn't long before things got a little complicated. As someone with no known interest in Lena I had to be careful not to get too close or show I had an opinion. Even from afar I was instantly aware that the man whom she shared the house with was becoming arrogantly vocal. I'd heard the disturbing rumours before, but now he was boasting openly of his dubious past. Common sense said to me he should have been more circumspect. The consequences would impact on him directly and soon.

3. Pure Theatre

London

Snippets taken from personal interviews given to Duncan Marwood, the editor of a best-selling Sunday Newspaper.

Charles Hanlan: Theatre Impresario, property developer, producer of the West End hit musical – Ever Searching.

C.H. – "That we're sitting and talking together must be a milestone in your paper's history. A test of moral fortitude perhaps? But if you print what I actually say and keep it in context, I may even become a subscriber."

D.M. – "Given that you feel you've been harshly treated, and I concede that in part my paper has been responsible for that, I wonder why you never made public statements to refute the rumours much earlier."

C.H. – "Couldn't afford the time to fight you. I may not be everyone's cup of tea and people's perception is always hard to predict. Given what was being inferred I would suggest that those with an average intellect saw the stories for what they were. 'Ever Searching' was so important to my daughter, I used the demand for tickets as a personal gauge. To say that 'There's no such thing as bad publicity' would be to over simplify the position we were in. It was a balancing act between protecting my family's privacy, or stirring up more unmerited interest."

Amelia Highland: Actress and Singer, a major star attracting world-wide attention.

A.H. – "I'm told by my vocal coach that I must have inherited my unique singing voice. I remember my mother singing as a soloist in a choir. That makes me sad but if she were alive today, I hope she could find pride in my performance."

D.M. – "What does the future hold for you now? After much speculation you're breaking away from your father."

A.H. – "Yes, but with his blessing. You in the press have tried to make out that he's controlling and had me under lock and key. As for what happens next, well, maybe I need to take a holiday."

Sherman and Rosalind Powers: Figure-heads of NRG Pictures, an independent film company based in New York.

S.P. – "It's no secret that I have been paying court to Miss Highland. It's not often one comes across a voice like hers when there's so much talent to pick from, both here and in America. I knew immediately I saw her that we could make films together. My wife and I are in total agreement on that."

D.M. – "So you haven't been discouraged by what has happened to her family in the recent months? The bad press hasn't sullied her potential to play the part of your wife, Rosalind, in her biopic for instance?"

S.P. – "Of course the situation is not…

R.P. – "I'll answer that, Sherman. Those are your suppositions, not ours, Mr Marwood. Keep your perspective and find scandal elsewhere for your reader's interest. Self-regulation should be your number one priority, or have you not been reading the papers. Instead of bugging people's phones you should de-lousing your whole business. Wouldn't you agree?"

Four metal chairs surrounded a square wooden table which was positioned in the middle of the stage. Four people sat on the chairs, each with space to deposit pen and paper, mobile phones, a half-smoked cigar in an ashtray, plus a small clutch bag and other paraphernalia. Four glasses and a jug of iced water were the centre piece to a boardroom meeting of some significance.

The house lights were up in The Theatre and maintenance to a row of seats in the circle was coming to a close. Soft lighting from the gantry above, shown down on to the stage without casting shadows, just as they were designed to. The meeting would start but only when they were alone.

Of the four of them the two men were meeting in person for the first time. Charles got up from the table to speak with the maintenance crew. Sherman took note as the younger man moved across the stage and was forced to make unfavourable comparisons with his own fitness. The half-smoked cigar within easy reach was beginning to annoy him.

The women were the best of friends and talked animatedly across their shared corner of the table. Amelia and Rosalind were a generation apart and yet shared the same wicked sense of humour and rebellious spirit that got under the skin of their respective men. Rosalind was much loved. It was the reason that Sherman sat without complaint on his uncomfortable chair. Amelia was still bathing in the afterglow of acclaim from her run in 'Ever Searching'.

In many ways the two women's careers bore favourable comparison. Rosalind's rise to fame back in the day on Broadway gave her unique insight into Amelia's decision-making process. This was the last-chance saloon to be persuaded to give up the boards and go into the studio.

And that was when the conversation became interesting.

“I don’t think that we want it to be truly autobiographical. It gives us a basic premiss on which to work.” Rosalind nodded her head in agreement.

Both men were suddenly silent.

Amelia continued. “Rosalind has already said she doesn’t want to relive her life in film.” She took a couple of seconds. “I want to work in some capacity with NRG, but don’t you think we should both take a back seat for a while.” She spoke directly to her step-father.

“Where does that leave us then?” Charles sounded petulant but knew that Amelia was right. He could imagine how Sherman Powers must now be feeling.

“Let’s look on the bright side. Pick on the positives. Use all the tools at our disposal.” Rosalind took centre stage literally by standing up and talking directly to Charles. “We have this facility, and with your proposed refurbishments here in the future we’d have ample time to do the work.”

“And who plays the lead if not Amelia.?” Sherman would need some convincing.

“Katie Ley.” Amelia said automatically. “The story of an actress trying to live up to the hype, with all the trappings of celebrity mixed in with the dangers of pressure from outside influences. I could go on.”

“Why don’t you?” Rosalind came back to the table.

“Well actually that’s what I want to do. I’ve started writing.” Amelia was surprised at how strongly she suddenly felt. “I’d need help and collaboration. What do you think Rosalind? Something we could do together.”

Rosalind's smile translated her willingness and agreement.

Both the men remained silent, until Sherman shook his head and said, "No. I can see your enthusiasm, but this is too far removed from my original idea. I'm sorry Rosalind but I've reached a point…" He tried to choose his words carefully. "…where I'm finding it hard to focus on new ideas that may well have merit." He hurried on before his wife could argue. "Perhaps it's time for me to consider some of the offers that have been made."

Instinctively she reached out across the table which did much to promote emotion that threatened to overflow. "You don't need to prove your love to me, Sherman. I sure as hell don't want you to feel disappointed. Maybe we do need to look at all of this from a, well let's be honest, a more modern perspective."

"The girls might be right. I haven't said much for obvious reasons." Charles had been criticised for being too protective. "Maybe the story is better suited to television. A multi-part serial that could go into the finer details. Amelia's father, my old partner, would approve of that."

Suddenly things didn't seem so bleak and the four of them spoke avidly for some time. Sheman regained much of his composure but remained under surveillance. Rosalind was anxious but did her best not to show it. She kept her tone light but eventually referenced her husband's state of mind by saying to him.

"I think you're right, Sherman. Now might be a good time to exit stage left and learn some new lines we can both follow and truly understand."

*

4. European Travel

Austria

It wasn't an easy conversation to have. Or rather it was a conversation that was easy to prolong, but without the real hope of finding a satisfactory answer.

"Whoever said that knowledge is power can't have been in this situation." Joe Peterson rubbed at his face with both hands, trying to rid himself of his confusion. "The consequences could be huge."

Samantha Grant poured the last of the wine sharing it between them. "We could get drunk and await divine intervention." She dipped her head to check the levels were even. "No, I'm serious. This problem is for majors in philosophy or religion."

Just as she spoke the clock on the side of the church struck seven times and the sun dipped below the hills on the far side of the lake, responding to the time of the evening. Lights from the distant hotel were suddenly visible, reflecting off the calm surface of the water. A red glow in the sky gave warmth to the end of the day and kept the wine drinkers company.

"What time's dinner?"

"I'm glad we're staying in the village and not over there. I wouldn't fancy the lake-side walk in the dark." Sam shivered and reached for her coat. "I think they said eight."

"We wouldn't want you falling in." Joe stood up and gave her hug. "Not sure how gallant I'd be now that I know you better." He was running before she could hit him.

*

The Hague

Kaira Maes considered herself fortunate on many levels. In her late twenties she'd sampled life in many guises and been blessed with natural talents, many of those she had rightly inherited through her parents. Her father was Dutch, a former dentist, now a forensic scientist, while her Sri Lankan mother practiced acupuncture with a long list of clients. Her ability to pick up foreign languages was however something that even surprised and outshone them both. She sat next to Colonel Bradbury and peered over the top of her glasses, taking in the courtroom atmosphere.

Bradbury was glad of her company. Deceptively pretty, she made little effort with her appearance and seemed unclear of her identity in this regard, possibly due to her multi-ethnicity and quiet disposition. Her levels of concentration made her eyes squint ever so slightly and were not helped by the acoustics of the room, but he knew she rarely missed a thing.

Their flight from London Heathrow to Amsterdam had proved very civilised, pre-booked and planned as had the onward journey to The Hague by train. The special dispensation to attend The International Criminal Tribunal gave them opportunities as yet unexplained. Safe to say that the Colonel had serious interest in a particular case. Keira Maes had reasons of her own for being there, and had everything to do with the practise of genocide and International Humanitarian Law.

As the morning session quickly passed the mood within the room soon changed from formally calm to fractious. Most of what was said was in English, but the defendant spoke in his native tongue with a dialect peculiar to

Northern Sommovia. Keira scribbled notes in a pad resting on her knee and spent time in translating the asides and angry outbursts that the judge was doing his best to restrict. By the time the break for lunch was taken she had written a healthy essay that Bradbury was keen to read.

"This is going to get messy, Miss Maes." He handed back her notes. "File those but keep them safe from prying eyes."

They walked the length of the corridor outside the court room, stretching legs and flexing backs. Colonel Bradbury had to do more of the latter citing his age. Just at that moment a small group of men with angry voices entered the building and started climbing the stairs. They were soon surrounded by security and made no further progress.

"Northen Sommovians," whispered Kaira, loud enough for the Colonel to hear. "Saying something about distorted justice where one side is treated disproportionally and with bias." She frowned a little. "Only not quite said in those particular words."

"Let's get out of here, Miss Maes. We have major problems to consider. Do we know where Peterson is? I'll need to see him in person. There's a good chance that somebody has been careless and over confident. Even I understood when the prisoner shouted the name of the village. We need to get a warning out there to them."

Kaira checked her diary, but was pretty certain of her answer. "Peterson said that he and his girlfriend would be on holiday in Austria."

Bradbury considered his response before saying. "Good, I've always wanted to see Salzburg in late summer. Let's make it happen."

*

Austria

"There's only one person that I'd be prepared to talk to. Not that it would be fair on her." Samantha had weighed up her options. "But if anyone could offer an opinion that I'd be prepared to listen to, it would have to be from Rosalind Powers."

"It begs the question. When are you expected back? NRG must be missing you. What's the latest on this new idea for a film?"

"What am I going to do with you, Mr Peterson. Not only an expert in all you do for the Hanlan dynasty, but now a bone fide film producer." Despite her levity a small black cloud had descended on their conversation.

"One thing at a time, I guess. We both have employers that need some answers and fast." Joe had picked up on Sam's melancholy.

"Which employer takes your preference? Charles Hanlan or your Army friend, Colonel Bradbury?" Sam wasn't trying to be spiteful. "I get the impression that the choice to go to Sommovia was no last-minute decision."

"In some ways, even though we're on holiday, I'm still working for them both in equal measures. The problem is, in being loyal to one doesn't mean I'm being fair on the other."

They walked up from the lake shore towards a group of farm buildings situated in the middle of the village. Beautifully conditioned beef cattle munched on their hay and looked contented. They were worth a small diversion; a faint smell of manure was not in any way offensive. It reminded Joe of the lately purchased animals that grazed the pasture back home in Suffolk.

"Bradbury makes a habit of pointing the way but then expects me to use my intuition. Right now, I feel I'm sorely lacking in that. Maybe we should chat some more over dinner and then leave it for a day or two more. What do you think?"

Good question. Just how Samantha was feeling was probably best kept to herself. Besides, she was there to support Joe, wasn't she?

The large dining room had public and private spaces; the most sought-after tables were by the windows which looked out onto the lake. Sam and Joe were happy to be sat in alcove a few steps up from the main floor. It gave them privacy to talk without the fear of being overheard. Not much was actually said until the delicious soup and bread had been consumed and they'd considered their main course choice from the menu. The waitress in her traditional styled Austrian dress was very polite and attentive.

"I should buy you a dress like that. It would suit you very well. I think I might try the stew and dumplings."

"Don't push your luck, mate. Male humour can be so crass. Political correctness is something you'll need to take on at some stage in your life." Sam looked at the waitress once again. "I'm a size ten by the way. Come on. We said we should have a serious conversation."

Joe nodded his head. "Let's assume I've made up my mind to let Amelia Highland know that her real mother is still alive. I'd have to admit that her father was killed by a vigilante group in Sommovia and not in a car crash in Italy. Also, that her mother was wounded so badly she has no memory and appears to have other mental problems.

She's needed the protection of her close family. Oh yes, protected because she was a witness and could potentially identify those who carried out these atrocities. Add to that there are still factions at the very top that may want to silence her forever." He took a breath.

"Or. Say nothing. Lie to her because it would be better for her mother's safety, and besides her mother may never be able to recognise Amelia as her daughter." Sam felt strongly. "You've been put into an impossible situation, Joe. It should not be up to a relative stranger to make these very personal decisions. Amelia is a big girl now, and should be allowed to make up her own mind. Colonel Bradbury is probably using you as his intermediary so that he can stay one step removed and keep his shoes squeaky-clean. Who's he working with anyhow? No, it couldn't be the American government."

"United Nations, NATO." Joe corrected her. "There's an official list. Perpetrators of war crimes and a mandate to go after them all. I think you're right, though. But how perverse that someone with no memory could be the key witness in a crime that possibly implicates the country's leaders. The difference here is that we're talking about the good guys. Those that won the war."

Sam voiced a question. "Something must have changed to allow Bradbury to point you in this direction though. The latest names quoted in the news, even I've heard of. It's difficult to believe that Amelia's family have such important links."

The very next morning Samantha and Joe set out after their breakfast on a long trek up into the hills. Light green pastures were rich with grasses that rippled in waves to the occasional breeze. Much had already been cut for winter feed like hay and silage. Even the banks by the track-side had been exploited and the bounty collected by hand to minimalize the wastage.

The sun was unfiltered and it kept their progress honest; shade was their friend. Forty minutes later, the view from the top of the col overlooking a lake to the east was literally breath taking. Paddle driven ferries made patterns of motion on the water as they drove out from their station towards a busy town in the distance. It was easy to forget that people were working ordinary jobs and not on holiday. Sam wondered too if those that lived there appreciated the scenery that surrounded them, knowing that Salzburg was only an hour away.

That was when Joe's mobile phone rang. In answering it he moved away. Sam concentrated on the views of the hills reaching towards the horizon and tried to distance herself from the difficult decisions. Perhaps even now one was being made on their behalf.

Intrigue and suspicion got the better of her and she turned her attention to study the language that is a man answering a mobile phone and not being able to stand still. Her best guess was that Colonel Bradbury was coming up with another hairbrained suggestion. Joe looked back at her and made a face that suggested that their simple holiday plans had the potential to become much more complicated. Standing in the cooling shade of the trees, she couldn't wait to get moving again, whatever the direction.

"It's a fair trek down to that village at the head of the lake, but the map shows a pathway cut into the hill that zig-zags all the way down to the bottom." Joe took Sam in his arms and allowed one hand to travel below her waistline and give her a squeeze, if only to emphasise the last word he'd spoken. "If I told you that I loved you you'd only believe I was saying it to soften the bad news you think I have to tell you, so I won't say it. Come on I fancy some coffee and strudel. I can see the top of the path from here."

"You're an absolute bastard, Mr Peterson." Her American accent was always stronger when she swore.

Thirty minutes later they felt the flat of the land and were glad that their walking shoes had the grip and had cushioned their progress on almost vertical steps downwards.

"If you intend for me to climb back up there, you've got another think coming." Sam had a rosy tint to her cheeks. Her flax-coloured hair fell back into place with a flick of her fingers. "I should have taken my fleece off before. This coffee and strudel better be good that's all I can say." In reality, the beauty of the village and the quality of shops and restaurants set against a backdrop of blue water were having their desired effect. Even the earlier phone call was temporarily forgotten.

"The number eleven bus runs every forty minutes and stops not far from our hotel." Joe took her by the hand. "The service around here is always reliable. We could even go to Salzburg and slum it like locals instead of driving there and using the hire car. How about tomorrow?"

Samantha Grant reached up to give Jos a teasing kiss. "Is that where Bradbury wants to meet us?" She stopped short of kissing him again. "You'd better tell me what's really going on. I won't take no for an answer."

*

5. Medical Intrusion

London

The blue flashing light was the only betrayal that it had arrived. The middle of the night ensured that the roads around Hyde Park were almost empty. The parking area to the rear of the Randolph Hotel was sufficiently wide to allow the ambulance to turn around and back up to the entrance. The two paramedics walked quickly inside and were met by the night manager who guided them to the service elevator and from there to the fourth floor.

"The room is number 402. An American couple have been with us for a few days. Mrs Powers rang down to say that her husband was in acute pain, and thought he might have suffered a heart attack. Thank you for getting here so promptly. If there's anything you need, I'll be just outside the door. Here's your key card should you need to go in and out of the room." The elevator reached the fourth floor. "This lift will be at your sole disposal."

The two medics, one female, one male, gave thanks and were relieved at the manager's professionalism.

"You take a look at our patient and I'll talk to the woman. If it's as serious as it sounds, I think we'll have to take him in just to be on the safe side." Gail Parker sounded relaxed and confident.

Neil Shaw tapped on the door to 402 which was ajar and awaiting their arrival. Quietly and efficiently the two of them made their appraisals without fuss and with seemingly no hurry.

"He says he's feeling better now, and I'm happy to say he looks that way, but an hour ago I thought he was dying." Rosalind choked out her last words before sitting down on her side of the bed.

Neil introduced himself to Sherman and asked what had happened and if he was in pain, and at the same time gently lifted a wrist to check on his patient's pulse. "Nothing like this has happened to you before? I'll carry on with my checks but I think it would be safer if we took you in to be assessed."

"Hospital?" Sherman croaked rather than spoke.

"I think that would be as good a place as any."

Meanwhile, Gail spoke with Rosalind in hushed tones explaining what would happen next. "Your husband will be in good hands. Yes, perhaps just a small bag with his toiletries and a change of clothes. Is there anybody you want to call to let them know?"

Rosalind immediately thought about her choices. Charles Hanlan would probably be more appropriate if she considered their relative ages, but she knew in an instant who she'd prefer to have at her side. Amelia was capable, not that Rosalind intended to put upon her. So that was settled. She removed to the privacy of the bathroom to make a call to a residence just a few miles across London.

A sleepy voice picked up almost immediately.

"Should you have a mobile so close to your bed when you are sleeping?" Rosalind's voice nearly broke into a sob as she explained what was happening.

Amelia was wide awake. "I'll be there and we can drive to the hospital together. It makes sense not to travel in with Sherman."

"The ambulance crew agree it would be better to go in separately. They're about to leave any moment. I'm sorry I woke you but, in the circumstances…"

"Don't be, I'm glad I can help and try not to worry. Give Sherman a hug from me. Sounds like it could have been a lot worse for him."

Amelia sprang from her bed in a hurry. Concern for Sherman and compassion for Rosalind. Her recent experiences with her friend, Ellen Ward, were difficult to forget. Contacting her father would become a priority; he had access to all kinds of private healthcare. A good friend was in immediate need of their support.

*

6. Marin's Mix

It had been a weird week and one to remember but certainly not one to celebrate. As a postscript to recent tragedies, it has now become indelibly inked into local history. The man responsible for setting off such a chain of tragic events now has a reputation he could never have predicted or particularly wanted.

As a small-time farmer who had inherited property at the head of the valley, he was keen to cultivate his good fortune. Fallow ground was no help to his aim of self-sufficiency, as he liked to explain. Fine tilth and rich seedbed were a given. The unearthing of an antiquity of the war that had lodged itself in his machinery had caused him a few head-scratching moments. Others of a keener wit had called it a harrowing experience.

"Bloody heavy, mortar bombs are. I couldn't get a proper grip. Ended up dragging it between my legs to the edge of the field." It had seemed the simplest of solutions.

"What the f..." An incredulous friend not slow to express an opinion was drawn to point out how stupid and ultimately lucky he had been.

"What do you mean? You're always telling me time is money. I only had the headlands to do before I went home. I didn't want to travel back and waste diesel."

Continuing the argument would have been a waste of breath but the friend did his best to remain insightful. "You could have blown your bloody balls off, you f... idiot."

Next morning the bomb disposal unit saw the funny side but took the precaution of placing the shell and a newly wired detonator into a specially dug hole. They also made sure that everybody was far enough away before taking cover themselves and setting off the charge.

The explosion was clearly audible and surprisingly scary given that I'd been pre-warned it would happen. Windows on the tractor I was driving a mile and a half away, rattled and vibrated. The hole the mortar created was not that deep but had far reaching consequences. On further inspection remnants of bodies, some of women and children, lay in a line just below the surface. Another case of war crimes that would promote a pain-staking and much needed investigation. In practical terms the farmer's quest for self-sufficiency in this particular field would have to wait until the following spring at the earliest.

Two days later I submitted my request to return to university. Compassionate leave and their understanding had its limits. Needless to say, I felt torn. If finding war graves had not been bad enough, the fallout threatened to be serious. As a recognised and regular customer at the bakery, Deana the owner, was trusting enough to confide in me. Her sister, Lena had gone away and wouldn't be working in the café for the foreseeable future. She tried to keep her voice casual but I could tell that she was truly worried.

She actually told me, "I trust you, Marin," and went on to ask, "If I ever needed a favour?" I told her, yes, and gave her my number and address just in case.

Her family's history was finally catching up with the present day. Deana's practiced silence in front of other relayed that message quite forcefully. I sensed her anger as speculation and conjecture was scattered in every direction. I suspected Lena's experiences before the start of the war had to be a big part of this.

Deana pointed to the front page of the daily newspaper. 'General Indicted'. And 'War graves Found'. The war ended nearly seven ago and most of us had tried to move on with our lives. Weren't we who lived in a civilised world supposed to be making sure that this kind of thing never happened again?

On my way to the train station, I passed by Lena's house to take a look for myself. I found the experience emotionally charged. Looking to the washing line I couldn't even see a clothes peg, let alone bedsheets or a lace handkerchief.

*

7. Salzburg Trip

With the promise of rain later in the day, catching a bus to Salzburg was a good way to see the surrounding countryside, and all for less than ten euros each. Samantha had asked if Joe would prefer to go it alone but was relieved when he had declined her offer.

Over scrambled eggs, freshly baked rolls and large cups of coffee, they had spoken of what the day ahead might have to offer. Colonel Bradbury had suggested meeting in the Maribell Gardens but warned he had only two hours with them before returning to the airport. Unfortunately, this gave little clue as to his motive in making the journey in the first place. It had been on his suggestion that they'd gone to Sommovia and it was from there that Joe and Samantha had driven across two borders to holiday in Austria. The message that Joe received suggested that circumstances had changed in the Horvat family setup and probably not for the better.

"Good to see you both looking so well. You must be Samantha Grant. I'm Bradbury and let me introduce you to my colleague, Kaira Maes." Cordial handshakes were made by all. "Dry enough to walk whilst we talk. What a lovely setting, don't you think?"

"The Colonel approves of your choice of destination. He's always wanted to come here." Kaira was confident enough to speak without being spoken to first. Her wild curly hair looked untameable.

Small spots of rain came and went. It prompted Bradbury to set aside formalities and come straight to the point. "There have been certain developments at the trial of one of the Northern Sommovian politicians that might indirectly impact on the continued security of Miss Highland's mother. I assume that you made contact with the family when you went to their village. It seems that someone has been over confident or just careless with concealing her true identity and the ramifications of that are difficult to gauge."

"All was well when we left there a week ago. I spoke with her sister and reminded her of the scheduled trials at The Hague. She seemed well informed. I'm guessing the indictment of this General from the south has stirred things up. We agreed that the only person we felt might benefit from knowing that Lena was still alive was her daughter, Amelia." Joe was very matter of fact. "Samantha and I have been debating the ethics of that very decision ever since."

"Not easy for anyone to decide, let alone an employee of the Hanlan family." Sam was not impressed and it showed. "It seems that Jelena Highland no longer exists. That sounds rather crass I know." She tried again. "The injuries that Jelena suffered have left her with no memory of the person she used to be. I don't see that the powers-that-be, whichever side they're on, could see Lena as a serious threat or reliable witness."

"Very true Miss Grant. I would tend to agree, but we know to our cost that what is logical to you and me doesn't always ring true with certain elements who believe that in fighting a war there are no rules." Kaira Maes spoke with authority that belied her age. "I have personal experience."

Kaira removed her glasses and gave them a perfunctory wipe. Everyone else was silent and seemed transfixed by her task. "This has come out of the blue," she continued,

"Colonel Bradbury had no reason to suspect that her cover would be blown. On the contrary it was thought that this may be the time to reconcile Miss Highland to the rest of her family; hence involving Captain Peterson at this stage in proceedings."

Nobody joined the conversation. All may have wanted to but had been side-tracked into appraising the small package of energy that was Miss Maes.

"Suggestions?" Joe looked to the Colonel but ended up waiting for Kaira to speak again. It was a memorable moment as Bradbury held himself in check.

"I have plenty. It could be that this new find of war graves so close to the village is purely coincidental. I'm involved with a War Graves Finders group, and was due to go out there in the next few days to be part of the team."

"It doesn't sound like we have time to spare. I'll go back immediately." Joe spoke directly to the Colonel. "The implications could be dyer, made worse by my recent visit."

"Our visit, Joe." Samantha tried to console him and looked to Bradbury to back her. "Could it be that we've underestimated the strength of feelings out there in Sommovia?"

"Oh, undoubtedly so." Miss Maes said without hesitation, and struck violently past Colonel Bradbury into his own net.

At that rather appropriate moment, the faint sound of a mobile phone buried in a deep pocket broke the tension. Samantha retreated quickly, half turning and raising a hand of apology. On answering, a familiar voice sounded constrained and full of emotion. Rosalind Powers spoke, imparting first the bad news and then asking for Sam's help by way of an unscheduled return to London.

"Sorry to bust up your vacation, but I'll have to leave Sherman and fly back to the States." It was easy to hear Rosalind's downbeat feelings.

"Rest and recuperation. Suspected heart attack, bless him. Charles Hanlan is going to transfer Sherman to a private hospital for further checks and analysis." Rosalind broke down. "Oh Samantha, I should have seen this coming!"

Samantha heard her vulnerability and wanted to reach out. Ordinarily Rosalind exuded confidence and positivity but, in this instance, she'd been hit hard. No arguments. For Sam it was time to reciprocate in kindness.

By the time she re-joined the rest of the party, Colonel Bradbury was checking his watch and coming to a decision.

"A word with you Peterson. One minute Miss Grant, this won't take long I assure you." Light rain had started to fall with regularity. "We'll come and find you. Why don't you take some shelter? Miss Maes, perhaps you'd go with her." Bradbury was actually chuckling with laughter as he and Joe walked away. "She's a Dutch fire-cracker if ever I've met one. Works with this War graves Finders group all over the world. Her father is a forensic scientist and she has connections to other anthropologists working in Eastern Europe. Her ethnic background is a strong driver in her work but I don't think she's religiously active and I haven't asked her about it."

"How come she's attached herself to you?"

"Her language skills have been invaluable to the cause. My role is coming to an end, Joe. This is possibly my last hurrah. I've spent too long dealing with Sommovian politics and the United Nations to go elsewhere. Miss Maes is well thought of by her own government and with the new graves found near Jelena Highland's village, we've become a match made in heaven." Bradbury tried to sound contrite but failed. "Unconventional it may be, but I'm also not sorry I dragged you back out of your retirement. Making Jelena Highland safe is a heavy weight on my conscience."

Joe understood those feelings only too well. "Have we compromised a difficult situation and unwittingly drawn attention to a family that should have been left in peace?"

"I'm afraid that circumstances have overtaken us." Bradbury turned to face Joe. "If Kaira Maes' information is proved correct, the eyes of the world will be focused on that village in a very big way."

*

8. Field Craft and Planning

Sommovia

One cycle was all but over. The air was full of dust and the visibility, uncertain. Farmers and contractors were celebrating the end of the harvest. Only two rows of straw around the periphery of one particular field remained unbaled and purposely forgotten. It was a classic set up for an illegal burn. Even in a secluded part of the valley this was a dangerous pursuit and definitely not encouraged.

The abandoned excavator positioned in the centre of the field acted like a magnet. The man wiped the sweat from his face and took a swig from his bottle of water. At least on foot he could take the most direct route, the field was large and square-shaped. Remnants of stubble crackled and broke beneath his feet with every step.

Why they'd left the machine parked out in the middle of nowhere was a mystery and an inconvenience. Lending out his means of livelihood had been a bad idea but then he'd been given little choice. Once again, the fear and the intimidation bit into his stomach lining as if he'd been drinking acid rather than lukewarm water.

The bloody thing wouldn't start. There was plenty of fuel, but somebody had obviously been playing around in the engine compartment. Dust kicked up from the ground had stuck to the injectors and filters where the diesel had been allowed to leak and spray out. A loose nut or damaged o ring was causing the problem. Lena's cousin went to the tool box on the opposite side of the machine to get spanners and a pair of grips.

In truth he wanted a hammer to smash-in all of their heads. The threat they posed was as real as it had been back in the war. Nothing had changed; only his weakened resolve and being sure where his loyalties lay. Maybe he should flee the country once and for all. Funnily enough that was what cousin Deana had suggested.

A warm breeze was picking up from the south but gave little relief. His mind, along with his head, were buried inside his machine with a spanner in hand and swear words readily on his tongue. He was obviously unaware of the pickup as it entered the field trailing a wire cable attached to a burning tyre. The pickup bounced over old ruts and uneven ground as it made its way around the boundary. It was being driven too quickly but the driver seemed intent; he was prepared to put up with the discomfort.

By the time it had travelled all four sides of the oblong, wisps of smoke were being fanned into visible flame. The growing bright orange crackled into a serious fire. That was when Lena's cousin realised that his problems had worsened and his priorities had dramatically changed. This had nothing to do with being selfish. It was a matter of life or death.

The authorities made up of officers from the police and a single ambulance attended the scene. They met with the farmer who owned the land, who seemed genuinely shock and saddened. Small outbreaks of smouldering stubble and areas of rough grass kept the fire fighters busy for over two hours. Between them they discussed how lucky all had been because the fields down wind of them had already been ploughed. Of course, the farmer was very vocal in denouncing this kind of farming practice.

On moving towards the small excavator in the middle of the blackened field, all could see the damaged paintwork and cracked windows caused by the intense heat. What they had not expected to find was the body of the driver. Crouched as he was in a foetal position slumped forward over the controls, the incident had suddenly taken on consequences of a more serious nature.

There wasn't a mark on him; smoke inhiation had got him. Quite typical, so the fire chief had said. There was no denying the identity of the man who had only just returned to living in the community. A real tragedy even if he was not that popular. Could this be an accident? Who would want him dead? There was no denying that the fire had been started deliberately. The question remained, by whom?

*

London

The arrest of her step-brother, who had pleaded guilty to a charge of assault had played out rather too publicly in the press. Interest from outside agencies in the music business had been tempered in response to this. At the age of twenty-one Amelia felt she was in danger of becoming a one hit wonder now that Katie Ley, her stand-in from the outset, was making her own headlines in the show, Ever Searching.

"Good for Katie," was starting to stick in her throat as the reality of being unemployed struck home. "I've lost my sense of self-worth." Money wasn't the issue. "I thought I would be able to pick and choose. How insensitive I was to turn Sherman down."

Amelia paced up and down, wearing out the carpet. It was fortunate that there was room, as her flat in Kensington Green was large and airy and full of the things that made it feel like home.

Rosalind Powers noticed this and found that preferable to becoming mesmerised by Amelia's constant fidgeting.

"Don't for one minute start to blame yourself for Sherman's unfortunate dice with death. It's as much my fault as it is his own." Rosalind thought for a moment. "No, that's not quite right. Sherman was fully aware of the state of his health, but I didn't scold him as much as I should have. What's the British expression?"

"Becoming an old nag. I'm sorry Rosalind, but you're in little danger of being that." Amelia tried to distract her. "More tea?"

"I fancy something stronger." Rosalind shook her head in self-admonishment. "There, look. I'm as bad as my husband. No self-discipline." Her thoughts were jumping all over the place. "I'm so grateful to your father for talking to the right people."

"An advantage of building the hospital with his own money and knowing which strings to pull." Amelia conceded. "No idea how long it will take Sherman to recover though. There must be rules about travelling by air. It's something we'll need to check." Amelia sat down next to Rosalind on the sofa. "I guess you'll be going back to New York before he's ready. The hospital has everything covered this end, but Sherman is more likely to make a speedy recovery knowing that you're overseeing the important stuff at NRG."

"NRG Pictures has always been his baby. I'm only sorry that Hollywood never thought us good enough for one of the top prizes."

"Their ignorance has only added to the studio's cult status." Amelia was no expert but she'd done her homework. "What are the chances of selling the business?"

"I think we've agreed that it's time to move things on." Sherman had never previously spoken about retirement. "A serious offer is now on the table. It could prove to be a compromise that might yet satisfy him. It has to be taken at face-value. Toby, Sherman's nephew, is a burgeoning player in a Tv company making films by subscription. It's proving popular and very lucrative."

"So, with Sherman temporarily laid up, the negotiation process will be out of his hands and fully reliant on you?" Amelia could see a cloud of uncertainty descend on Rosalind. "Oh, if only I could be of help. I am going to miss you."

"Don't." Rosalind leaned over to give her a hug. "This is not the right time to tell you how important you've become to me. Maybe later, over a glass of wine, when neither of us have a care in the world." She sat back. "First things first, have a word with Samantha and sell her your ideas. She's probably as confused as the rest of us."

"When do you expect her back from her holiday in Austria?"

"In light of what has happened to Sherman, I've asked her to be back as soon as she can."

Amelia smiled and was happy to admit. "Well, we'll both be glad of that, I'm sure."

*

9. Marin's Mix

They said prayers for Deana's cousin in the church on Sunday. A tragic death among many that had preceded it. Another victim looking down on the rest of us poor sinners. Listening to those around me, the mindset of most had become more insular. Keeping secrets was the watchword and default setting in a village that had re-infected scars. It suited Deana that Lena's name was kept out of any mainstream discussions.

And strangers were what the village would have to put up with for the foreseeable future. The surprising find of the graves on the edge of the forest would bring the attention of the outside world to our enclave. Although supposedly self-sufficient, the specialised group of archaeologists and anthropologists would have to access their supplies via the roads in and around the village. Security was tight enough to discourage the curious from entering the area and the farmer on whose land the graves were found was placed under immediate arrest. The feeling amongst the locals was to keep their distance and promote their innocence by showing a lack of interest.

First post on Monday I received a formal letter from the university in Mezlar, inviting me to continue with my music studies, beginning in the Autumn later that year. The sense of relief to be moving away was palpable, there was nothing to keep me. The light of the summer was beginning to fade fast. A change of scenery before the bleakness of the darker days of winter had to give me the promise of new beginnings.

The only cloud on my horizon was leaving the memory of Lena behind me. I swore on the day I took the train to the city that I would never forget her. She deserved that from me.

Big clumsy fingers, the bi-product of my recent manual labour was the only part of my physique that the teacher of woodwind, Helen Matic was interested in. It was a blow to my fantastical ego and frustrated my libido as I found her sophisticatedly attractive, if ultimately unattainable. Dextrous exercise, she informed me, might allow my oboe to become useful once again, but duets were totally out of the question. Instead, I was encouraged to join the university choir. Her suggestion; I listened very carefully, and realised I'd been given a chance to justify my place amongst the elite.

Older than most, with less talent than most, the first few weeks were a jolt that had me rattled for a while. Shared accommodation could have been problematical but gave me access and insightful knowledge as to what was happening on-campus and in the city. Nightlife was the biggest part of the university scene and proved to be quite eye-opening to a country boy like me.

And that's where I had to be careful. It would have been easy to believe the hype and the generalised extremes of student behaviour. Of course, the usual drink and drugs were available, but the more discerning never let them be essential. They became a comfortable backdrop to learning about the people around me and taking the time proved so beneficial. By mid-term I would become part of something truly wonderful that kept me on my toes and eager to learn. Academia was just a part of it. Contacts

I was making there would see me right, now and into the strangeness of my future.

Sometimes I even forgot to feel sad about what had happened to Lena and her cousin but that was about to change. Incredible, really.

*

10. Holiday End

Kaira Maes looked at herself critically in the full-length mirror and tried to decide if the new purchases really suited her. Certainly, the beautiful printed sets of underwear, chosen in haste from a fashionable shop in the centre of Salzburg, had been totally influenced by having Samantha Grant as her companion. Whether she would have spent that kind of money on clothes that nobody else would see was doubtful. She had only capitulated under heavy persuasion. The shirts and tops and the figure-hugging designer jeans had been easier to choose once the seal on her caution had been broken. How she would repay the debt she had accumulated on the American's visa card was something to feel guilty about now and celebrate later once the balance had been settled.

"I would encourage you to travel with Mr Peterson. Go directly with him. Leave for Sommovia in the morning, he has a hire car at his disposal." Colonel Bradbury had made it sound so simple. "I'll get all your clothes and equipment sent on. Why waste a day when we need to assess the situation as quickly as possible? You can meet up with your own people almost directly once you're there."

Kaira took another look at herself in the mirror and wondered what her 'own people' might say regarding the change to her image and in particular what this new bra was doing to her cleavage. Something that been so inconsequential had seemingly taken on a life of its own. She breathed in heavily and straightened her back to accentuate the effect, deciding by way of researching further to delay putting on her shirt. In the course of moving back and across her bedroom she swivelled to check the fit of the new jeans and immediately regretted not splashing out on a second pair.

The hotel where Samantha and Joe Peterson were staying had a beautiful setting and each room had wooden balconies which were adorned with rows of potted flowers. The room itself had a four-poster bed and a bathroom to die for. Much would likely change over the next few days. Sharing a motorhome was the best she could hope for when she met up with the rest of the team. The news from Sommovia was encouraging if finding evidence of hastily dug graves could be referenced without sounding too offensive. All the evidence would need to be processed and forensic techniques used in thorough and scrupulous ways over the whole site. Not much need for designer jeans where she was headed for. No doubt her father would be waiting in his laboratory to gather and separate the DNA samples for identification purposes. Thousands of people were still missing; it was imperative to find them, however hard that might prove to be.

There was a knock on her door that brought her back to the here and now and without thinking she walked over and opened it.

"Sam and I are going to the bar for drinks before dinner. Why don't you join us?" Joe Peterson blinked his attention from her chest back to her face.

It took Kaira a few seconds to realise that she wasn't properly dressed. She tried and failed to stay calm by casually crossing one arm diagonally across herself, adjusting her glasses. "I'll be right down," was the minimum she felt comfortable in offering before slowly closing the door. "You're an idiot, Kaira," escaped her in hushed tones lest Joe hear her mumblings. Not that she was a prude in any way, but what would her mother say if she could see her now? After all there was very little privacy when she worked on site and that was somehow seen as acceptable. It was just that for the first time in a long time she'd taken the trouble to take pride in the way she looked. She could only hope that Joe would not think her too obvious and forward. Tomorrow they would be spending the day together in rather close proximity. More importantly, what would Samantha be thinking just about now? She hurriedly picked up a shirt.

"A simple apology, Kaira. But don't ramble on. It'll only make you look more guilty." She went back to the mirror adjusting the collar, but was undecided on how many buttons should be left undone at the top. In other circumstances, not a problem. Somehow the more that she gazed at her reflection, the less she recognised the person she thought she should see. Given more time and clean clothes of her own, she would have changed and been more comfortable.

Joe and Samantha were chatting quietly at a table with a couple of beers in front of them. They were dressed casually but looked good, particularly together. The welcoming smile never left Samantha's face as she assessed the new clothes that Kaira was wearing, and she looked so pretty herself. Kaira could feel her cheeks glowing as she walked over to join them.

"What'll you have?" Joe was on his feet and going to the bar.

Kaira walked with him and whispered quietly. "Sorry about earlier. I simply forgot where I was."

Joe could see she was serious. "No worries, absolutely not. Go sit and relax. Have a beer or a glass of wine, perhaps?"

Kaira joined Samantha at the table watching for any adverse reaction there. "I'm so sorry you have to go back to London. Your boss; is he okay?"

"There's never a good time to be ill, but I'm guessing this is something that has been building for some time. He's getting the very best of care from the doctors. I'm losing a few days of holiday but that's nothing in comparison. I'm meeting up with his wife, Rosalind, before flying back to the States. We have negotiations to make in selling NRG Pictures."

Kaira digested this information and voiced another concern. She wanted to make things easier for all if she could influence them. "When will you and Joe meet up again? Perhaps I could track Lena and her family down and save him a trip. This new site I'll be working is only a few kilometres away from their village."

"It's complicated. I'm not sure how much your Colonel Bradbury has told you, but Joe has his own responsibilities. He knows Lena's sister and his dilemma of when to tell Amelia that her mother is alive makes it a difficult situation." She shrugged her shoulders in pure resignation.

Joe returned to the table carrying one beer and a glass of orange cordial. He placed the beer in front of Samantha, the cordial he gave to Kaira and explained that he had a coffee on its way. "Got a long way to drive tomorrow."

Somewhere between finishing her meal and sipping some water from the bottle she'd placed on her bedside table, looking on the bright side had faded away. Sam recognised the uniqueness, where work had been reduced from top spot in her thinking and been replaced with feelings of inadequacy. “Dammit,” Kaira Maes had made her feel jealous.

A woman, no, still a girl in reality, if only a few years younger than herself, she had spoken so openly and passionately about her work. Forty thousand people missing and unaccounted for across the region that had seen so much conflict, including thousands of mixed-race families massacred in one town alone only weeks before they might have been saved. Sam was aware how strongly Kaira felt being attached to an organisation that would try to move heaven and earth to find them. It had become part of her, encouraged by her father. Somehow the morbidity she described in finding bits of bodies that had been moved from grave to grave had been fascinating and compelling. The perpetrators trying to conceal the evidence of their crimes. Human DNA the pieces, like putting together a jigsaw puzzle. And not once had she shown any anger or a wish for revenge.

Kaira was refreshingly naïve in some of her social behaviour. If her glass of orange cordial had had a couple of straws, it wouldn’t have seemed out of place. Innocent eyes were framed by glasses that gave the impression that her eyesight was deficient, when she rarely missed a thing. The tumbling curls of her unruly hair hid a hearing aid and she favoured one side when she listened intently. She rarely looked away from your lips when you were talking. Sam had seen her father do very much the same thing, an easy habit born out of having an accident as a child. It could actually be quite alluring, having someone take the trouble to listen without looking away. Joe seemed quite taken; no that was unfair.

Sam rolled over and lay on her side. She listened to the sound of water in the shower and then Joe cleaning his teeth. They were comfortable and stable, weren't they? The sex was still very exciting. She wouldn't want to not have him around, but that prospect was looming. The events of the last two days had robbed them of time for talking about the future. And now that future seemed more uncertain and weirdly unreal. Joe was going back to Sommovia, while she would go back to work in New York. There was much to be done and Rosalind Powers would need all the help that Samantha could give her. She desperately wanted to be useful.

When Joe joined her in bed, she stayed facing outwards with her back to him. He said nothing and tried not to touch her.

"I'm just sad, that's all." Sam spoke in a whisper. "I want you to miss me."

Joe put an arm around her middle. "I could say I do already." He rested his head on the pillow and listened to her breathing until he was sure that she was sleeping.

Later, in the blackness and quietness of the night, gentle fingers awoke and aroused her. That she wanted him was obvious and in return he gave her completeness without asking for anything in return.

*

11. Coping Somehow

Rosalind Powers was getting her "shit" together and was whipping up a storm, while her husband remained stable in hospital. Phone calls to the office in New York had created an impetus at board level to setup meetings with opposing executives who had NRG in their sights. This had proved the easiest thing on her list to complete. Constant reminders from her husband were predictable and sometimes unwelcome, while the sight of him attached to a heart monitoring machine put everything else into context. She visited him often and was still able to resist pulling the machine's plug from its energy giving socket, but that didn't stop her from threatening to do it.

"Thank God Samantha flies in later today. Sherman you're meant to be taking it easy." Her exasperation was half hearted. "The sooner you get out of here the sooner you can be a pain in the arse and get a few dollars more for the business we've worked so hard to make a success of."

"There's only one way to keep the company in the family, we both know that. Unfortunately, my nephew and his bosses are aware of it too. Maybe it's a compromise worth making. They're good at what they do and I know that Tobias would be in a good position to influence the artistic direction."

"Sherman, once we sell to them there will be no guarantee of anything. You'll have to accept that we've had our time and maybe that's the way it should be."

Sherman Powers looked at his wife, and not for the first time had to agree she was probably right.

*

Charles Hanlan's in-box was full, memos piled on top of one another and leaning like a certain tower in Pizza. Sally Stewart was fidgeting, wondering if her stacking procedure would prove adequate enough. Decision-making appeared slower than usual and there was still plenty that needed Charles' consideration on that particular day. Top of the hit parade; Katie Ley was not feeling well and a long-term question loomed over the strength of her voice. Her talent was undisputable, but it begged the question as to how Amelia had managed for so long, day after day.

"We may have to bring the renovation program at The Theatre forward. I know the clamour for tickets is huge, but this kind of situation justifies our decision not to take pre-bookings too far into the future."

"Katie says she'll be better after the weekend. Her stand-in is doing a very fine job, by the way." Sally understood the ways of the theatre. "Audiences get so disappointed when they've come to see a particular actor." She wanted to be more positive. "A small blip we can get over, just like we've done in the past."

Charles nodded his head. "Amelia is going back with Samantha Grant and Rosalind Powers. She wants to be part of the negotiations when NRG is finally sold. She feels beholden to them for all they did for her." He was referring in part to the intimidation Amelia had suffered at the hands of her step-brother.

"Mrs Powers has definitely been a great influence on her." Sally Stewart had seen the evidence for herself. "Amelia is much more aware of what is going on around her."

Just at that moment Charles' phone began to ring, a personal number that only family and close friends would have been given. Sally reached across the desk to answer and act as a buffer. She was not fazed when she recognised the voice on the other end of the line.

"Sally? It's Joe Peterson calling from Austria. I've got a bit of a crisis and need to make some changes to my plans. Is he there?"

Sally proffered the receiver towards her boss and whispered, "It's Mr Peterson."

Charles sat up straight in his chair. "Okay Joe, what's going on." The trust in his man was implicit. "You're supposed to be on holiday, remember?"

"Well as it happens, I'm on my way back to Sommovia. I'm at the border in Austria, heading south. I've been hijacked by my previous boss in the Army." Joe was reticent. "Certain information has come my way through the Colonel and it has implications for you and your daughter."

"Spit it out Joe." Hanlan's interest had been piqued. Something must have happened to one of Amelia's family. From the tone of his Joe's voice, he could tell it was serious.

"There are complications... Mr Hanlan, are you still there? I have some surprising news concerning Amelia's mother... ". For a couple of seconds there was a loss of signal. "... Best not to say more over the phone. Give me a couple of days..." The line went dead.

Charles put the phone down back in its cradle. A jumble of emotions drained the blood from his face. Not someone prone to over-reaction he felt weak and slightly paralysed. Without saying a word and waving away Sally's concern, he eventually managed to rise and walk away from the office.

Minutes later, Sally watched as Charles exited the building on foot and started wandering aimlessly up the street. It was only then that she picked up the phone and dialled Joe's mobile number back.

"Mr Peterson, this is Sally Stewart. Yes, I can hear you clearly. Can I take a message or should I get him to ring you straight back?" She stopped to listen. "Yes, it has come as rather a shock to him. No, he's gone from the office. Do you want to tell me what you can and I'll pass it on to him later?"

Joe had thought about that. "There's a man from my Army days, a Colonel Bradbury, he can supply you with further information. He's expecting your call. Look Sally, I've got to go. Just wanted to let you know that I'm going to be delayed for a few days more." He paused and listened to her next question. "No, I wouldn't say anything to Amelia; not just yet. I'm going back to do what I should have done in the first place. Little point in upsetting her as well as her father."

Back on the border, Joe walked steadily back to the car that he and Kaira Maes were sharing. With every step he was convinced there was no other option. The time for secrecy was over. Somebody close to Lena, had become careless. How easy was it to forget that powerful people, had supporters helping to hide their true identities.

*

In typical style Colonel Bradbury was wearing his casual clothes in a very formal way. Jacket and tie were as standard, while the crease of his trouser appeared as dangerous as a knife. He gave the park bench a thorough inspection and checked the branches above him for birdlife. He made sure Charles Hanlan was sitting comfortably before taking his own place next to him. Dappled light from the trees was a filter to the heat of midday, but there was little breeze to renew the air at ground level. Red buses and black taxis provided a back-ground noise that was not too overpowering. An occasional scooter the only major distraction to their conversation.

"One thing I should make plain from the very start is that we are dealing with circumstances that are outside of our normal control." Bradbury spoke with consideration while looking straight ahead. "As with Captain Peterson when he first came to see me, I have to be consistent and cautious about how much information I'm able to pass on."

Hanlan tried to be non-committal but had adopted a pose of stillness that threatened to erupt at any moment.

"I appreciate your patience but had you not employed Peterson this information would probably have never come to light." He stood up and encouraged Charles to do the same, sensing that it might release some of the tension and give them the chance to look each other in the eye.

Colonel Bradbury went on to describe Joe's first visit to the village in Sommovia and meeting with Deana at the café where Amelia's mother worked. Yes, Lena was Lena Horvat, or rather Jelena Highland as Charles best remembered her. The Colonel spoke of her injury and her near-death experience and how it appeared to have affected her memory and mental capacity. He would have preferred to have glossed over the reasons why her family had hidden her for so long but knew instinctively that Hanlan would not let that happen.

"The Deana who you refer to, I have actually met out in Sommovia, but that was back in the eighties before the start of the war. What I'm having trouble in understanding is why she never let us know that Jelena was still alive?" Charles spoke with increasing passion that had a personal edge that went beyond his concern for his daughter.

Bradbury picked up on this immediately. "You knew the Highlands quite well I believe?" And answered his own question. "Hence becoming their daughter's guardian. Her extended family never challenged your adoption of Amelia?"

"They were happy believing that she might benefit from the advantages that I could offer her. Although born out there she was ultimately raised in Britain but I have always encouraged her to stay true to herself." There was a hint of irritation in his voice that belied a self-defence mechanism. "I have always tried to do what I thought Amelia's mother might have wanted for her daughter..." Charles' voice faltered.

"It's my opinion that the family have acted similarly by protecting Jelena. To all intents and purpose, she should have died from that head-shot. Just another murder victim in a part of the world that has witnessed so many atrocities of a similar kind. Only in this case the perpetrator became an important and influential name in his country's history." The Colonel hinted at his disgust but remained full of realism. "His cult hero status during and after the war cannot be overstated. Unfortunately for him the policy decisions of his former allies in government have had to change. Such is the power of the country's need for financial security. In his capacity as an Army General, he's become one of the most important political pawns in their negotiations with the European Union."

This made little difference to Hanlan. "Is he the one that pulled the trigger? The one who meant to kill Jelena?" Continuing with his train of thought he asked the obvious question. "And if it was him, then what was his motivation?"

Bradbury hesitated but then nodded his head as if responding to decisions he'd only that minute made. "We're talking about a man who wore a similar uniform to the one I wear, who perhaps forgot that his country was not yet at war. Probably off-duty and almost certainly not acting under orders, maybe he decided to take matters into his own hands. This is all conjecture, you understand. The authorities will neither confirm or deny any wrong doing."

Hanlan put the pieces together. "Jelena was just a witness?"

"That's what we believe, and of course Maurice became a victim too. Almost certainly he walked straight into the aftermath and was killed through mistaken identity or as part of the cover-up." Bradbury took a breath and turned it into a sigh. "And covered up it was. Sanctioned at the highest levels of government; that is until he was recently indicted. It's now no secret that we're talking about General Berislavic."

"Why isn't he in prison?"

"In simple terms he's gone on the run. Tipped-off by the very same people who supposedly want to arrest him. This is the game they play. It's been suggested he wants time to prove his innocence."

Hanlan said little in response, understood the situation as best as he could but had one question left for the Colonel. "How bad is Jelena? If as you say, she has truly lost her memory, why can't we go in and get her out?"

"Peterson is on his way to do just that but I've warned him he'll be putting himself at risk." Bradbury knew that Jelena's family would need to agree and it would have to be done in secret. Not easy when there was no knowing how incapacitated Amelia's mother may yet prove to be.

"I would suggest you say nothing to your daughter; her mother is still in danger. Peterson will do his best to make an appraisal and we will act accordingly." Bradbury cleared his throat in a familiar manner. "I say, we, with reservation. As a servant of the British government, I cannot be linked with anything that would be deemed illegal of course."

Hanlan chose to ignore this, and reasoned he could rely on Joe. "I understand he's not travelling alone. What has Miss Maes got to do with this situation?"

"Ah, Kaira Maes." The Colonel considered his choice of words. "In layman's terms she's a finder of graves and a collector of evidence. She is my unofficial link and ears to the ground that I can no longer walk on. On a personal note, and I don't mean to upset you, she's there to investigate some newly found graves on the edge of the village where Jelena was living." He paused to emphasise his next sentence. "It could be that she may yet find the remains of your good friend Maurice Highland."

*

12. Marin's Mix

Some of my fellow students were getting used to the sound of their own political voices. The extremely emotive subject of the tribunals in The Hague seemed heavy material for those of us in the arts. Like it or not the whole country was debating the wrongs and the rights of crimes that had potential to turn heroes into criminals. I tried to keep an open mind as a tribute to the memory of my girlfriend.

My sadness was mirrored by many others who had felt threatened, even in the capital, Mezlar. Air raid warnings and indiscriminate sniper fire from vantage points anywhere on the ground had been common. As a mature student looking to be accepted in a younger environment, I tried to balance my world-weary outlook with some popular pride in the region's new and growing identity.

The learning experience at the University was all-consuming. It was evident that I would never make a career out of performing music, and yet it was the subject that remained closest to my heart. Arranging gigs and getting musicians together was more in-tune with my character. The influence I was gaining with my fellow students was viewed with suspicion in certain quarters. The more courageous had to concede that I was offering them alternative opportunities outside the campus where experience was king. Some even got paid and they weren't complaining.

Proof I was no rebel with a cause came with gentle persuasion. The internet became a friend in widening all our learning spectrums. Even the most traditional minds eventually cottoned onto its easy power. Popular music was fast becoming more than just what we heard on the radio.

One particular tutorial on the influence of big-time musicals on Broadway and in the West End proved a turning point of personal significance. The publicity machinery of the country was looking for new blood to infuse feel-good factors into everyday life. In sports we had our football teams and tennis players to be proud of, so why shouldn't the cultural world get its own important shot in the arm.

Interesting articles and interviews started doing the rounds from one particular show. A small tit-bit of information got me thinking and prompted some research. That's when my gorgeous tutor began to take more of an interest, if only to commend me. Still no dating, more's the pity. Formulating plans kept me awake at night. "No Marin, concentrate on your work."

I chose to ignore the lure of new technology and rely upon the written word in an old-fashioned letter. In some ways it became a curriculum vitae; an application for a non-existent job. I made a strong case for a world-renowned theatre impresario to pass on his knowledge of a business that had captured my imagination. His daughter's links to my country's heritage must have helped my entreaty to become a formal invite. The University were keen to be seen as forward thinkers. If nothing else the endeavour brought myself closer to Helen Matic. I sought her advice and we worked on my English. She became the official link between the University and Charles Hanlan, should he take the trouble to respond. And respond he certainly did.

*

13. Following Orders

Crossing fields at speed had been damaging to man and machine alike. The pickup's lack of decent suspension had caused the passenger to slip a disc. It was real enough to worry and annoy the driver who had more important things on his mind. Orders were there to be carried out. A snapped alternator belt was just another spanner in the works to disrupt his schedule.

"Get that fixed while we still have light. I'll come myself, tonight." The boss was unnaturally calm.

Later, the driver slowed as they approached the entrance to the cottage. A single light shone from somewhere inside but gave no proof that the dwelling was occupied. The boss who was carrying a double-barrelled shotgun and spare cartridges did not appear too concerned. The driver's weapon of preference was a crowbar. Despite being indirectly responsible for one killing that day, he had no appetite to use this on a woman's head.

Parking further up the road and hidden by roadside trees, the driver made sure the pickup was positioned for a speedy getaway. Nothing would be left to chance. The woman named Lena had not been seen at the cafe since the discovery of the gravesite and he took comfort in this. Keeping his feet on soft and noiseless ground, he followed in the wake of his boss. The stillness around him pervaded the open spaces and made him feel claustrophobic. After some minutes they arrived at a side door that led out to the garden. Now was the time to be brave.

The crowbar made short work of the lock that gave-way a little too easily in the driver's opinion. The smell of petrol should have been a dead giveaway. Using a small torch, he shone a small cone of light inside the kitchen. Sounds of scuttling and shadowy movement plus the slam of a door startled both to such a degree that the boss pushed past and raised the shotgun to his shoulder.

"No Slav...", was all the driver had time for when the gun went off, both barrels. The explosion was instant and in an enclosed space the roll of flames quite devastating. The driver was blown clean off his feet and out through the door back into the garden. When he finally came to, the house was on fire. He endeavoured to gather his senses and regain some semblance of hearing. It was time to get away. Movement from just inside the door pricked his conscience. Instinctively and without ceremony, he reached down and dragged his boss out of the flames.

How they made it back to the vehicle was a mystery. Shot gun and crowbar discarded, the driver dragged his passenger most of the way. It was a miracle that he was even alive. First things first, make good their escape and quickly; any injuries, however bad, would have to wait. The cottage was now an unmissable beacon to anybody in the near vicinity.

The pickup shot forward and continued on at speed, inspiring single-minded concentration. A calming cigarette helped to mask the smell of burnt flesh. The boss was in a bad way. It couldn't be helped; the lack of suspension be damned.

*

Joe controlled the Audi A4 with satisfying ease, making good use of autobahn and motorway limits. His front-seat passenger felt safe despite clenching the occasional leg muscle in response to some late braking and compensating accelerations. Kaira's eyes flickered towards the car's speedometer in fascination and some excitement.

Once back across the border, she sensed that Joe had a sense of purpose. "It can't be easy coming back to this country, knowing what you know and seeing what you've seen. I'm surprised you've done this voluntarily." Kaira spoke as they slowed for some traffic lights up ahead. "I think we need to make a left here by the way." She studied the map one more time to be sure.

"I could say the same about you, Kaira. Dealing with death and documenting the evidence can't be considered as straight forward." Joe hesitated. "I guess we both wrap ourselves in the detail and try not to take on emotional baggage."

"With science there's a detachment that comes from having to be very sterile with the evidence and processing the data. My parents came from different cultures. Considering my father's background, I guess it's become a bit of a calling. I think of us as dedicated puzzle solvers."

Joe made his turn to the left just as the lights changed from green to amber. "When I joined up, I'd never have guessed that there would be war in civilised Europe again so soon."

"But you still get involved. Why?" Kaira kept her eyes on the road. She didn't want to seem too pushy.

"It's a job that needs doing. Others are in trouble." Joe was thinking about Lena as much as anybody else. "It's part of what I do."

As daylight faded, mist began to gather in the low-lying areas between the tree-topped hills. Joe drove the road some five miles out from their final destination and felt at home. An air of nervous tension grew to a pitch as lights showed in house windows. Cresting a rise and continuing down into the village all seemed normal until they reached its centre. All the streets were deserted and the atmosphere, subdued. In the distance a single column of smoke rose into the sky.

The café was shut, no surprise there perhaps, but so too was the restaurant and bar further down the road. Joe parked up and took in the scene.

"Where are your people staying, Kaira? In the village or are they self-contained?" He kept his attention focused outside of the car.

"The initial set up is that we keep together on site and preserve an area around the graves until we get proper security. We're not always accepted with open arms. People get very suspicious." Kaira reached for her phone. "Is it okay if I give them a call. They'll have mobile accommodation at our disposal, with some food if we want it." She picked up that Joe was watching the café. "Is that where Lena works?"

Joe was about to reply when a torch flickered briefly into life. The pedestrian gate by the side of the café was now open and a woman was beckoning to them. Seconds later, she'd gone again.

"We're expected. Come on let's go." Joe switched off the car's internal light before encouraging Kaira to get out. "Keep close." He took her hand and led the way, pushing through the side-gate and entering an alleyway. "Probably best to slide the bolt across and make it secure."

At the far end more light glowed through a half-opened door. It acted as some kind of silent invitation. Kaira followed his instructions and kept instep behind him.

Opening the door and entering into what at first glance looked like a storeroom, they stopped to get their bearings.

Joe spoke first. "With your permission." A shadowy figure stood half hidden behind some carboard boxes. He'd recognised her immediately. "Deana, it's Joe and I'm with a friend." He could see the barrel of a rifle pointing in no particular direction but definitely held out in front of her.

"Dobra vecer, Mr Peterson." The voice was calm but its intonation was asking all sorts of questions.

"Good evening to you Deana, good of you to look out for us." Joe replied, never taking his eyes off of the gun. "Is now a good time to introduce you to Kaira Maes." Joe stepped to one side to allow a full view of the young woman standing behind him. "She's here to look after your newly found war graves."

There was no immediate reply.

"I'm guessing there's been a problem?" Joe persisted giving Deana time to consider her options. Despite the relative darkness, deep shadows under her eyes and scratches to the side of her face seemed to be painful.

"What brings you back so soon? I can't believe you love Sommovia so much." She spoke in perfect English. Something she hadn't undertaken to do the last time they'd met.

"Well, we came here to warn you." Joe still spoke in her own language. "But I'm guessing we might be too late."

"An understatement if ever I heard one. Lena is missing and our cousin is dead. I'm hoping you weren't responsible, whether you meant to be or not." Deana's strength began to crumble. "What the hell is going on, Joe?"

She turned and stiffly walked away. "You'd better come in, but bolt that door behind you. I'll make us some coffee and you can explain why you've a different girlfriend in tow." She deposited the rifle into a broom-cupboard on her way into the kitchen. "I rather liked the look of Samantha."

Kaira was about to protest but Joe stopped her with a gesture and a smile. "Do you take sugar?" he asked her.

"What?"

"Deana will make you coffee with loads of sugar in it unless you tell her not to." Joe continued with his warning. "And don't, whatever you do, refuse one of her cakes when it's offered."

Kaira frowned. "Or what, she'll point a rifle at me?" She was still trying to adjust to the crazy hospitality on offer.

Deana's hearing was superior to Kaira's. "No need. I have plenty of sharp knives in the kitchen. Come girl, sit down at the table."

After a moment's hesitation, Kaira decided to do just what she had been asked.

"And you, Joe." Deana proffered a mug in his direction. "I have a story to tell you." She tried a tentative smile. "But first, let us drink our coffee. It is the most important thing, I think."

*

Southern England

Charles Hanlan appreciated the kindness meant by Colonel Bradbury's honesty, but the truth behind his revelations was painful to hear. Salt had been liberally sprinkled onto an open wound. The mention of his old friend and business partner, Maurice Highland, had raked up the ashes of previous disasters and made them catch fire again. Only a few weeks ago Charles had contributed to a newspaper article in which he'd confessed his love for a woman he'd no right to have feelings for. It felt like a punishment of perversity to know that Jelena was alive and that nothing had changed about the way he felt about her.

Following his meeting with Bradbury, Charles went down to the river in the hope of clearing his head. Leaning over the embankment wall he stared at the light on the waves that rippled and sparkled until his eyes were full of tears. Time became precious; somewhere between there and the end of his walk back to The Theatre he made a serious resolution. He had to be proactive. Now to work out the logistics and plan all that might be needed. Just as important was who to include in his burgeoning plan.

Both the Colonel and Joe had warned of involving Amelia at this stage of the proceedings. Charles saw little or no alternative. He reasoned that while there was a chance of a positive outcome his daughter had the right to choose for herself. He couldn't imagine her not wanting to be reunited with her mother. More importantly, she would never forgive him his secretive nature and stifling protection, whatever his motivation and care.

Charles reached for his phone and prayed that she'd left her own switched on. Fortunately, the connection was immediate.

"Don't get on that flight for New York, whatever you do… I don't care if you've just arrived at Heathrow… There's something that needs our attention… I know you're thinking about your future… The future is very important, but right now we need to take care of the past."

The conversation was a short one. Charles was on a roll.

Sally Stewart had her orders. "Get through to Nick Sayers and don't stop trying until you succeed… please." This was more like it. Charles Hanlan speeding through the gears.

Decision one, meant that renovations to The Theatre were to be brought forward to start almost immediately. The postponement of 'Ever Searching' for a week or two would force a public apology wrapped in technical and safety excuses. Reimbursements to all those affected, plus the offer of discounted admission on their next visit was a small price to pay. Hanlan's strict policy on advanced bookings had come into its own.

Decision two, "Nick Sayers speaking. Is that you, Sally?… No, good to hear your voice. What can I do for you?"

"The boss wants to speak to you… Naturally, and to see you as soon as possible." Sally had been given carte blanche to negotiate on Charles' behalf. "Fancy a trip to Europe?" She was hoping that he was at home in New York and not out on assignment. "Not exactly sure of all the details, but take it from me it could be life changing for a certain individual very close to his heart."

Nick didn't have to ask. Without her being aware, Amelia had become a focal point of much that was taking place in his personal life at Stress Magazine and beyond. "How soon do you want me to be in London?

"Could you make it tomorrow? I know that's unlikely." Sally was trying to be realistic.

"I'll do my best." He tried not to sound too enthusiastic. "Tell your boss he owes me big time."

*

Rosalind Powers had to believe that her husband's progress would be gradual following his procedure. They wanted to keep him in under observation and treat him with antibiotics for a small infection. Normal procedure and no need for alarm; that was what the doctor had said.

It made her realise how important it was to trust in true professionals. With this in the forefront of her mind, she began to abandon both her travelling companions at the airport, explaining it was for the greater good.

"I know what I'm doing and there's no point in trying to persuade me otherwise. I'll talk to Tobias and buy us more time by playing hard to get." She was referring to the tricky business of preserving NRG Pictures' legacy. "In any case Sherman should be there to fight his own corner. His nephew should respect his uncle's predicament." She turned to Amelia. "Families, eh?" She put her own concerns to one side. "Your father needs you, and you need a friend in Samantha. I know I sound as if I've been taking something illegal, but in time you'll come to agree with me." Rosalind made clear she wasn't going to take no for an answer.

Turning to Samantha she opined. "Besides you never got to finish your holiday. Whatever the outcome just be sure you look after each other. You are the future…" Rosalind never got to finish the sentence as both young women crushed her in a loving embrace.

"If you're sure…" Samantha was about to argue.

A nod of her head sufficed as part of Rosalind's answer; it had to. A shooing motion and a certain look in her eyes quietened any further objections.

"Okay we're going." Samantha said in surrender, wanting to make more of their goodbyes.

Rosalind took her place in the queue for Passport control and was careful not to show any lack of resolve. The strength of her love had made her feel fragile. In a few hours' time she and her life-long partner would be many miles apart, where days before, she'd nearly lost him forever. Perhaps that was why she had made Samantha to go with Amelia. They were younger and more vital; one of them was becoming too independent for her own good.

"Imposing your will on others?" Rosalind spoke to herself and smiled. "By the look on their faces, I'd say they were quite pleased." Amelia had still needed persuading despite her father's last-minute call.

"Sorry madam, did you say something. Boarding pass and your passport please." The young man in his B.A. uniform, had the time for a smile.

"Just thinking about relationships. I didn't mean to speak aloud and I don't mean to pry but are you in one yourself?"

"Well as it happens… Why, are you offering, madam?" He coloured deeply, thinking he had over-stepped the mark. "I shouldn't have…"

"Don't you dare take that back. Taking risks are important." Rosalind regained her passport and moving away spoke over her shoulder. "It's what keeps us young at heart."

*

14. Meetings and Secrets

He had lost patience with Libi. The silence between them had been deafening, the disconnection complete as she replaced her old-fashioned phone in its cradle. So, that was it. This was no way to live their lives.

Since his return from England, Nick had stayed home and been more discerning in his work-choices. Life in the city had turned into a sabbatical verging on becoming a second honeymoon. No efforts had been spared on either side of the bed and that attraction remained even now.

Perhaps it was depression, or fear of commitment? He hated that phrase. Libi was a successful business woman. It wasn't in her nature to just quit. Always the leader, always the rescuer, maybe she figured that her role in their relationship was finally done? Simply put, she feared that one day he would outgrow his need for her.

Nick touched down in London for the third time in as many months. There'd been no sight-seeing out of the window, as the four engine Airbus made its approach into Heathrow. Too intent on doing his research. The same stuff he'd skimmed over the last time he'd been asked to do it. Samantha had provided the relevant updates along with well-deserved criticism for his lack of attention of detail.

Hearing her voice had been a welcome boon. The seriousness of the ongoing situation had negated the temptation to discuss anything of a personal nature. Charles Hanlan had provided a car and a driver with a list of things to do and places to go. Settling back in his seat he took in the dubious views of the northern M25 heading east towards his first port of call. Ipswich was still more than an hour away.

"It's actually a pub on the edge of the river." Hanlan had informed him. "Marsha Ivanovic is staying with a friend who lives close-by. Of course, you'll be expected to buy her lunch. I'm told the menu is varied but be careful what she drinks. Amelia reckons alcohol makes her volatile."

"No more than when she's drinking tea, I assure you." Nick replied peering out of the window looking for road signs. "So, be more specific. What makes you think she'll spill the beans to me? Previous experience tells me I'll not be in charge of the conversation. That's if she'll talk to me at all."

"Don't worry about that. I decided to bribe her with a trip back home to Sommovia to see Amelia in a Christmas concert."

This was interesting news on so many levels. "How have you wangled that at short notice?" He hoped he might be asked to go there himself.

"I've decided to reward persistency, recognising something of myself in another; a student who won't take no for an answer. It's a university that has tentative links with my old pal, Maurice Highland."

Nick wondered in view of the circumstances, if Charles was doing this more for his daughter or for himself. The unspoken name of Jelena was infused in every thought.

The driver had turned off onto a backroad. "Okay. Look, we've made good time. I'll call you later. Preparation is everything. I need a few minutes to steel myself for the encounter with Ms Ivanovic."

Whatever his true motives, Charles Hanlan was instigating a plan in his own inimitable style.

Nick couldn't wait to talk to Amelia and gauge her thoughts on her latest trials and tribulations. Being part of a dysfunctional family and seeing her step brother go to jail hadn't been easy. West End stardom with the promise of making films in America had to be balanced against the disturbing events that had overtaken her as a teenager. Now to be told that her mother was risen from the dead, only to go missing again; you just couldn't make it up.

He became present once again as the chauffeur slowed the car and made a left turn. Not long now before he'd have the pleasure of meeting with Marsha Ivanovic for a second time. A proud woman who'd been forced to flee her country during the second world war. If she'd not been a musician and teacher, he thought she'd have made a talented General. Nick allowed himself a smile and began to gather his thoughts. With the main road behind them, a narrow lane that had subtle twists and turns led them gently downhill. Scrub trees and mature woodland to the side restricted the view forward; their cautious progress heightened the expectation. When they finally broke back into the clear, there were low-lying boathouses and the occasional cottage that gave rise to partial civilisation. The next one quarter mile was a revelation, as if the modern car had literally warped back in time.

A visible strip of water was preceded by the smell of the river and Nick was amused to see his driver hesitate at the sight of tidal mud and seaweed on the road. Nearly down to the water, the tarmac gave up and morphed into rough track of rubble and hardcore. Old boathouses and barges dominated the foreshore and cast derelict reflections on slow moving and riven-like surfaces on the water. Beyond this the river was wide and constant with masts and buoys defining its width. Back on the land and behind low brick walls, patches of grass were the dry-berths for small rowing boats and sailing dinghies. Untidy boatyard buildings spoke of quiet chaos where everything had its own place if you knew just where to find it. Everything 'Ship-shape and Bristol fashion' had no obvious meaning here; not to a land-lubber like Nick. But what a place to photograph.

The pub was already busy and the outside benches and tables were mostly taken with diners enjoying their food. Nick ducked his head and entered the contrasting light of inside. He blinked allowing his eyes to grow accustomed while searching the bar and its adjoining room for the lady he'd travelled this far to interview.

*

15. Beautiful Alcavar and More

Amelia sat in her pyjamas hugging her knees to her chest and stared into the distance of another world. The small Island of Alcavar off the coast of Sommovia was making an impression that she would have found difficult to immediately describe. The taxi ride from the small airfield to the old town and its harbour had been a revelation. No jams, no potholes and no stress of being caught in the wrong lane. The final descent into the new marina area had been full of picture postcard moments. Beautiful boats bobbing on blue sea drew them onwards.

Beyond the harbour other smaller islands became apparent, bathed in the late afternoon sunshine. Water taxis and small ferries were busy and looked to be an adventure in themselves. Amelia was rather glad she had someone to share it with but randomly allowed herself to wonder how Rosalind was getting on without the help of her trusty sidekick.

Movement outside on the balcony beyond the bedroom's sliding door brought Amelia back to the here and now. Not for the first time she wondered at the sacrifices that others were making on behalf of her family. Sam had not long ago risked her own life and now Joe Peterson and her Aunt Deana were potentially putting themselves into danger.

Sam was talking to Joe, her mobile phone an appreciated link and an essential friend. From the snippets of muffled and quiet conversation, Amelia figured he must be trying to allay her fears. In reply, Sam's words of frustration were easy to decipher. Once the call was over, she remained leaning on the railings taking in the array of brightening lights reflecting on the water as evening descended into deepening darkness.

Amelia gave her some privacy before sliding the balcony door open. She was keen to offer her companion some well-intentioned advice. The balmy night air was comfortable and kind. "Can I point out that if you stay out there much longer, you're going to freeze your tits off. Come on in and stop being a stranger."

Samantha managed a smile, left the door ajar but closed the curtains as though seeking protection. Soft lighting in the room gave its generous space some welcome intimacy. A proffered glass of red wine was the ultimate prop in cosiness and she joined Amelia by sitting on their king-sized bed. They'd been fortunate to find a late cancellation as all the hotels on the island were fully booked. The hotelier had recognised their immediate need and had apologised that the four-poster couldn't be made into single beds.

"The town is hosting a huge regatta. The day after tomorrow you will see racing and a very busy harbour." He raised his hands in a sorry admission and excused his inadequate translation. "Boats in the marinas, they are full as well." In passing he made casual inquiry as to whether either had a partner who would be joining them later.

In a bid to save themselves embarrassment Samantha explained how their plans were open-ended. Whether her partner would get to join them would ultimately decide on how long they were staying. A dig in the ribs prevented Amelia from making comment about being part of a threesome. At least she was seeing the funny side of their strange predicament.

Sam took another sip of wine before settling her head back on the pillow. The call from Joe had not been reassuring. As new relationships went theirs was proving problematical. It had definitely moved on from its honeymoon period. The girl lying on the bed beside her was part of the reason for that. Looking after her interests was proving as stressful as it was enlightening. Sam was aware of questioning eyes that kept their focus.

Finally. "Well, what's the score?" Amelia had kept herself in check. Sam's subtle facial expressions and animated movements only added to her endearing and reassuring qualities. The same athleticism that had been used to plunge into the black waters of a river in Suffolk to save her step-brother were now telling a conflicting story between support for someone she cared for and needs that were purely selfish.

Samantha took a breath before springing from the bed to pour herself a refill. She finally relented and spilled her news. "Joe has made contact with your aunt who now reports that your mother has gone missing. There's no sign of her in the village at all." She stuttered into silence.

Amelia was growing impatient. "Spit it out. I'm prepared for anything. Really. I'd be surprised if things didn't get worse before they get better. They will get better, won't they?" She held out her own glass for her share in a top-up.

"Your mother's house has mysteriously burnt to the ground and the man she was living with has been killed, possibly murdered." Sam didn't hold back. "Apart from that, everything is absolutely fine."

Amelia digested the unfortunate news with a sigh of exasperation. "Why can't we just go there and see for ourselves. We've come to this island because my father insisted. It couldn't be that he's doing his best to keep us out of harm's way?"

"There has to be more to it than that. Joe and your aunt are working closely together." Samantha glossed over the dangers. Not going directly to Sommovia now seemed sensible even if it was indeed a ploy. "Remember, we're here to do our bit too."

"I know." Amelia was trying not to sound too petulant. "So, this possible link between my mother and Alcavar; how important can it be?" She still sounded edgy.

"Don't be cross with me. You promise?" Sam bit her lip. "I'm waiting for a call from a mutual friend of ours. It might help explain more about why we've come here. It's no good looking at me like that. If I knew more, I'd tell you."

"My bloody father up to his tricks again." Amelia wanted to scream. "Next you'll be telling me that Mr Sayers is on the case and then we can all be one happy family again."

A look in Samantha's eyes was enough to give the game away. It prompted a "you've got to be f…g joking". Amelia immediately held her hands up in apology but she'd become agitated with pent-up fury.

A change of scenery was in order. Suddenly the need to go down to the key-side and find a place to eat took precedence over anything. A hurried change into jeans and jumpers later, they crossed over from their hill-top hotel and descended a series of stone steps to the road below. The sight of restaurants full of diners helped relax the two young women who were suddenly torn between choosing where to eat and wanting to explore further.

The hotel manager hadn't lied to them. Pontoons full of yachts and motor cruisers lined the quayside on the far side of the road. They stopped to stare at some of the luxury that was making quite a show. One boat in particular moored stern on to the quay gave rise to a fantasy that helped rid any latent tension left between them.

"It's absolutely beautiful and large enough to make a home in." Amelia spoke in awe of the decadent seating and polished wood that gleamed under the cabin lighting. In truth the accommodation just forward of the cockpit was as big as her own London apartment.

"Sail around the world and never put a foot on land. If you had time and the money." Samantha stared into the sky looking at the height of the boat's two masts and all the rigging.

"Need a captain and a crew." Amelia drew an appreciative glance from one of the latter who was standing in the cockpit drinking a cup of coffee. "Let's be honest, we couldn't even afford to fill it up with diesel let alone buy a week's holiday aboard." Amelia made them laugh.

They moved away and thoughts of what might have been cooking in the galley returned their thoughts to finding vitals for themselves. Steak and chips and a glass of red wine was the order of the evening. A waiter with a twinkle in his eye made a fuss of them and some of their fears and troubles were briefly forgotten.

Walking back to the hotel Amelia took Samantha's hand in her own. In doing so she made a silent promise to protect and nourish their friendship as something infinitely precious. The wine had broken cautious barriers, but was making their progress a little unsteady. If Sam found the physical contact uncomfortable, she wasn't letting it show and much to Amelia's relief did not try to take her hand away.

Back in their room they both showered and changed ready for bed. Amelia was first, a whirlwind of action that only calmed after her toothbrush had been returned to its glass. Wrapped in a bath towel Sam was quiet efficiency. She moved quietly, folding discarded clothes as she went. Returning from the bathroom in t-shirt and clean knickers she was aware of Amelia watching her from the bed while still pretending to read a magazine.

She stood in front of a mirror and used her finger tips to comb through her slightly damp hair. Raising her arm accentuated the swell of her breast and she felt her nipple gently rub against the thin white cotton that covered it.

Slowly Amelia climbed out from under her duvet to stand within touching distance of Samantha. The look of confusion on her face expressed an awkwardness in choosing the words that might excuse and explain the intimate touch of her hands. Samantha held her breath and turned to face Amelia as excitement chased away the surprise. A smile accented her acceptance and permission.

With trepidation in her eyes, Amelia moved to mould her body against her friend's. Of similar heights they fitted well, the softness of their cheeks touched and then pressed together. In a moment of tenderness, Amelia's need to feel physical intimacy had overtaken her natural inhibitions and the fear of taking the lead. She'd moved beyond flirtation and teasing; bypassed them altogether. If it hadn't been Sam she was holding, she might have tried to step away.

They stayed close, neither felt stifled or restrained in their movements.

"It's okay. I need some of this as much as you do. No, don't worry, don't even go there. I've got you and I think we deserve this. Something for us to share."

Their faces were just centimetres apart until Amelia felt brave enough to close the gap and brush her lips against Samantha's. Tentative at first, it felt as if it was the most important kiss of her life. Inhibition and self-loathing were suddenly lost in undiluted and latent passion.

If Sam felt any embarrassment, she made sure that Amelia was not aware of it. To be fair and protective to both of them, she matched the receiving of pleasure with a commitment to give it in return. It was as much a revelation to her as it was a healing process for Amelia.

When they talked of it later, lying beside each other and relaxed in exquisite afterglow, Amelia appeared shy but deeply grateful. She admitted it had been akin to losing her virginity.

"I know I always appear confident and sometimes flirtatious, but when it comes to being intimate the wiring that controls my emotions are full of loose connections. I'm all false bravado and bluster. That's the first time I've ever initiated a true act of passion." Her cheeks were pink and she looked shyly at Sam's naked body. "I felt I could trust you. Being sexual with you was so lovely and didn't make me feel dirty. Not like before… when Lloyd took advantage."

Samantha felt she should respond but knew she could not fully understand Amelia's sentiments and confusion. Instead, she decided to be open and truthful. "I wanted to be compassionate… No, that's the wrong thing to say." She tried again. "Initially I wanted to be supportive, but when you kissed me, I don't think I could have stopped. Haven't figured it out as yet. It may prove to be a once in a lifetime experience, who knows?" Sam couldn't look directly at Amelia. "But it's something I'll treasure forever..."

Amelia lent in and kissed Samantha's cheek and gave her a grateful cuddle. "My father became very adept at scaring away any potential boyfriends I might have had. You know, trying to protect me." She snuggled down and encouraged Samantha to do likewise. "He wasted his time. I never would have consented. Not until now. You and Nick are the only ones I have ever trusted, not that I would have ever slept with him." It was a surprising admission that took Amelia a few seconds to digest. "I only hope that I haven't messed up..."

Samantha butted in. "Don't you believe that for one second. I'm a big girl and can make my own decisions." As if to accentuate her point she turned and kissed Amelia. A kiss that turned into a passionate embrace, that went further than both had imagined could happen again. It left Samantha drained. Settling down to sleep, she realised that she had many questions to answer. How many times had she said to herself, "Amelia Highland can do that to you in the blink of an eye."

*

Southern England

A large glass of red wine was the only adornment to a table top that had seen a great deal of use judging by the geography of its surface. Biology was not an issue; everything was spotlessly clean. Marsha Ivanovic twiddled her fingers on the stem of the vessel in front of her and appeared transfixed by the colour captured inside it.

"Looks like you could do with a drink for yourself." She observed Nick with some reservation. "You've been putting in some air-miles."

"Well, if you're buying?" Nick watched as fiery eyes shot up to lock onto his own. He put his hands up in surrender.

"No don't spoil it. I like the fight." Marsha's harsh exterior relented; a little twitch of her lips gave her away. "But while you're up there I'll have another. They know what I'm drinking. Oh, and put one in the bin for my friend Nikki, who's going to join me for lunch after our little chat."

Nick swapped knowing glances with the woman tending the bar before returning with two glasses of the same vintage. "I thought I'd join you." He settled back into his seat.

Ms Ivanovic exuded a confidence that had nothing to do with her age. She was sure of herself, yes. Some found this disconcerting. It helped hide her vulnerability. "So, what do I owe the pleasure of your company and more importantly where is my former student and why is she not desperate for my company?"

Nick had to smile at this and explained that Amelia was taking a short break in the Adriatic, otherwise he felt sure she'd want to be here with him. "But only to be with you, I assure you."

Ms Ivanovic said something in her native tongue but never gave him a translation.

He decided to move swiftly on and come to the point of their meeting. "Jelena Highland…" he hesitated.

Marsha cut him off. "She's dead. What's the problem?"

"Well, that may have been true in some people's eyes but as of two days ago she was still alive."

"I repeat myself. What's the problem?"

"She's gone missing and you don't seem surprised by anything I've just said."

"Probably just a case of mistaken identity." Marsha's depreciation of a confusing situation was priceless. "And what has this to do with me?"

"Does the name Gabriela Simic mean anything to you. I believe she was a student in Jelena's year. Maybe you don't remember." Nick tried to bait her.

"I remember her very well." Marsha took it hook, line and sinker. "Couldn't sing a note, and I never tried to make her. Too much for the world of music to bear. But a nice enough child. I know Jelena missed her when she left to have her baby." Marsha had lost her caution.

"You wouldn't happen to know where she went or even better, where's she living now? Only it could be important." He could hear Charles' voice echoing in his ear.

Marsha put the pieces together. For the first time in an age, she felt uncertain and knew that it probably showed in her demeanour. She studied Nick a moment longer, needing to be persuaded. "How important?"

"A cliché I know. A matter of life and death. Important enough for me to travel half way round the world to ask the question." He held his hands up in surrender. "I'm guessing you've made a pact of secrecy. Very sensible, if the little that has been told to me is true."

"You're sure it's the Adriatic?"

"The Island of Alcavar, to be exact." Nick held his breath. A certain colonel had been doing his homework.

"My guess is that Mr Hanlan has unscrupulous friends in high places, hence your question and Amelia's choice of destination." She breathed a deep sigh that sounded something like relief. “Sounds like you know the answers before you’re asking the questions.” She took a large sip of wine before speaking again.

“Keeping secrets becomes a habit. It’s not easy to trust strangers in war and more particularly peace-loving friends who might become careless. Lives can depend upon the silence.” Marsha sought his understanding. “Remember, I had to leave my home for another.”

“Much like Gabriela Simic has had to do.” He watched as the old lady nodded. “Circumstances do change. I understand that some secrets are best kept secret, believe me I do, but it could be that in this case Jelena is calling out for assistance. You must be aware of this infamous General who’s been in the news lately. We think there’s a connection.”

“Wanted by the war crimes tribunal. If he’s guilty, then about time too.” She took a sip of wine and waited for a reaction. “Yes, I know he was a hero for my country, but some things are inexcusable in any fight you have with your enemy. What’s he doing? Trying to sweep it up under the carpet by getting rid of the witnesses.”

Nick shrugged in agreement and let Ms Ivanovic confirm some of Charles Hanlan’s assumptions. Her words were like a code and her flow of information was a trickle, unlike her consumption of wine that required him making a further visit to the bar.

“She goes by the name of Brie Sanchez. She lives in a small cottage in a fishing village not far from the old town but that’s all I know. I communicate with her only two or three times a year and always through an intermediatory. Somebody she probably works with. The address is some office at the Port Authority. If it helps, she sends me a picture of a small tug boat. Don't ask me why but I think she finds it significant and somehow personal."

Nick digested the information and gave Marsha his thanks. On settling the pub bill, he paid in advance for any food that Marsha and her friend might want later. His final memory of that day would be watching her toddle across the room to find another table, one with a view of the receding tide and boats moving on the river. He thought that even if his trip from New York had been a long haul it had been worth all the effort. How often did one have the pleasure of meeting with a truly unique character like Marsha Ivanovic.

*

Sommovia

Heavy rain thrummed on the roof of the café and within minutes rivulets of water were flowing down the street and into the gutters. Joe Peterson checked the covered walkways and beyond for signs of human movement. He was treated to distorted reflections of street lamps on shiny tarmac surfaces; nobody stirred. Returning to the kitchen he watched Kaira treat the wounds on the side of Deana's face.

This did not stop Deana from talking. "Gentle touch, your young lady has. My impressions of her are getting better by the second. I see why you brought her along." Deana was making light of her injuries and doing her best to get a rise out of Kaira. The latter was intent on her work.

Joe was intrigued to see her cope without alarm or fear to the riling. If the kitchen light had been brighter, he might even have seen Kaira blushing deeply with feelings she'd not had enough time to process.

He picked up his unfinished coffee. "So, what happened to the cottage? An accident or arson? Looks like you tried to save it single-handed. I hope to God you knew she wasn't trapped inside?"

She shook her head "The firemen confirmed that straight away, but the fire was deliberately started." Deana seemed calm enough. "We always knew she'd be better off out of the way. Lena may appear slow but she has a mind of her own."

"But you went looking anyhow. You took risks." Joe was being perfectly reasonable.

Deana gave the slightest of nods and received a depreciating look from Kaira who was still trying to swab her face with antiseptic.

"Sorry if I'm hurting you. Am I?" Kaira asked but seemed unconcerned.

"Yes, as it happens, but not as much as when I fell down in the rubble." The smell of burning and marks on her face evidence of her concern and panic. Her words, the first sign of self-depreciation. "I'll be honest it brought back bad memories." Deana was through with the nursing and got up from her chair to sit in another one opposite Joe. "I knew all along it would come to this. Our government has done a U-turn and is looking for people to blame."

"Indicted to appear at The Hague, convicted of crimes against humanity. Yes, we know who General Berislavic is." Kaira came over to join them. "Colonel Bradbury says his followers are still loyal. His influence reaches far and wide. If your sister remains a target, you've done well to hide her this long."

Deana took this as some kind of compliment. She offered Kaira a tight smile. "My cousin got careless and started shooting his mouth off, boasting of the help and information he gave the authorities. I told him it would never be over until the right people were safely behind bars, but he felt he deserved better; that he'd waited long enough. I admit, living with Lena must have been stressful but it was as much for his own good. Burying bodies during the war was not a life to be proud of. Justice has caught up with him now. I can't waste my sympathy. It has to be kept for Lena." Deana tried her best to sound defiant.

"This General and his cohorts surely can't believe she'd be able to give evidence against them." Joe remembered clearly how damaged Lena had appeared. "When we spoke before, you mentioned Lena's friend, Gabriela. I know she has a grown-up son. Surely that's a significant connection."

"And something must have changed to make him act this way." Kaira was all too aware how dangerous and desperate people in power could be. "He could have done this much sooner. Think of his status at the end of the war. The world was his oyster." Despite her words she didn't sound impressed.

Deana had considered that and had a ready answer. "Because the status quo has shifted since the indictment. For Slavco Berislavic to have had a baby with a mother of mixed-race was in certain quarters, an embarrassment verging on being dangerous. No offense, Miss Maes. I don't need to remind you of the discrimination that still remains. That man's hypocrisy has been our protection providing we kept silent." Deana felt like spitting. "Don't get me wrong, I'm proud of my birth-place. The deaths of innocent people are nothing for anybody to be proud of."

"I'm glad you say that," Kaira spoke with her usual strength of feeling. "Many would disagree. Those in the northern regions with strong ties to the former dictator, for instance. The instigators of the war want the General taken down. His name is synonymous with victory, but if it can be linked to the final atrocities, he'll go from hero to zero and a prison cell. Perhaps, there's nothing left for him to lose, except a desire to destroy anything and all that might help prove him guilty."

"We could debate this forever." Joe could see they were making little progress. "I need to make calls and give a couple of people an update on our situation." He reached out over the table and touched Deana's hand. "Why is it you don't seem as worried as I thought you'd be? You know, that Lena could be in danger." He gave her smile but took his hand away. "I know you've received a blow to the head but I can see your mind is still ticking over."

Deana's reply was short and to the point. "Lena never did like that cottage."

16. Marin's Mix

Planning for the visit of Charles Hanlan became compulsive and I focused on very little else. My course work suffered as a result. On the upside, collaborating with my tutor became joyfully addictive, made easier when I whole-heartedly agreed with her suggestions. Taking time off seemed a luxury we couldn't afford, but honestly, the hard work was done. There was a danger of wearing oneself too thin as Miss Matic consistently made plain.

And she was right. By the time I got off the train and got a ride to my flat in the village I still called home, there was little left in the tank. Mumbled greetings and making apologies to an elderly neighbour, I shut my front door on the world. Deep sleep interspersed with tinned fruit and the occasional coffee became a necessary and staple diet. No time, no energy, all the cupboards bare, and nothing else easy to prepare. Famine loomed as the sun went down on my second day and shopping would need to be done. Even students need some fresh food once in a while.

That someone should take an interest was no big surprise. Neighbours of a certain quality do tend to look out for one another. No, it was the identity of my food-saviour, armed as she was with a brown carrier-bag, that really took my breath away.

The light outside the front door shone down on her head that was cocooned within the hood of an oversized fleece. I noticed that her hands that cradled the bag were only just visible, poking out from rolled-up sleeves, while the garment's waistband had become a hem that hung halfway down her thighs. Wisps of what I thought was bleached-blond hair framed her face, they were actually grey. Her face remained in the shadows but I knew instinctively who she was.

No words were spoken as I opened the door and invited her in. Her movement was hesitant, as though she was testing uncertain ground. Coming to rest in the centre of the living room she looked towards the windows implying her discomfort. Closing the blinds before turning on the lamp by the chair seemed to satisfy her silent bidding. Without further invite she walked into the adjoining kitchen and deposited the contents of the bag on the only worktop available. The smell of fresh bread and cakes was wonderful. She'd even brought butter and some jam.

My self-disgust at the lack of any acceptable housekeeping was made worse by her obvious confusion that nowhere seemed clean enough to put things on. Warming to her task she pulled her oversized fleece over her head and searched for a place to drop it. I thought for one moment she might try the bedroom, but thankfully she chose the arm of the sofa. Returning to her mission in the kitchen, it seemed she'd made herself comfortably at home.

It was at that point that I spoke her name, Lena, as if in part of a question. She turned, came over, and kissed me on both cheeks as if we were old friends. I heard her mumble something and then correct herself before saying my name, "Marin." If I'd expected her to burst into easy conversation, I would have been disappointed. Sensing that she owed me an explanation she took breaths and prepared to make a concerted effort.

"I want to say and explain all to you. I have much difficulty…" She was necessarily simplistic and spoke with an engaging lisp. There was measured delay but a lyrical rhythm in how she articulated thoughts into words. At no point did she become frustrated but I made sure that I never tried to jump in and finish one of her sentences. My patience was rewarded as Lena grew in confidence.

"They killed him…"

"The man that you lived with?"

"My cousin… not nice man, but he looked after me."

"You have been hiding? But where?"

"In caravan, where they do the digging. I have to be careful. Can't stay there now. Too many people…"

Lena had been resourceful but the odds of detection had outweighed her hopes of long-term safety. Forensic teams had gathered at a pace in the last few days with the hope of identifying the bodies. World news was already reporting that the task had been made more complicated as this was a second-hand grave-site. The bodies had been moved as the frontline of combat had developed over time.

While Lena made us more coffee, I went to tidy my bedroom. When I returned, Lena indicated her need to go outside and asked that the lights be turned off while she did so. Retrieving a plastic bag full of clothes, it was clear she was asking to stay. I had one more important question.

"How best can I help you?"

Lena bowed her head and I thought she might become tearful. We drank our coffee in silence. She held her cup in both hands and took sips that gradually revived her spirits. Sitting on the edge of the sofa with her knees together in perfect symmetry, her floral-printed summer dress sat across the top of her knees and hung down either side of her tanned legs. Its V-necked top showed flawless skin from her neck to the top of her breasts. She looked like an innocent girl. The more I stared at her the more she reminded me of someone I'd seen quite recently.

*

17. Digging and Delving

International War Grave Finders camp

They knew it wasn't going to be easy or straight forward. Local opinion in a place that had guarded its secrets could never be that welcoming. On the contrary, feelings towards the outsiders were biased at best. No hotel and a lack of offers to rent accommodation, made self-efficiency inevitable; to some within the group, preferable, even if that meant camping out in fields nearest to their work.

Kaira lay on her right side and listened with her good ear proffered to the immediate world around her. As mobiles went this latest incarnation of her home was more luxurious than she'd been used to. Night-time noises drifted in through an open window above her while the silence from within was a constant. Joe Peterson was definitely not a snorer. His choice to make a bed in the main living room compartment was generous and gave Kaira her privacy. That was a good thing, right?

It had been too late to talk to the team leaders the previous evening. A meeting over breakfast had been scheduled. All who attended spoke of the need to ramp up their security not only for the sake of the excavations but also in and around the campsite. Already one of the smaller storage caravans had been broken into.

"Nothing of real value was taken, except for an old bicycle that we strap on the back of it and use for our own convenience." The team leader tried not to sound too angry. "We're still waiting for the specialist machinery to arrive before making a concerted start. There's plenty of prep to do in the meantime." It was easy to be careful after the event.

"I don't need to remind you that that every scrap of evidence could be vital."

Kaira winced at the choice of words that the director had chosen. If she was going to be kind, she might have said it was a form of gallows humour.

Despite his impatience Joe was glad that he waited for Kaira to return to the home. They began putting together information gained from her colleagues with what they already knew from Deana. A report of a lone cyclist on the dirt roads that bypassed the village had piqued their interest. A visit from local police enquiring into the break-in made their suppositions seem real.

"I'm confused as to why the cottage was burnt to the ground." Kaira noticed that Jeff was ready to leave. She wanted to keep him talking.

"Deana hinted that she thought it was a sign." He explained. "The authorities confirm that nothing of importance was found in the wreckage. The shot gun and crowbar found dumped in the garden remains a mystery. Petrol was used; the obvious accelerant. The property had no real value. Deana always said it needed to be knocked down. Apparently, her cousin was a slob and treated it like a workshop. Lena was always washing and cleaning. They found one of his old motorbikes, burnt out in the middle of the living room."

"You think that Lena could have been responsible for burning her own home down?" Kaira was fast reaching certain conclusions. "Seems to me that her competence has been underestimated."

Joe wholeheartedly agreed. "What better way to hide in plain sight? Problem is, the deception probably no longer exists and could make her enemies desperate and angry."

"This general who's gone on the run needs to be found and quickly. We should speak to Colonel Bradbury as soon as we can."

"Nick Sayers, a reliable man by all accounts." Bradbury was at work very early. Other offices were still empty and the lack of interruption a boon. He held the phone tightly to his ear. The reception was patchy at best as if Joe was in the middle of nowhere.

"I gather Hanlan sent him on a fact-finding mission and he's come back with something useful. Enough to alter our plans accordingly?" Joe had made his own mind up.

By chance the Colonel was rearranging papers on his desk. "Could be. Interestingly enough I received a tip-off from my Spanish counterpart in Barcelona. Captain Nunez, a good chap. Used to play water polo against him. We've kept in touch." It was an unusual aside from a man that Joe had never got to know on a personal basis.

"Tells me there was an incident on a local ferry. Suspected heart attack. The man died but his identity papers proved interesting. The island has Spanish connections but is now under Sommovian governance. The man was definitely Eastern European with a military background and served under Berislavic. Nunez knew I wanted checks made on traffic heading east." He tried not to sound too enthusiastic.

Joe gave this some thought before replying. "There's two ways of reading this, sir." He was only too aware that Samantha and Amelia might already be in danger.

"With respect, if we can find Miss Simic then so can the general and his supporters. We can't be sure whether this man was sent ahead or is part of a backup team. In my opinion, we should get Miss Highland and Miss Grant out of there."

"Or we use the fact that they're already there to our own advantage." Bradbury was playing devils-advocate. "Look Peterson, other agencies are in charge of this. We're bit-part players at best."

"I want to make more of Miss Maes's involvement. We need to know who's at risk." Joe was adamant. "I'm guessing she knows more than she's letting on."

Bradbury spoke calmly. "Go carefully, there's only so much pressure you can reasonably apply. Meanwhile, I'll speak with Hanlan again. Not easy, Peterson, whatever we decide to do. It's a fine balancing act."

"We can't afford casualties, Miss Simic included. I need to get to this island. Alcavar, did you say? Apart from Lena, all the likely victims are there."

"Send her a warning but give Miss Grant the chance to come up with some definitive information. I'll be honest with you, Peterson. Our involvement in this needs to see a return if we're to be taken seriously. Give them proof and the authorities may include us."

Joe had to trust that Bradbury had no personal motive in the decisions they were making. Responding to order was easy as a professional. "I'll get a message to Miss Grant but I should be as honest as I can. I'm sorry but we'll have to abide by her wishes."

Bradbury had to agree. "Do that and leave the rest with me. Another few hours may make the difference. I have a plane at my disposal, ready to go at a moment's notice."

He paused and thought more of Joe's concerns. "No, you're right. I'll come out straight away. Be on hand and if needs be we'll travel to the island together. It's the best I can offer."

*

Alcavar

Buffet breakfast was a sumptuous and tempting affair. Both women selected orange juice as a starter and made themselves comfortable on a table looking out onto the patio and beyond. Shimmering blue water was visible through gaps in the pines. Encouraged by Samantha's choice of scrambled eggs and rashers of bacon, Amelia forwent the healthy option of muesli and fruit. She added cheese on top of her bacon that drew a frown of disappointment from Sam who thought she'd missed out.

"Do you want some? I'll get you some. We might not eat again until this evening." Amelia got up from the table and returned with two slices of gouda and two freshly baked rolls. "This really feels like we're on holiday. I want more of this. I want… I'll shut up and eat."

Sam supressed a laugh and covered her mouth with a napkin. She continued looking at Amelia who was busily chewing and wondered what else she had been about to say.

The early morning air made their skin tingle as they took their coffee out and sat in comfortable chairs on the patio. She was thinking of getting a refill when Samantha received her first call of the day. It was Charles.

"Tell my daughter to turn her bloody phone on, will you please Samantha." He turned down his voice a notch or two. "She's okay, isn't she? Not too upset with all this news concerning her mother? It can't be easy for her."

"She's coping okay. I'm finding things to distract her." Sam raised her eyebrows a little guiltily and proffered her phone to Amelia who shook her head and spoke without moving.

"Hello father. Wishing you were here."

"Don't be fooled, she hides her feelings too well when it suits her. If she gets out of hand, she probably needs a good hiding. You have my permission." Hanlan cleared his throat and sounded emotional. "But seriously, down to business and I'm sorry to have to tell you this but we haven't heard from Joe. It could be a time-difference thing but his old army boss promised to get in touch as soon as he got word. You've met Kaira Maes?"

"Yes, in Salzburg with the Colonel."

"She told Bradbury he left the camp an hour ago to meet up with Deana Horvat." Hanlan made his choice. "The picture is unclear but Nick has done well with Marsha Ivanovic." He wanted to be cautious but Samantha was persuasive.

"Gabriela Simic now goes under the name of Brie Sanchez. She definitely lives on the island." Charles relayed all that Nick Sayers had told him. "I don't want you doing anything to put yourselves in danger. Wait until we've heard from Joe, I think." After a few parting pleasantries the line went dead.

"Always forthright and to the point." With a flick of her eyes, Samantha let Amelia know it was time to move on from their comfortable lethargy.

Both decided on a change of clothes before going into town. Once back in their room, Amelia found a message sent up from reception; something about a late cancellation. There'd be time to talk to Sam later about that.

"Why the sudden hurry?"

"Lots to do and much to discuss." Folded clothes were quickly dispatched into drawers. "Come on, get your butt moving."

The walk into town gave them choices. They could keep high and go through quiet residential streets or down steps and tarmacked slopes to the harbour's edge. There was a headland just down from the hotel that looked west and gave views of the ferry port and small cruise ship moorings. Amelia took hold of Samantha's hand and decided to be brave.

"Are you happy, I mean sharing a room? I know I'm not tidy like you, but well… what do you think? Another one might become available." It was the first time that she had alluded to their unusual situation. "I'm really comfortable, I have to say." She tried to sound non-committal, as if Samantha's answer wouldn't really matter.

Crossing the road created a moment where Sam could reflect and decide what was most appropriate. Her on-off relationship with Joe was governed by the width of the Atlantic and led to moments of frustration and a share in short-lived gratification. The trip to Sommovia and then onto Austria had seemed like a holiday romance.

The real question remained; did she feel guilty for being intimate with Amelia? Could she have refused the young woman's need to be loved? Reliving the physical consequences that had proved intoxicating gave her exquisite pain. How to be comfortable and committed, not settling for safety but not being constantly on edge. She thought that Amelia probably craved the same.

They both looked down from the top of the cliff. The tourist boats and leisure craft were becoming busy, creating patterns of wash that criss-crossed one another.

"Let's go this way." Samantha had seen something below them that took her interest. "I'm perfectly happy where we are, but we can always ask at reception." She too had picked up the message but was happy to let her roommate decide.

"No, I'm fine if you are. It's a nice room with good views." Amelia appeared to brighten. "Where are we going?"

"Down there. See that bright orange boat tied up to the key. Gabriela Simic has a thing about tug boats, apparently."

The large paved concourse gave room for easy walking without the need to check one footstep before taking another. The tug boat with its bow and stern covered in protective tyres sat tall and proud and was held to land by two single lines. A man with a sea-faring cap and Spanish badge was checking a coil of rope as the two women approached. It was fascinating to be this close to an integral piece of the harbour life. It looked as if the boat was being readied for action.

"Buenos dias, Senor. Hablo muy poce Espanol." Samantha's mixed accent of American and Spanish brought a smile to the master of the boat.

"Como esta."

"Muy bien, gracias." Sam's knowledge of the language came to a sad end. "Captain, I know you must be busy but I was wondering if you've heard of a woman by the name of Brie Sanchez. She seems to know your boat very well."

The master was proud and shrugged his shoulders as if to say that no one should be surprised by this. Everyone knows of the orange tug.

"Who do I speak with and why do you have this question?" He tried not to show his interest but was swayed by the attention he was receiving. He felt it best to reciprocate in kind. The darker one, he noticed, was wearing a short dress that was blowing in the strengthening breeze. The other woman asking the questions had intense looking eyes visible beneath the peak of her cap. Her golden tan was even and made her skin glow.

"She's a friend of a friend. We've been asked to get in touch and say hello." Samantha explained and became aware of a younger pair of eyes looking down to them from the doorway of the wheelhouse.

"I'll ask around if you like. I have to go now. We have an old gas and oil tanker coming into harbour soon." He touched the side of his head in a casual salute and disappeared down through a hatchway.

Sam and Amelia looked at each other in disappointment and were about to walk away when a voice shouted down for them to wait where they were. The young man shimmied down a ladder and came to the side of the boat.

"See the harbour tour boat with the yellow hull. Meet me there at twelve-thirty." His order was brief and quite simple. Without a backward glance the young man returned to his duties and implied that the girls should not hang around.

Sam got the message and led Amelia away. "Don't look back but I'd say we're on the right track." She looked at her watch. "In the meantime, we've got time to kill. Let's go back into town. I don't know about you but I could do with something to drink. It's hotter than I expected."

"A boat trip sounds good to me." Amelia sounded upbeat. "What was it that made him come down and speak to us?" She answered her own question. "He must have heard the name you mentioned to the captain."

"I'd put a bet on it." Sam rested her hand briefly on Amelia's shoulder. "Come on, this way. Those flight of stairs must lead us somewhere."

Amelia walked in step and close by, seeking occasional touches that would not appear too obvious and yet were reassuring. She glanced briefly at Samantha and smiled. If she'd looked closer, she might have seen her friend's eyes misting over.

Cold lime cordial and a small cake became their impromptu lunchtime snack at a café that had gorgeous views of the harbour. They watched as the orange tug helped turn a small freighter on its axis. The tyres that acted as a nose in the bow of the boat pushed the much larger ship until it could reverse its way along the dock on the far side of the water.

At twelve noon they ventured back down the stone steps and bought tickets to ride the yellow tour boat. Amelia adjusted the strap on her new baseball cap and offered herself up for inspection.

"Good choice, it fits well. Your new disguise?" Sam looked deeply into Amelia's eyes and given the chance would have said more.

They walked slowly forward to join a small queue of holiday-makers ready to take to the water. At twelve-thirty sharp the young man from the tug boarded with seconds to spare and in passing spoke to some of the crew. They all seemed to know him. He even made time to flirt with the girl who was selling iced-lollies at the refreshment bar. When he finally approached Amelia and Sam, he came armed with three of differing flavours. Choices made and seats taken out of the sun, he began with a question.

"You mentioned a name to the skipper, but I wonder if you can give me another?" Dark eyes in a sun-burnt face looked with lazy intensity and made ready to judge their reaction. He stared at Amelia in particular, as though encouraging her to be the one to answer.

She duly obliged. "Gabriela Simic. Is that who you mean? She was a friend of my mother's when they were young. If I had to make a guess, you're probably her son."

"Let's say that's true, then why do you need to see her? What's she to you?" His face was expressing emotion as though he wanted to say 'she's been through enough already'.

"I understand you might not trust us. Truthfully, we don't know the full story." Amelia looked to Samantha for support. "My father asked us to come so we can make you aware of recent developments."

The young man took his time and looked over the water in the direction of the other islands and beyond to the open sea. Dark features and his brooding demeanour could not disguise his youthful appearance. If this was Luca Simic then he'd be only a couple of years older than Amelia.

"If what you say is true then why not just send a message. Why come here in person?"

"Like you we need to be cautious. We have important information that your mother deserves to hear in person." Amelia turned to Sam showing signs of distress. This was a familiar theme that needed fixing, and soon.

Sam jumped in. "Maybe if we could see Gabriela and she was happy to talk of the past." She whispered something into Amelia's ear.

"You can say it aloud. No need to keep it a secret." The young man's eyes never left them for a second.

"We were wondering if you remembered where you lived before coming to the island and who your mother worked for?" Amelia asked a loaded question.

The young man tried to laugh "Why is this suddenly important?" He was becoming increasingly defensive.

"All I can tell you is that our intentions are from the heart." Amelia sounded suddenly wistful. "You want to protect your mother, but these things are rarely that simple. They certainly weren't for my mother."

"It would only be for five minutes." Sam jumped in. "She could come to our hotel or we could go to her home. Your call entirely." She could see he was weighing up the options and understood that once chosen there'd be no turning back.

"Sorry, we never introduced ourselves properly. I'm Sam and I think you know who this is."

"Luca Sanchez." A small smile crossed his face as he spoke directly to Amelia. "My mother said you'd be beautiful." He stood up and beckoned them to follow. The tour boat was slowing just beyond the harbour limits. "They feed the fish here. The boat has a glass bottom if you're interested." He shook hands with both of them. "I must go now but I'll contact you at your hotel tonight."

In the blink of an eye a small power boat approached and drew alongside where he stood on the dangerous side of the safety rail. Luca waved to the crew of the tour boat and with one easy stride stepped onto the smaller craft just as it reversed back and away. Two seconds later and with the wheel hard over the driver accelerated the boat into a turn with white water accompanying the roar of its engine.

"Well. What do you think?" Amelia held onto Samantha as the boat rocked in the newly created waves.

"About the fish or do you mean Luca?" Samantha spoke instinctively. "Quite a catch for you, Amelia." She was aware that she was still being clung to.

Amelia watched as seagulls circled and dove to the surface of the water scooping up the food that the fish were too slow to get to. "Happy where I am, thank you." She paused for a second. "How does he know which hotel we're staying at?"

"Well Mr Sayers what have you got to say for yourself?" Sam sat with her legs in the sun and top half under the shade of a parasol. She whispered into her phone. Other guests were lying close by and enjoying a lazy afternoon by the hotel pool.

"I hear you've been in Suffolk again. Is there nothing you won't do to get your hands on a pint of local beer."

"Nothing changes, working as usual. Back on my own. It's a long story. Sucker for a dollar and can never say no to a pound." Nick's voice was full of acceptance. "Been speaking to Amelia's old music teacher who also worked with her mother back in the day. No doubt the info was passed onto you. How is it going out there on Alcavar?"

"What a beautiful place. We found the Simic boy, or at least he found us. Hoping we might join up with his mother. Luca says he will contact us later tonight, all being well."

"And Amelia, how is she coping with all that's knew and surprising."

Samantha blushed to her root tips, not knowing what to say. She watched in fascination as the said actor climbed out of the pool. Sun glinted off droplets of water that covered her torso and her gorgeous legs. Sam saw that

Amelia's bikini was charmingly respectable while her own mind and thoughts appeared to be anything but.

Holding her phone in one hand she passed her glistening friend a spare towel with the other. She whispered "it's Nick", and had her means of conversation immediately confiscated. "Don't get my phone wet", did nothing to quell the obvious delight and relaxed manner with which Amelia walked away out of earshot. Samantha watched as she turned, making faces that told a story of lightweight banter and the swapping of up-to-date news.

It wasn't long before Amelia returned to Samantha's chaise-long. The words that were spoken had become more intense and serious. She sat down next to Sam and asked her to take over once again. Amelia listened in on the rest of the conversation as she dried her hair.

"No, I've not heard from Joe… No, I'm not happy… Yes, I've already agreed that with Amelia. We're here for that very reason. Now we know who we're looking for… No, that's no excuse… Yes, we're going to be extra careful." This time it was Samantha who was making faces. "You're going where?… Doing what?… Okay, I'll pass that onto Amelia." With a few last words and a wish for him to travel safely, Samantha disconnected the call.

Amelia looked expectantly at her. Folding her towel, she sat down, borrowing space on the chaise long as Sam pulled her legs to one side in invitation. "Come on then, spit it out."

"Well, there you go then. Did you know that Nick is going to Mezlar. Apparently, your father has accepted an invitation from the music department at the University to give a talk on 'Ever Searching'. Nick is covering the event."

Amelia nodded her head as though it might have been something they'd discussed.

"Were you also aware he's thinking of giving an impromptu concert and hopes that you haven't forgotten how to sing." Samantha waited for a reaction.

A slight smile played on Amelia's lips, followed by a look of concern. "You'll be coming with me. I need a manager who can be a friend." She spoke without thinking. "I spoke to Rosalind and she thinks it would be ideal. You know, she said you could be closer to Joe…" Her thoughts and voice faded away as the reality of their situation cut through and pin-pricked the holiday balloon. "Suddenly nothing matters but being with…" Amelia felt a hand on her arm as she looked away and tried to be calm.

"So many things are happening and quickly." Samantha's own thoughts were confused and unsettling. "You know Nick has split up from Libi, this time for good." She addressed what she considered to be a delicate subject. "You get on very well with him and I know there's an attraction between you both."

"But he can only be a friend." Amelia shook her head. "He's too mature and I don't mean, old. I could never be his girlfriend, I'm sure of that." She turned the question back onto Samantha. "It's you that I'm worried about. I mean, honestly, and I know we've been naughty just the once, but what about you and Joe? Is it forever? How do you tell?"

Sam was aware that her world had been reduced to the small shade of the parasol that they shared. Something that had germinated in New York as part of her job had suddenly grown roots and needed to be nurtured. She was certain of nothing.

"When I was on the phone just now and I watched you get out of the pool..." Sam took a deep breath and wondered whether to continue.

"Please go on. No more secrets."

"Well, I felt like crying; still do. Never saw anything as beautiful. Don't want to lose you by making the wrong choices." She stifled a sob. "And we aren't even together. I'm meant to have a boyfriend." She shrugged her shoulders. "I guess you can sense my confusion."

Amelia was silent while she gathered her thoughts.

"The way I feel now makes me think I've lived in a bubble. What happened between me and my step-brother seems like a different life. It hasn't scarred me like you might imagine, I promise you." She squeezed Samantha's hand. "I'm finding out about myself all the time. During the last six months, you've given me constant support, without question." It was Amelia's turn to show feelings that were becoming vital. "And I kind of love you for that."

Both took deep breaths and let in the rest of the world around them. Splashes made in the pool and waitresses collecting glasses from nearby tables became audible once again. It gave them respite and excuses not to say something that might embarrass the other. It was suddenly rather hot, even in the shade.

"I want to kiss you for saying that." Sam felt grateful and embarrassed all in one go. "We should probably get moving. Have a shower and be prepared to hear from Luca."

"I can't wait for that."

"What for?"

"To be kissed." Amelia stood up and grabbed her bag from the other chair. "Oh, and have some dinner." She received a playful pat on her bum.

Samantha gathered her own things together and watched as Amelia walked across the grass heading back to the hotel. The outline of her body showed through her lightweight dress. "Well, here we go." She spoke to herself and sauntered in the wake of her roommate. It was only late afternoon and there was no need to rush.

Not so. Not in another's opinion. She could feel her stride getting suddenly quicker as Amelia beckoned her forward and held out her hand. They tried to stay modestly apart as they climbed the stairs to the first floor. Nerve-endings tingled as their progress down the hall became less than casual. Once inside the privacy of their room, towels and shoulder bags lay where they landed as they stood together on the cool tiles, inches apart. Curtains were drawn with outstretched hands and the soft safety of the bed was there if they chose it. And suddenly they were coy.

"I've got you. I understand. There's no need to worry. When the time is right." Amelia embraced the hesitation. She knew her inexperience would have easily disappeared in passion and greed. "Let's give ourselves time." Their limits of respectability were in danger of being tested again. She stepped back to give them both some room.

The depth of feeling and preferences were understood without words. A sense of anticipation remained. Bikini tops and bottoms were naturally discarded.

"You're wiggling suggestively on purpose." Sam giggled as a release of tension. "Maybe I should get that other room."

"No, sorry, don't do that. Look, I've stopped."

"Looking but no touching. I think I can do that, just about."

From then on in, questioning eyes and small nods of approval set them right when either one felt hesitant. Even when they'd both showered, they respected the small space between them on the bed where they lay wrapped in their robes.

The first to offer something that truly made sense was Amelia. It wasn't much but it did make them laugh. "F… me. Is this what it's like to be mature." She gently nibbled Samantha's shoulder. "I'm suddenly hungry."

Samantha was happy to reply in kind. "Sorry madam but that's temporarily off the menu."

*

18. The Enemy

Where was she?

Joe Peterson drove out of camp and followed his nose along unmade tracks that by-passed the village. Although proving herself quite self-sufficient, finding Lena was imperative for his own sense of well-being. If as he surmised her choice had been to come this way, she must have had good reason. It couldn't have been easy riding a bike on a surface this uneven.

Not for the first time he cursed the low-profile tyres on the hire car as he tried to avoid large stones and deep potholes. He was just thinking how inadequate puncture repair foam and a battery powered pump would be when the sound of a rifle firing two shots overtook his senses. The car kicked to the right as a nearside tyre was blown out and destroyed. By the time the car came to a halt Joe was already out of the vehicle, rolling to his left and into a ditch that ran alongside the road.

Up ahead a red pickup crept out from the deep cover of undergrowth and turned towards the crippled Audi. It finally came to a stop twenty or so metres away from where Joe was lying. He peered from his meagre place of cover and watched the passenger door being opened. His puzzlement was matched with exasperation as Lena emerged with her hands held to her head. A figure behind her was urging her forward with the muzzle of a gun pointing at her back.

"They will hurt me badly. Only talk… to you… not kill you." Lena spoke in her native tongue so that her captors would understand she was complying with their wishes.

Joe considered his options and decided he had none other than to surrender himself to the threat of the gun they had on Lena.

"Not hurt you, old blue beret. Yes, want answers, same as you." With Lena safely back in the passenger seat, the gunman's weapon was lowered, inviting him forward.

He stepped out from his place of cover and approached the man who stood to one side of the truck. Two things happened simultaneously that did not bode well. The driver re-started his engine just as Joe became conscious of movement from the back of the pickup. The face of a man who'd been laying down rose above the tailgate. Eyes were sending signals that Joe never truly understood as the pickup suddenly reversed and knocked him down. Some part of the tailgate slammed into his right thigh; a rear wheel came within centimetres of crushing his head.

As the dust settled the man with the gun reached down and took Joe's phone from his shirt pocket. The smirk on his face showed a certain satisfaction. "You should never come back. Once a blue-beret, always a puppet." The man spat into the dirt and placed his foot on Joe's injured leg. "They don't pay you enough for this, eh?"

An hour later the man with singed hair continued to drive in silent contemplation. The flame throwing explosion that had destroyed the cottage was indelibly inked into his memory. Any anger he felt towards Lena for her part in nearly killing him and his boss was kept under wraps for now. He'd overreacted when knocking the British soldier down. It had only encouraged his comrades to get their blood up, something he'd been trying to avoid. But then old habits die hard in the face of the enemy.

The pickup's progress on the motorway was deafening. The sound of treaded tyres humming inside a tin can running on hard rubber made the high revving engine almost indefinable. The man sitting next to Lena carried a hidden revolver but let it be known he had her covered. She sat by the window but knew the door was locked from inside. With a slight turn of her head, she could see Marin sitting on a makeshift seat in the back. The third man of the kidnapping party must be there too, no doubt with a rifle by his side.

They were heading north-westward towards the coast. It was a road, coincidently, she'd driven many times before. Taking holidays when she was young was a past she could not remember. Living in the here and now, her mood was getting more desperate. They wouldn't even stop to let her get out and go for a pee.

It was dark when they finally arrived at their destination. They had eventually stopped for fuel and Lena had been allowed to use the service station toilets providing she was accompanied by revolver man at all times. In sharing the cubicle, he'd been neither fazed by his vigil or taking the opportunity to relieve himself too, as she was forced to look on. His proud stream, she noted, had put her own self-conscious trickle to shame.

The smell of the sea permeated into the depths of the old warehouse that played some part in a boat building business. At present it was empty save for the remnants of old life-raft cannisters and rubber dinghies, both well past their sell-by dates. Each had been stripped of their life-saving medicines and aids, like torches and flares. To both Marin and Lena, the air inside the building seemed colder than they'd been used to inside the pickup. Lena clung close to her companion both for warmth and a sense of comfort. Nobody was inclined to speak. Their captors endeavoured to stay relaxed as they waited.

The cigarettes that had been a staple diet amongst the three kidnappers were soon stubbed out as the sound of an outboard motor was heard approaching. A mobile phone bleeped and was answered. The man with the rifle and the driver went to a side door and looked out at the water. The atmosphere had suddenly changed and the body language of the man with the revolver became business-like and expectant.

Raised voices acted like a warning of impending trouble. The sight of a man who was bald and probably in his sixties did nothing to dispel the sense of foreboding. Followed by a collective of bodyguards, the warehouse became instantly more crowded. Lena instinctively gripped Marin's arm as the well-known figure of General Berislavic walked slowly towards her. His eyes never left her for one second. She flinched involuntarily as he reached out and traced the outline of her scar on the side of her head.

"Well, I thought you might have died. All this time. Really, you should have died." He shook his head and looked both amazed and disappointed. "You may be damaged goods, but you still have value." Berislavic spoke in an aside to the man who had driven the pickup. "He was foolish to underestimate the spirit of this woman." And then directly to Lena. "Maybe it would have been kinder, yes? Only you know how much your life has changed." He stroked the scar one last time. "You're too proud to admit to it. I can tell by the look in your..."

Lena kept her eyes on the general's face, tried not to blink and look fearful.

"If it weren't for you... well, my son might have enjoyed his life. Not become so angry. It's hard to say. You had the courage to stand up to him." Again, he made contact with Lena's face, this time cupping his hand under her chin. "Now, you must tell me all that you can." He touched her gently. "There's still time to save your friend, Miss Simic. My son needs luck but I fear it's about to run out." Dropping his hand, he looked concerned. "Disaster can happen as quickly as a bullet fired from a gun. Of all people you should understand this. Come, yes come, we must go to my rescue. Yes, I'm in trouble too. And yet there's much we still have to do."

Berislavic took Lena by the hand and began walking back towards where he'd entered the building. By the door he turned and spoke to Marin. "I don't know who you are but you have just become a very important person. Yes you. You know who I am. They put my picture on the news and in the papers, so go to Mezlar and tell them what you have seen. Remember, I'm no monster. Tell them that. Make sure they listen. General Berislavic asks this of you with a promise that nothing unpleasant will happen to Miss Jelena here. At least I can try." He laughed with no enjoyment. "I helped win the war but I'm no miracle worker."

*

19. Marin's Mix

Tell who, and tell them what? The late-night bus made few stops on its way back into Mezlar but gave me time to reflect. The thugs who had knocked the ex-soldier down had received the full wroth of their new employer's disfavour. I had watched the General's shoulders sag in disappointment when they admitted what had been done. He accepted the mobile phone that they'd taken as some small compensation. Certainly, I was being treated with more respect now. The driver with the singed hair even dropped me off at the bus station and gave me money for the fare.

Settling back in my seat my mind wandered back to the night before when all this surrealness had started. How could I explain and find the words to match the sentiment.

... I'd been wide awake with wonder at how this woman had found me. Was it for rescue or just respite? Lena's trust in me was naively child-like and yet she appeared full of steely determination. In choosing the sofa she left me no alternative but to take to my own bed. Chivalry was dead before I could to show myself off in a good light. When the bedroom door swung inwards, her movement had been quiet. She climbed onto the mattress beside me and pulled the duvet up to her chin and lay on her side facing me. She said nothing but I'd grown accustomed to this.

I tried to make out her expressions but the darkness made it impossible to see if her eyes were open or closed. We must have dozed off as I listened to her breathing, because the next thing I felt was the trace of her lips on my neck. Her subtle scent and delicate touch made my reactions immediate as my hands reached out purely to comfort and protect her. My last conscious thought was how her petite frame belied the strength of her spirit.

The experience was real enough and still lives with me now. The pleasure that I took in her trust of me acts like a balm during the bad times. I'm only sorry I wasn't there for my girlfriend before she ended her life. Others have said that there was nothing I could have done for her. I'm not so sure. Should I have made more time for her? What little we understand when we're young...

The bus went over some rumble strips and shook me out of my revelry. From a special kind of intimacy to kidnap. Yes, there were guns and I was scared but I never felt threatened. I'll never forget the look of the men's faces as they bundled us into a pickup. I chanced to see my neighbour, the one who gave them the tip-off, taking her reward in folding currency. Some people are greedy and full of shame. At least she'd had the decency to wait until Lena and I had showered and eaten some breakfast.

There had been nothing said about sharing a bed and I was glad about that. I stole looks at Lena as she'd sipped her coffee and thought she looked undamaged. Her face never showed much expression but her eyes could still twinkle. They looked bright and holding hands was allowable. It gave us a link that spoke volumes as we continued on a bizarre journey together.

That all ended in the warehouse by the coast. Now they'd taken her and I had no idea where or how to help. Or did I? I sat up straight in my seat and took comfort from the fact that if they meant to kill her the deed would have already been done. It seemed I was heading in the right direction after all. Visitors from a foreign land that I'd helped to invite to this country. Could it be they were the people General Berislavic was referring to?

*

20. Getting Together

Fully Comprehensive Insurance was written into the hirer's contract but was not important right at that moment. In his present condition Joe was only trying to divert himself. Any sensible conversation with the hire car company must prove interesting. The four-wheel drive Audi drove better in reverse as the front tyre finally shredded and fell away. Joe had taken minutes to drag himself back to the car's open door. Selecting gear had been painful and driving left foot down on the accelerator, he'd used his rear-view mirror for guidance. His leg felt badly swollen and he'd be incapable of walking properly for a couple of days. Even longer if the bastards had broken anything.

"How did the accident occur, sir?" and "Oh, you claim you were shot at by a gunman using a rifle." and "Did you manage to exchange details. By the way, you owe us half a tank of diesel."

These thoughts and his main hope that Kaira Maes would still be in camp had for the most part kept his mind off of the pain. Fortunately, there'd been no further complications except for a grinding sound coming from the front suspension. Pot holes be damned. He drove as fast as his leg would allow him.

Eventually, Joe parked at an angle beside Kaira's mobile and shut his eyes, giving himself a moment to recover. That proved to be all he was allowed as the young woman herself opened the door and gasped her enquiries. Leaving him for a few seconds she returned with painkillers and two colleagues who took physical charge and control. Joe found himself being lifted inside Kaira's new home.

"Don't worry, there's a doctor on site." She winced and was totally in tune with Joe's discomfort. "When you're ready you can tell me what happened." She put a reassuring hand on his shoulder. "I should say that Colonel Bradbury has been trying to get a hold of you. He landed in Mezlar not long ago and says he's on his way." She adjusted her glasses, pulled back her hair and tied it in a ribbon before blushing profusely. "I'm going to take off your trousers. I hope you don't mind but the doctor will need to see it."

"It might be swollen." Joe tried to inject some humour and undid the buckle of his belt. "Be careful of the zipper, won't you."

Despite the situation Kaira giggled and only just refrained from saying anything more. She leaned across him, tugging at his shirt to release his jeans. The blue and purple bruising on Joe's thigh made her gasp.

Despite the pain Joe tried to grin but finally laid back and gave in to her administrations. Towels and plenty of ice were the short-term solutions.

"You couldn't be in better hands." The doctor, a full-time member of the group handed back his patient to Kaira. "Plenty of bed-rest. Don't wear yourself out." As he left Joe's side he added. "And that includes you too, Kaira." He shut the door behind him.

Kaira blushed again. "He thinks that I'm an innocent. So, what do we do now?" She filled another plastic bag full of ice and set it down gently just above Joe's knee. "They took your phone, obviously. We should try and warn all your contacts. Particularly Samantha and Charles Hanlan. Make sure they know you're safe."

Joe lent his head back on a pillow. "Right now, I could do with a scotch or brandy. Whatever you can get your hands on. Ring Bradbury back and tell him what's happened. Not that he can do much to help us. Give me an hour and then we'll go find Deana, make sure she's okay. Maybe tell the Colonel to meet us there." He made sure Kaira understood his commitment. "Right?" He waited until she nodded. "And while we're doing that you can fill me in on who you're really working for."

Kaira inwardly smiled. She'd need to make a call of her own. The time seemed right and she thought Joe was due. His injury was an unwanted complication but not a disaster. Everybody else needed to keep their nerve and do their jobs.

"Okay. Scotch on the way. Makes better use of the ice which you seem to be wasting." She adjusted towels to keep him dry and leaned over Joe to re-adjust another pillow. "Anything else I can do for you?"

Pain relief could come in many guises. Joe had views of smooth skin and knew he needed to be careful. How appealing are those who are beautifully naive. "I'll think on that and let you know."

"Following his indictment, Berislavic's lawyers have been working twenty-four seven maintaining his innocence." Colonel Bradbury turned to Joe. "Between you and me, stealing your phone allows him to contact us directly. My guess, he'll turn himself in but only when he's good and ready."

They all sat in Deana's café sipping coffee and sampling home-made cake. "Very good, by the way." Bradbury took another bite and understood that placating his host was no easy task.

Involuntarily, Kaira Maes reached up to her hearing aid and wished the Colonel would turn down the charm. She expressed an opinion they could all share in.

"There's no doubt we're being played by his supporters. Negotiations between government officials and Dutch Special Forces are taking place as we speak. These high-profile trials have to be justified by results." Kaira was entering new territory. "It doesn't help much, but we're in a privileged position because we're close to Lena and Gabriela." She watched as Deana became indignant. "It may not seem that way to you. At least we can be confident of being kept in the loop."

"You think so. I'm so glad it's working out for you." In her anger Deana got up from the table and bumped into Joe's bad leg that was propped up on another chair. His wince of pain did nothing to calm her. "So, what are we doing here drinking coffee? Let's go. You want me to bring my rifle? I'm ready, come on let's get moving. I want my sister back."

Bradbury smiled and tried to disarm her anger and bravado. "Pack a bag, we can leave in ten minutes. Bring your toothbrush and clothes for a few days." He turned to Joe. "I assume you'll be wanting to tag along. It's that or stay behind and deal with the car-hire company."

Bradbury's driver had certainly drawn the shortest straw. Left with instructions of where to find Joe's car, he was sure of being abandoned and forgotten, maybe for ever. Never slow to pick up on another's misfortune, Deana had perked up and was happy to inform him which keys were which to lock up the café. Tomorrow's customers were going to be a disgruntled group unless he was into baking bread. Her final instructions left him thinking it was easier to take orders from the Colonel than it was from Deana. Her insolent air-kiss as they departed did nothing to improve his mood.

"It's true we've been given dispensation to speak with the Special Forces Team. How cooperative they'll be remains to be seen. They have a base at Port Central and a presence on the Island of Alcavar itself. It takes about an hour by fast ferry between the two." Bradbury drove with infuriating calm that seemed to put Deana on edge. Her, "you can go faster", had little effect on the speedometer as she gave direction from the front of seat of the car. He noticed she wouldn't stop fiddling with air-vents and every conceivable button on the radio.

Bradbury politely pointed out he was listening to the woman's voice on sat-nav.

"I know the way. You don't need her. My family have property not far from Port Central. Alcavar is a beautiful place." It was hard to tell if Deana's heart was beginning to thaw. "You have a first name? I want to know more. If we find my sister alive, we may become friends. Who knows?"

"Just call me Colonel for now." Bradbury sounded cautious. He kept his eyes on the road but allowed himself a glance in the rear-view mirror, seeking assistance.

Joe Peterson's silent advice seemed to be one of acceptance. His back-seat existence was one of ice wrapped in towels that seemed to be helping his leg. His threshold to pain was greater than his wish to ignore Kaira Maes who was studiously becoming a very competent nurse. Admitting her links with Dutch armed forces had not been that surprising but was incongruous with her gentle and physical nature. What she lacked in experience she made up for with her intelligence and fearless honesty.

She seemed okay with the status quo; Joe duly noted this and made him inquisitive. Kaira and Bradbury understood the games that were being played, whilst he was still missing bits of a complicated puzzle. It was obvious that his own opinions meant little or nothing. Controlling his own destiny suddenly seemed mightily important.

Thoughts of Samantha flashed up as warning signs. Difficult subjects could no longer be ignored. New York and Britain were hours apart. Living in Suffolk was fine but not easy to impose on another. His work at Sedge House was all but complete, and helping Amelia had been a short-term agreement. Despite the present situation, it would be untenable moving forward.

Being back in Sommovia these last few days had sparked feelings of unfinished business within him. Through her work finding these war graves, Kaira had forged links with powerful agencies and made herself indispensable. He looked at her now and felt self-indulgent for the care she continued to show him.

"I should try to bend my knee and get the blood flowing." He kept his tone understated while Deana remained engaged in conversation with Bradbury up front.

Kaira was unconvinced as he delt with the obvious pain. Although alive to the touch of his hand on hers in his silent message of thanks, she found herself wishing she could read his mind as easily as his lips.

Forty minutes later they pulled over at a convenience store on the approach road into Port Central. Deana was hungry, Kaira had requested the chance for privacy and Joe wanted the chance to stretch his legs. His best foot forward produced an awkward limp as Colonel Bradbury looked on in silent sympathy. Beyond them, the land dipped down to the docks with its warehouses and cranes. The Island of Alcavar drew and teased their attention out on the sea.

Kaira returned sooner than expected. She looked flushed with excitement. “I’ve just a made call to my Dutch colleagues. The General was sighted earlier today boarding a luxury motor cruiser, right here in Port Central. They tracked the boat by GPS and it docked in Alcavar late this afternoon.”

She made use of Deana’s absence and kept her voice low. “No sign of Lena, though. I did as you requested and asked that we be brought up to speed. The Dutch commander is waiting for us at the ferry terminal buildings.”

Bradbury became animated. “And Berislavic is definitely on board this motor cruiser?”

“He’s not been seen out on deck but the boat has been under constant surveillance.”

“This is better. Let’s hope our luck holds. We’ve precious little time left to decide what to tell Deana. Damn and blast it. What’s the General done with Lena? Find her and this could all be over.”

“Could she be on board as his hostage?” Lena was Joe’s priority. “Let’s wait until we’ve met with the Dutch officials at Port Central.” He saw Kaira nod in agreement. “The only ferries to Alcavar go from there, one tonight and one in the morning. Having Deana with us may yet be a godsend.” Joe wrinkled his nose, trying to make sense of what the General might be up to. “I hope there’s method to his madness. Berislavic can't possibly believe he would go undetected."

At that moment Deana returned to the car with a bagful of shopping.

"What are you all staring at?" Taking her choice of sandwich, she handed the rest over. "No fighting, just pick what you want. Not happy? Then, go buy your own." She checked her watch. "We should get going."

Port Central proved to be a small but busy hub of industry protected from the open sea by a rocky spit of land. On the fore-shore, traffic consisted of lorries reversing into unloading bays. Freighters at anchor out in the harbour were points of interest, waiting to discharge their cargos. On either side tourism was king. Old-fashioned hotels clung to the cliffs and wooded hillsides in a functional way; a one fits all approach to the architectural choices of the day.

Side-door entrance to the ferry terminal, although private was no shortcut to beating the system. An increased police presence made security painfully slow. Colonel Bradbury and Miss Maes disappeared into an office and did not return for over an hour. Of more concern was that Deana Horvat was also taken away. Joe sat alone and felt he should be doing something more constructive. When Bradbury returned to the room, he was already on his feet.

"It's complicated and at the same time, fascinating." Bradbury, who carried a plastic bag in one hand pointed the way to a quiet corner. There were traces of confusion and an awkward smile on his face. "With the help of Miss Maes and in the presence of government officials I've just had a very interesting conversation with the General."

"Berislavic?"

Bradbury nodded. "He's making good use of your phone but doesn't speak much English. I think we understood each other, as far as it goes." He took a breath. "In passing he asked after your health."

"Very considerate of him, I'm sure." Joe kept his voice even.

"I assured him our interest was purely personal and hoped that Lena Horvat was well and would be returned to her family shortly."

"And I take it he definitely has her?"

"Claims he's doing his best to protect her."

"From himself? I don't understand."

"Protecting her from his son." The Colonel cut short Joe's next question. "We have to accept the General's demands and abide by the country's stage management of the affair. The Dutch are seething by all accounts. It means we have more hoops to jump through but I can see no alternative. It's all been pre-arranged. He'll hand himself over, when the time is right. Whatever his demands are, we must all go to the Island of Alcavar."

"But Lena's okay, right sir?" Joe was not going to settle for hearing half of the story.

Bradbury nodded. "You were right. She's his insurance policy. Until his son is accounted for, he maintains she's safer with him. It suggests to me she was on board the cruiser."

"And Deana?"

"Ah, Miss Horvat. Despite a thawing in our relationship, she won't be joining us. If all goes well, we've agreed to meet up later. A promise or a threat? I couldn't be certain." Bradbury smiled with affection.

"Come, let's find the industrious Miss Maes. She's negotiating our departure arrangements." The carrier bag the Colonel had been holding all the while made a familiar clinking sound as they walked away. "I've been given some duty free to take with us."

In the skies above the Adriatic Sea a commercial flight on route from London began its scheduled decent into Mezlar. Passengers, many flying for business or returning from the same pursuit in London were accompanied by Nick Sayers. Journalist and intrepid traveller, he thought that if he saw the inside of a plane again soon, he might need oxygen or something stronger. True to form the numbness he'd felt as he boarded the small Boeing was gradually turning into familiar fluttering's of excitement that threatened to make him a liar once again. A leap of faith into the unknown was good for the soul. He was to be met by a representative from the university with a promise of dinner and a good hotel. The music teacher, Helen, who was Australian by birth but with a European surname had sounded enthusiastic, which had to be a good thing.

Nick folded away his table in front of him and made sure his seat was in the upright position and prepared himself to cross-check and land safely. Touch down was smoothly done and lights in the terminal showed the way through customs to the exit.

"Good flight, Mr Sayers? Hi, I'm Helen Matic from the University of Mezlar. Good to meet you."

Her handshake was firm and as sincere as her welcome. Shoulder length hair framed a face that had hazel brown eyes and a smile that came naturally and quite often.

Nick thought her pleasant and fell into easy conversation. Or was it nerves making him ramble?

"Mr Hanlan regrets he can't be here in person but has asked me to fact-find and with your cooperation organise future proceedings. He's very keen to put a feasible package together that will be of benefit to the University." Nick was aware of Helen Matic's full attention. "I'll shut up immediately. I sound like a lawyer who's about to close out a deal." That made her laugh at least.

"Don't worry, Mr Sayers. We're so pleased to meet you. You're a journalist with Stress Magazine. Am I right?" Miss Matic's Australian twang was still perceptible despite her time spent in Sommovia. "We've been studying an article of yours in my tutorials. You're to blame. It really started this hairbrained scheme in the first place. One of my students, Marin, you'll meet him later I hope, was the catalyst and the driving force behind it all. He's put all his energies into this and seems to have taken it on as a personal labour of love. I sent him home to get some well-deserved rest. I'm hoping he'll be back tomorrow."

Nick nodded and reminded himself that he should remain circumspect and not reveal too much. "As you are aware, Mr Hanlan has invested much in his theatre work and would be pleased to contribute something back to his daughter's country of birth. All being well, he hopes you'll get the chance to meet her in the not-too-distant future."

"I understand you've come here via a trip to England. You must be tired. I'll drop you off at your hotel. In any case it's too late to see the university this evening." Helen drove the city roads with confidence born out of enjoyment and familiarity.

Nick felt his stomach rumble. "I could do with something to eat. Perhaps if you have no further plans, we could have dinner together and continue with our conversation there." As soon as he said it, he wondered if he'd been rather forward. He was about to dilute the offer by assuming her caution when she spoke next.

"Good idea. Time is short. I know a good place not far from the hotel. Do you want to drop by and get rid of your gear first. We could have a drink in the bar and then it's all but a short walk around the corner."

After a hectic day that had been full of potential hurdles, Helen Matic was making life seem like a canter on the flat. Nick was happy to sit back and relax in her capable hands. "You don't ride horses, do you?" He asked. "I know, silly question."

"Well, as it happens…" She smiled but didn't answer the question. "Do you? No? I didn't think so." Helen thought dinner was going to be interesting, come what may.

*

21. Marin's Mix

It was after midnight when I got back to my university digs. A hidden key that I'd never used before came in handy. Obeying the first rule of sharing, I put it back without hesitation. A quick shower and then to bed had been my only option. Perhaps if I'd had my phone, I could have… well, made some calls, but to whom? And besides, there was no way of accessing the numbers. Only one seemed relevant and was indelibly inked in my memory. My music tutor, Helen Matic, would have been a great sounding board. Better to be fresh and surer of myself.

I could only hope the General would be as good as his word and keep Lena safe. Memories of my journey with her lay just beneath the surface of my conscious thoughts. I felt I had responsibilities now, weird as that may sound. The bus trip had given me time to reflect on that.

Early next morning I went out armed with my credit card and some borrowed cash. I felt I should be ready for anything. Time was precious and contact with Miss Matic essential. Never normally late, I watched her enter the building seemingly animated and excited. She was in company with a tall, good-looking man who was doing his best to keep in step beside her.

"Hi, Marin. Just the person we were hoping to see." Her voice was spirited and gay. "I want you to meet Nick Sayers, a journalist from New York. He's here to represent Charles Hanlan, the theatre empresario." Helen words began to slow and she looked at me intently. "What is it? What's going on?"

*

22. How Revealing

"Good afternoon, Miss Highland." The receptionist looked up from her computer screen but did so as she hit 'return' with something akin to a flourish. "I was just about to call you. You have a message. The courier asked me to deliver this letter in person."

Amelia took the white envelope with her name on the front of it, hand written. A small stamp of a tug boat in the top left-hand corner gave the sender a name. She refused the impulse to open it and put it safely in the pocket of her shorts.

"I'm just going for a walk but thank you. Oh, and I meant to say that Miss Grant and I will be taking dinner in the hotel tonight, if that's possible."

"Yes, no problem. I'll book you a table for two. Just to warn you, the restaurant will be full. The regatta is starting early tomorrow. But no problem, we'll find you a place." She clicked a few buttons and double-checked the screen. "I'm afraid the option on the additional room has already gone. I can see here a late booking was made this afternoon." She looked to Amelia to judge her reaction.

Amelia showed no concerns while concealing a blush of embarrassment. "I'll see you later, and thanks for the message." She walked out into the late afternoon sunshine and lengthening shadows. The heat in her face betrayed the uniqueness of her situation.

She walked down the road towards the lookout point which always gave great views of the harbour in both directions. Bright light shimmied and reflected off the water as the sun approached the western horizon.

Warm colours and a gentle breeze were in tune with the end of the day. Motor cruisers were queuing at the re-fuelling dock having returned from their day trips somewhere around the island. In the other direction the old fuel and gas tanker remained at her birth. An outline of gantries and pipelines were difficult to see without squinting directly into the sun.

Amelia had forgotten her sunglasses. Rosalind had phoned and it had seemed appropriate to leave Sam to speak with her employer in private. So much to consider. What might happen to NRG Pictures could influence all of their futures. Samantha's in particular. So many questions. Amelia wanted to swear in happy frustration.

All was good between them; they wanted to be sure. No rush on the physical. Once might be forgivable but twice? No way. How would people she knew react? What would her mother say, if and when she finally got to meet her again? Dare she even hope that she was alive?

Amelia turned to look back at the hotel. A young man was walking up the slope towards her. She felt a tingle of nerves as he tried not to stare. Shorts and a t-shirt left much of her sun-kissed skin on view to be appreciated. Not that he acted in any way to make her uncomfortable. That in turn led her onto a whole different subject; was she gay? Samantha was still in a relationship with Joe Peterson. And yet?

The young man nodded as he walked past and continued along his path. She thought his stride and posture showed an inner confidence. He was proud of his youthful good looks. So why couldn't she readily accept his admiration for what it was. Too much in the spotlight, the fame could become addictive to some, but not to her. Not to a self-proclaimed introvert.

Her step-father's protection, the need to grow and become more self-sufficient consumed her. Recognition was no more than a happy twist of fortune in her eyes. Now there were real decisions to make without a mentor and female guidance. Not forgetting Samantha, but then she was part of the problem.

Amelia could follow the young man. It wasn't too late if she ran. They could have a drink, have some dinner, go back to his place and make love and all would be well.

A flash of flax-coloured hair shone in the last rays of sunlight as a familiar figure walked through the trees heading in her direction. Amelia caught her breath and stifled a sob of grateful expectation. She reached inside her pocket for a tissue and found the letter instead.

"You look as if you've been crying. I thought I might find you here" Samantha saw the moisture in Amelia's eyes.

"Think I've got a fly in my eye."

"Here, let me have a look." Sam turned Amelia's face towards her and searched for the offending insect. "Blink a few times."

Amelia's tears ran down her face and she turned away in fear of showing too much weakness. "The sun's in my eyes." She heard herself sound a little angry. The next thing she felt was a gentle slap on her bottom.

Sam couldn't help but laugh as Amelia turned around in mock horror. "Have I told you how important you've become to me." She raised her eyebrows and offered Amelia a spare tissue. "And you need to blow your nose before I kiss you. What's in the letter? Not Luca Sanchez wanting to whisk you away for a romantic cruise on his tug?"

"Jealousy will get you nowhere." Amelia dabbed at her nose. "Just to show how not interested I am, I'll let you read what he has to say. Besides, I've nothing glamourous to wear at the captain's table." Amelia leaned against the nearest wall and grimaced in put-upon pain. "That hurt, by the way." She assessed the damage to her bottom with one hand as she gave Sam the letter with the other.

"Rubbish. A mere tickle, when you probably deserve more. Come to think of it your father suggested it as a form of keeping you in control. I don't want to sound weird but your ass does make a wonderful target."

"Hmmn… read the letter, why don't you."

Their short walk back to the hotel was full of serious discussion. The message was short and to the point, with reference to an early bus ride up the coast, the name of a street and a house number. And that was all it said.

"Someone is being cautious. Should we be too? In some ways I'm excited and yet I know we've got to be careful." Amelia had regained her composure. Feeling so vulnerable and alone in that moment and then seeing Sam, as if right on cue, had been powerful.

"Are you talking about Brie Sanchez or something more personal? It's a lot to take in. Your mum who you thought dead is found alive. You've learnt distressing things about your past and you're wondering if it's affecting the choices we're making right now. I say we, for obvious reasons." Sam took a deep breath. "I think good decisions come from being in a positive place. Live for today is a cliché." She took hold of Amelia's arm. "I cried earlier because, well, I feel happy. Makes no sense, I know."

Amelia changed their direction and headed to the top of a familiar flight on stone stairs. "Let's go down to the water one more time before dinner."

Samantha wasn't about to complain. She followed her friend as she skipped down to the bottom, and crossed the road to their favourite walk along the jetty. There was no way of telling how Amelia was feeling until she drew alongside and saw the smile on her face.

"I got scared. I've never had to question whether I'm normal or not. I just get on and do. Life in the last two years has had familiar routines. Performing in front of an audience or sitting at home on my own, the times I remember best are being with Mary and Jimmy Paxton… and now with you."

"Don't forget your father."

"Yes, he's my greatest supporter but it's time to move on. Besides, he needs a life of his own. In some ways he might be more excited about seeing my mother than I am."

They walked past their favoured restaurant and saw the waiter pull two chairs back in invitation. A little flirtation and two generous glasses of wine poured made the world a happier place. The view of beautiful boats and their owners saluting the sunset with their own choice of beverages was a prelude to what promised to be an exciting race-day.

"We should agree not to get too paranoid." Samantha tried to look serious. "Honestly, if I could choose who I'd want to be sitting here with me now, it would be… now let's see." She burst out laughing and held up her hands in case Amelia decided to throw something. "Come on, drink up. I'm hungry and we've an early start in the morning."

"What was the news from New York? Rosalind alright, I hope."

"Interesting developments and maybe good news for NRG. Sherman is on the mend and should be allowed to fly home…"

The waiter picked up his tip and looked with admiration and a feeling of loss as the two women waved and sauntered away. No point in trying to explain it without sounding base. It must be a natural phenomenon.

*

"Sometimes I wish that we could all speak without words. Be telepathic." Kaira Maes was aware that her hearing aid needed to be recharged.

It was the first time that Joe had seen her show any frustration in this regard. They stood together by the exit doors to the ferry terminal and away from the public gaze. Out in the compound, government vehicles were lined up ready to act as land-born ferries. Any desire for clandestine travel would now be tempered with local and sceptical security. Nothing was being left to chance.

Despite Kaira's protestations to her senior Dutch colleagues, the decision stood; they wouldn't be going to the Island until first thing in the morning. Instead, they must overnight at a swanky villa just outside of Port Central. Colonel Bradbury was travelling separately but in tandem with the Dutch Special Forces commander. Another meeting was scheduled to take place at the safe house. Within twenty minutes all parties were back on the road inside blacked-out people carriers heading south along the coast road.

"Your levels of concentration are something else and would put most people to shame. Take a time out, it won't be long before you arrive at your accommodation." Joe felt her head rest on his upper arm. She hadn't asked and he'd not refused. Perhaps this was what she was referring to. 'Speaking without words…'.

"You won't be staying."

"Not invited. I'm only getting a lift because Bradbury requested it."

Back at the terminal in the gathering darkness, a lone man with singed hair hidden under a peaked-cap was the last foot-passenger to board the evening ferry heading to the Island of Alcavar.

"Colonel Bradbury speaking. Ah yes, Captain Nunez. We're here at Port Central and in good time, I believe." He broke off and listened for what seemed an eternity. "I'm glad you've been put in the picture. We appreciate your diligence and cooperation." He reached for pen and paper. "Not until Saturday morning. The ferry to Alcavar goes an hour earlier than normal. Yes, a change of schedule to accommodate the end of season regatta. I understand the two women you refer to have been on the island a couple of days but not met with Miss Sanchez." He felt obliged to update Nunez with the latest intelligence.

"We now have a secondary and potentially more serious threat. Yes, Slavco Berislavic, the General's son." He looked around the large living room at his audience. "This changes the dynamic and makes Miss Sanchez's security crucial. All is in place. I'm grateful for the cooperation of both Sommovian and Dutch officialdom; and of course, your loyalty." Bradbury had one more point to make. "No, I understand. I fully appreciate that Brie Sanchez and her son have dual nationality. I want to emphasise that we'll need to be vigilant across the whole of the town… As ever, adios and good to speak with you." The Colonel closed down his call and without looking round hoped that he had been clearly heard by all.

There were mutterings amongst the assembly as the Colonel looked on with steady concentration. He waited patiently for reaction from the Dutch Special Forces commander. He was sat on the edge of a desk on the opposite side of the room with a government representative while Miss Maes had her head bowed taking notes. A high-ranking policeman from the Island was an interested but silent bystander. If arrests were made it would be he who would ultimately be in at the kill. The use of force on Alcavar had been previously discussed and deemed a last resort option if all else failed. Public safety with a high percentage of foreign visitors present was of the highest importance.

"My men are already stationed in and around the harbour. Our yacht, although entered in the regatta is there to keep up with appearances. We're using it as a mobile command centre. What is of concern to me is that my target is there ready for the taking." The Dutch commander could barely hide his impatience. "Doing deals with the General wasn't part of my plans."

"I appreciate the information he's provided complicates the picture. Sighting his son shows us he's serious." Bradbury looked to others to step in and make the case. "I'm sure efforts will be made to cover every eventuality. I understand that Slavco Berislavic may well have sought medical assistance on the mainland. I have no way of knowing if this is relevant." He waited but in vain. "I'm not prepared to put Miss Highland, Miss Grant and now Brie Sanchez at further risk. I've made myself clear to you, sir. I'll say no more here or try to undermine the operation, but every precaution must be taken to protect them at all costs." His last words although spoken to the Dutch commander were aimed at the room in general.

A steely two-way stare cooled the air. Kaira Maes removed her glasses and checked both lenses for non-existent contamination. Interpreting the silence was unnecessary. She couldn't make herself look up from her work. It took her ages to replace her eyewear. A stubborn spot on one of her lenses, the answer to her problem.

"Duly noted." The commander didn't sound best pleased.

Bradbury coughed to clear his throat in a bid to rid the room of residual tension. "The General is keeping the where-abouts of Lena Horvat as one of his bargaining tools. We have to take his concerns about his own son at face value. My feelings? This is all about damage limitation."

The Commander had done well to not react with cynicism. His mission made more complicated with an arrest count suddenly doubled. He slowed his heart rate but still looked resigned. The last few days had been wearing for all and it looked like negotiations would continue with the Sommovian officials right until the end. Finding Slavco Berislavic may yet prove to be the biggest prize.

"So, how did that go?" Joe who'd been excluded from the meeting sat on the side of the swimming pool gently exercising his legs in the water. The safe house appeared to be a government owned refuge for visiting dignitaries and those who should be afforded the luxury of guaranteed privacy. The perimeter walls kept prying eyes to a minimum and hidden cameras were part of a proficient security system. The pool had underwater lighting and subtle spots gave the courtyard intimacy. “Your Dutch team leader doesn’t give much away.” It was a statement that contained a question for Kaira.

“Chosen especially for jobs like these, so I’m reliably informed. Colonel Bradbury has had dealings with him before. I haven’t.” Kaira wanted nothing more than to dive into the pool, or at least to sit beside Joe.

“Put some shorts on.” He’d noticed her hesitancy.

She returned a few minutes later, her legs bare and only a shirt to cover her modesty. “I bought you a towel if you want a swim.” She offered Joe a hesitant smile and sat herself down, feeling the latent heat from the poolside tiles through her knickers. Leaving a respectful gap between them, she could still see the residual bruises on Joe’s leg. He looked more comfortable and she contented herself that the cool water would do him some good.

“So how long has all this been in the planning?” Joe spoke quietly so as not to be overheard. “None of my business; I’m retired I know, although lately it doesn’t feel that way.” He lifted his right leg out of the water. “Perhaps I got lucky after all?”

Unsure of her answers Kaira chose to ignore the questions. “You must miss it; not being fully involved must be difficult.” She was conscious of his study. “Yes, you’re sitting on my good side.” Instinctively she put her finger to her deaf ear. “A few hours recharging and I’ll be back to full power.”

“I never doubted that.” He knew she took her lack of hearing seriously. “I gather you’re not allowed or just don’t want to explain your full involvement in this operation.”

Kaira removed her glasses and was going to use the hem of her shirt to clean them when she put them aside, out of the way. "You make me self-conscious. I wish I was as beautiful as your girlfriend, Samantha." She tucked unruly strands of hair behind her ear and decided to be bold. "I thought you would make the perfect couple but now I'm not so sure."

"Oh, yes?" Joe was more amused than offended. "You just come right out and say it. No, no worries, I think it's an attractive quality." Joe was about to touch her when he thought better of it. Distracted, he encouraged her to get back to the issue in hand.

Kaira had started and then stopped undoing shirt buttons. "I have language skills that the War Crimes Commission wanted to make use of. I agreed to aid liaison with foreign countries, particularly you Brits and eventually got assigned to Colonel Bradbury. Like him, this is my last job before I return to my work for the War Graves Finders group." She sounded relieved and committed to that. "Berislavic's arrest is deemed necessary by his superiors. Peace and politics need deals doing if his country wants to be a part of the European Union. No negotiation there."

"And the General becomes a bargaining tool? A sacrifice. In your opinion, is he a wager of war or just a war criminal?

"Berislavic? I can't speak for him or his honesty directly but his actions helped bring the fighting to an end. His superiors want EU membership and the UN and Europe want convictions that reinforce their political stance on human rights. The same rights that went by the wayside for so many when their peace-keeping became a travesty. The whole region has had their share of victims. Now the world wants redemption and justice when it's too late for so many, particularly those of ethnic minorities and mixed race." She shrugged her shoulders. "The trials are taking place in my country. I've lost people that were close to my family." She sighed. "I'm going in for a swim."

When the last button was undone, she took off her shirt and plunged into the water. A flurry of leg-kicks did their best to soak Joe before she settled into a quieter and proficient breast stroke.

He watched her turn at the far side of the pool and glide beneath the surface, not emerging until she was once again by his side. Her underwear helped define the shape of her body beneath the water's surface.

"Could you pass me my towel, please." She blinked her eyes and focused on making an exit from the water as gracefully as she could. The strength in her arms and muscled stomach made that look easy. She glanced down to see that all she wore was still in place. "I think I've gone see-through. Towel please, now, Joe."

Kaira padded back to her room leaving a trail of inviting footprints which Joe may have followed had it not been for Colonel Bradbury wanting a quiet word.

"How is the leg? Fit for tomorrow?" He seemed unnaturally hesitant. "On your suggestion, I've made inquiries into private boat hire. I've got details of a fishing vessel that can drop you off if you still want to go."

"You won't be coming?"

"Not the unofficial way, no. I've made too much noise to be seen breaking rules at this late stage. I'm travelling on board Port Central's customs launch with the big boys.

Hopefully tomorrow may prove significant. I'm expected back in London on Monday."

"I might be needing a lift, if you don't mind, sir. All being well I'll have to go back and speak with Charles Hanlan. Hand in my notice."

"Are you certain? What about your girl? Miss Grant, I mean."

"She'll be fine. Instinct tells me I'll get to meet with her tomorrow. We must rely on the Dutch team to do what's necessary." He thought for a moment. "And what about Miss Maes, what's her role going forward?"

"They've decided to acquiesce with the General's demands and put her aboard the motor cruiser. She's to stick like glue to Berislavic until it's all over." Bradbury could see that Joe wasn't happy. "My guess is he wants to make a public display of his innocence and cooperation." He struggled to keep his contempt under control. "I suppose I can't blame him. His son will supposedly try to stop this from happening. Probably fears his father will apportion blame in attempt to clear his own name. Miss Maes has researched this obsessively. A good soldier who got results but could not control all who he led. Your injuries are a small testament to that. The real crime was committed against those villages that were shelled in the final storm that had no mercy. The men who you ran into used to be under direct command of Berislavic's son, Slavco. That's why he remains the biggest threat to Jelena Highland and her old friend Gabriela Simic."

"Don't forget her son Luca."

"You're right. I wonder who's actually more responsible. The General or his son? Deana's cousin mysteriously dead and threats made towards both of the Horvat sisters.

Whichever way you look, there's cruelty here that has been left unchecked for far too long. Now that the General is part of a deal, others must fear they'll be made into scapegoats. Courts of law demand facts and proof of guilt."

"So, get rid of the evidence. Every man for himself; this Slavco character with the most to lose. Any new intel on what he did?"

"Sent missiles into an undefended village. By then the chain of command had broken down with blood-lust. The General appears to go around hoovering up Slavco's messes. Could be mentally unstable, certainly a shadow of his father's making."

"So, Alcavar is to be the lure that Slavco can't resist. Gabriela and Jelena, the bait. The General a hook."

"In case you were wondering, I was outvoted two to one by the Sommovians and the Dutch that Amelia be allowed to travel to the island. More honey in the trap; Miss Grant, an innocent bystander. This is all about saving face and propaganda."

"That would explain why the General isn't already in custody." Joe reasoned. "His own government have a majority of voters to appease. Giving up a hero will not be popular. And Slavco. Do we know for certain he's not already on the island?"

"It would appear so. All staged and cleverly choreographed where everybody taking part gets a medal." Bradbury paused in his usual fashion. "I knew nothing of this but it could make the difference between his spending months or years in jail before an appeal is heard."

"He'll plead guilty?"

"No, not at all. But he knows the court will find him so. Open and shut case."

"And his son?"

"For the sake of peace, they need to apprehend him tomorrow... without fail."

"As your last hurrah, you couldn't have had a more complicated job." Joe would hate for a reputation to be destroyed in its final chapter.

"Bad timing and good deeds that backfire happen all the time, Captain." He began to walk away from the pool. "I hope you said your goodbyes and made plans to meet with Miss Maes again soon. You won't get bored with her around. Don't delay any longer. Still waters run deep and she's been rather quiet of late."

Joe listened and realised Bradbury was probably right. He'd tried to flick the off-switch on his army background and found it almost impossible. Charles Hanlan's employment of him, an antidote whose potency was fast running out. The estate in Suffolk, an enjoyable interlude, his best efforts to keep tabs on Amelia Highland and her family, the real reason for any job-satisfaction. No, that was unfair. The physical demands of working the land had been addictive. His on-off relationship with Samantha Grant... a wonderful diversion. That was really being unfair on her.

In his last moments at the safe-house and with strict disregard for privacy and decorum he'd made Kaira scramble for her towel. In that moment she'd been more real and revealing to him than if she'd just stood still and been angry. To his credit Joe had turned his back and given her time to rectify the situation. Hurried explanations and an agreement to meet soon must have given Kaira hope that she had made an impression. Too early to talk about that. She'd certainly made him feel responsible towards her.

Was one kiss, cheating? He'd felt her tremble and instantly knew he must move away.

And move away he did in the direction of Port Central. Nobody in authority at the house took much notice or tried to stop him. They even took the trouble to call him a taxi. Listening to Bradbury's advice he travelled about five or six miles along the coast road to an address set back in a pocket of homes overlooking the bay. At the final junction someone was waiting for him. Joe tried to supress a smile and easily failed.

"What took you so long?" Deana Horvat beckoned and without further preamble led the way back across the road.

"Had some goodbyes to make." Joe eventually caught up. "You and the Colonel are as bad as each other. Where are we going now?"

Deana pointed to the lights in the distance. "Across the sea and far away. I have a friend with a boat and he owes me many favours." She didn't elaborate. Instead, she seemed to take pleasure in that Joe was still limping. "Come, it's a ten-minute walk, if you think you can make it."

"You're all heart, Miss Horvat."

"I know, a heart of stone."

A tarmac path led them down to a small jetty where they found a lone fishing vessel tied up on single lines. Lights in the wheelhouse announced that someone was waiting for them. Nothing was said as they stepped aboard but once under way, while Joe kept to himself, Deana seemed relaxed and made time to flirt and converse with their host. Borrowed waterproof coats were essential as misty rain fell in showers. Ahead of them lay the Island of Alcavar with its lights sparkling in the murk and semi-darkness. An hour or so later green and red buoys flashed their welcome and identified the channel with its dangers to either side. The man in the wheelhouse spoke briefly on the radio and was duly invited to dock at a refuelling pontoon. Joe was told to go below and stay out of sight while they took on both diesel and water.

Twenty minutes later the boat was expertly reversed onto its own designated mooring space. It would give them a wonderful outlook over the rest of the harbour come the morning. The owner nodded towards Joe and kissed Deana before heading inland to the comfort of his own bed.

"A friend of yours? You seemed close." Joe proffered a thumb in the direction of the town.

"A friend of a good friend, let's just say that." Deana motioned for Joe to find comfort in their meagre surroundings. She in turn made use of the galley stove and kettle.

"You never felt like getting married and having a family?"

"Is that an offer, Mr Peterson?" Deana frowned at him. "Spoilt for choice, aren't you, without adding me to your list."

"You may have a point there. But come on Deana, you must have had chances of your own."

"Too busy. When my father died, for a time I oversaw his business interests as well as running the café. I also still manage the rental property where I picked you up this evening. That and looking after my sister has meant making sacrifices. The war didn't help. But I do alright, don't you worry about that."

Both settled down to rest. The aroma of coffee laced with brandy acted much like an antidote to the fish-infused air of the cabin.

"And Lena, how bad was she after getting shot?"

"She's a hundred times better today than she was. The shock she suffered made her completely shut down. Didn't try to speak for two years, or maybe just couldn't." Deana shrugged her shoulders. "She still has good days and bad."

"You took a lot on, Deana."

"I had help."

Joe gave pause to show his support.

"Bradbury tells me that at the time of her attack, things were hushed up to protect the General. Now he and his son are both back to haunt you all over again. The world calls for justice and we're made to play these games." Joe waited for her reaction.

It duly came. "Give me a gun and I'd shoot the guilty myself."

*

23. Race Control and Tactics

In the translucent pre-dawn light, harbour life began in earnest. Fishing boats were landing their catches and hungry gulls swooped for the scraps. The end of season regatta had attracted expectant crews and racing boats from near and far. Flags from many countries flew at masts with their sails set ready for competition. Even now as Joe surveyed the scene through binoculars he'd found in a locker, a fifty-foot yacht left her moorings and headed for the open sea.

"If you're right then she's come from the same part of the marina as the General's boat." He handed Deana the binoculars as he continued to watch the yacht slip past without fuss or ceremony.

"They stick out like a sore finger." Almost opposite the Dutch Special forces team were busy folding sails and washing deck windows while keeping a lookout. Deana didn't sound too impressed by what she saw. What Slavco Berislavic might achieve in this very public place she couldn't imagine.

"You've a good eye, but to be fair they're not trying to hide their existence."

Before Deana had a chance to reply things began to get interesting. In from the sea the island's large and powerful Customs boat entered the harbour. Its dark blue hull and blacked out superstructure made it look menacing as it slowed and moored on the far side of the water. A low-level pier of concrete it tied up to was backed by non-descript buildings which in turn made them interesting.

Joe took charge of the binoculars once again and was able to focus on the first person to disembark. He glimpsed a figure wearing her hooded jacket walking towards a waiting car. The same car that ten minutes later dropped her off at the end of the pontoon where the General's boat lay silent. Kaira Maes was making contact with the enemy.

He watched intently as she made her way down the floating pontoon carrying her shoulder bag in both hands as if it were a balancing aid. She made him smile with her vulnerability that was strangely endearing and yet, her strengths made her highly capable. No questions on that score.

There was no one at the rail to greet her, so she climbed aboard uninvited. Once on deck she seemed to hesitate but then quickly disappeared through the rear cabin door. And then, nothing. Joe felt the urge to run to her. Deana came up beside him and asked what he could see.

"What's the quickest way to get over to the far side of the harbour?"

"By boat, of course."

"Have we got one? I could row there in minutes. Something's wrong, I can tell."

Just as he said it, Kaira came back on deck with a phone to her ear. The binoculars magnified her agitation and she seemed to be searching all around her. The General had obviously gone.

*

24. Marin's Mix

Miss Matic has her own office within the music department. It's perfectly formed but rather small, as the three of us were finding out. Having my tutor in such close proximity felt nicely weird and disturbing. I noticed she had no trouble rubbing shoulders with the journalist. I suppose I couldn't blame her for that.

"The warehouse was definitely Port Central based. There was signage all around us and he definitely came to us by water; I heard a small boat's outboard motor."

Nick Sayers spoke next. "This doesn't make a lot of sense to me. I was told the General is a threat to Jelena and not the guardian angel he's claiming to be."

"I'm supposed to tell 'them' what he's done and what a good guy he is. Who are 'them'?"

"Or 'they'." Helen Matic made a grown-up suggestion. "Maybe I should call the police and let them deal with this."

Mr Sayers shook his head. "And get tied up in red tape. No, I don't think so." He sounded a note of caution. "I hate the thought that Jelena may be in danger but there's still a chance we could cut some corners here. I'll try and get a message to the right people." Mr Sayers sensed my agitation. "Marin, isn't it? What's your connection to Jelena Highland."

The office was becoming stuffy and rather warm. I remember mumbling something about being from the same village and tried to move the subject away from his question.

"So, Lena is Amelia Highland's mother? Thanks to Miss Matic's lectures, I think I recognised that fact some time ago. I just wasn't brave enough to believe my own eyes."

"You never confronted her?"

"No, I never did. Conversation with her isn't always easy, but..."

"Yes?"

"I can't help worrying. I need to know she's safe." I heard the words catch in the back of my throat. Mr Sayers didn't look up from his phone, while Miss Matic put her hand on my arm to give me comfort without fully understanding why it was so important to me.

*

25. Rough Waters

Light showers of rain overnight had left their mark on the pavements and deserted roadways. Cars were parked but their owners were nowhere to be seen. Alcavar's harbour was the focus of all the attention that morning. The bus terminal in the centre of town was quiet even for a weekend. Bus number thirty-two, left on time and Amelia and Samantha were joined on their journey by only one other passenger. Sitting in silence they took in the scenery as the road wound through low hills and gently sloped valleys. The occasional farm house and small tracks leading to somewhere unknown were points of interest along the way. Signposts and speed restrictions hinted at the final stop on the outskirts of a fishing village and when the bus pulled over the doors automatically opened.

They walked along the road in comfortable silence and then on sand covered paths. They briefly held hands and saw the sea where it touched the shore in a crescent-shaped bay that had its own island. Small craft and unused, colourful buoys bobbed up and down in a swell that was gentle and regular. A café situated in amongst a few trees was ready to open. When asked, the lady cleaning tables gave them general directions and pointed inland.

The main street, so called, was no wider than a lane and seemed uncertain of its own way between fisherman's cottages, some flats and apartments that had rental signs tied onto balcony railings and garden gates.

In their search Samantha finally pointed to the right and they started to climb. The cottages became houses and in looking for number nine she realised they hadn't much farther to go. A large white van with insignia saying Port Authority, Alcavar, was parked in a lay-by opposite a blue front door which had a letter box with a tug painted on its side. Brie Sanchez was a proud parent and lived in a two-storey dwelling.

They waited all of twenty seconds, from their first knock to the blue door being opened. Ms Sanchez was of medium height; her hair was naturally brown with hints of grey. Her skin, with scatterings of freckles was dark and smooth with slight creeses at the corners of her eyes. These eyes that studied Samantha, opened in surprise as Amelia made herself known from behind. Brie gave an audible gasp and then a small shake of her head.

"I don't believe it. You look like my best friend back when, well, when life was not so complicated. Please come in. Oh, tell me it is you." She turned once again. "We don't have much time. I have to work today and my son is already out on the water setting out the course of today's race."

Brie walked ahead and went into the living room that had enviable views of the bay and the sea beyond. "Winds from the north means the race will head south and then east along the coast. A safer route and more people will get to see the boats that way." She bade them sit down. "Oh Amelia, how beautiful you are. Your mother would have been so proud. Can I get you a coffee? I need a moment to compose myself."

Amelia took a breath and looked back at Sam. It was the first time that anybody had spoken of her mother in such an emotional way and yet said nothing at all. Did Brie know that her friend was still alive? It was a question that must be broached and soon.

"We were at school and university together, that is until I fell pregnant with Luca. Sorry its only instant." Brie handed out the mugs of coffee and sat herself down in a single chair. "My boss at the Port has told me that I was to expect visitors. Says there's danger." She made a face that showed her disbelief. "From Luca's father. I'm not sure why and why now. I thought perhaps he might have died during the war. Perhaps you can tell me. I always thought he could find me if he really wanted to. So, what's changed?" She put her cup down on the floor. It was too hot to hold.

Samantha tried to take the lead. "We have so much to tell you but it's important we understand more about your situation." Her words felt lame.

Brie looked from Sam to Amelia. "You want to know what happened to your mother?"

"This is new to me and in some ways disturbing… I'd be so grateful if you could explain as much as you know." Amelia spoke quietly but felt guilty when Brie began to cry. "I was told she died in a car crash with my father."

"I watched them both get shot. I was told to say nothing." She tried to calm herself. "Jelena's family, your family Amelia, helped me escape after their deaths. They were so good to me. I was so sorry when your grandparents passed away and …" Brie dabbed at her eyes with a handkerchief. "I stayed on at their holiday home for a couple of years longer. Nothing changed there. Then out of the blue I was offered the chance to come here, to live and work on Alcavar. War was coming, I couldn't refuse."

"You say my parents were shot. But why?" Amelia tried not to sound impatient.

"Yes. She came back thinking she could support me and stand up to Slavco. He'd bullied and coerced my parents long enough. He said he wanted to take Luca." Brie shook her head at the memory but there was a flash of defiance in what she said next. "But we used signals and words like we'd always planned, me and my parents. I knew immediately something was wrong."

"What do you mean by that?" Sam was intrigued.

"My father specifically asked me to bring Luca with me. He would never have said that; it was something we'd agreed on. A way to keep him safe."

"Like you say, a sign. This Slavco, had he not tried to do this before?"

"The war was coming. My parent's ethnicity and the fact that he'd slept with me made him a hypocrite of the worst kind. I don't do religion, but in his world, prayers would not have saved him."

"I'm so sorry, that's terrible." Amelia wanted to reach out. "I'm sorry if this brings back bad memories but it's important to all of us."

Brie took a deep breath. "Jelena calls and tells me she's on her way from Italy, but she got delayed and I get to my parent's house before her. I remember parking in the lane outside but he's waiting there, standing in the dark. Slavco was furious that Luca is not with me. I tell him this is no place for a ten-year-old boy, but he won't listen and knocks me down." She points to a small mark above her right eye. "I'm bleeding. I can hardly see." She sobs and wipes her tears away.

"That's when Jelena arrives. She has no thought for her safety. She comes to comfort me calling Slavco all the bad names she can think of." Brie takes a breath and waves Amelia's concern away. "No, I must finish but you may not want to hear what I say."

"It's okay, please go on." Amelia was holding herself rigid. Sam wanted to reach out to both women.

"It's dark and then lights from a car fill the lane. Slavco and Jelena are shouting and then he hits her too. I hear a terrible noise and she falls to the ground. I can hardly believe it." Brie re-lives the moment.

Then, another man comes out of the darkness, a piece of steel in his hand. He hits Slavco from behind. Not on the head, he would have killed him, but up between his legs." Brie shuddered as she remembered the sound and tries to make herself laugh. "He was not so good when he got me pregnant. I doubt he's ever had sex again in his miserable life."

"This man, who hit Slavco. Who was he?"

"I never found out for sure but I've always assumed he was your father. Yes, I'm so sorry, but while he's helping Jelena, Slavco gets up on his feet and launches himself on top of them. They struggle and then I hear a shot. I see Jelena crumple; I think she feels nothing but your father... I'm so sorry, he holds his chest before he goes down..." Brie can't finish. She buries her face in her hands.

Amelia kneels in front of her mother's friend and tries to console her.

"I must have passed out." Brie looks confused but reaches out and strokes Amelia's face. "The next thing I remember, I'm in the back of a large car. I'm blindfolded with some kind of bandage, but I smell leather and expensive cologne. There's a man sitting beside me telling me I'm going to hospital, making me promise to say nothing. He whispers that if I do as he says my family will not be harmed. And then nothing." She holds her hands out, palms up. "They leave me on the steps outside the hospital. A small concussion and a few days in bed and then I'm back with Luca in my apartment, your grandfather's apartment," Brie corrects herself. "Did you know that, yes, I'm there as if nothing has happened."

"And what about the man you saw get shot?" Samantha voiced the thing that had been on Amelia's mind. "Perhaps your parents know more?"

"If they do, they would never tell you. A promise is a promise in their world. I think that's the way they cope. Unlike me they didn't get to just disappear." Brie looked at her watch. "We should go. I have much to do. Today will be busy in the harbour."

They all stood together a little self-consciously.

"I want to give you a hug. May I?" Brie reached out briefly to Amelia. "You've made a good impression. My son likes you and it gives me joy to finally meet you. Come on, I'll give you a lift back into town if you'd like that."

Samantha and Amelia took a moment standing beside the port authority vehicle waiting for Brie to shut window shutters and lock doors on her house.

"Do you think we should tell her now?" Amelia had no conviction one way or the other as what to say about her mother.

"Not sure, but probably, no. You need to see her and believe it for yourself, first things first."

Further conversation died away as Brie skipped across the road towards them. "We can get three in the front. Strap yourself in." Negotiating tight turns was part of her make-up and Brie kept the conversation light until they were on the open road heading back to the harbour. "My life's been in Alcavar, I try not to look back. I only ever kept in touch with Jelena's music teacher."

“Marsha Ivanovic?” Amelia became animated. “I saw her a few months ago. She helped me when I was at school, before things took off with ‘Everlasting’. That’s how we found you. Your letters, they’re monogrammed with a tug boat. It helped us a lot.”

“I try to understand this. Why look for me now? What’s changed? Not that I’m unhappy to meet you, and you too Samantha.” Brie still looked concerned.

Neither passenger responded straight away. “It’s complicated”, would’ve sounded inadequate. Both looked at each other, one seeking the blessing of the other. Inevitably the truth had to come out.

“My mother did not actually die when she was shot.” Amelia spoke her revelation kindly.

Sam tried to help. “It’s true. A few weeks ago, I met her sister, Deana. Jelena was there at the family café. She has some difficulties with her speech and memory, but she looked happy, I think.”

Brie shook her head and kept her eyes on the road.

Sam filled the silence. “And then this famous General was indicted for war crimes. You must have seen it on the news. He fled the authorities before he could be arrested. We think Luca’s father is under suspicion too. That’s why we’re here.” She ran out of steam and like Amelia waited with trepidation for a response.

The van turned left onto the main road. “Okay.” Brie was very matter of fact. “Let me drive now. We will not speak until we get to the harbour.” Her face that was set in determination gradually relaxed into a smile. “Thank you for telling me. One thing is true enough. Jelena has never been dead to me.”

Armed police stood in small groups and were tasked with stopping all vehicles in and out of the gated dock area. Sometime during the night, the oil and gas tanker had left port for other islands in need of its cargo. Beyond the compound, activity on the water was verging on the chaotic as tall masted craft that had filled marinas were now fit for purpose and ready to sail in competition.

Brie Sanchez was in her element, fielding phone calls and answering radio messages. It helped her to be busy; she needed time to absorb all that she had learned that morning. As was her want in stressful situations she'd made a concerted effort to tick off her priorities, one item at a time. Top of that list, her son. He remained on board a pilot's boat just beyond the harbour limits monitoring the first two legs of the race. Last reports suggested wind and sea conditions were favourable and that quick times should be anticipated.

All was well and she was about to take a breather when a SOS was relayed to her office via the pilot's boat radio.

"Pilot boat two, receiving you." Brie spoke slowly and clearly.

Through the static and engine noise, a voice she recognised as Luca's answered giving their call-sign. "We have a report of a man in the water. We're heading south toward the second leg marker. Has anyone reported a crew member missing? We will update you when we know more." Luca sounded untroubled, even confident.

GPS and radar checks were made and all known positions of boats taking part were duly noted. Contact with race control was made to see if they could supply further information. The office became a hive of activity as colleagues joined Brie to give assistance where it was most needed.

In the background the port authority commander spoke in hushed tones with a representative of the Dutch Special Forces. Both were concerned and alert to the proceedings. Both agreed that putting an armed presence on board the pilot boat might yet pay dividends. The consensus had been to plan for every eventuality and be thankful when nothing happened.

When Brie Sanchez dropped them back at their hotel, she left both her passengers with so many unanswered questions. They watched her drive away and wondered at her strength of mind and keenness to go into work.

Their early start that morning meant they'd missed out on breakfast at the hotel. Suddenly their favourite key-side café held more appeal than usual. Samantha checked her watch.

"They'll be starting the main race in half an hour. We may get to see some of the action up close and personal. What do you think, and more to the point how are you coping?"

"Always happy to have breakfast anywhere with you." Amelia wanted to hide her true feelings. "I'm going to need time to digest it all and I don't mean the food. Honestly, I'm fine, but thanks for asking. You know I couldn't be doing any of this without you."

Samantha studied the menu and vowed not to burden Amelia with her own insecurities. She told herself to keep things light and realised the last few hours had not been easy for either of them. "I think I'm going to have some cheese and ham with my coffee."

"Am I being too greedy by wanting it all." Amelia's foot made contact with Sam's calf. "You, my mother, my work. What if I have to compromise; how does that work out?"

"Not sure I can answer you with any certainty. Perhaps, for the time being, forget the first and the last and concentrate on your mother. If I were making predictions and had anything to do with their outcomes, then the first and the last will take care of themselves."

Just at that moment a waiter approached their table. They ordered their food and sat back in reflective silence to watch the action out on the water. Yachts of varying sizes with sails to match, mostly white but some red, some brown and the odd flash of blue, were making their way to the start line just outside the harbour entrance. Small speed boats with bright orange flags were acting like well-trained sheepdogs. All except one, which was heading the wrong way and had come from the opposite side of the harbour.

Samantha's eyes were concentrated and sharp but she found it hard to believe exactly what she was seeing. "Holy sh…, it's Joe and look, he's got Deana with him. Look, see, that has to be your aunt. Can you believe it?" She pointed with her arm fully outstretched. "There, going towards the marina." Both she and Amelia jumped up from their table, began by walking and then broke into a run. They were sure that the key-side pathway would converge on a point where the boat must surely land.

A flurry of legs and flying hair made a picture that was in keeping with the speed that Joe and Deana were making across the water. Sam let fly with another 'Holy sh…' as she looked forward and saw Kaira Maes standing on the deck of a large boat a hundred or so metres away. They were still sprinting when they got to the gate at the end of the pontoon that had been carelessly propped open by a box of supplies. Both women steadied and slowed as they turned immediately left onto the floating parking lot. Both runners and speed boat incumbents arrived alongside the cruiser with almost perfect timing. In unison all looked to Kaira Maes and waited for an explanation as to why she stood alone and had blood on her hands.

"Good to see you. Glad you got here so fast. Come aboard, I think I may have killed someone." Kaira held her glasses in one hand and did her best to remain calm. "Please Joe, come quickly."

The cabin at the rear of the motor cruiser was full of fixtures and fittings. Plush leather upholstered seats were long enough to lie on and the cream-coloured curtains were a perfect match to the rug that covered the floor. The only thing out of place was the body of a man who lay face up and bleeding. Joe recognised the driver of the pickup. Perversely he thought the rug that had cushioned his fall would need cleaning and quickly.

Kneeling beside him was a woman with grey hair who was dipping tissues into a bowl of water. She appeared intent on reviving her prostrate patient. Kaira breathed a sigh of relief as he suddenly came back from the dead. His broken nose seemed in keeping with the rest of his features including his badly singed hair.

As all eyes assessed the scene, Amelia stepped forward and knelt down beside the woman to help wash away the residual blood from the man's face. They worked as a team and in harmony.

It seemed only fair to give the mother and her daughter room to work. "You must have hit him pretty hard."

Joe didn't hide his admiration. "Disfigured but alive. I'm impressed Kaira."

"I panicked. He came out of nowhere. I thought he meant to do me harm." She put her glasses back on which allowed her to clutch her injured hand. "I think I've broken some fingers." Her knuckles and wrist were already swollen.

From behind them Deana spoke for the first time. "Maybe I should be more like my sister and become your nurse for a change." She suspected fear. "What? You don't trust me?" She wasn't about to take no for an answer and ushered Kaira into the galley.

Up and until that moment, Joe and Samantha hadn't spoken a word to each other. Neither seemed inclined to open the bidding, but Joe did give her a pat on the shoulder to gain her attention. "Here comes the cavalry. Stand back. They may not be in the mood to take prisoners." The sound of heavy boots preceded the Dutch Commander who followed his team's advance down the pontoon. Joe ushered Samantha to one side but used himself to block immediate access to the rear cabin door. The boat leaned to one side as muscle and brawn walked up the gangway.

"I haven't had time to look but Miss Maes says the General is not aboard. You'll find your colleague inside the galley being tended to by Miss Horvat. Nothing serious." Joe had a word of warning. "There are also two women inside caring for the General's sidekick. No threat there but you should know his nurses are Amelia Highland and her mother." He thought it about time to step aside.

"Mr Peterson." The Commander allowed himself a tight smile and a begrudging nod of his head.

Joe pushed his luck. "When you've finished your search, we should probably speak."

Back inside the cabin the two women had succeeded in getting their patient upright. Although groggy and in pain, the man had recognised Peterson, the ex-army man. He spoke only once but sounded contrite. If he was using them as part of his plea for leniency, his words were certainly well received.

"You're here for Slavco Berislavic. No more worry there, he's dead. Died last night. Didn't survive the fire at the cottage."

The Special Forces Commander who was close enough to hear nodded his head. He looked grim but somehow satisfied. "Time to stop playing games then. Where's his father?"

"I think I can help you with that." Joe spoke through the open door and beckoned for the commander to join him back out on deck. "Early this morning I watched a large yacht called 'Hydration' leave harbour before all the others. They're mooring was in this part of the marina. Could be he jumped ship. I made a note of her registration." He handed over a small scrap of paper.

"There's no need to panic." Deana's voice was clear as she and Kaira followed the commander out into the open. "He's out there, racing." She gestured to the yachts beyond the harbour limits. "He'll keep to his word and play his part in this put-up deal." She actually laughed. "Unless he drowns first. I get the impression he wants to see his grandson before he goes to prison."

"And you know this, how?" The commander was fast reaching the end of his tether.

"Because he said so and Dejan never breaks a promise. Not ever."

In the same moment as Deana stopped speaking, two gulls called to each other as if imparting a joke, one to the other. The Commander looked skyward as if he might become a target but was only struck by the irony of their inappropriate calls. Others might have laughed but he couldn't allow this, not until his feet were safely back on dry land and he had his prisoner in custody.

"Dejan is it? I'll see you all for questioning later. My men will escort you over to the Port Authority Buildings. It's time to bring this charade to an end. Peterson…" He pointed in Joe's general direction but did not turn to face him. "Make sure there are no more surprises, if not for your own sake, then for your Colonel's."

*

26. Rescue and Port Authority

Bradbury coughed apologetically and spoke in hushed tones.

"They've picked up a survivor. They'll bring him in when the race has cleared the second marker. Shouldn't be long now according to Miss Sanchez."

"Well, according to the General's sidekick, it won't be Slavco Berislavic they'll rescue. Died of his injuries sustained in a house fire. You know nothing of this?" The Dutch Commander's mood hadn't improved. "We're trying to get corroboration through official Sommovian sources but it's like trying to get blood out of a stone. Now, that's your problem not mine. I came for the General and he alone. Miss Horvat assures me he'll give himself up after his boat has won the race." Sarcasm bubbled to the surface. "I understand you know Miss Horvat quite well, but not well enough to be partial to her secrets."

"Sorry to say my involvement with Deana is recent." The Colonel couldn't help his good humour. "I think she has a thing about uniforms but in this case, the General outranks me. I might sound flippant but believe me, nothing is ever simple in this part of the world. Keep out of politics, don't act with children or animals and don't visit the Sommovian Provinces if you want a dull and staid life."

Now that Lena was safely in their protection, Bradbury could see the means to an end. "Reel the big fish in and I can go home too, remember that. And don't be too harsh on Deana Horvat. She's worked for her family in exceptional circumstances since well before their senseless war began. Who was there to protect her then? Certainly not you and I as peacekeepers." He held his hands up in surrender. "That's a whole different story, I grant you. Talk to her nicely and you'll hear stories that might make you think about this operation you're running and why we continue to play these games."

Out at sea, just south of the second marker buoy the coxswain turned into wind and slowed the pilot boat down. This gave them no more than headway against the current of oncoming waves. Whoever was in the water was waving and seemed well prepared for the dangers of potentially drowning. By accident or by design, his wetsuit and life vest showed forethought and a certain aversion to risk. Clinging to a floatation aid gave proportion and the impression to the onlookers that they were going to rescue an over-inflated Michelin man. As one crew member was heard to utter, "That thing would be a danger to fast moving shipping of any size. Not a porpoise, more like a whale."

The technical importance of plucking out this patented advertisement for safety gear without doing him bodily harm concentrated minds. The idea of using a hoist situated in the stern of the boat seemed as good a way as any. To be successful, the whale would be required to slip into a harness set on the end of a line. "Well, that's not happening. He's a floating blob with no control of his own movement. Give him a motor, he could drive himself ashore."

In Luca Sanchez the boat had a strong swimmer who was fully trained in rescues of this kind. Given the chance he would have volunteered. Being the youngest and fittest crew member, he reacted to an order and duly plunged into the sea. Speaking later he commented on the jovial spirit of the man who acted as if he were relaxing on a blow-up sunbed. It was only when the floatation aids and vest were stripped away that they recognised the full figure of General Berislavic in his not so becoming wetsuit.

Guns seemed superfluous but a member of the Dutch Special forces none the less made his presence known and kept close. "No concealed weapons." That much was immediately obvious. The need to frisk the prisoner down was considered an obligatory if somewhat odious task, not helped by the amount of rubber on show. The General took everything in his stride and persisted in praising his single-handed rescue at the hands of his grandson.

Luca Sanchez looked on as if the man must have received a concussive blow to his head. Quickly dried and changed he continued with his duties none the less.

"Pilot Boat Two to base. Alcavar, do you read me?"

"Loud and clear. What's your position?" His mother's voice remained professional.

"Rescue successfully completed. Returning to harbour with a man now aboard who claims to be General Berislavic. He says you have interested parties awaiting his return. He's unhurt as far as we can tell and under constant watch. Says… Tell Gabriela Simic, he can't wait to see you again."

"Message received. Over and out."

Brie Sanchez and Gabriela Simic, two incarnations of the one, asked to be excused and went outside the office to cry for very different reasons.

The offices at the Port Authority on the Island of Alcavar had witnessed many things but nothing quite like this before. A team was quickly set aside to oversee the end of the regatta and the safe return of all yachts taking part, while a private room at the back of the building was prepared to host an international gathering of some note. Given the recent history of the region, Sommovian officials of all rank and file had thought it only natural to be present. Lawyers for all the interested parties jostled for table space. A sense of self-importance filled the air. All but one had their minds fully focused on legal constraints. Dejan Berislavic was the exception to the rule. He had no trouble getting a chair and was undoubtedly the centre of attention. Dressed once again in uniform more becoming to his rank, he sat contentedly with Kaira Maes beside him who would translate his every word.

"Did you know my yacht is called 'Hydration'? I don't know why I chose the name. Maybe because of my thirst for life. I think she won her class today." He was certainly proud of that. "They sailed as if their lives depended upon it. I was sad to leave them. But what better way to spend an afternoon in the company of my grandson and see him at work." If his chest could have expanded further it probably did at that moment.

"Very impressive. I've spent my life in trying to encourage all of my family. Now that I've lost my son, I can endeavour to spend more time with my youngest descendant. I hope one day he'll understand and except me without obligation. I've tried to do what's right from the very beginning."

For the first time since he'd started talking, the General looked world weary. "Oh, do shut up and go away." One of his lawyers was becoming insistent. "I've spent too much time keeping silent. Gabriela Simic and Jelena Highland deserve the truth." He tried to placate those who were there to represent him. "Don't worry I won't speak of the fighting except to say that my son subverted my orders and acted as if the war gave him some divine right to play the almighty." He wiped a single tear from his eye.

"I'm no racist, don't label me by faith or by colour. I'm just a human being human. Go to any war grave across this country of ours and ask the occupants which God was looking after them when they were killed. And maybe which Church they prayed in before they were raped and tortured." True silence descended on the onlookers. "Yes, it's distasteful and we should try to forget our differences. I fought for survival and a peace to take us forward. How can I be expected to control the outcome of every action, when the Gods of all faiths fail their followers so miserably." Berislavic rose stiffly from his chair.

"Perhaps it's us who twist their teachings to fit our selfish ways." He was aware of impatient movement behind him. "Time to go? I have one more favour to ask. Is Miss Deana Horvat still in the building? I need a personal word."

Government officials stood to one side to let the General, preceded by Miss Maes to pass. "See you in The Hague. This will be my last dedicated action for my country before I retire. Judge me as a soldier with your head and as a father with your heart. That's all I ask." With that Berislavic left the room.

Out in the corridor and surrounded by their police escort, Kaira walked a couple of paces in front only to round on the General. With her good hand she slapped his face. Strong men grabbed her and she winced in pain as she was taken quite literally in hand.

"That's for your son. You've lost him now and not before time. When you're in prison, you might think of the hundreds of innocent families that still grieve for their mothers and daughters he executed." Despite her ingrained anger, she spoke with clarity and control.

Berislavic understood every word. To the police he asked that she be released. He tried to speak a little English but had to give up. "I have no words that will make up for your loss. Only deeds, perhaps, if I get the chance." He tried to show compassion. "Not easy, but young lady, go now and move on with your life. I know who you are. At least the people you work with can make a difference and give closure to those that live lives in continual despair." With a nod of his head, he excused himself and walked on down the corridor with his following entourage leaving Kaira behind.

"Come, come with me." Colonel Bradbury who'd witnessed what had happened, gently took her by the arm. "There's someone waiting for you outside." A few paces later he took a chance. "You're officially fired by the way. Our goals have been achieved and the General's right; you do have more important work to go on to."

The Port Authority buildings were bathed in some late afternoon sunshine. The Colonel pointed toward the distant coast of mainland Sommovia which appeared in blacked out shapes as a ball of deep red sank slowly and inevitably towards them. A man wearing a pair of ill-fitting sunglasses was standing on the quayside looking out over the shimmering sea. He seemed to be waiting without making that obvious.

"I sat on them when I drove that speed boat earlier." He didn't look down as she sidled up beside him but just reached out and pulled her closer. "I need to speak with Samantha. I owe her bigtime for the last few months." Joe took the sunglasses and perched them on the tip of Kaira's nose. "Can you be patient? I need to explain and make my goodbyes." With that he bent his head and tried to kiss her.

Hesitancy had nothing to do with the way Kaira acted. Simply, the sunglasses slipped off her nose and got in the kiss's way. A second attempt proved much more successful. The sunglasses fell to the ground and were left there unheeded for some time.

From an upstairs window Samantha Grant also watched the sun dip towards the horizon. Sadness filled her heart knowing that her relationship with Joe was at an end. It was something she could have predicted and he and Kaira actually looked good together. Why then, was grief her overriding emotion?

It seemed only fitting. Whatever happened between her and Amelia, it shouldn't get in the way of mourning the loss. "How grown up." She whispered the words and held back tears. They would come later and lift the burden of any guilt she still felt.

In an adjoining room, mugs of tea were sipped to quench thirst, while hungry stomachs grumbled. Deana hoped some sugar might help to replenish her lack of energy. "What I wouldn't do to be back home at the café." She turned to Amelia. "Have you inherited any of your mother's skill in the kitchen?"

"Bloody hell, that reminds me." Amelia's thoughts of food sparked sudden panic. "We never paid our bill at the quayside restaurant this morning. And where is Samantha? Why isn't she here with us?" There was mild panic in her voice.

"She's giving us some family time and talking with Mr Peterson." Deana raised her eyebrows but decided to keep her questions and more importantly her opinions to herself. She brought Amelia's thoughts back inside the room. "Let's be frank, you're going to have to take some time getting reacquainted with one member of our family. Drinking tea fixes most things but helping you bond with your mother again may take something more substantial."

Both women looked to Lena who was studying maps and charts framed on the walls of the boardroom. Seemingly in a world on her own, none the less she'd acted with unexpected compassion towards the General's sidekick and taken particular notice of Brie Sanchez when she'd greeted Deana and Amelia like long lost friends.

Brie, who had just entered the room had picked up on this. Her own approach had bordered on indifference by totally suppressing her excitement and joy at seeing Jelena alive. It must have been difficult and yet she'd made unexpected progress by being a proper stranger.

"When I first came here, we used maps like these all the time. Now it's all on computer." She pointed to an intricate chart showing the harbour entrance. "I think it looks like a piece of art. So cleverly drawn. What do you think, Jelena?"

The use of her real name induced no reaction but Lena was taking everything in, even if she felt no reason to reply.

Brie took no offence. She turned to the others. "We're all finished here. You're free to go and I don't need to remind you not to breathe a word of what's gone on here today. I have personally vouched for us, so please don't make them send me to prison."

Her face brightened. "Luca is trying to play down his status as a hero. Provided he plays ball and keeps to the official story, the Sommovian authorities are happy to relinquish their hold over us. There's not much more to say." She held up her hands and smiled with relief.

"Good for you, Gabi. We're all starving here." Deana took control. "Any chance we can get back aboard the General's boat. Apparently, my sister was bought some new clothes to make up for her abduction." She unenthusiastically picked at her armpits. "I could do with a shower and a change myself."

"Got some spare clothes back at the hotel, if you're interested. Might find something to fit you at a stretch." Amelia realised what she'd said and stifled a giggle as she made haste toward the door. She ran straight into Samantha. They stopped inches apart and stared at each other. Amelia could see uncertainty in her friend's eyes.

"Bloody hell. I thought I'd lost you forever." She launched herself at Sam who did well to keep her balance. "Are you alright? I feel as if I've deserted you; I'm so sorry." She whispered the last bit and squeezed the American in a tight embrace. She finally stepped back as if to gauge the effect the day must have had on her friend.

"That bad, eh?"

Sam encouraged Amelia to walk with her. "Me, I've nothing to complain about. Managed a quick chat with Joe. He seems fine and as usual said nothing contentious or blameworthy. Bless him, but sometimes I wish he'd get angry. At least then I'd know I did make a difference." She took a deep breath. "And yet, how can I blame him for anything. It was me who cheated."

"As far as you know." Amelia was quick to point out. "And I'm totally to blame for that. Maybe there was a bit of truth-avoidance going on between you when you were still together."

"A short-term deal that had no future, so why continue? You could be right."

"Aren't you two hungry? Stop moping about and go pay your bill at that restaurant." Deana was taking no prisoners. "Get it where you can. With anything long term, be friends first. That's my advice."

Nobody was prepared to argue, especially on empty stomachs.

"Is that what happened with you and the General?" Amelia ran for the exit with a fast-moving Aunt in close pursuit.

"Cheeky cow."

"What does it feel like to be free at last?" Sam sat in the front of the thirteen-seater coach alongside Brie Sanchez. They were parked close by the General's cruiser and were waiting for the Horvat sisters and Amelia to return.

"No difference really. I've always felt safe here." She considered the rest of her answer. "I think deep down I always knew the General was our guardian angel. You only have to look how proud he was of his grandson today. During the war this island was always well protected. It didn't matter which side you were on, Port Central and Alcavar were deemed no-go areas. Maybe that's why the General chose it specifically for me and my son."

"Do you think it was him who rescued you and Lena when she was shot?"

"Good question that only he and Deana can answer. He'll never admit to it for obvious reasons.

"Because he'd implicate himself in the shooting of Maurice Highland?"

"That and much more. Slavco Berislavic was a racist and violent man. Despite that Deana reckons he may not have meant to kill Maurice. Dejan to this day maintains it was purely accidental. No one will ever know for certain. The incident was hushed up, that's true, because the opposition were looking for excuses to start a war and our side needed time to prepare. Two years made a huge difference to getting onside with our allies."

"Presumably the Americans and by association the British were in on the subterfuge. Joe always thought his old boss, Colonel Bradbury, knew more than he ever let on."

"Who knows. If it wasn't for Berislavic I'm sure Lena would never have survived. Deana says he paid for her hospital treatment and re-habitation. Getting my job with the Port Authority on the island was a done deal even before I was interviewed. My house in that fishing village you visited, bought and paid for. I only found this out recently. I thought it came as part of my work package." Brie smiled. "I've been lucky in so many ways."

"The General too perhaps. Although it's easy to forget he just lost his son." Samantha tried to put herself in his position. "Maybe it's come as some kind of relief."

"Slavco was an unhappy man out of uniform. Perhaps he should have died in the war and been remembered as a defender of our way of life. Instead, he'll be blamed for genocide and ethnic cleansing; a butcher of innocent women and children. All those that didn't fit his vision of purity."

She paused and took a deep breath. "And yet he was happy to sleep with me. I wasn't important. Getting pregnant was not part of his fun and Luca became the evidence that could be used against him. I pray he didn't kill all those women and children because of his failings with me."

Sam reached out and put a comforting hand on Brie's arm. They sat in silence for a minute or so. "Silly question, I know. Which name will you use; Brie or Gabi?"

"I'm used to Brie, that's how I'm known and I see no reason to leave my life on Alcavar. The island has been good to me. Seeing Lena again fills my heart with joy, but as you can see, we're two different people now. Luca is settled and happy. I suppose if he wanted to return to the mainland I might have to think again. He's off to the yacht club party this evening and has been asked to give out end of season awards at the prize giving." She was proud of that. "The island has a new celebrity, at least for this weekend. He loves being on the water and the boys he works with are brilliant with him. He'll be disappointed that Amelia is not available. She's a sweet girl and for somebody that famous quite down to earth. I think you'll make a good match."

"Not sure how it happened and can't believe how uncertain I feel right now. Don't get me wrong; try and take her away and I would fight for her. Does it change who I am and should I be acting differently?" Sam was quite serious. "I don't want to take advantage if she's vulnerable. Let's be honest Brie, you survived a bad start but that didn't change your preferences or persuasion."

"I never gave it a moment's thought. True, my parents didn't disown me but I think they were relieved when I left home. Like I said I got lucky and have been self-sufficient. I'm grateful for Luca, if not for his father's involvement." Brie could see Sam hanging on every word she spoke. "My gut tells me you'll not want to be without her. Ah, I see that hit home. Give yourself time. You both need to get back to work. That'll be a good start."

Never had a truer word been said in Samantha's opinion. Their conversation was brought to a close. "Here comes trouble."

Deana led her sister and her niece back to the coach. They were escorted by a Sommovian official who'd been there to lock up the General's cruiser. "Could have slept in there if it weren't for the buffoon that came with us. What a palace that boat is. You should see the clothes he bought for Lena. If I lose a few pounds, I'll be pinching a couple of items, that's for sure."

"I wouldn't bet on that. Mama seems quite protective of her stuff." Amelia smiled at her mother. "She's held onto those bags as if her life depends upon it." Any offer to help had been rejected out of hand. "Let's get back to the hotel. We can chat up the manager and you can all use our bathroom before we have dinner."

*

27. University (Marin's Mix)

"Ever wanted something bad enough you'd actually kill for it? Or be prepared to let somebody else die for your cause. European Union membership is a prize your country has made its priority." Nick Sayers spoke candidly.

I had been reading the latest copy of a national newspaper. Recent statements attributed to the General had been carefully leaked.

… "I don't want Gabriela Simic's thanks, she deserves mine. My links to her family will help validate my innocence. Anybody I attacked were true enemies and legitimate targets. What happened in those final days was a tragedy of our own making. The North and South of the country eying up the land in between. Win at all costs and take the prizes." …

"This I find interesting." I showed the paper to Nick and did my best to translate what I'd just read.

… "I gave my son too much love and protection. Gabriela and my grandson Luca are proof to the world where my sympathies lie." …

Nick didn't seem surprised. He invited my insights as a resident student.

"His arrest has divided opinion. When you spoke before about sacrifices, it's him that our government has decided to put forward as a token." I was yet to be convinced.

Nick made no judgement. At last, I had somebody I could open up to over the death of my girlfriend and her family. He'd listened with sympathy and agreed to highlight these issues in the future. I was grateful for that.

"Well, the next few hours should prove most enlightening." I wanted to move our conversation back to the here and now. Miss Matic who had suddenly appeared in the doorway looked at both Nick and I as if to say, "What are you two up to."

Without further words from either of us we followed her down numerous corridors to the central lecture room. The place was crowded just as I knew it would be. The banked seating shaped in a semi-circle was filled with students and tutors alike. All were drawn by the rarity of meeting entertainment royalty in person. Four chairs centre stage were as yet unfilled. Miss Matic climbed the few stairs from the floor with a microphone in her hand. I'd never been more nervous or proud as a hush fell over the whole room.

"Everyone; good evening to you all. We have some special guests I know you're eager to meet who have come a long way to be with us tonight. Maybe Sommovia can claim that we have one of our own returned to the fold. We can perhaps ask how she feels about that. That, and so much more. Please give a heartfelt welcome to Amelia Highland, Katie Ley and Mr Charles Hanlan.

Applause rang out as all three walked onto the stage.

Charles came down front and centre. "Language can be a barrier but I find music rarely is. I'm told that most of you here tonight understand English. I'm sorry I can't reciprocate in kind, so please forgive me. My daughter does speak a little Sommovian but I'm told it's mostly the swear words you use here; apologies once again. Before we start in earnest, I'd like to say thank you to a few people. Miss Matic for her diligence and work behind the scenes to getting this thing done. The University for our invitation of course, and most of all to you, for your love of music and theatre." Charles was at ease while he waited for the clapping hands to quieten.

"The individual whose brilliant idea it was to disturb me from my comfortable desk in London doesn't want his name to be mentioned so instead I wrote it down." He held up a piece of paper which had MARIN scrawled on it in felt-tip pen. "Thank you for being there for my daughter's mother in such dangerous circumstances." He looked to me without emotion. "You and I will speak later."

I sat there stunned and felt myself sink deeper into my chair. I wondered what Mr Hanlan might want to talk to me about. I'd seen Lena back in her rightful place at the bakery. The whole village was pleased that the recent unrest had not diminished her baking skills. Bread and buns, the thing I most looked forward to was seeing her smile.

"Nothing lasts forever." Charles Hanlan's voice brought me back to the room. "We as a company have important news. I want you to be the first to hear it. If I take you back in time, 'Ever Searching' had a purpose that honoured the love that I felt for Amelia's mother, my friend and partner, Maurice Highland and the bond that our two families have always had. In the beginning, Amelia and now Katie Ley have kept this alive along with those who work at The Theatre. We want to take this forward and to do this we need your help. We want to bring the creativity that you all buy into and take it to a wider audience. This will include collaborations with universities just like yours and being able to loan out our expertise. We have new partners based in America who want to buy into the franchise and make film and tv out of our original ideas. An extended family if you like. NRG Pictures have joined forces with a television network headed by Tobias Powers."

"Why am I telling you this? Because there are so many facets to what we do that need new skills that you can provide. We can't all be the stars of the show. If by chance we do make it, then we represent the rest of the team. I've explained this to my daughter at length but she still doesn't get it."

I could see that father and daughter sparked off of one another. I looked to the younger, more animated version of a friend I had recently made and wondered how much they had in common. Both were having to start all over again.

Now it was Amelia's turn. "I know Christmas is still a couple of months away but this year will be different for our family. After years spent apart, having my mother back has made me realise the importance of the people you chose to keep close. Now I've met you."

As she pointed towards the audience, she could have been her mother reaching out to take back that lace handkerchief.

"There are many who have worked behind the scenes for no other reason than their loyalty to my father. It couldn't be for money. He doesn't pay us that much." Amelia was striking back amongst the laughter. "Come on Katie, you can earn your crust now."

Miss Ley stood beside Amelia and acknowledged a loyal band of support. "We'd like to request your indulgence and in particular those members of your famous university choir. I sing your praises. We'd love to join you in celebrating Christmas Eve by being a small part of your wonderful concert in the Cathedral here in Mezlar. It's rather short notice, I know, but we'd be honoured and grateful if you could find room for us in your hearts. One night only, I promise."

The roar of approval was deafening.

28. Mezlar and Beyond

The night of the concert, the city had come alive with throngs of people visiting the winter markets, eating street food and celebrating Christmas Eve with good cheer in the bars. The doors to the cathedral were kept open and all were made welcome. News had travelled far and wide and extra seating had been imported. Students from the university had gathered in the square despite the cold. Those not normally fans of choir music had none the less come from their homes to take in the heady scent of celebrity. Hopes of hearing Amelia Highland in fine voice were deemed good to excellent. Apparently, the sound checks had been out of this world.

Nick Sayers was back in the city he'd not long ago left. Saying goodbye the first time to newly made friends had been astonishingly emotional. He'd admitted to shedding a tear as the aircraft left Sommovian airspace and thought it must have been a reaction to a change in cabin pressure.

And now nearly all the players were back together again. Nick had the best seat in the house. A thorn between two roses, with Helen Matic on one arm and Samantha Grant on the other. With the sight of snow falling outside in the square, he might have believed the atmosphere was spiced with a hint of romance. Swirling eddies made the cathedral a wonderful place to shelter in.

Samantha had been keen to meet up with Amelia and Katie before the performance started. From previous experience Nick had learnt to steer clear of dressing rooms, especially Amelia's. He had the strangest of feelings that Samantha would be greeted with open arms.

It made perfect sense; they'd always been good friends and their attraction to each other was bound by no rules.

Helen had agreed to pick up him from the airport as before. Same route into Mezlar, the same hotel. A room booked as a double, two suitcases and the thought of pushing the beds together. Their agreement had been to take things slowly. He hadn't checked his watch but it was all of five minutes from unpacking to having their resolve sorely tested. Out of respect for the vows they'd made to each other, both had found reasons to keep busy in checking phones and diaries. The evening stretched before them.

Charles Hanlan approached and cosied up to Samantha before whispering in her ear. He seemed relaxed and even happy. Nick was inclined to temper his opinion. Seeing Lena alive but knowing that he must be dead to her memory, was tragic. Perhaps Charles harboured hopes that she might yet snap out of her amnesia.

If anyone had made a significant impression on Lena it was Marin. Always attentive, he dealt well with her frequent moods of introversion. In a crowd they would naturally gravitate towards each other and find common ground that was theirs alone.

Joe Peterson didn't do Christmas concerts; not really his style. Kaira Maes did come to the city and met with most of the group a couple of days before. Joe was back in Britain tending to his father who had appendicitis. She explained how a turn in the weather, bringing thick snow to the region, had temporarily put a stop to their sensitive work. According to her, Joe had been the perfect fit into a team working in unusual circumstances.

Rosalind Powers kept a watchful eye on Samantha, not knowing whether to blame Joe for the breakup of their relationship. If she knew that Samantha had acted before she was pushed then she kept that to herself.

Sherman was a notable absentee. He'd stayed in New York while practising in behaviour more associated with a man who has a "doggy ticker." Rosalind explained further.

"When I spoke to the doctors in London I asked if they would be inserting sense or stents into his wonderful heart."

Amelia was sad that he and Marsha Ivanovic had not made the trip.

"My home is in Britain now. I severed my ties in Sommovia. No point in raking up the past. Come visit me in Suffolk, sometime before I die, but only if you can make it in time." The message was loud and perfectly clear, just like the old woman's sarcastic wit.

Although the last few months had been a strain on Amelia, she'd kept her spirits high. She'd integrated well with Toby Powers' new Tv company. New York would now become her home for half the year at least. Her working relationship with Rosalind, remained vital for both of them.

As Sherman gradually relinquished his grip on the company, Samantha had taken up the reins. Her public persona was one of steady control, but privately she was dealing with the ebb and flow of her emotions. As someone who knew her best, Nick had the impression that she was trying not to fall in love. When she and Amelia greeted new friends from the university in Mezlar's beautiful cathedral, both searched and found each other. The briefest touch and they seemed happy to move away again.

Deana Horvat continued as a force of nature. Nick had been fascinated when trying to put an article together for Stress Magazine, and questioned her directly. With the trial of General Berislavic due to begin the following year, getting her to speak even off the record was impossible, unless it suited her purpose. Considering the things she has done in her life, he pointed out it would be remiss of him if he didn't document some titbits for posterity. After some consideration, she thought he was probably right.

Putting Brie and Deana in the same room became a masterstroke of luck as far as Nick was concerned. The common dominator was their love for Lena, and their share of hatred for Slavco Berislavic. The counter-balance to all the negativity was Luca Sanchez.

"Thank the Lord, he takes after his grandfather. Dejan had to do the dirty work and lead proud men against our enemies. Even now there are people who want to go back to an era of dictatorship, where they don't have to think for themselves." Deana had been her usual forthright self.

If anyone had the right to judge the General, it was her.

"I confronted him outside in the hospital grounds. I held a rifle to my shoulder until my arms ached. He calmly told the medics to care for Lena as if she were one of his own." Nick had been stunned. "He made a simple admission of his son's involvement and promised to care for Gabriela and Luca." Only the force of gravity and his abject apology had finally made Deana lower the gun.

Interestingly, she was not prepared to talk to him about the death of Maurice Highland. Did she care that he was dead? Yes, of course. "I may be considered tough but I'm not unfeeling. He interfered in something that was not his concern and paid the price." She left it at that.

She went on to explain how within a matter of weeks the Horvat's property outside of Port Central had a long term let, paid in advance. The transaction was done via an independent agency and Deana had been in no hurry to identify her tenant. "The General told me not to bother."

Gabriela's protection from Slavco was guaranteed as promised. "She was headhunted by the Port Authority on the Island of Alcavar. After the war, Dejan bought his cruiser just to be close to his grandson. Gabi here, had no idea."

Nick recorded the verbal gold and wondered how he should approach the subject of Lena's life post the shooting. In some ways it had all been staged without her full knowledge and understanding. Deana was prepared to admit that making her share a house with her cousin had been a mistake, if only done as a means to an end. Disguising their identities had been temporary. In reality, Slavco had been too busy winning the war to understand she was still alive.

"During those final days of conflict when he subverted his father's orders and destroyed a village, he severed any hope of Dejan's protection. It nearly killed him." Deana confessed she'd watched as a proud man crumbled. "From that moment on, Slavco lived in fear of his father."

Nick found how easy it was to get sidetracked and put any concerns for Lena to one side. Bottom line, he hoped she was happy. He wrote some thoughts down while they were still fresh in his mind

"She communicates, but only to those who deserve her attention. Marin is one and Deana is a constant without showing outpourings of affection. Amelia and her mother getting to know each other will be fascinating to behold."

Nick considered Lena's future. "There's hope there, I believe, and it may hinge on what happened towards the end of the Christmas Eve concert. I was privileged to witness an incident that in isolation may have been disregarded."

All the audience were wrapped in joyful concentration. Katie Ley had just performed a solo from the London show when Amelia came back on stage. She began to sing a lilting folksong that many would remember from their early childhood. The key notes were hit in perfect pitch and emotion filled the air.

Quite unexpectantly Lena rose from her seat on the end of the aisle and began to approach the stage from the side. If it hadn't been for Samantha, security would have probably intervened and broken the wonderful spell that had been cast. She sat on the stone steps leading to the stage and watched intently as Amelia captured her audience with an easy power and control. She never let her eyes wander for one second.

But Amelia's did, and seeing her mother close by, walked slowly towards her. That was when her voice began to falter. Had the choir not joined in singing the final verse, the song may never have been finished. Amelia sat beside her mother and took hold of her hand. She gathered herself for the final lines and made sure she finished strongly.

Guided by Sam on one side and by her daughter on the other, they returned Lena to her seat. Holding hands had become mandatory and they stayed like that until all was calm between them. Amelia kissed her mother's cheek before returning to her place with the rest of the choir.

Like most of the audience, Nick forgot to breathe.

With the magazines monthly deadline approaching, Nick went with Rosalind to the Horvat family village.

Kaira Maes had not overstated the recent weather conditions, as thick snow made the driving tricky and slow. Strong winds in exposed places had caused drifting and reduced some roads to single tracks. It had taken twice the normal time to get there.

Strong coffee with brandy and a choice of pastries, freshly prepared, made the café some kind of Santa's grotto. They were both made to feel very welcome. Rosalind sat by Nick's side and took in the scene with wide-eyed interest and a growing love for the quaintness of village life.

"Sherman would hate this. Too laid back for him by half. The only village he's really comfortable in is Greenwich." She got up to remove her heavy coat and settled comfortably back down. "I could get used to this."

"A few years ago, you could be dodging a sniper's bullet or tripping over a landmine. Don't be fooled. These recent grave finds are a powerful reminder."

"I guess it's easy to dismiss what happened to those who are so far away." Rosalind had known people that had died in the twin towers, so wasn't immune. "Why do we treat each other so cruelly?" She sighed. "You have to admire Deana's resilience in looking after her sister. Strong woman, that one."

She went on to voice a concern that Nick had already identified. "No recriminations from Amelia that she was kept in the dark for so long? She's lived with a mix of extremes to say the least."

"From devastation to darling of the London theatre scene and now working with you in New York. I've heard no complaints. I think she understands the dilemma her aunt found herself in."

Nick wanted to broach another delicate subject and thought he could rely on Rosalind to be straight with him. "And moving in with Sam?" It was a statement with a question attached.

As expected, Rosalind came through. "That is a surprise, but I think in a good way." She took a sip of coffee. "Sam was young when she first came to us. She became my friend and ally in a traditionally male dominated world. I'm glad to say she's met that challenge without betraying her lovely caring nature."

He nodded in agreement. "I'd have to say that a few weeks back I felt she'd lost that desire. I even wondered if she might move away and live on a farm with Joe Peterson."

"Maybe I encouraged her to do just that. She needed time off from us at NRG to find what was important to her. Looking back at the risks she took in Suffolk, the person she most cared for was Amelia. Yes, we paid her wages and she always kept the faith, but throughout, the one thing she craved was to make things right for that young lady."

Nick couldn't argue with that.

"I know what you're getting at." Rosalind took her time. "What those girls have is desire. If they can make each other as happy as they feel in their own skins, then bring it on."

The door to the kitchen swung open and an aproned Amelia came to where they were sitting armed with two slices of traditional Sommovian Christmas cake.

Rosalind smiled. "We were just talking about you."

"Now there's a thing. Don't you get bored with that subject?" She tucked a stray strand of hair behind her ear. A dusting of flour adorned one of her eyebrows.

"More importantly, I want to know why Nick is finding it impossible to leave the comforts of Mezlar. Mature students are welcome at the University, I realise that, but what's your subject and who will your tutor be?"

Nick accepted her ribbing but was happy to allow Rosalind to admonish Amelia for her cheek and disrespectful nature.

"That reminds me. Marin flies out to London to meet up with my father. You'll remember that Charles promised him a position within the company. They intend to set up a number of workshops to integrate new talent from universities into the business. Marin will likely oversee one of these in Mezlar. Should be exciting."

Amelia seemed to have a tick-list she'd decided to shorten. "Sam sends her love by the way. Working hard with Toby." She sighed for effect. "Sorry, I'm feeling a little Sam-sick."

Nick took the bait. "Not making you ill, is she?"

"No, I just miss her, silly." He was happy to see that the tip of her tongue was still delicately pointed.

*

Postscript

Cold winter sunlight made the day presentable. Snow chains were essential. Family and friends made their way to the burnt-out cottage in a variety of vehicles fit for purpose. Men from the village had cleared a pathway from the roadside down to the remnants of charcoaled timbers that lay between tumbled down bricks and mortar. All that passed by had the whiff of fire in their noses. They took their time until the depth of snow under the pines made walking more comfortable. Deana led and seemed certain of the way.

The edge of the forest was naturally created and gave rise to gaps in the trees. Rosalind walked on Nick's arm and they followed close behind the Horvat family. The silence around them was broken by a small flock of birds calling from the safety of high branches. Their simple song and flashes of colour were welcome amongst the bleakness.

At the top of a small rise, they could look down on a small, iced over pond that was surrounded for the most part by reeds and clumps of evergreen bushes. To the left and in amongst the heads of low grasses, stood a cross on the top of a beautifully carved headstone.

Deana kept on walking but Amelia who was holding her mother's hand came to a halt. Her throat felt tight and her legs were suddenly heavy.

"Amelia, your father is buried here. Only come down if you want to. Life is for the living but you deserved to know that he was taken care of. I promised Dejan I'd show you." She touched the headstone and gently brushed some snow away revealing a simple inscription.

Her job done, she walked back up the slope making to pass by Nick and Rosalind who out of respect had held back. “Feel free if you have need to see for yourself.”

Rosalind walked on and stood beside Amelia and Lena. Nick stayed where he was.

“Place gives me the creeps, if I’m honest. How many times can you say you’re sorry.” Deana breathed in and suddenly seemed tired.

“If you’re referring to what happened to your sister all those years ago, then I’d have to say Lena got some revenge.” Nick could only imagine the devastation caused by the fuel induced explosion. “Whether she meant it or not, Slavco Berislavic went to hell that night.”

Deana smiled but it never reached her eyes. “I’ve heard you use the expression a number of times before. How do you say it now?” Deana paused for thought. “Ah yes. Off the record, no matches were needed. I should know. It wasn’t Lena in the cottage that night but me. Think about it, he wanted to kill my sister. Yes, for him, a horrible way to go. Always was a hothead, and that’s being kind to his father. One spark was all that was needed.” Her respect for Dejan seemed constant.

“One thing to remember and one thing only.” She touched Nick’s arm and leaned in, closer. “The gun wasn’t mine and I never pulled the trigger.”

About the Author

Mark Robinson has a passion for travel, and research for his books has taken him from the world of Art and theatre to beautiful countries with complex pasts. Mark is a keen observer of human nature and finds modern history an inspirational background for his fiction. He now resides with his wife, Amanda, in Hampshire.